SACRIFICIAL PRINCESS AND THE King of Beasts

6

Yu Tomofuji

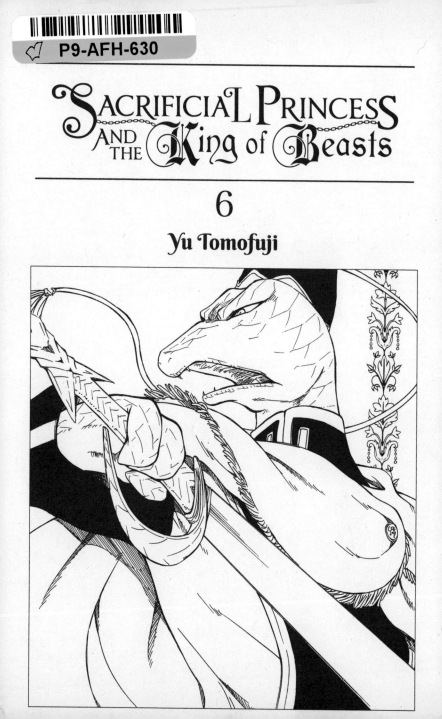

SACRIFICIAL PRINCESS AND THE King of Beasts

6

contents

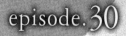

episode.30

SACRIFICIAL PRINCESS AND THE KING OF BEASTS

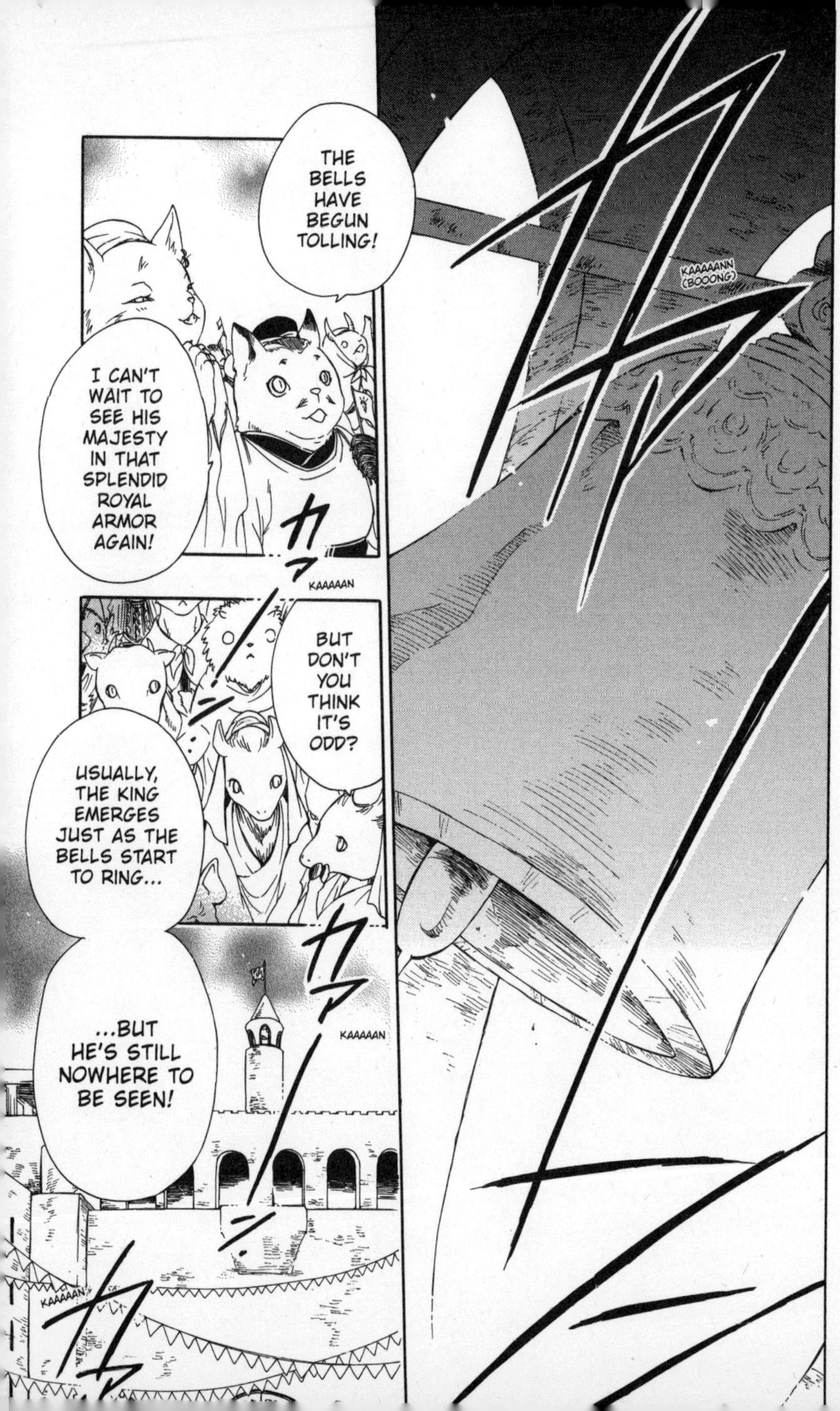
KAAAAANN (BOOONG)
THE BELLS HAVE BEGUN TOLLING!
I CAN'T WAIT TO SEE HIS MAJESTY IN THAT SPLENDID ROYAL ARMOR AGAIN!
KAAAAAN
BUT DON'T YOU THINK IT'S ODD?
USUALLY, THE KING EMERGES JUST AS THE BELLS START TO RING...
...BUT HE'S STILL NOWHERE TO BE SEEN!
KAAAAAN
KAAAAAN

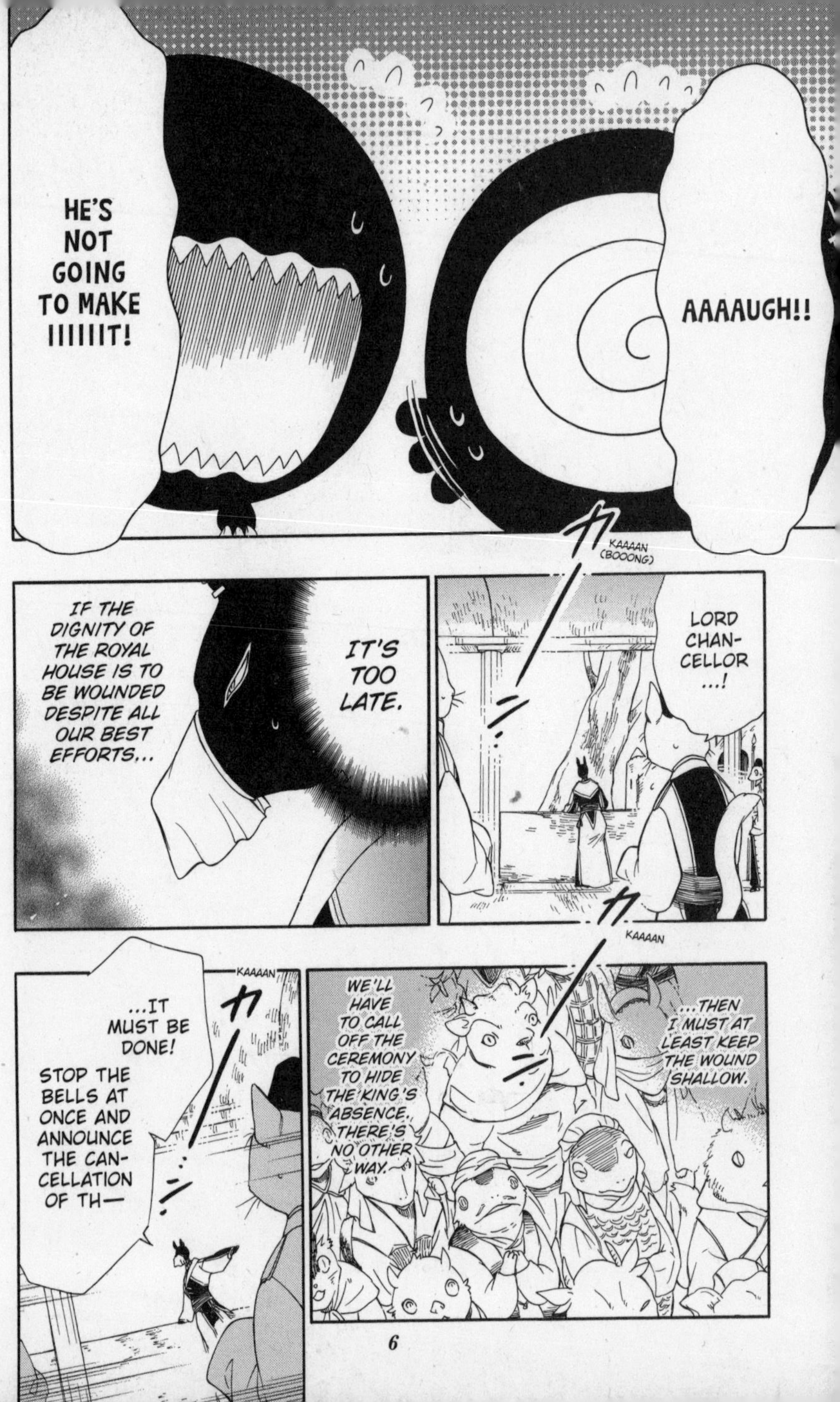
AAAAUGH!!
HE'S NOT GOING TO MAKE IIIIIIIT!
KAAAAN (BOOONG)
LORD CHAN-CELLOR ...!
IT'S TOO LATE.
IF THE DIGNITY OF THE ROYAL HOUSE IS TO BE WOUNDED DESPITE ALL OUR BEST EFFORTS...
KAAAAN
...THEN I MUST AT LEAST KEEP THE WOUND SHALLOW.
WE'LL HAVE TO CALL OFF THE CEREMONY TO HIDE THE KING'S ABSENCE. THERE'S NO OTHER WAY.
KAAAAN
...IT MUST BE DONE!
STOP THE BELLS AT ONCE AND ANNOUNCE THE CAN-CELLATION OF TH—

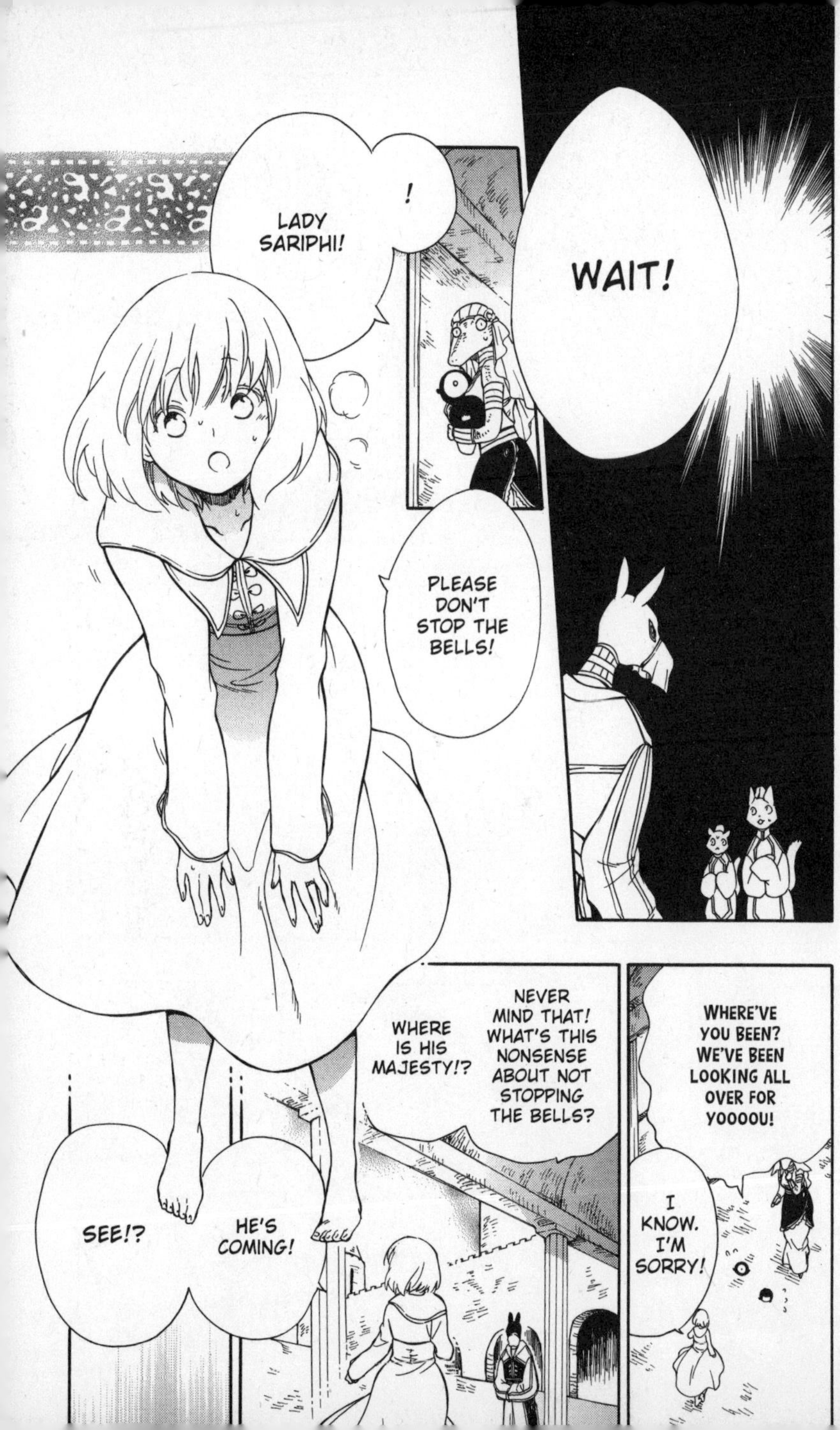
WAIT!
PLEASE DON'T STOP THE BELLS!
!
LADY SARIPHI!
WHERE'VE YOU BEEN? WE'VE BEEN LOOKING ALL OVER FOR YOOOOU!
I KNOW. I'M SORRY!
NEVER MIND THAT! WHAT'S THIS NONSENSE ABOUT NOT STOPPING THE BELLS?
WHERE IS HIS MAJESTY!?
HE'S COMING!
SEE!?

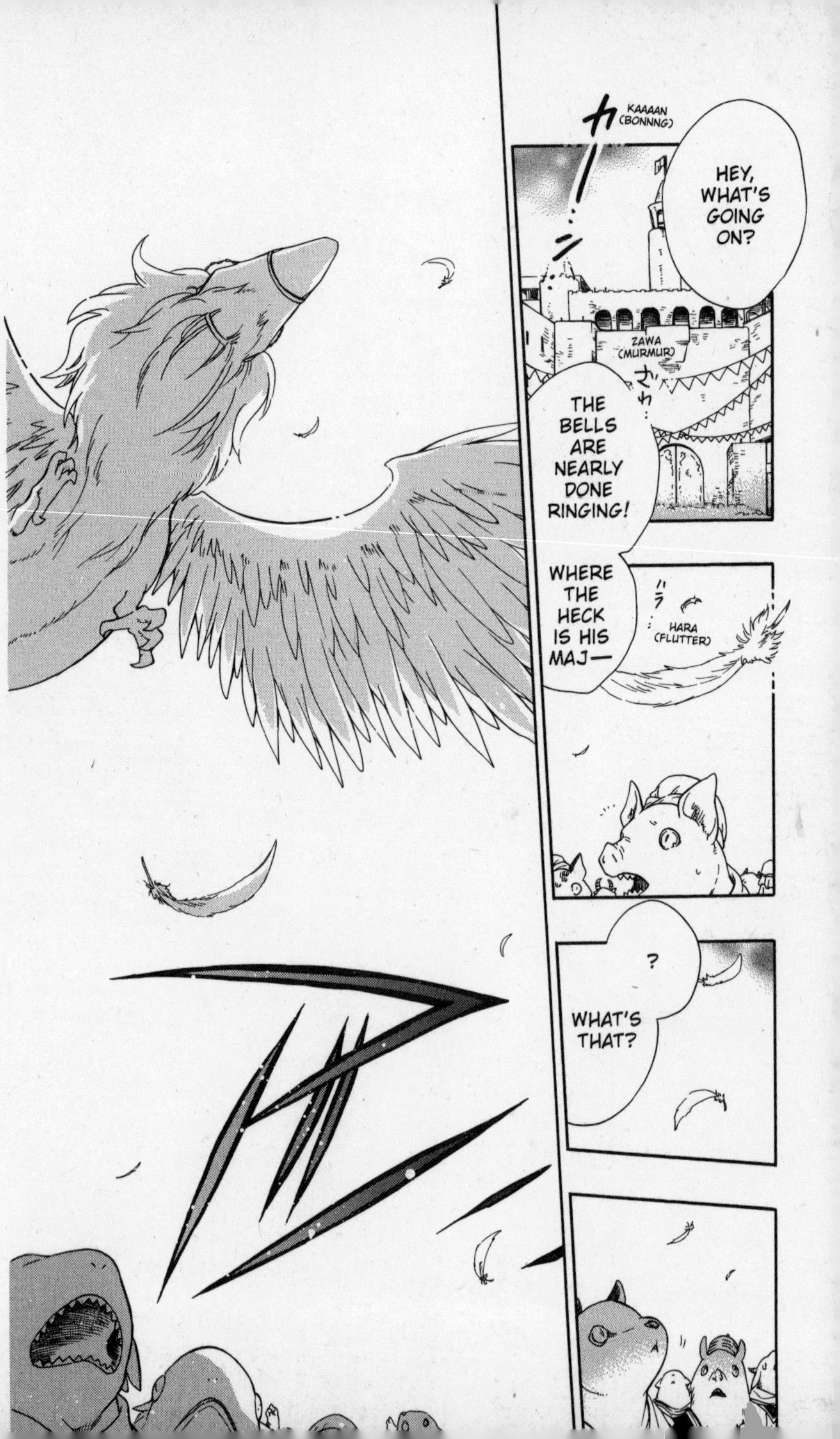
KAAAAN (BONNNG)
HEY, WHAT'S GOING ON?
ZAWA (MURMUR)
THE BELLS ARE NEARLY DONE RINGING!
WHERE THE HECK IS HIS MAJ—
HARA (FLUTTER)
?
WHAT'S THAT?

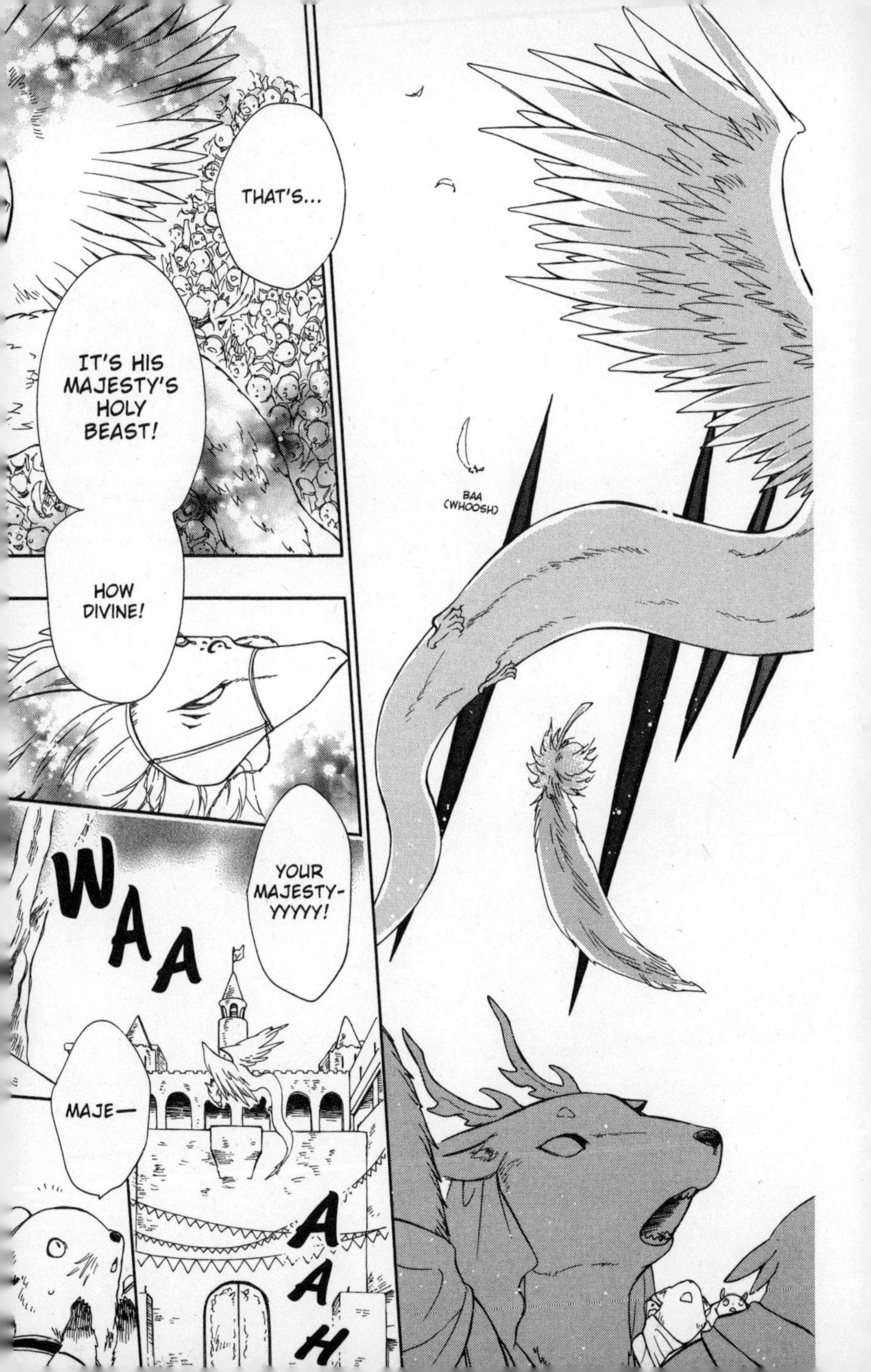
BAA
(WHOOSH)
THAT'S...
IT'S HIS MAJESTY'S HOLY BEAST!
HOW DIVINE!
YOUR MAJESTY-YYYYY!
WAA
MAJE—
AAH

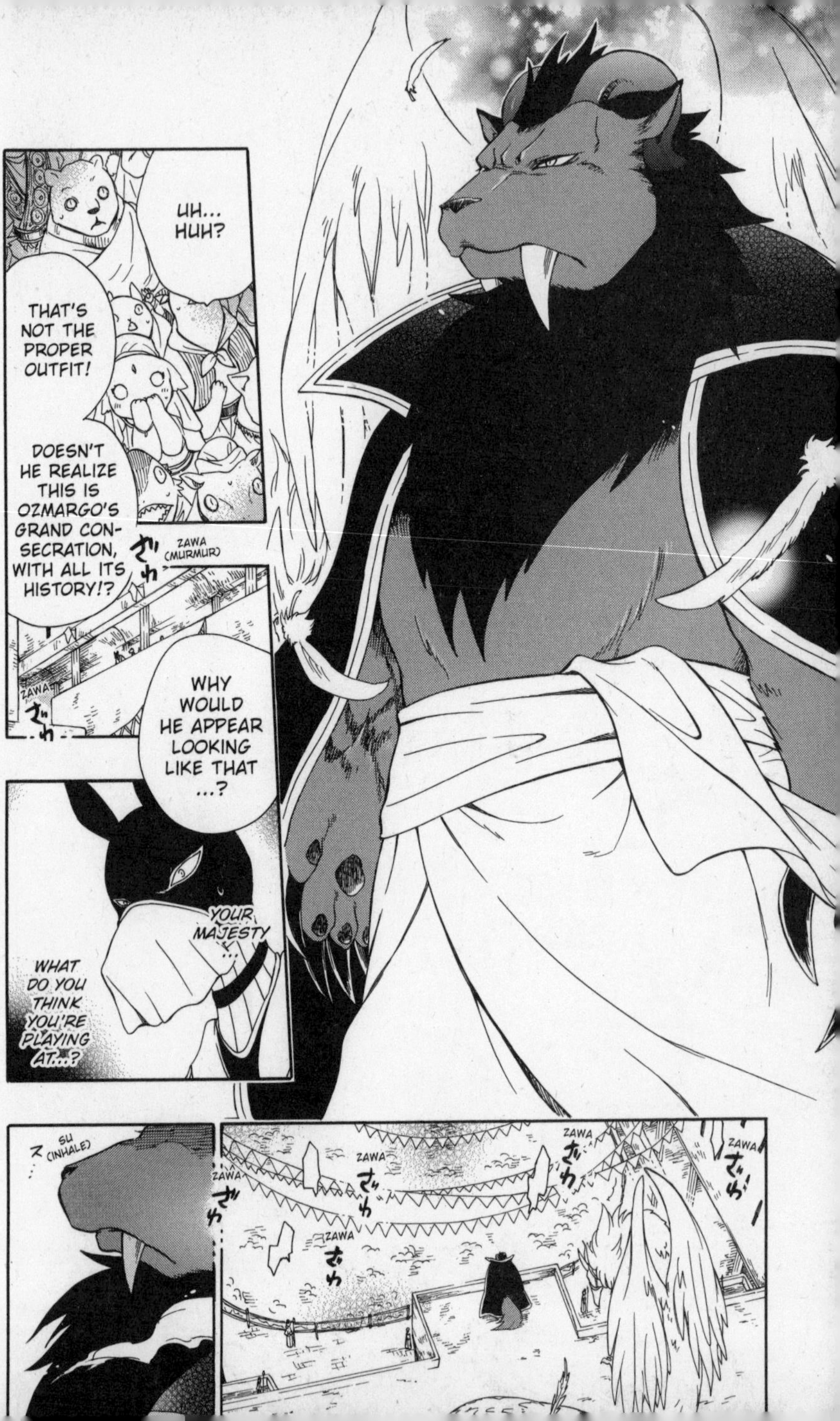
UH... HUH?
THAT'S NOT THE PROPER OUTFIT!
DOESN'T HE REALIZE THIS IS OZMARGO'S GRAND CONSECRATION, WITH ALL ITS HISTORY!?
ざわ ZAWA (MURMUR)
ざわ ZAWA
WHY WOULD HE APPEAR LOOKING LIKE THAT ...?
YOUR MAJESTY ...
WHAT DO YOU THINK YOU'RE PLAYING AT...?
ざわ ZAWA
ざわ ZAWA
ざわ ZAWA
ざわ ZAWA
ざわ ZAWA
ス... SU (INHALE)

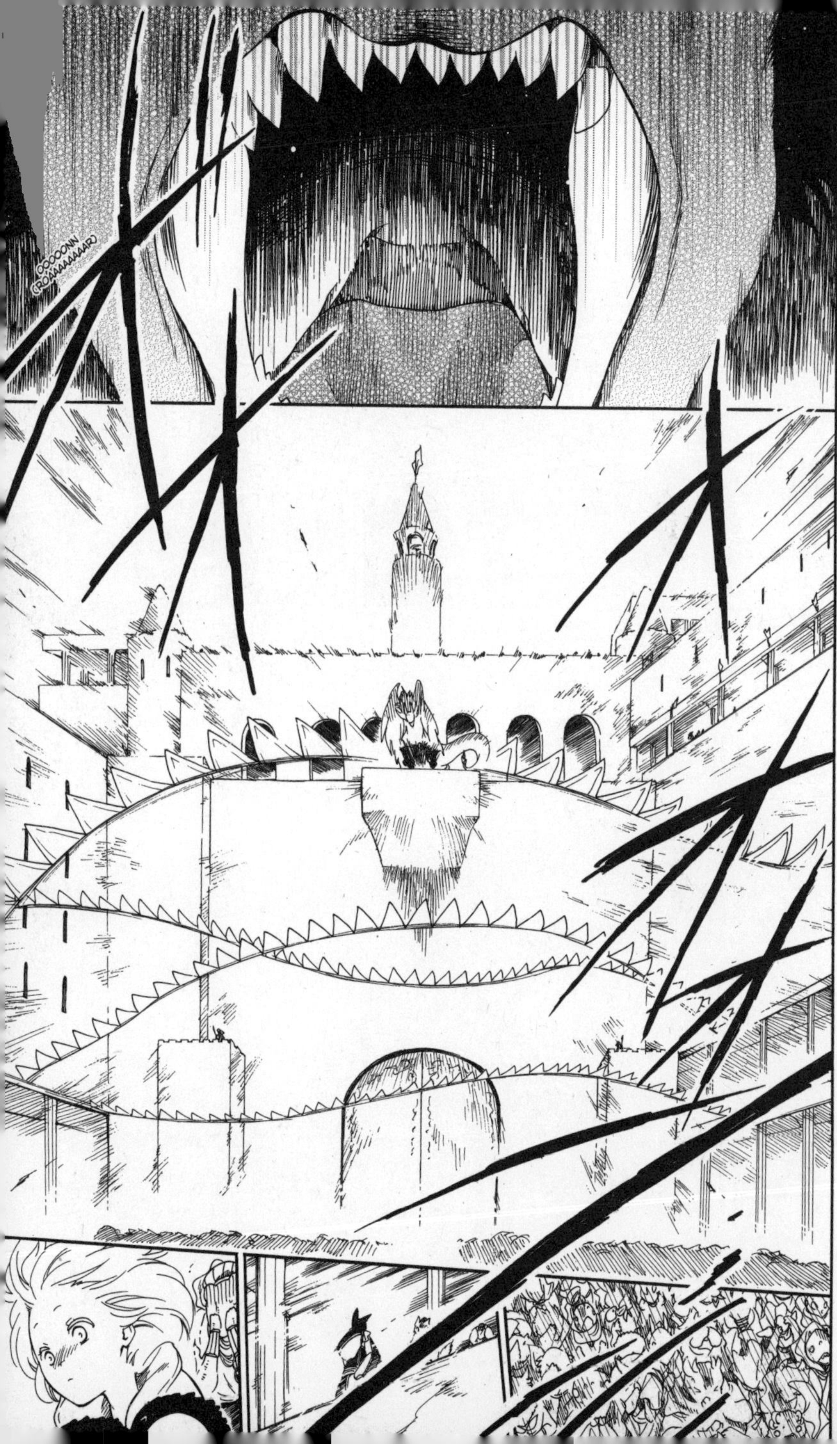
GOOOOONN
(ROAAAAAAAAR)

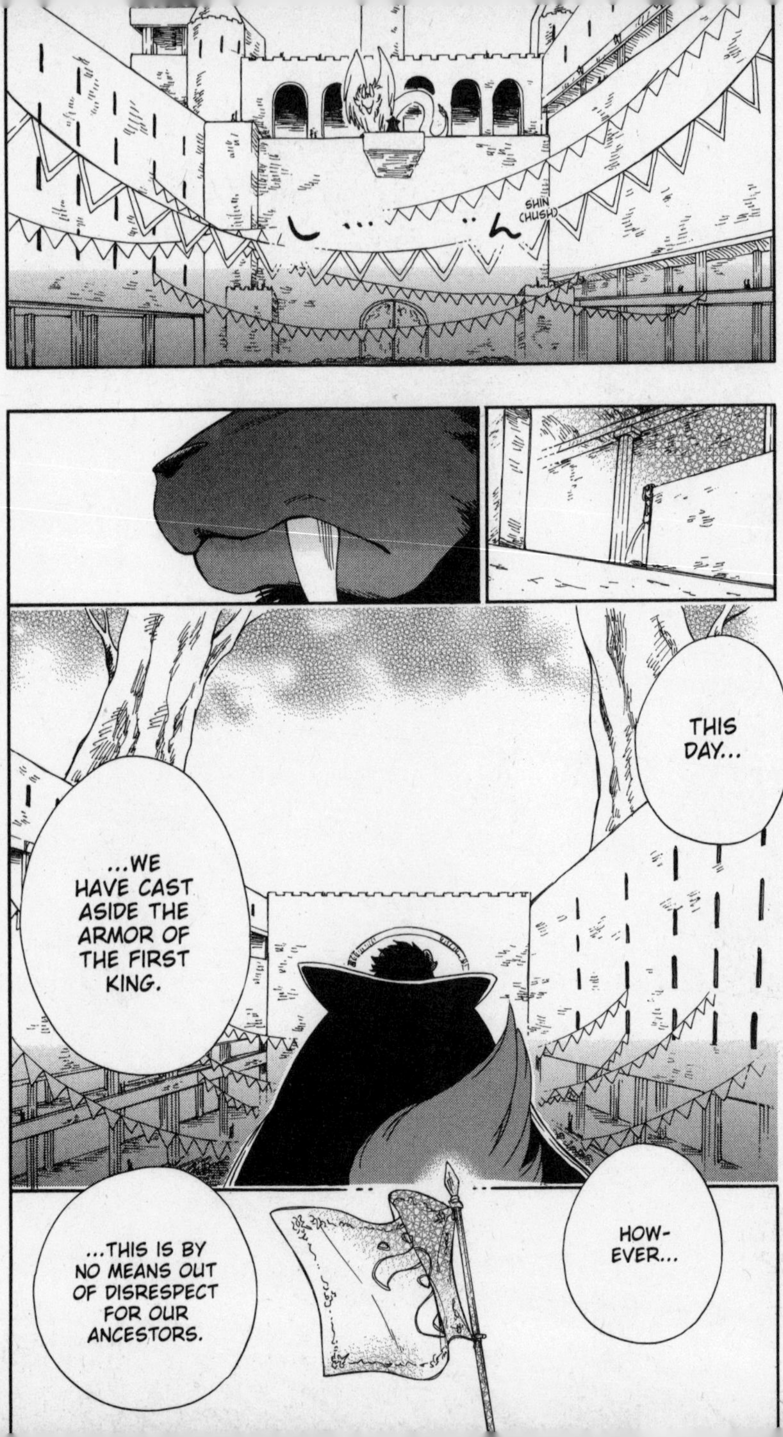
SHIN (HUSH)
THIS DAY...
...WE HAVE CAST ASIDE THE ARMOR OF THE FIRST KING.
HOW-EVER...
...THIS IS BY NO MEANS OUT OF DISRESPECT FOR OUR ANCESTORS.

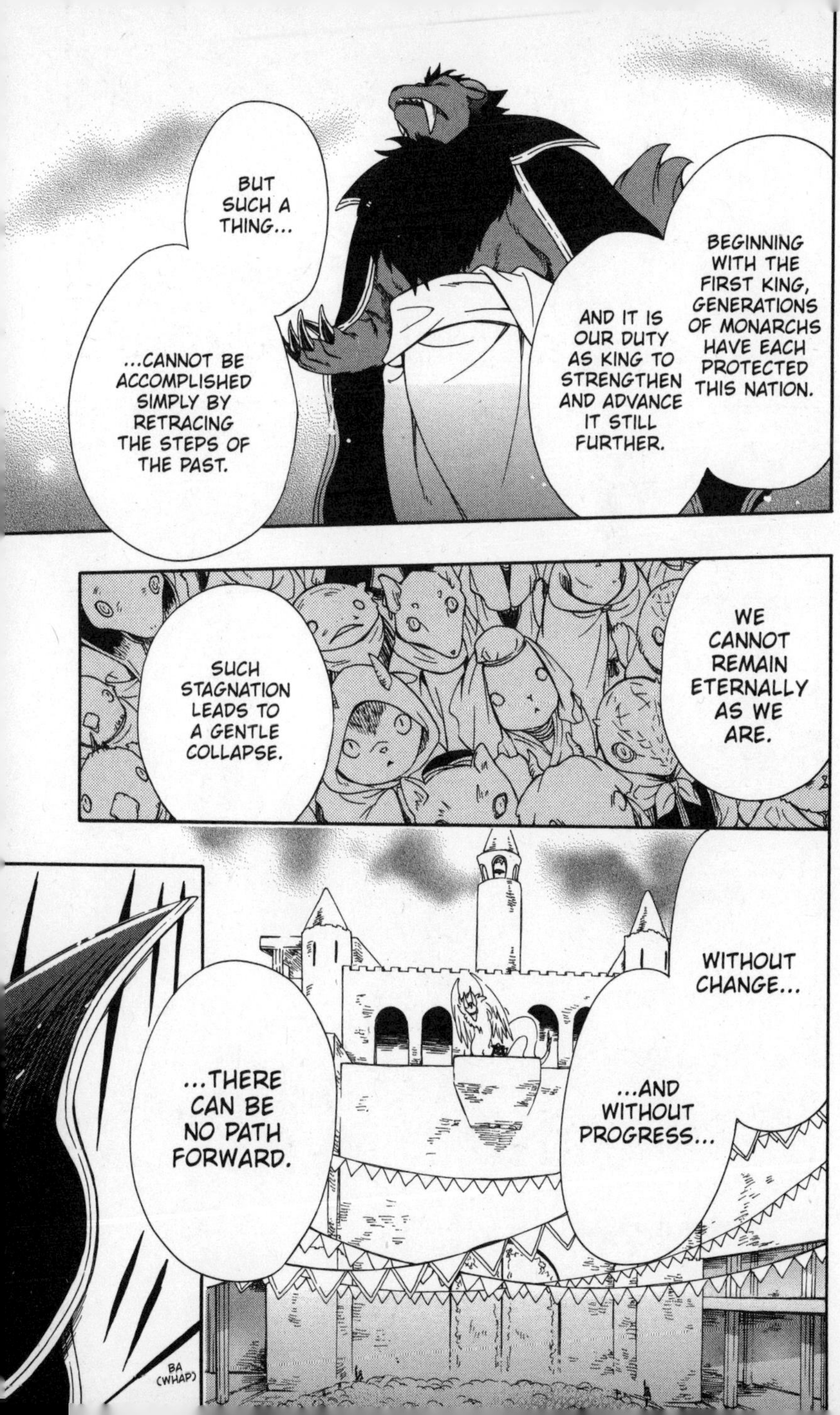
BEGINNING WITH THE FIRST KING, GENERATIONS OF MONARCHS HAVE EACH PROTECTED THIS NATION.
AND IT IS OUR DUTY AS KING TO STRENGTHEN AND ADVANCE IT STILL FURTHER.
BUT SUCH A THING...
...CANNOT BE ACCOMPLISHED SIMPLY BY RETRACING THE STEPS OF THE PAST.
WE CANNOT REMAIN ETERNALLY AS WE ARE.
SUCH STAGNATION LEADS TO A GENTLE COLLAPSE.
WITHOUT CHANGE...
...AND WITHOUT PROGRESS...
...THERE CAN BE NO PATH FORWARD.
BA (WHAP)

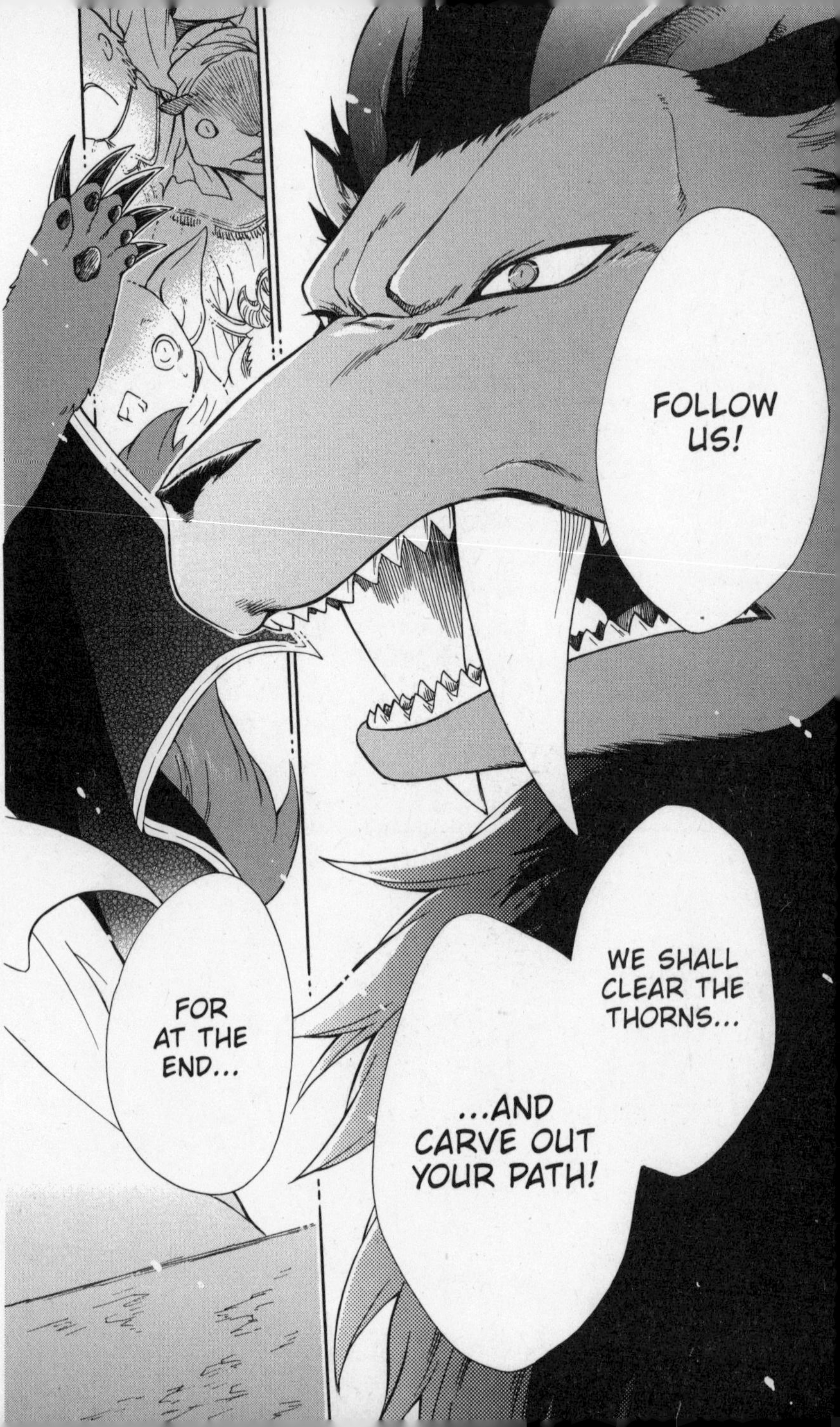
FOLLOW US!
WE SHALL CLEAR THE THORNS...
...AND CARVE OUT YOUR PATH!
FOR AT THE END...

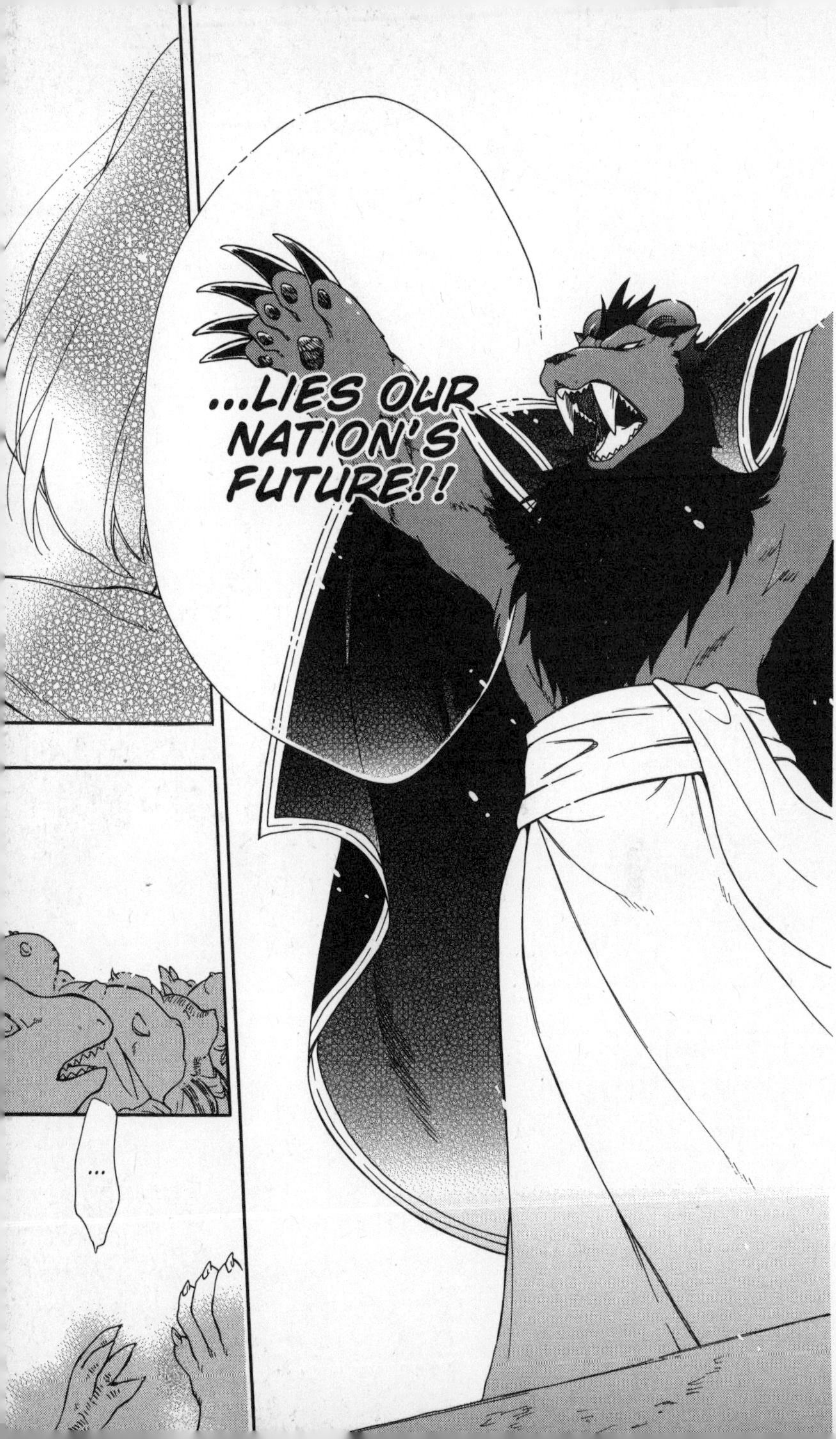
...LIES OUR NATION'S FUTURE!!
...

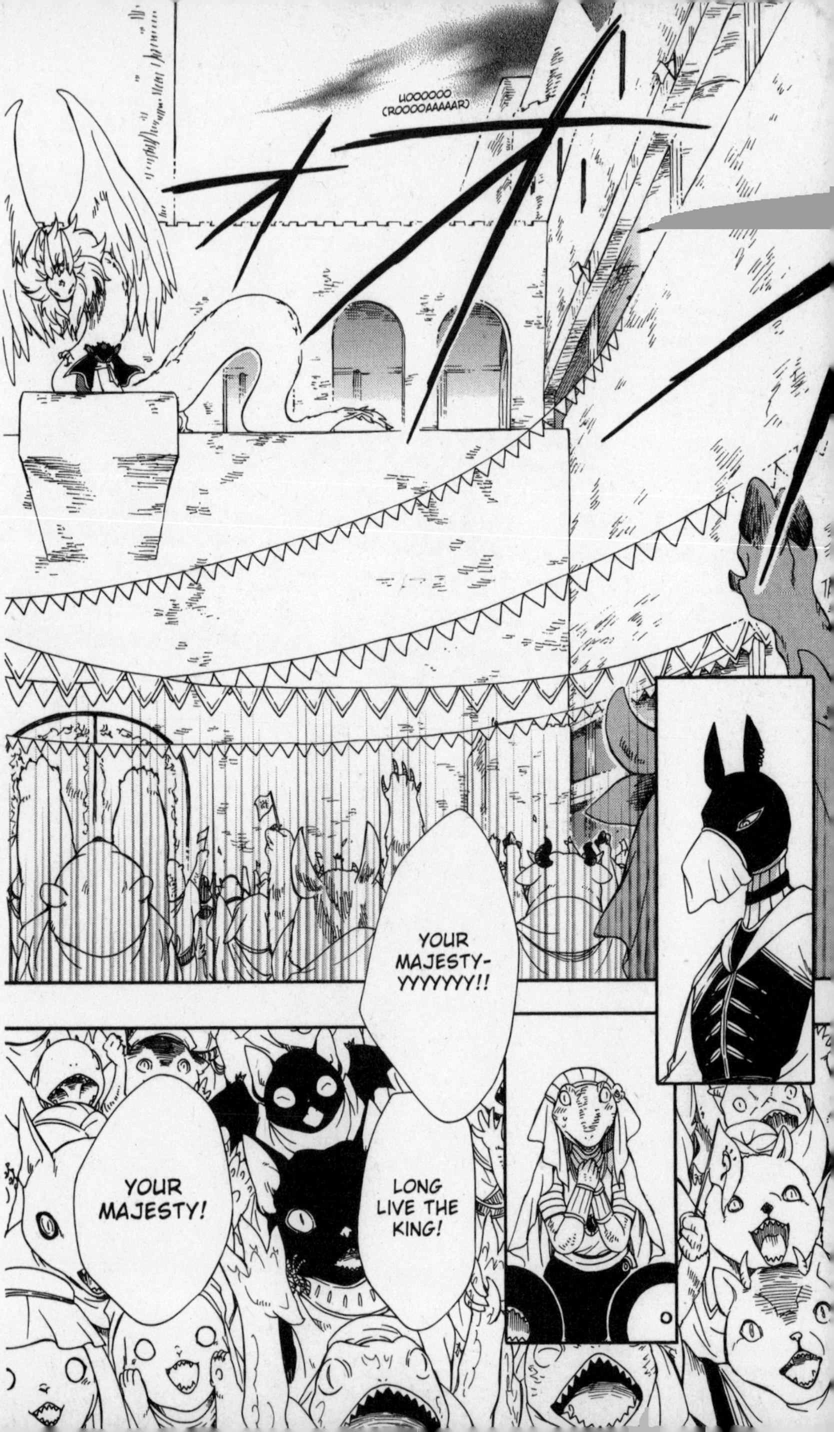
UOOOOOO
(ROOOOAAAAAR)
YOUR MAJESTY-YYYYYYY!!
LONG LIVE THE KING!
YOUR MAJESTY!

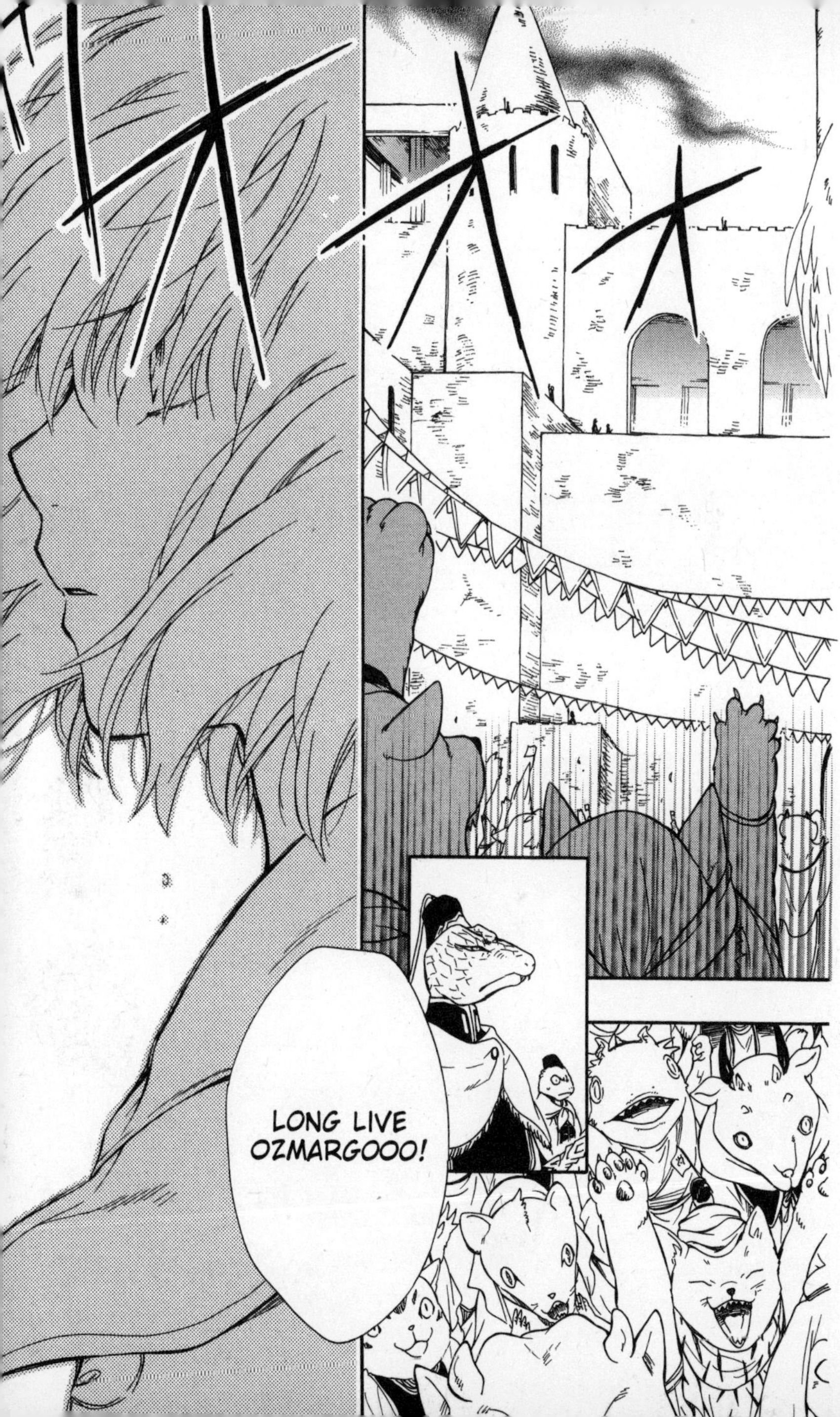
LONG LIVE OZMARGOOO!

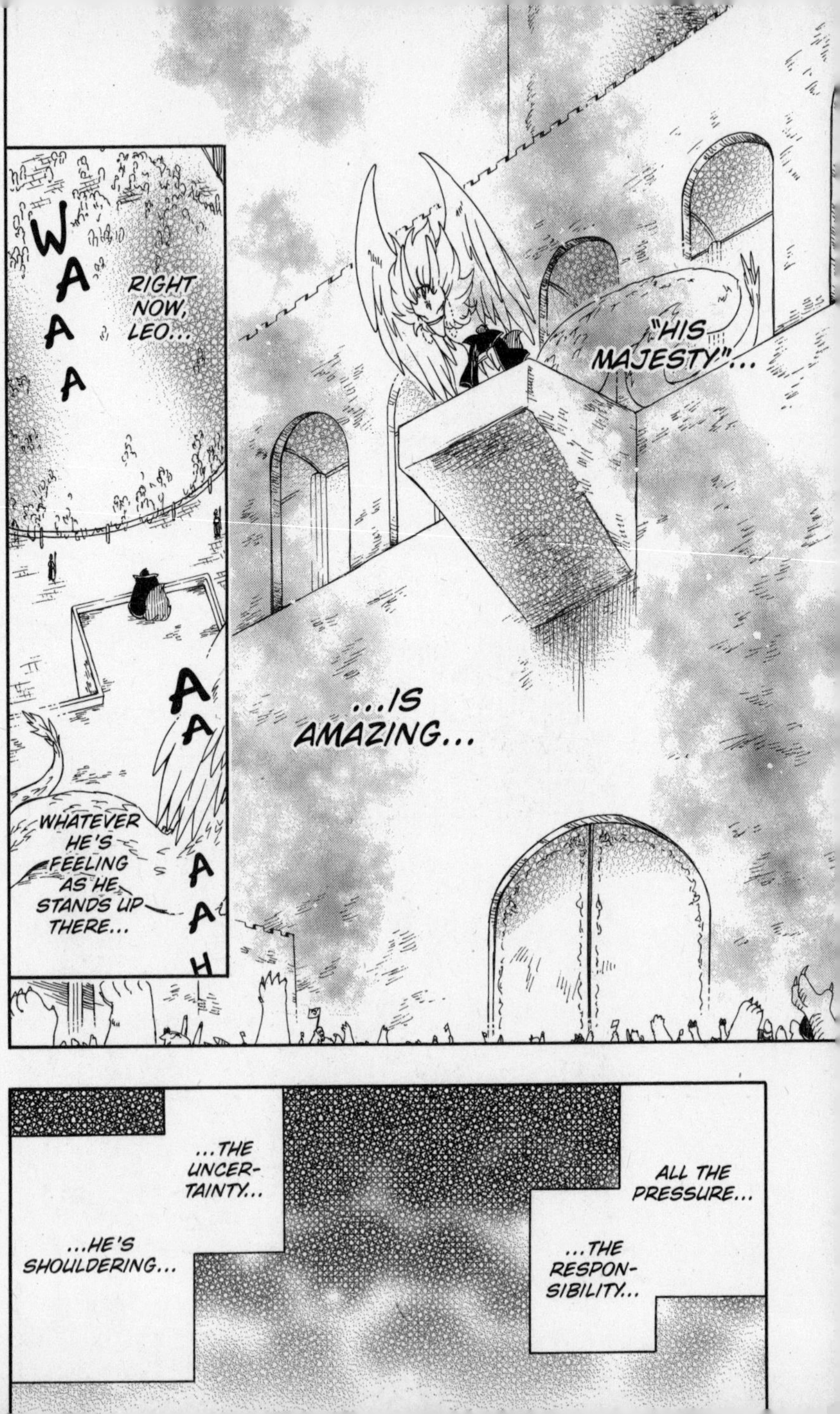
RIGHT NOW, LEO...
"HIS MAJESTY"...
...IS AMAZING...
WAAAA
AAAAH
WHATEVER HE'S FEELING AS HE STANDS UP THERE...
ALL THE PRESSURE...
...THE RESPON-SIBILITY...
...THE UNCER-TAINTY...
...HE'S SHOULDERING...

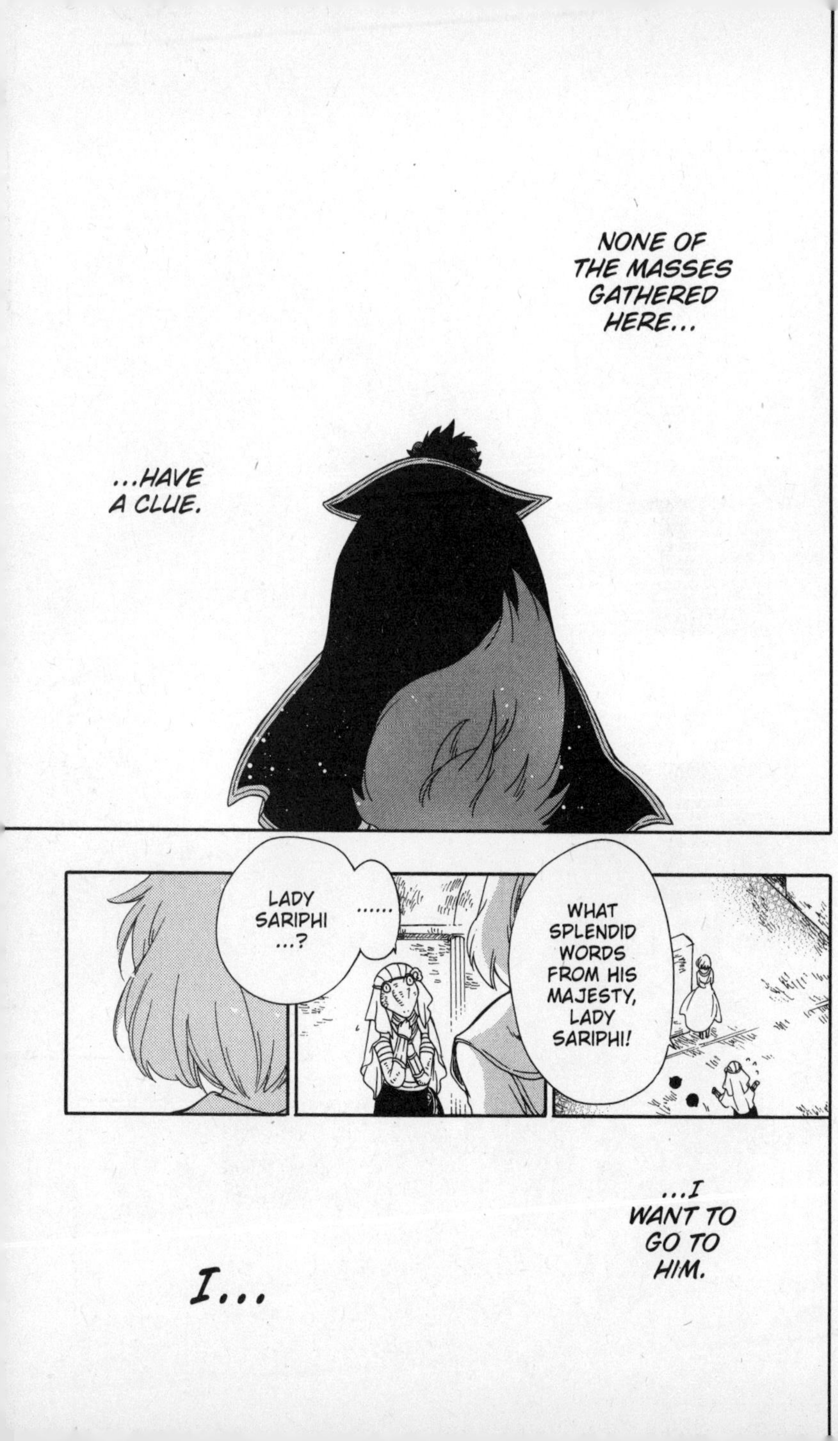
NONE OF THE MASSES GATHERED HERE...
...HAVE A CLUE.
WHAT SPLENDID WORDS FROM HIS MAJESTY, LADY SARIPHI!
......
LADY SARIPHI ...?
...I WANT TO GO TO HIM.
I...

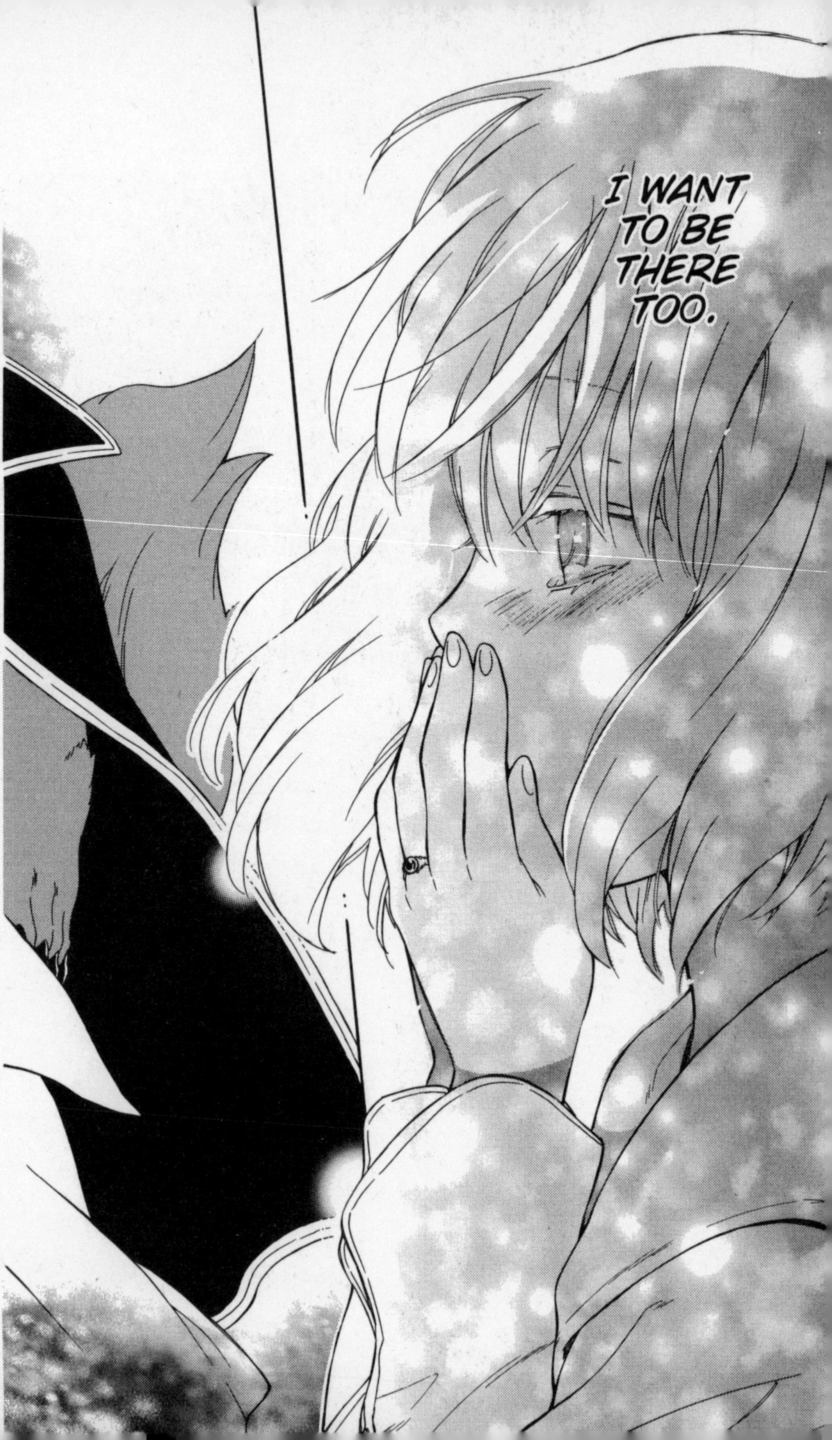
I WANT TO BE THERE TOO.

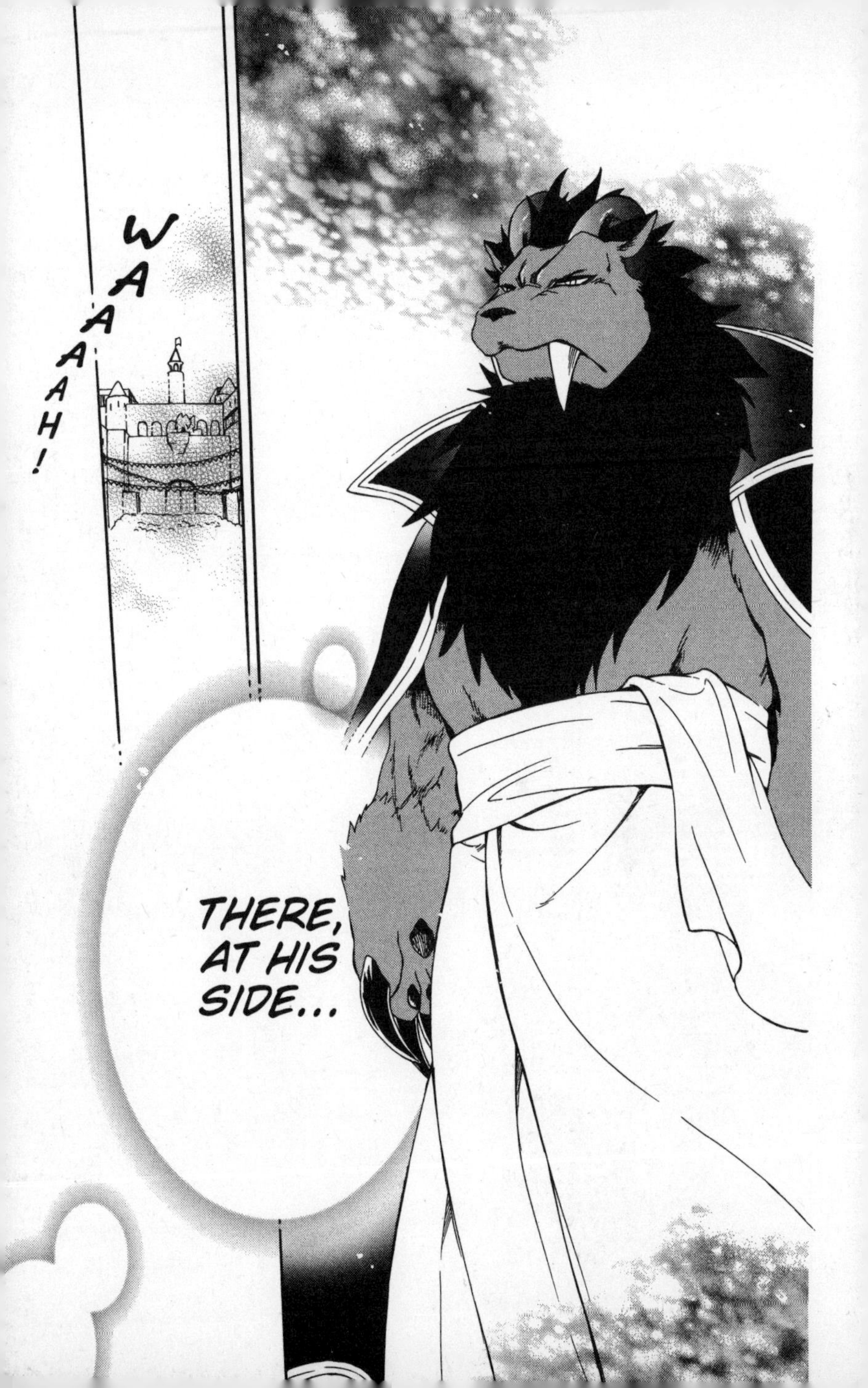
THERE, AT HIS SIDE...
WAAAAAH!

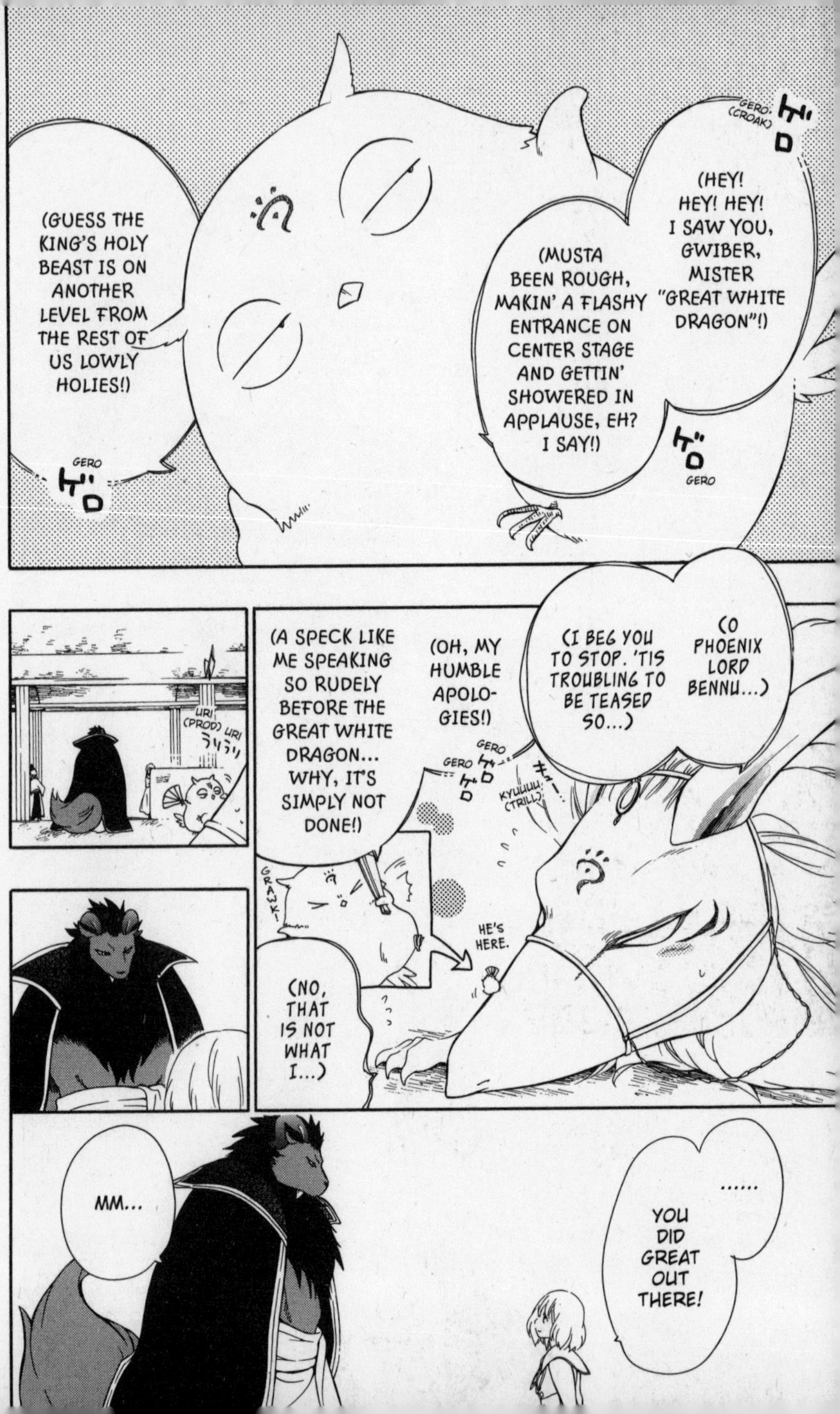
GERO. (CROAK) ゲロ
(HEY! HEY! HEY! I SAW YOU, GWIBER, MISTER "GREAT WHITE DRAGON"!)
(MUSTA BEEN ROUGH, MAKIN' A FLASHY ENTRANCE ON CENTER STAGE AND GETTIN' SHOWERED IN APPLAUSE, EH? I SAY!)
ゲロ GERO
(GUESS THE KING'S HOLY BEAST IS ON ANOTHER LEVEL FROM THE REST OF US LOWLY HOLIES!)
GERO ゲロ
(O PHOENIX LORD BENNU...)
(I BEG YOU TO STOP. 'TIS TROUBLING TO BE TEASED SO...)
(OH, MY HUMBLE APOLOGIES!)
(A SPECK LIKE ME SPEAKING SO RUDELY BEFORE THE GREAT WHITE DRAGON... WHY, IT'S SIMPLY NOT DONE!)
KYUUUU (TRILL)
GERO ゲロ
GERO ゲロ
GRANK!
HE'S HERE.
(NO, THAT IS NOT WHAT I...)
URI (PROD) URI ウリウリ
......
YOU DID GREAT OUT THERE!
MM...

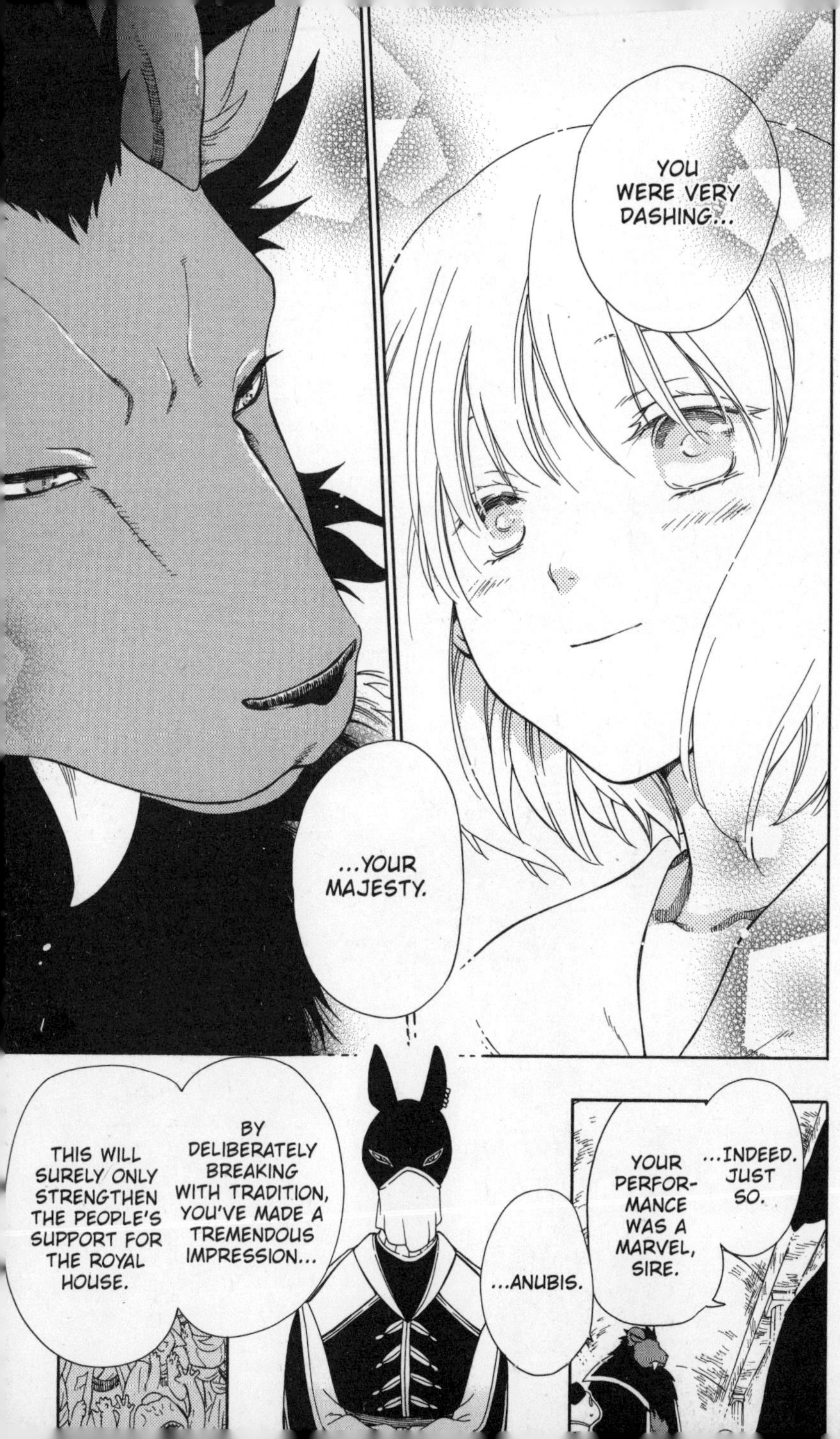
YOU WERE VERY DASHING...
...YOUR MAJESTY.
...INDEED. JUST SO.
YOUR PERFORMANCE WAS A MARVEL, SIRE.
...ANUBIS.
BY DELIBERATELY BREAKING WITH TRADITION, YOU'VE MADE A TREMENDOUS IMPRESSION...
THIS WILL SURELY ONLY STRENGTHEN THE PEOPLE'S SUPPORT FOR THE ROYAL HOUSE.

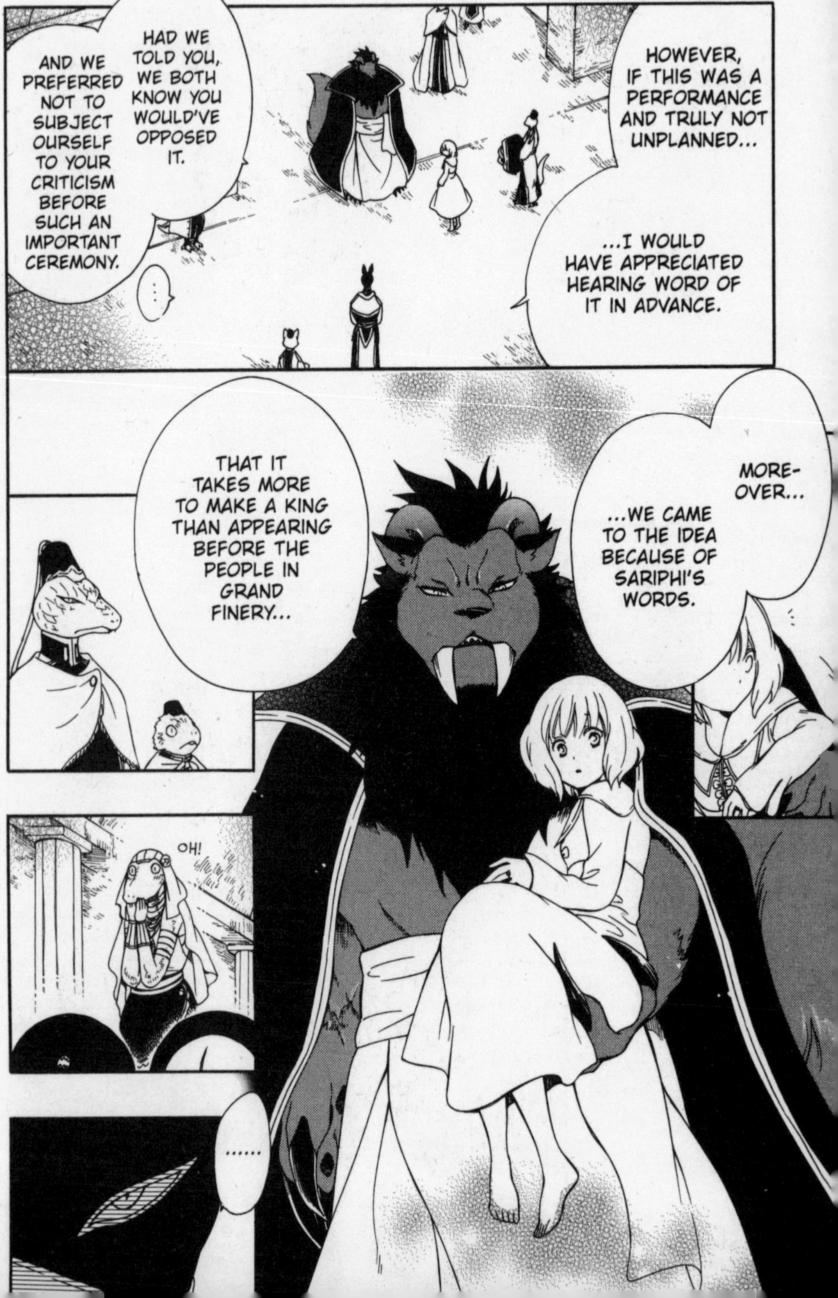
HOWEVER, IF THIS WAS A PERFORMANCE AND TRULY NOT UNPLANNED...
...I WOULD HAVE APPRECIATED HEARING WORD OF IT IN ADVANCE.
HAD WE TOLD YOU, WE BOTH KNOW YOU WOULD'VE OPPOSED IT.
AND WE PREFERRED NOT TO SUBJECT OURSELF TO YOUR CRITICISM BEFORE SUCH AN IMPORTANT CEREMONY.
...
MORE-OVER...
...WE CAME TO THE IDEA BECAUSE OF SARIPHI'S WORDS.
THAT IT TAKES MORE TO MAKE A KING THAN APPEARING BEFORE THE PEOPLE IN GRAND FINERY...
OH!
......

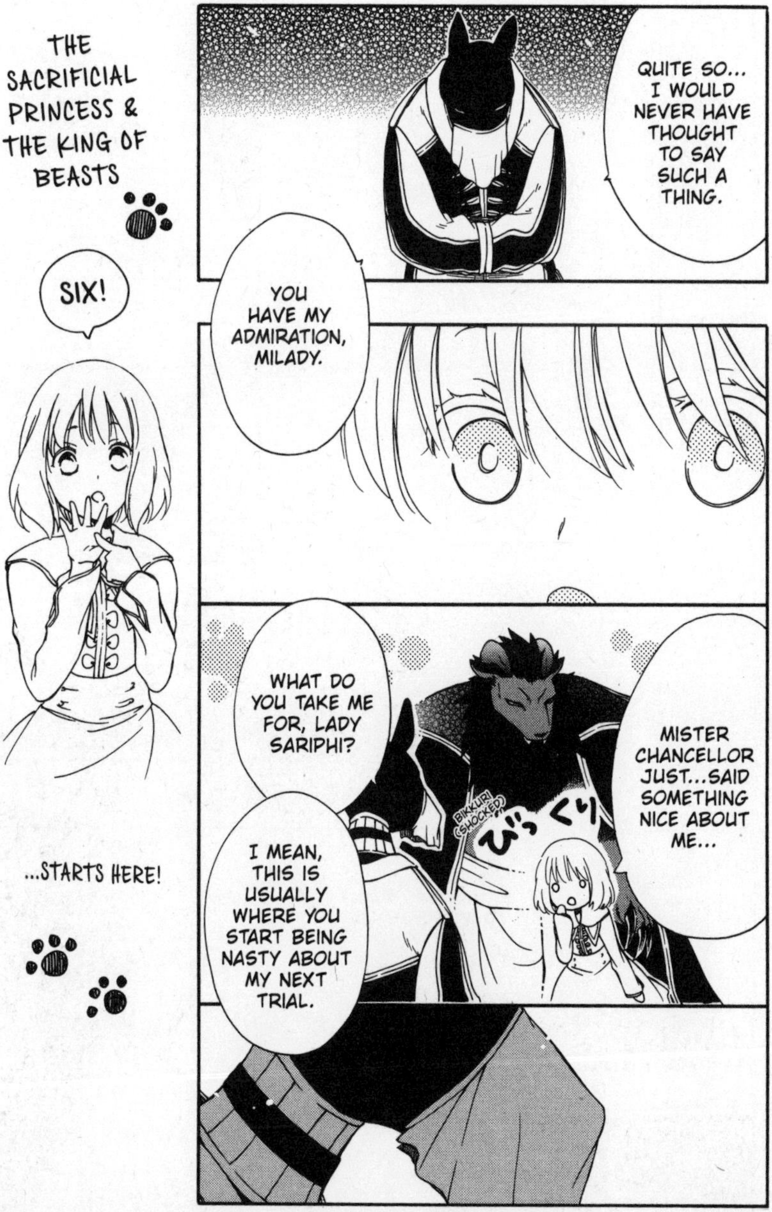
QUITE SO... I WOULD NEVER HAVE THOUGHT TO SAY SUCH A THING.
YOU HAVE MY ADMIRATION, MILADY.
MISTER CHANCELLOR JUST...SAID SOMETHING NICE ABOUT ME...
びっくり
BIKKURI (SHOCKED)
WHAT DO YOU TAKE ME FOR, LADY SARIPHI?
I MEAN, THIS IS USUALLY WHERE YOU START BEING NASTY ABOUT MY NEXT TRIAL.
THE SACRIFICIAL PRINCESS & THE KING OF BEASTS
SIX!
...STARTS HERE!

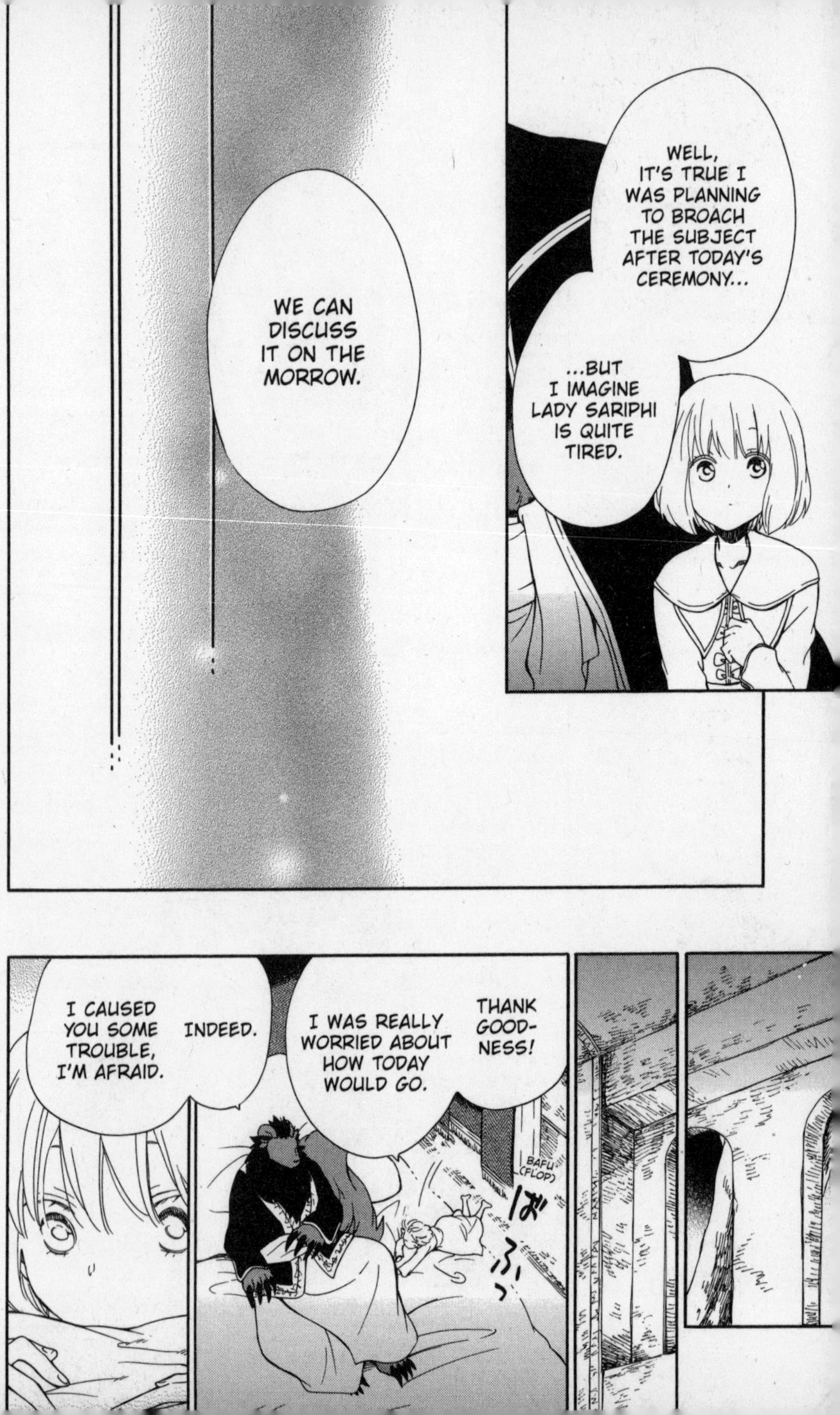
WELL, IT'S TRUE I WAS PLANNING TO BROACH THE SUBJECT AFTER TODAY'S CEREMONY...
...BUT I IMAGINE LADY SARIPHI IS QUITE TIRED.
WE CAN DISCUSS IT ON THE MORROW.
THANK GOODNESS!
I WAS REALLY WORRIED ABOUT HOW TODAY WOULD GO.
BAFU (FLOP)
ばふっ
INDEED.
I CAUSED YOU SOME TROUBLE, I'M AFRAID.

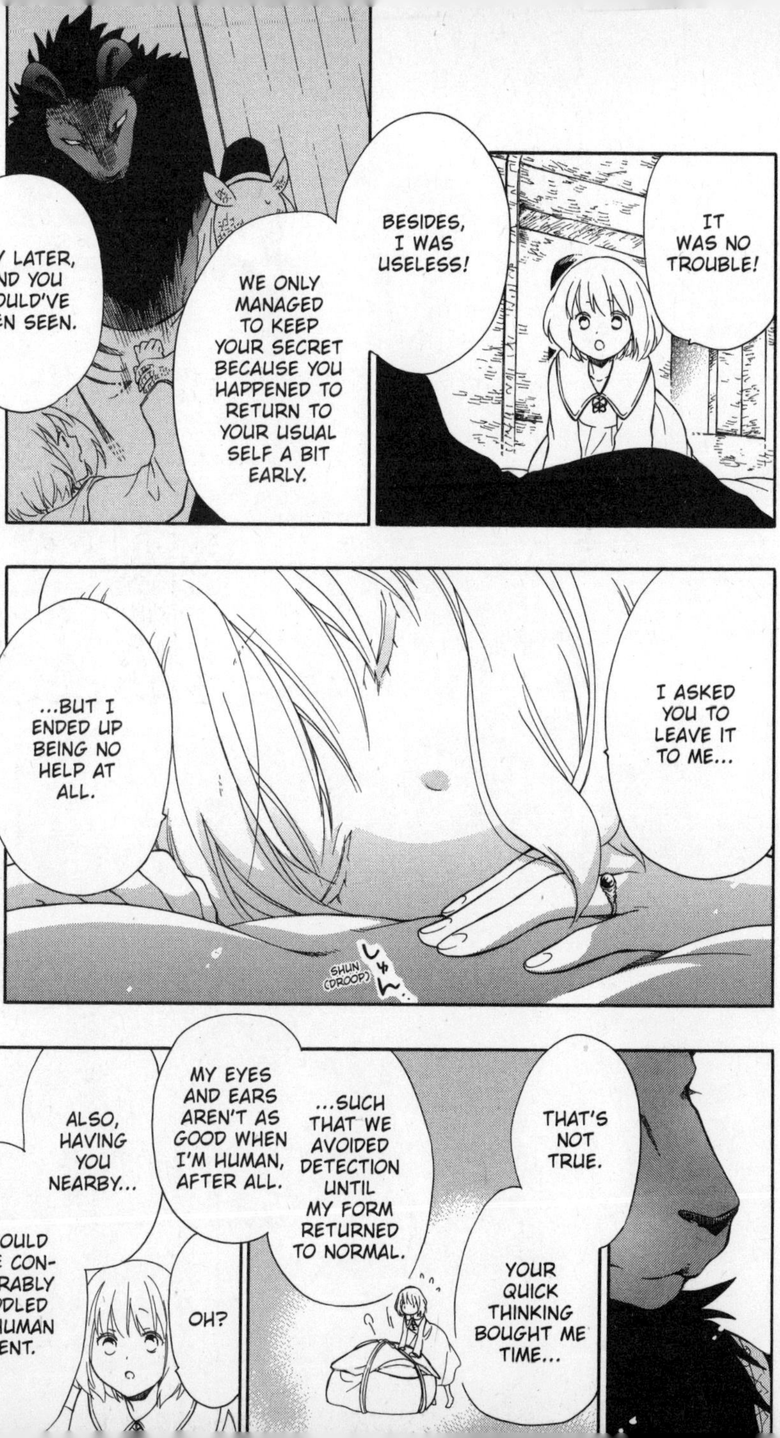

IT WAS NO TROUBLE!
BESIDES, I WAS USELESS!
WE ONLY MANAGED TO KEEP YOUR SECRET BECAUSE YOU HAPPENED TO RETURN TO YOUR USUAL SELF A BIT EARLY.
ANY LATER, AND YOU WOULD'VE BEEN SEEN.
I ASKED YOU TO LEAVE IT TO ME...
...BUT I ENDED UP BEING NO HELP AT ALL.
しゅん...
SHUN (DROOP)
THAT'S NOT TRUE.
YOUR QUICK THINKING BOUGHT ME TIME...
...SUCH THAT WE AVOIDED DETECTION UNTIL MY FORM RETURNED TO NORMAL.
MY EYES AND EARS AREN'T AS GOOD WHEN I'M HUMAN, AFTER ALL.
ALSO, HAVING YOU NEARBY...
OH?
...WOULD HAVE CON-SIDERABLY MUDDLED MY HUMAN SCENT.

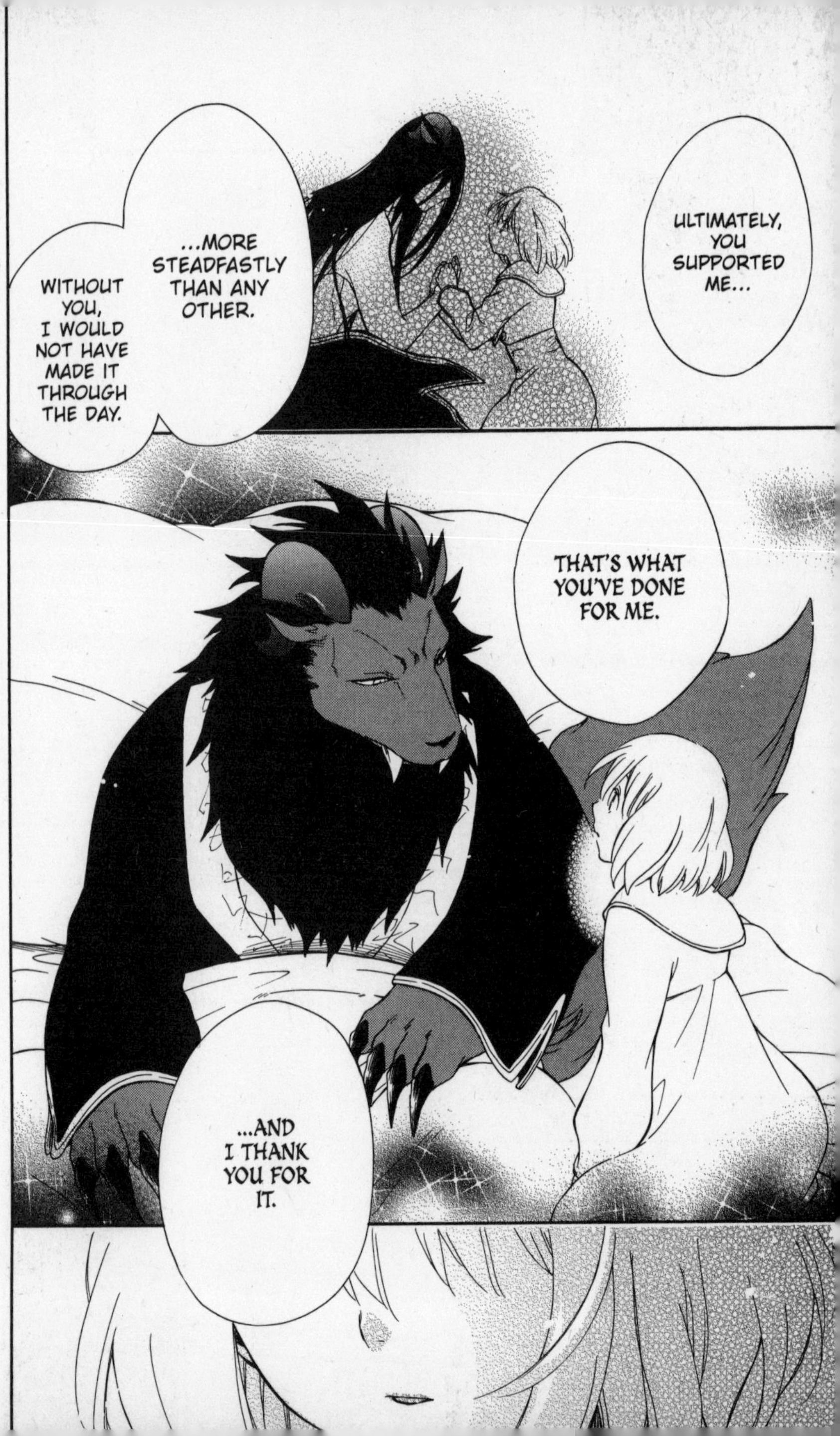
ULTIMATELY, YOU SUPPORTED ME...
...MORE STEADFASTLY THAN ANY OTHER.
WITHOUT YOU, I WOULD NOT HAVE MADE IT THROUGH THE DAY.
THAT'S WHAT YOU'VE DONE FOR ME.
...AND I THANK YOU FOR IT.

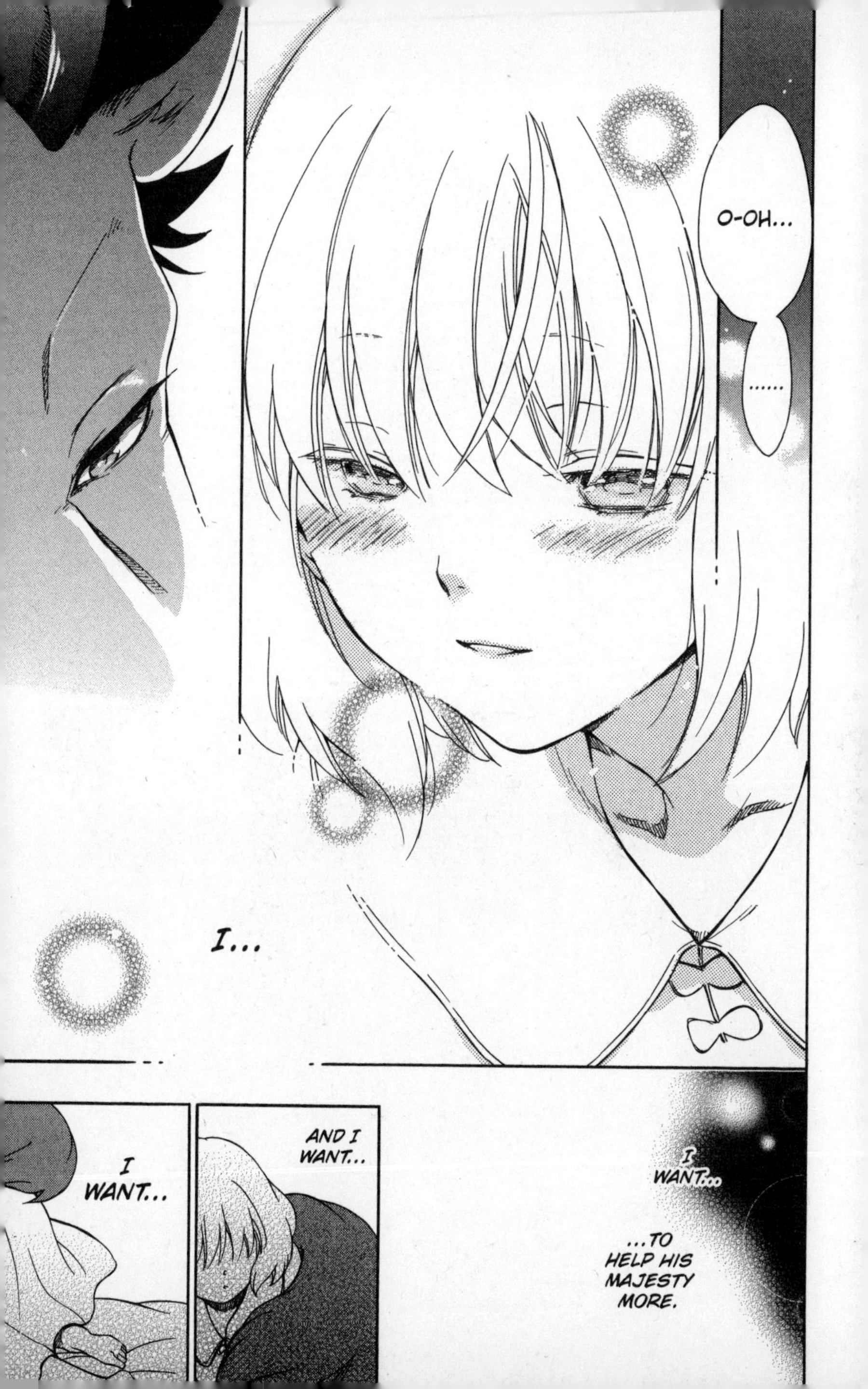
O-OH...
......
I...
I WANT...
...TO HELP HIS MAJESTY MORE.
AND I WANT...
I WANT...

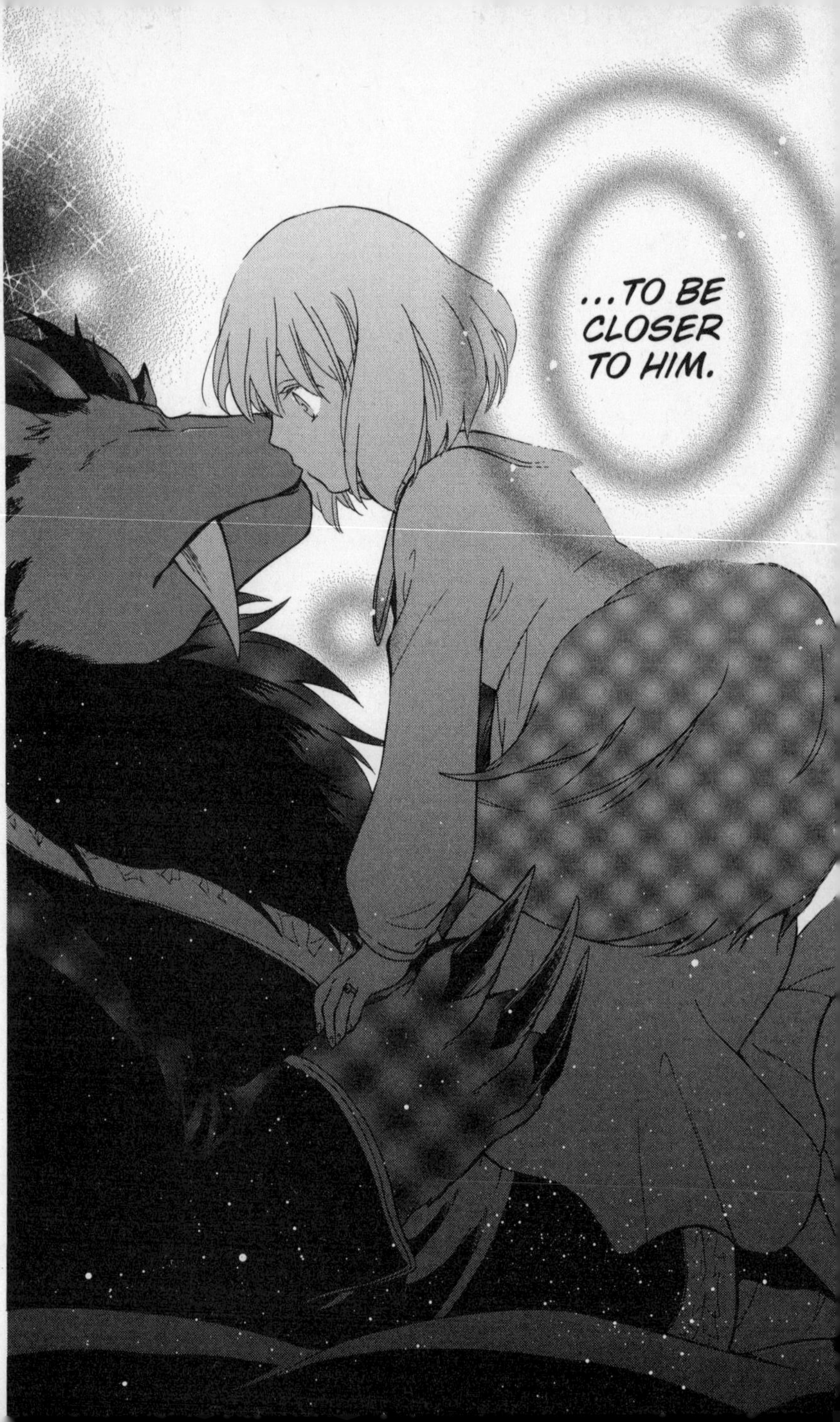
...TO BE CLOSER TO HIM.

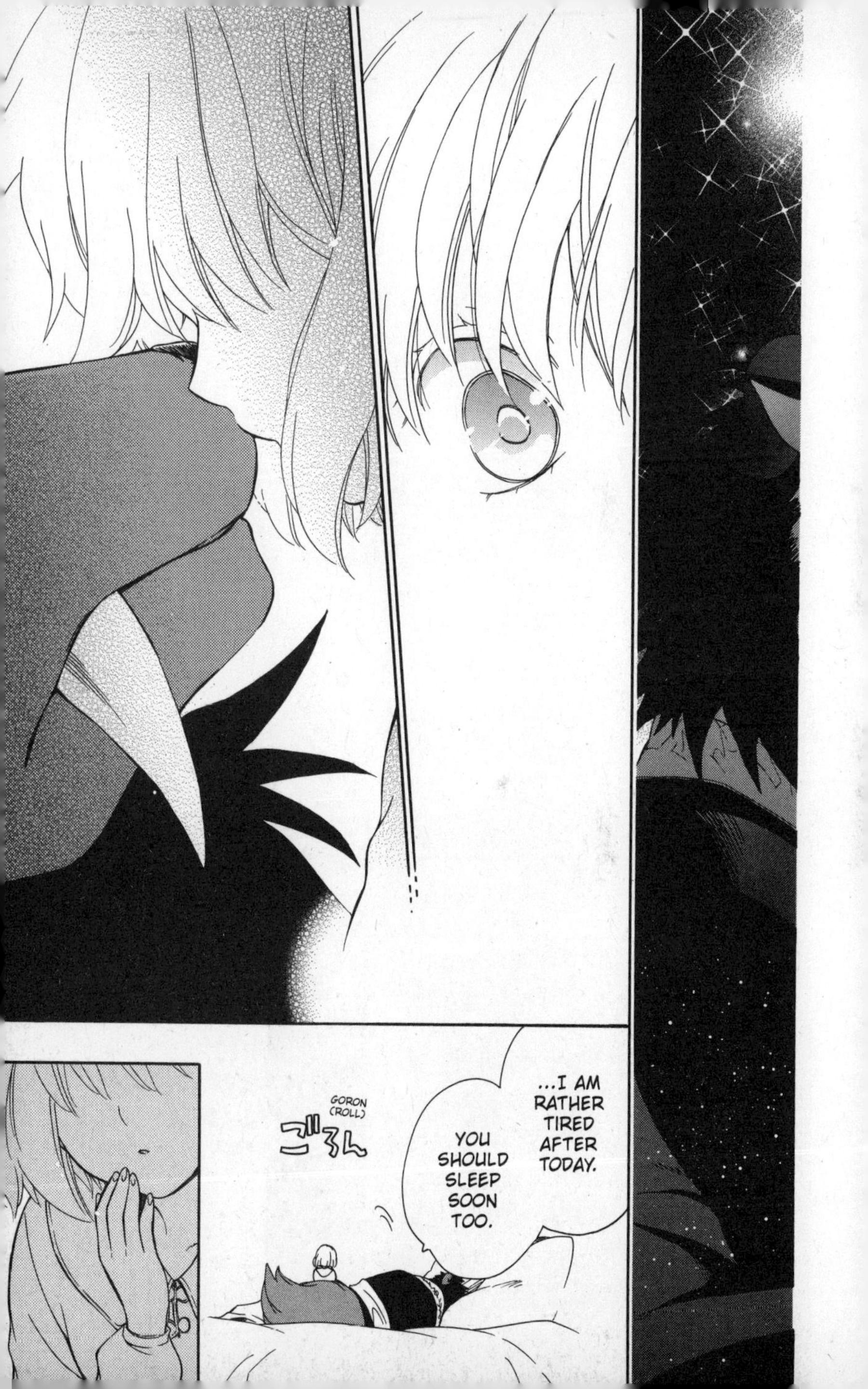
...I AM RATHER TIRED AFTER TODAY.
YOU SHOULD SLEEP SOON TOO.
ごろん
GORON (ROLL)

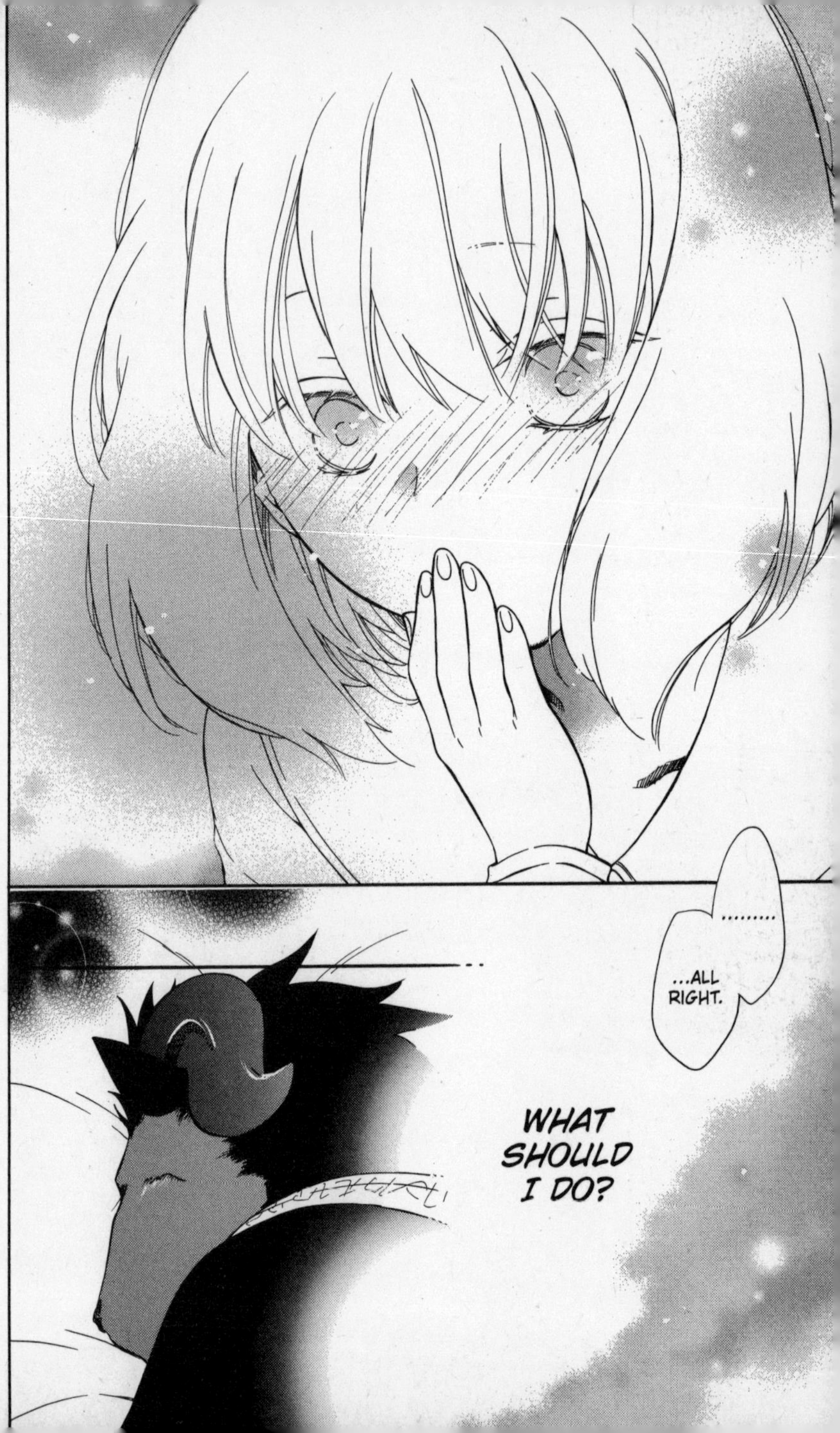
....
...ALL RIGHT.
WHAT SHOULD I DO?

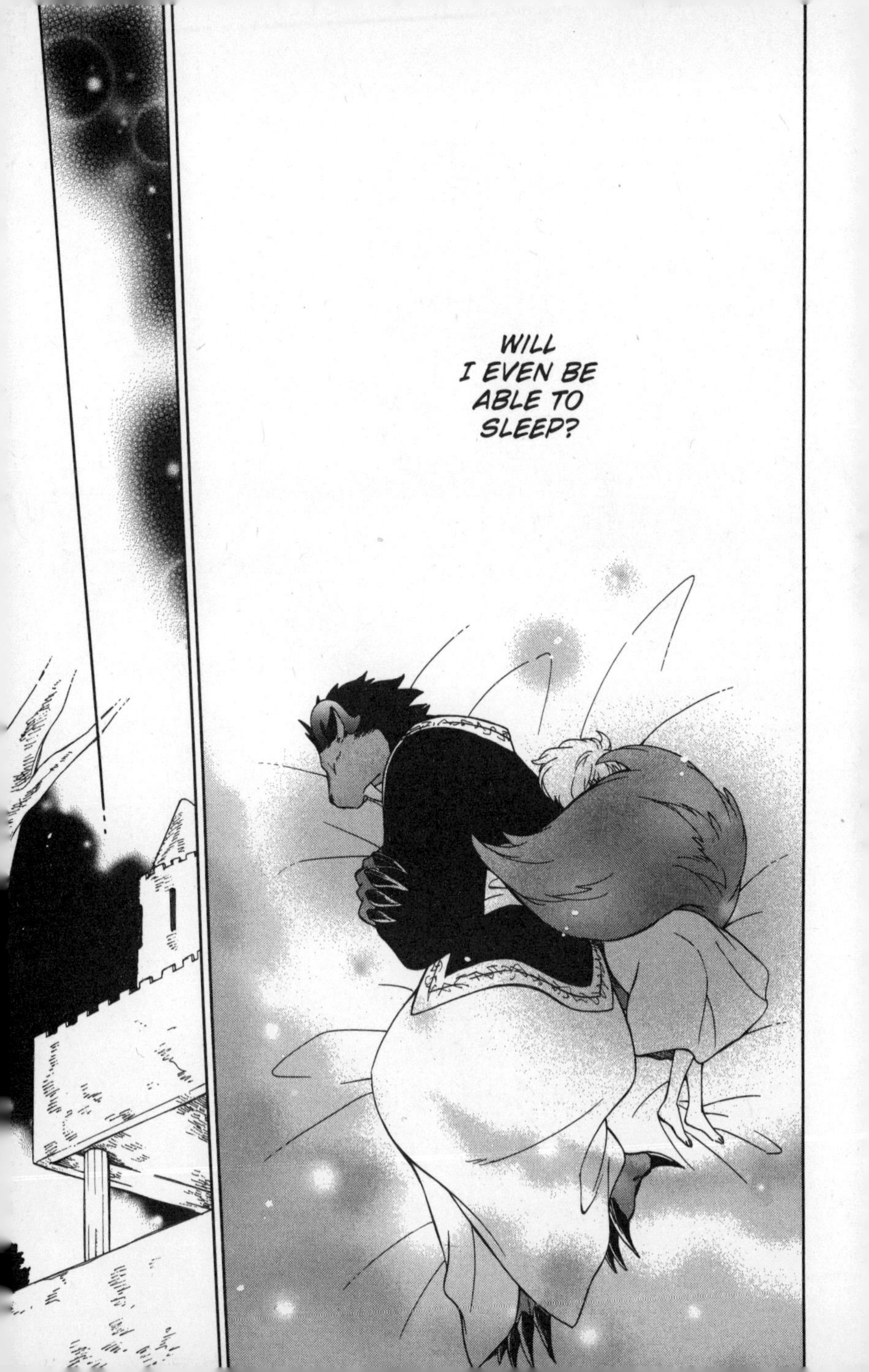
WILL I EVEN BE ABLE TO SLEEP?

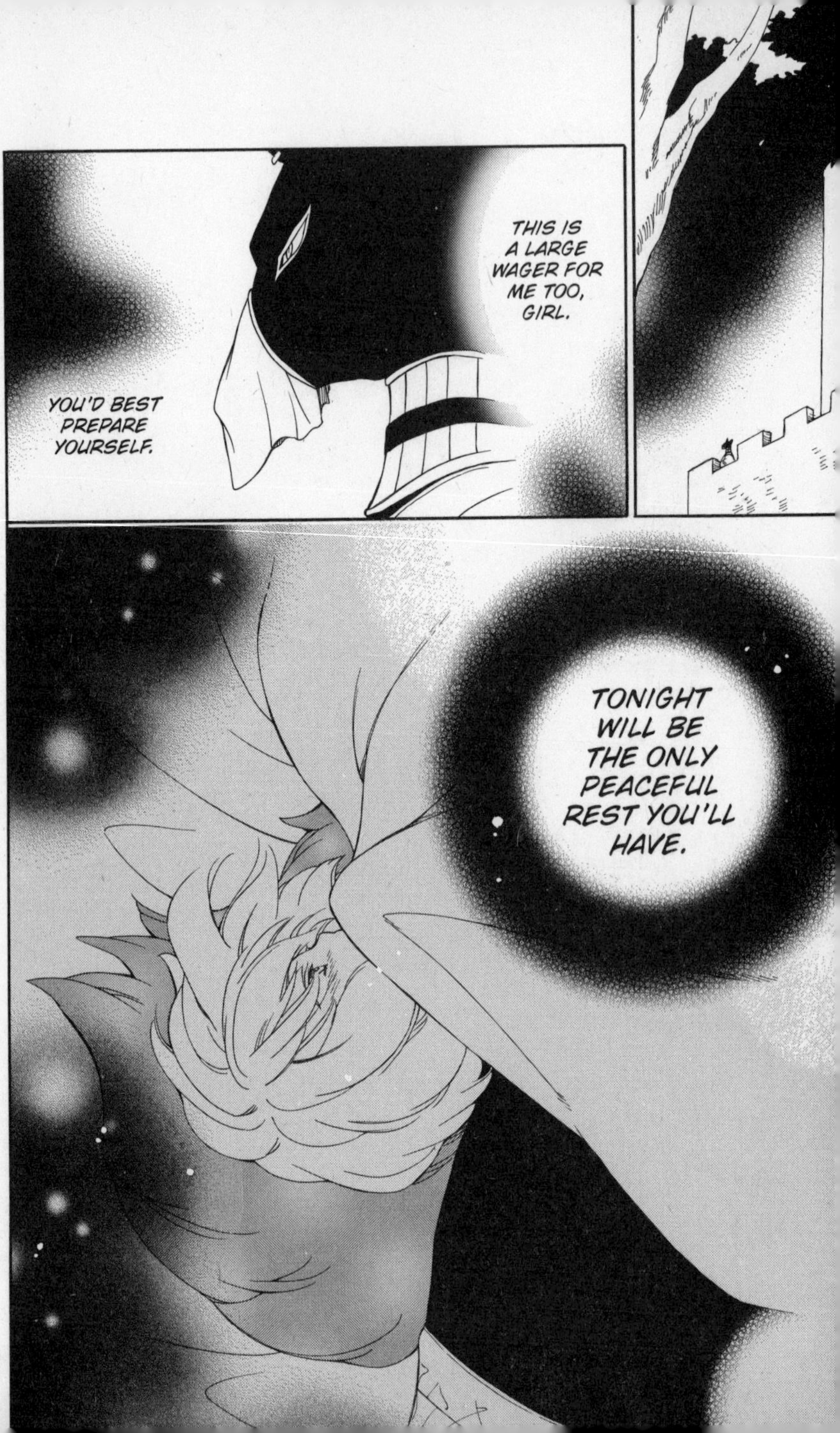
THIS IS A LARGE WAGER FOR ME TOO, GIRL.
YOU'D BEST PREPARE YOURSELF.
TONIGHT WILL BE THE ONLY PEACEFUL REST YOU'LL HAVE.

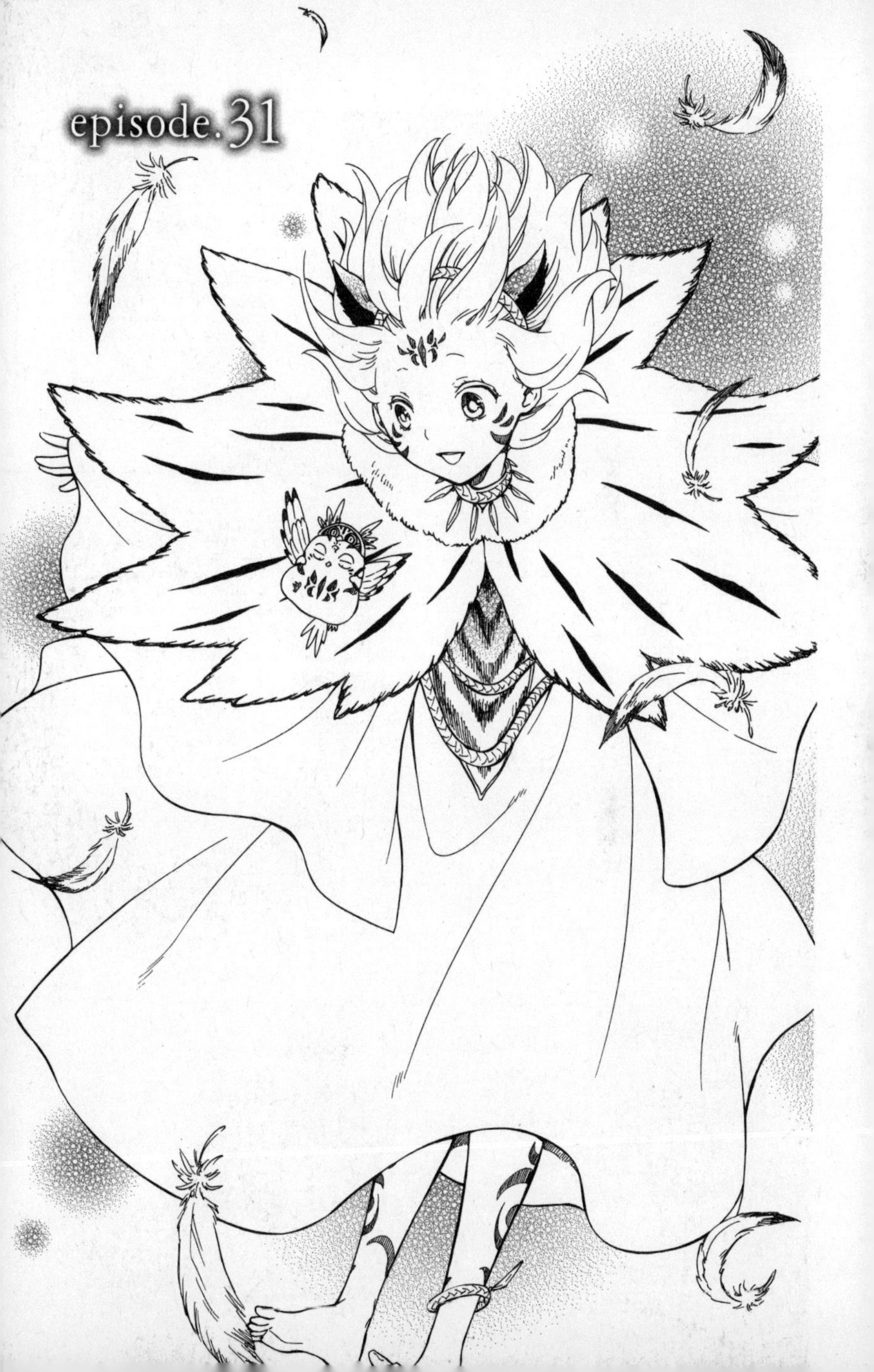
episode. 31

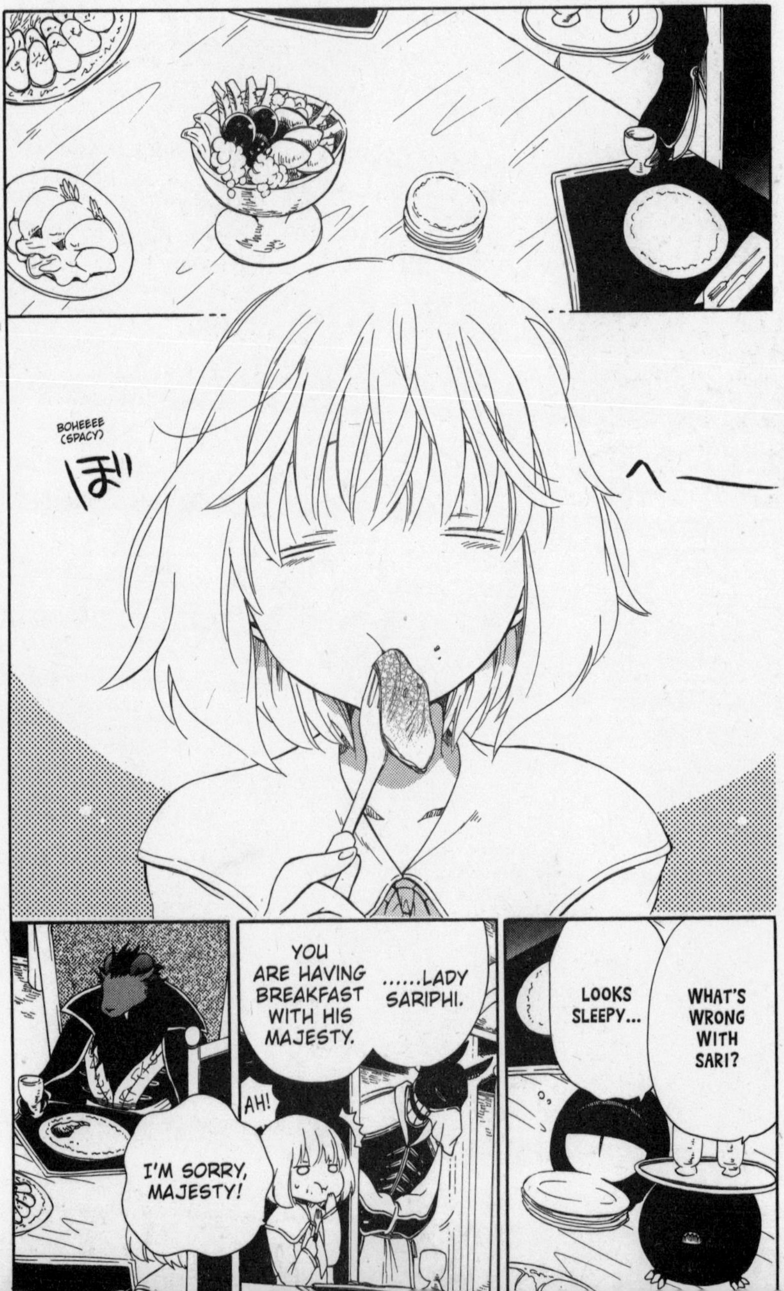
BOHEEEE (SPACY)
ぼ
へーー…
WHAT'S WRONG WITH SARI?
LOOKS SLEEPY...
......LADY SARIPHI.
YOU ARE HAVING BREAKFAST WITH HIS MAJESTY.
AH!
I'M SORRY, MAJESTY!

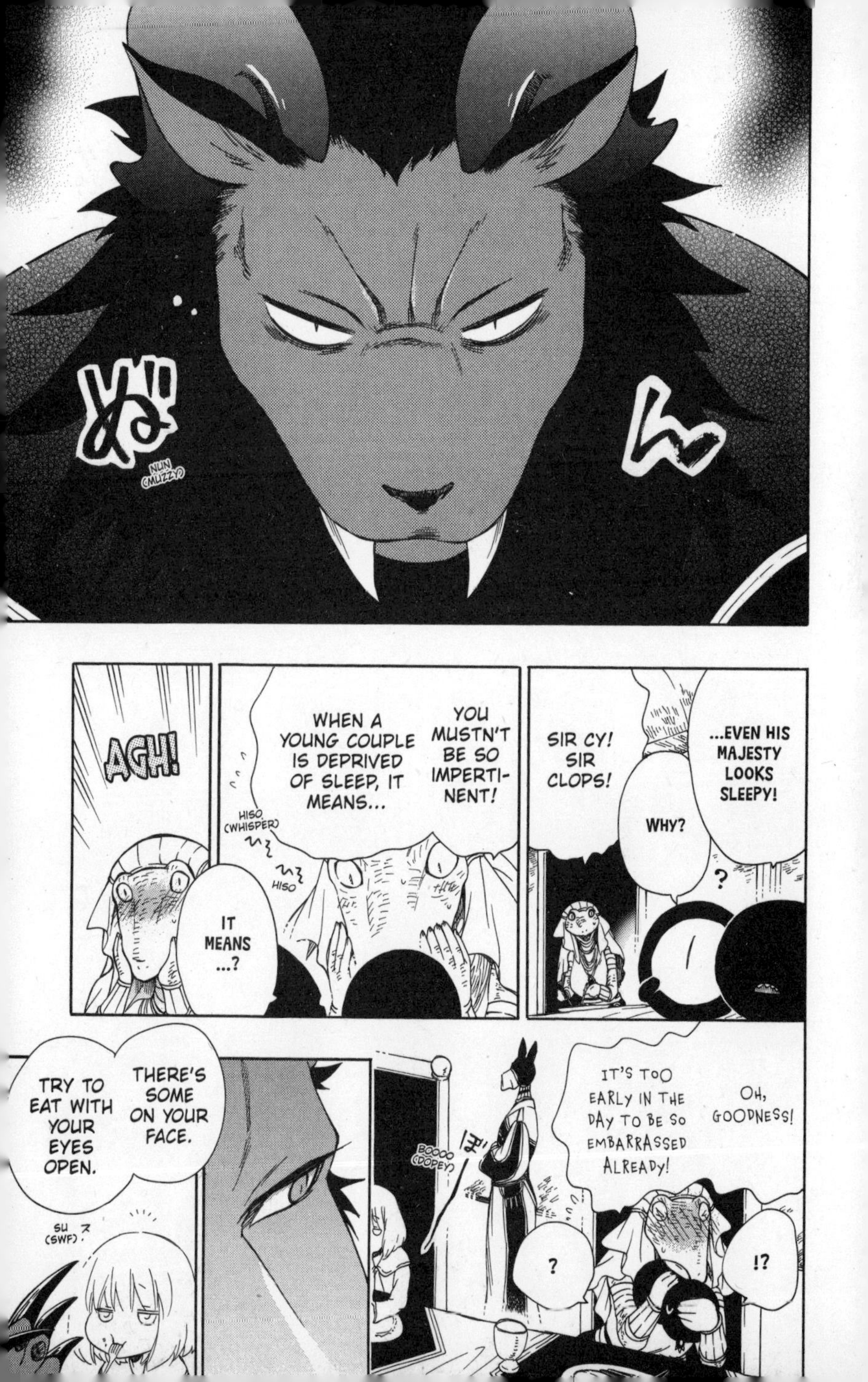
ぬん
NUN (MUZZY)
...EVEN HIS MAJESTY LOOKS SLEEPY!
SIR CY! SIR CLOPS!
WHY?
?
YOU MUSTN'T BE SO IMPERTINENT!
WHEN A YOUNG COUPLE IS DEPRIVED OF SLEEP, IT MEANS...
HISO (WHISPER)
HISO
AGH!
IT MEANS ...?
OH, GOODNESS!
IT'S TOO EARLY IN THE DAY TO BE SO EMBARRASSED ALREADY!
BOOOO (DOPEY)
!?
?
THERE'S SOME ON YOUR FACE.
TRY TO EAT WITH YOUR EYES OPEN.
SU (SWF)

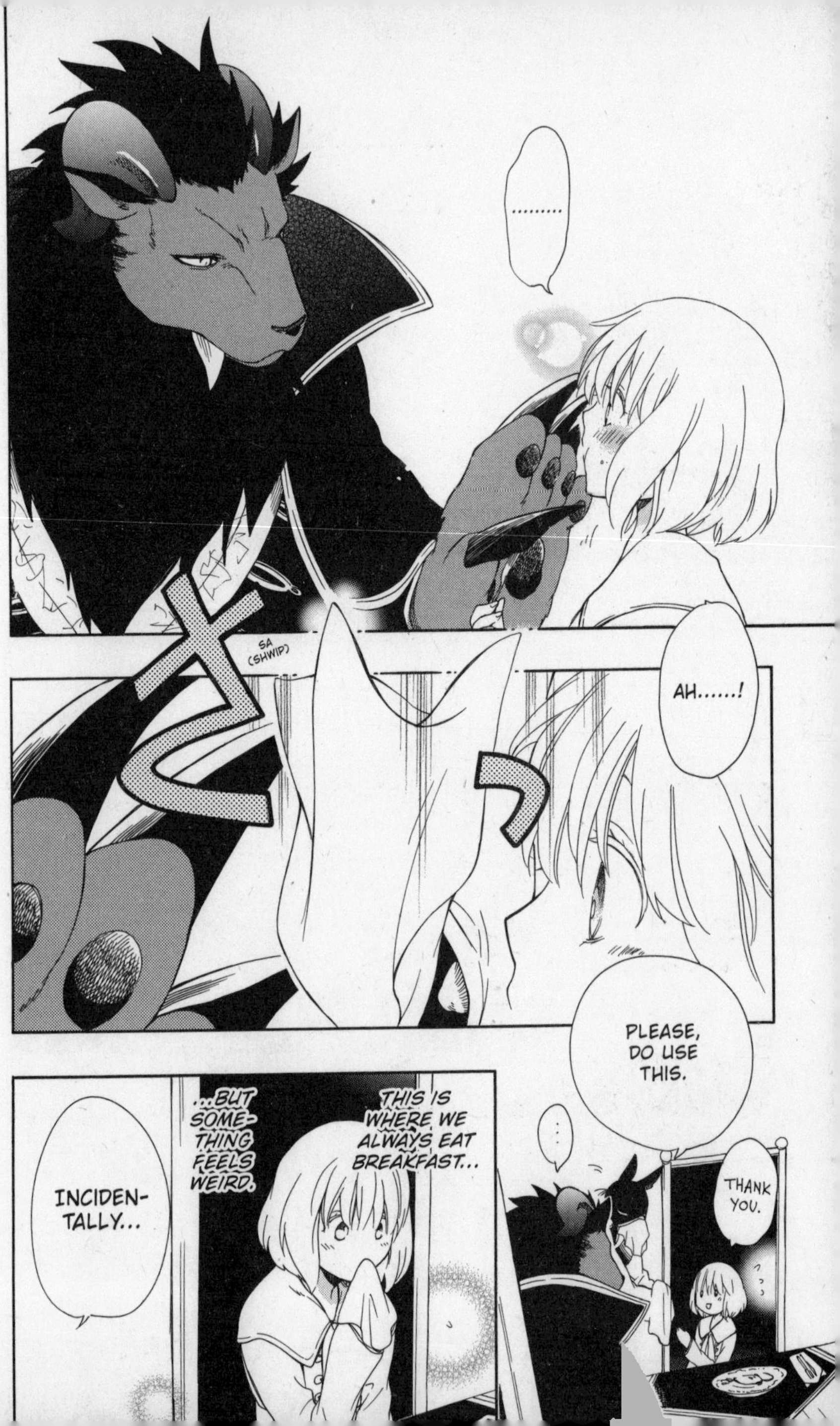
....
SA (SHWIP)
AH......!
PLEASE, DO USE THIS.
...
THANK YOU.
THIS IS WHERE WE ALWAYS EAT BREAKFAST...
...BUT SOMETHING FEELS WEIRD.
INCIDENTALLY...

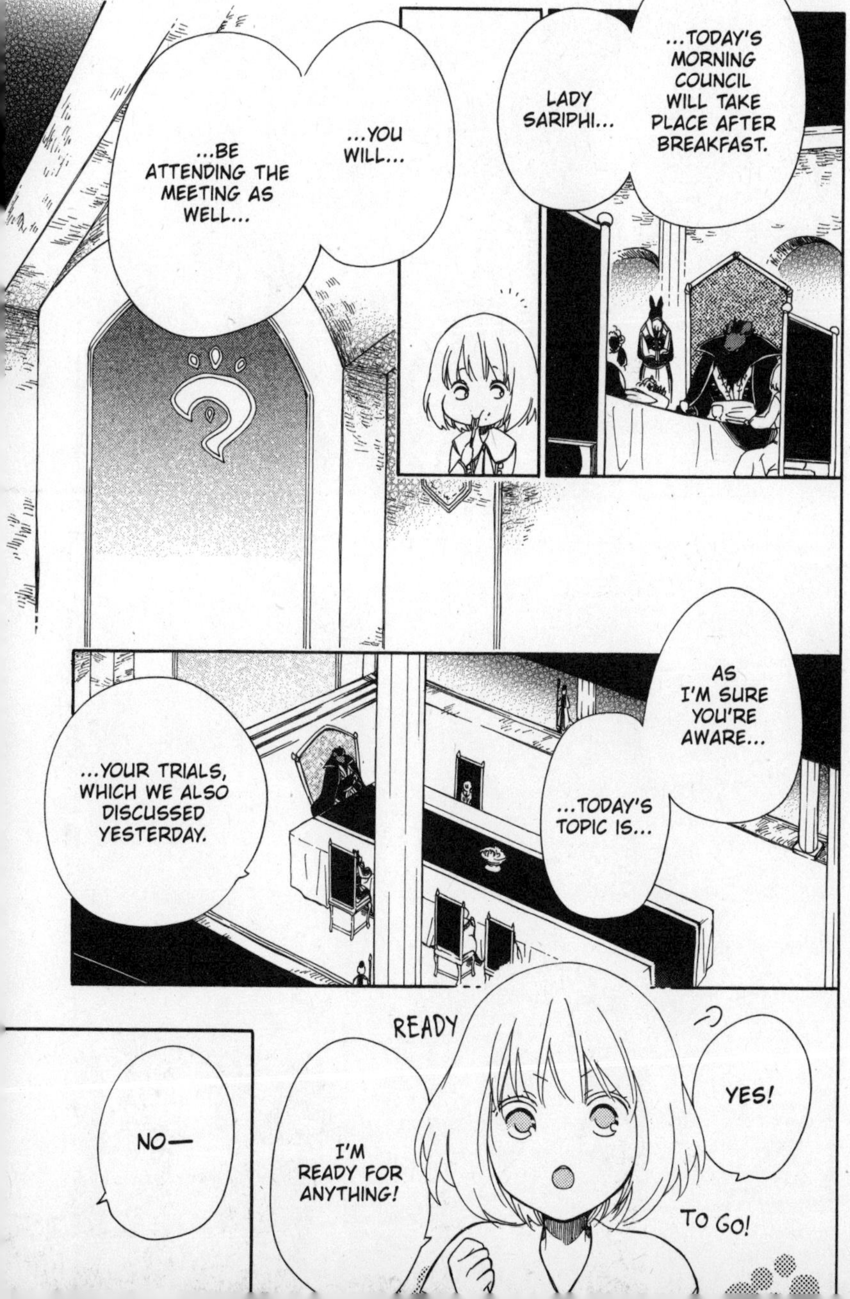
...TODAY'S MORNING COUNCIL WILL TAKE PLACE AFTER BREAKFAST.
LADY SARIPHI...
...YOU WILL...
...BE ATTENDING THE MEETING AS WELL...
AS I'M SURE YOU'RE AWARE...
...TODAY'S TOPIC IS...
...YOUR TRIALS, WHICH WE ALSO DISCUSSED YESTERDAY.
YES!
READY
TO GO!
I'M READY FOR ANYTHING!
NO—

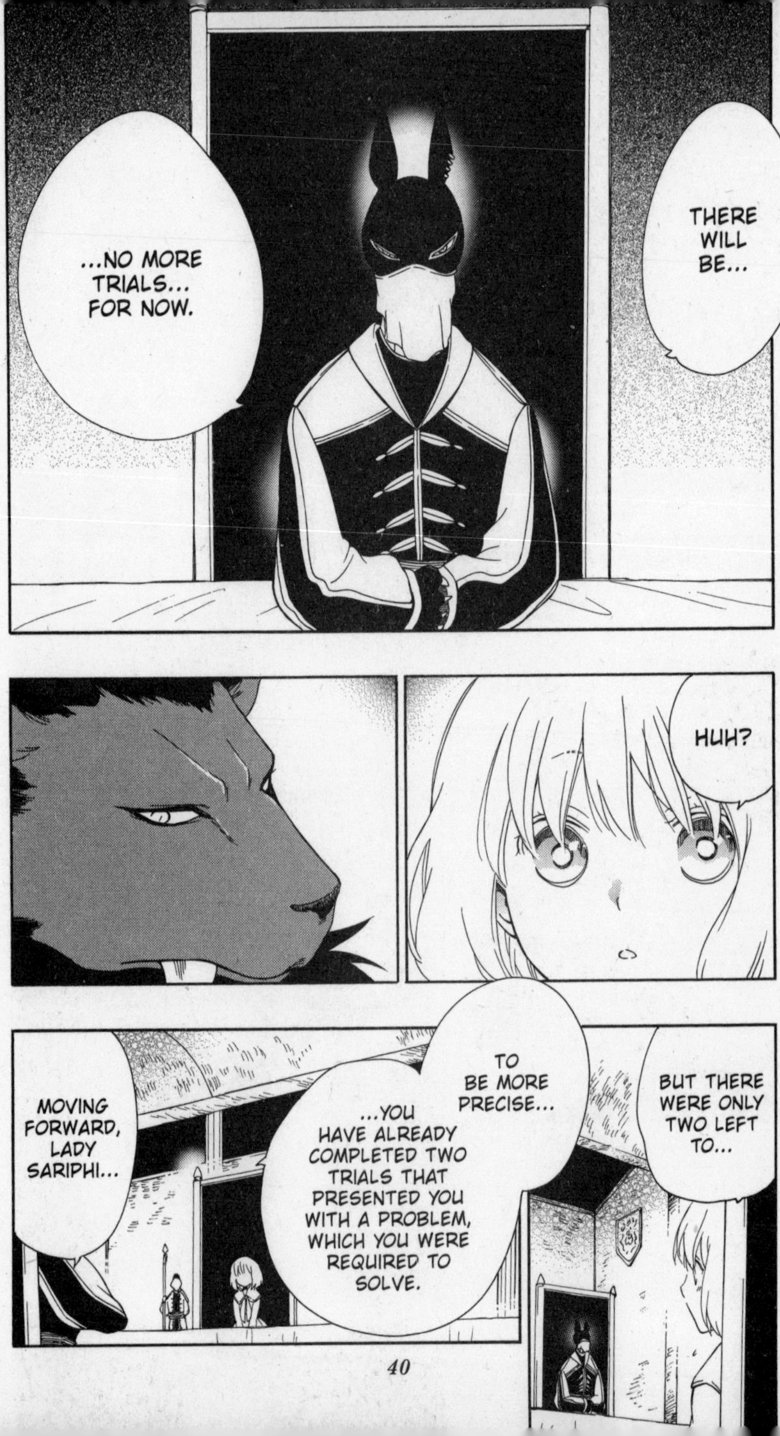
THERE WILL BE...
...NO MORE TRIALS... FOR NOW.
HUH?
BUT THERE WERE ONLY TWO LEFT TO...
TO BE MORE PRECISE...
...YOU HAVE ALREADY COMPLETED TWO TRIALS THAT PRESENTED YOU WITH A PROBLEM, WHICH YOU WERE REQUIRED TO SOLVE.
MOVING FORWARD, LADY SARIPHI...

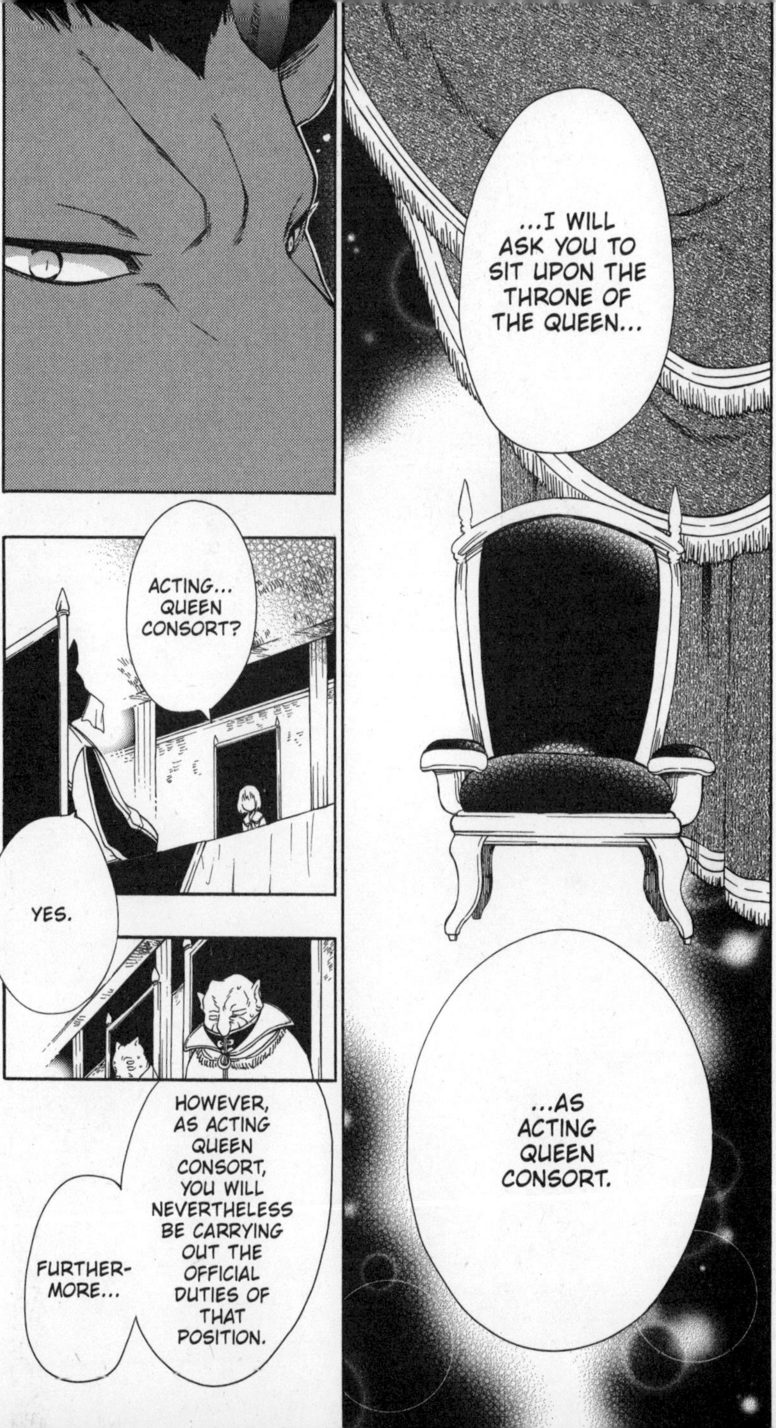
...I WILL ASK YOU TO SIT UPON THE THRONE OF THE QUEEN...
...AS ACTING QUEEN CONSORT.
ACTING... QUEEN CONSORT?
YES.
HOWEVER, AS ACTING QUEEN CONSORT, YOU WILL NEVERTHELESS BE CARRYING OUT THE OFFICIAL DUTIES OF THAT POSITION.
FURTHER-MORE...

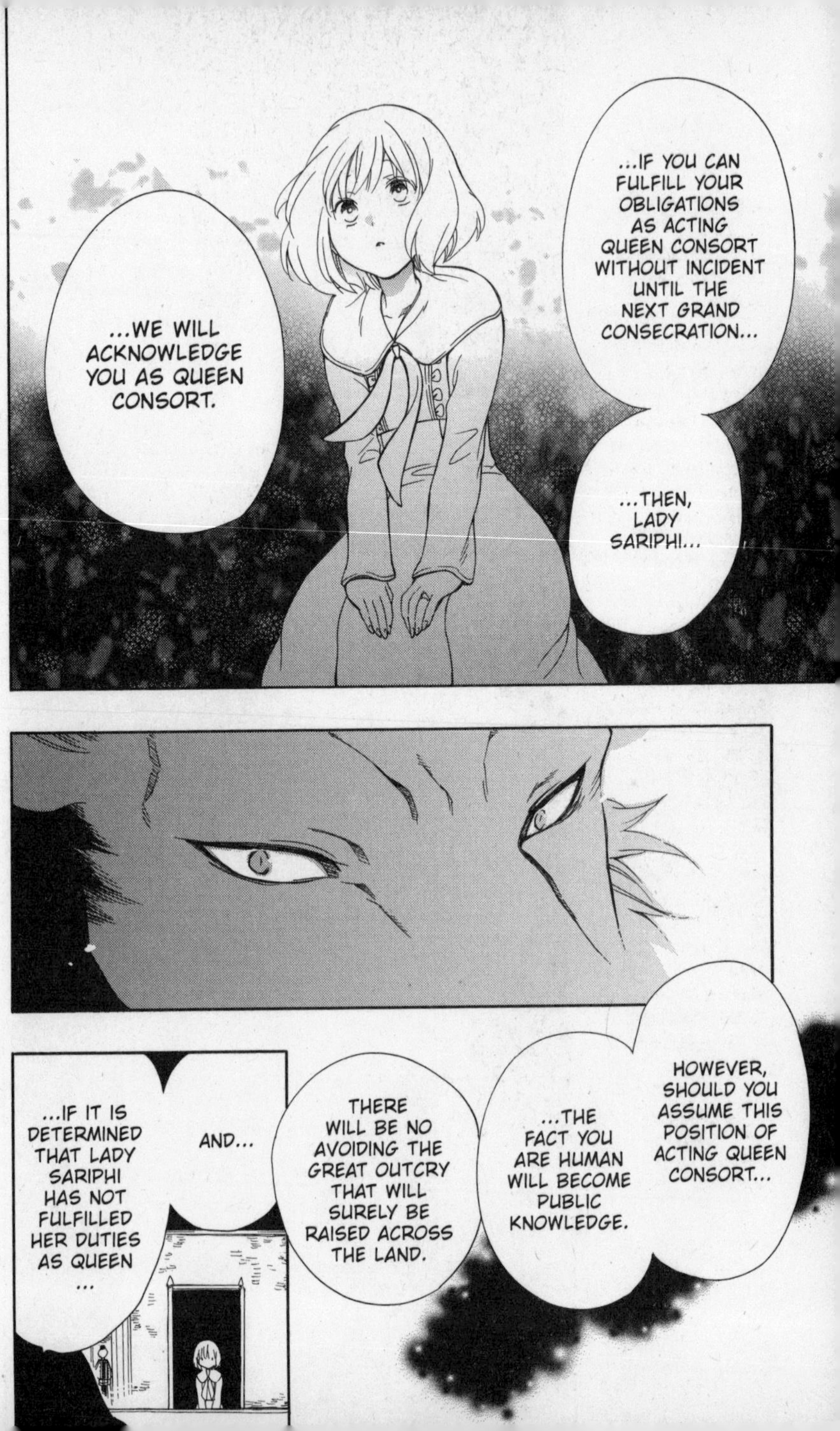
...IF YOU CAN FULFILL YOUR OBLIGATIONS AS ACTING QUEEN CONSORT WITHOUT INCIDENT UNTIL THE NEXT GRAND CONSECRATION...
...THEN, LADY SARIPHI...
...WE WILL ACKNOWLEDGE YOU AS QUEEN CONSORT.
HOWEVER, SHOULD YOU ASSUME THIS POSITION OF ACTING QUEEN CONSORT...
...THE FACT YOU ARE HUMAN WILL BECOME PUBLIC KNOWLEDGE.
THERE WILL BE NO AVOIDING THE GREAT OUTCRY THAT WILL SURELY BE RAISED ACROSS THE LAND.
AND...
...IF IT IS DETERMINED THAT LADY SARIPHI HAS NOT FULFILLED HER DUTIES AS QUEEN ...

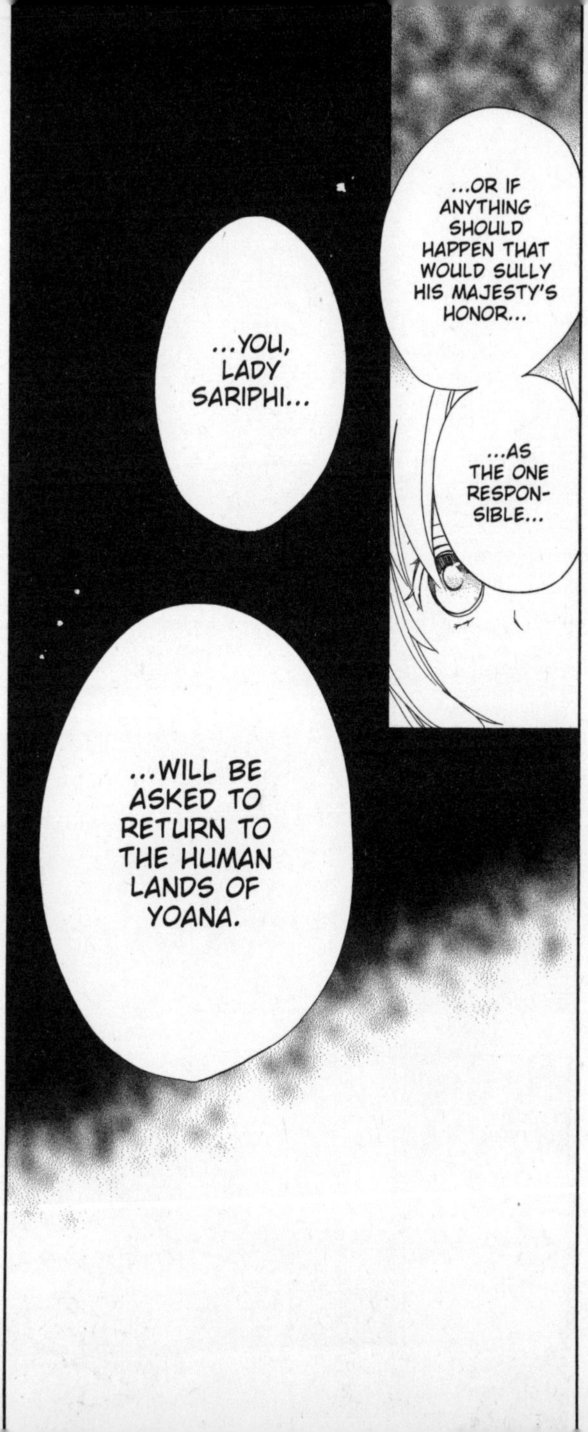
...OR IF ANYTHING SHOULD HAPPEN THAT WOULD SULLY HIS MAJESTY'S HONOR...
...AS THE ONE RESPONSIBLE...
...YOU, LADY SARIPHI...
...WILL BE ASKED TO RETURN TO THE HUMAN LANDS OF YOANA.

AND WITH THIS, WE PLUNGE INTO VOLUME 6 OF *SACRIFICIAL PRINCESS*.

AND NOW THERE'S GOING TO BE A DRAMA CD, OF ALL THINGS! I NEVER IMAGINED THE DAY WOULD COME WHEN ACTORS AND OTHER PROFESSIONALS WOULD RECORD A STORY I WROTE. I MEAN, THE FIRST CHAPTER WAS MEANT AS A STAND-ALONE! IT FEELS LIKE A MIRACLE TO ME JUST GETTING TO CONTINUE THE STORY THIS LONG. I'M TRULY GRATEFUL.

I GOT TO WATCH THE EDITING OF THE DRAMA CD, AND IT WAS INCREDIBLE BEING UP CLOSE TO SEE THE SKILL OF THE PROS WHO WORKED ON IT. IT'LL DEFINITELY BE ONE OF THE MEMORIES THAT FLASHES BEFORE MY EYES WHEN I DIE! YAY!

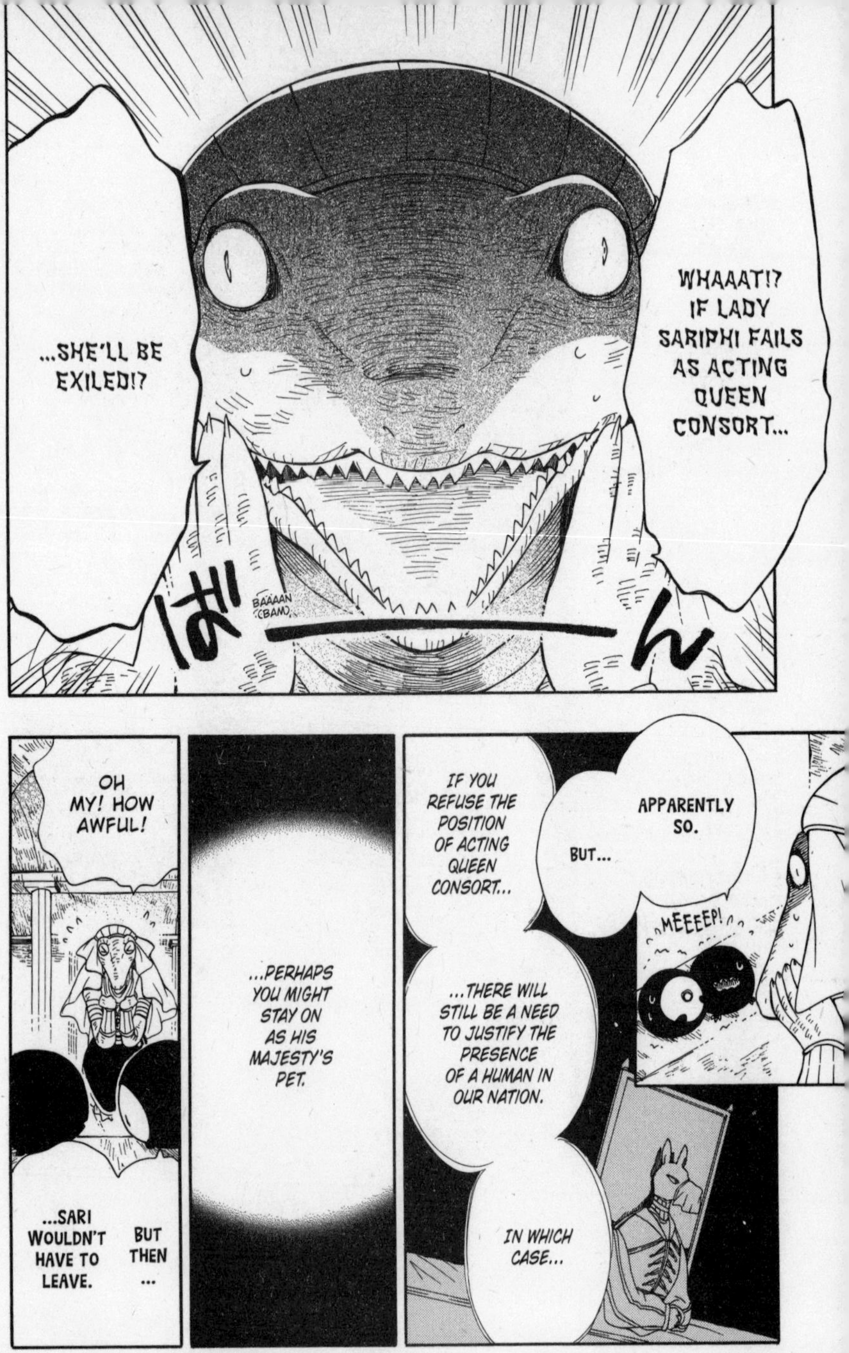
WHAAAT!? IF LADY SARIPHI FAILS AS ACTING QUEEN CONSORT...
...SHE'LL BE EXILED!?
BAAAAN (BAM)
APPARENTLY SO.
MEEEEP!
BUT...
IF YOU REFUSE THE POSITION OF ACTING QUEEN CONSORT...
...THERE WILL STILL BE A NEED TO JUSTIFY THE PRESENCE OF A HUMAN IN OUR NATION.
IN WHICH CASE...
...PERHAPS YOU MIGHT STAY ON AS HIS MAJESTY'S PET.
OH MY! HOW AWFUL!
BUT THEN...
...SARI WOULDN'T HAVE TO LEAVE.

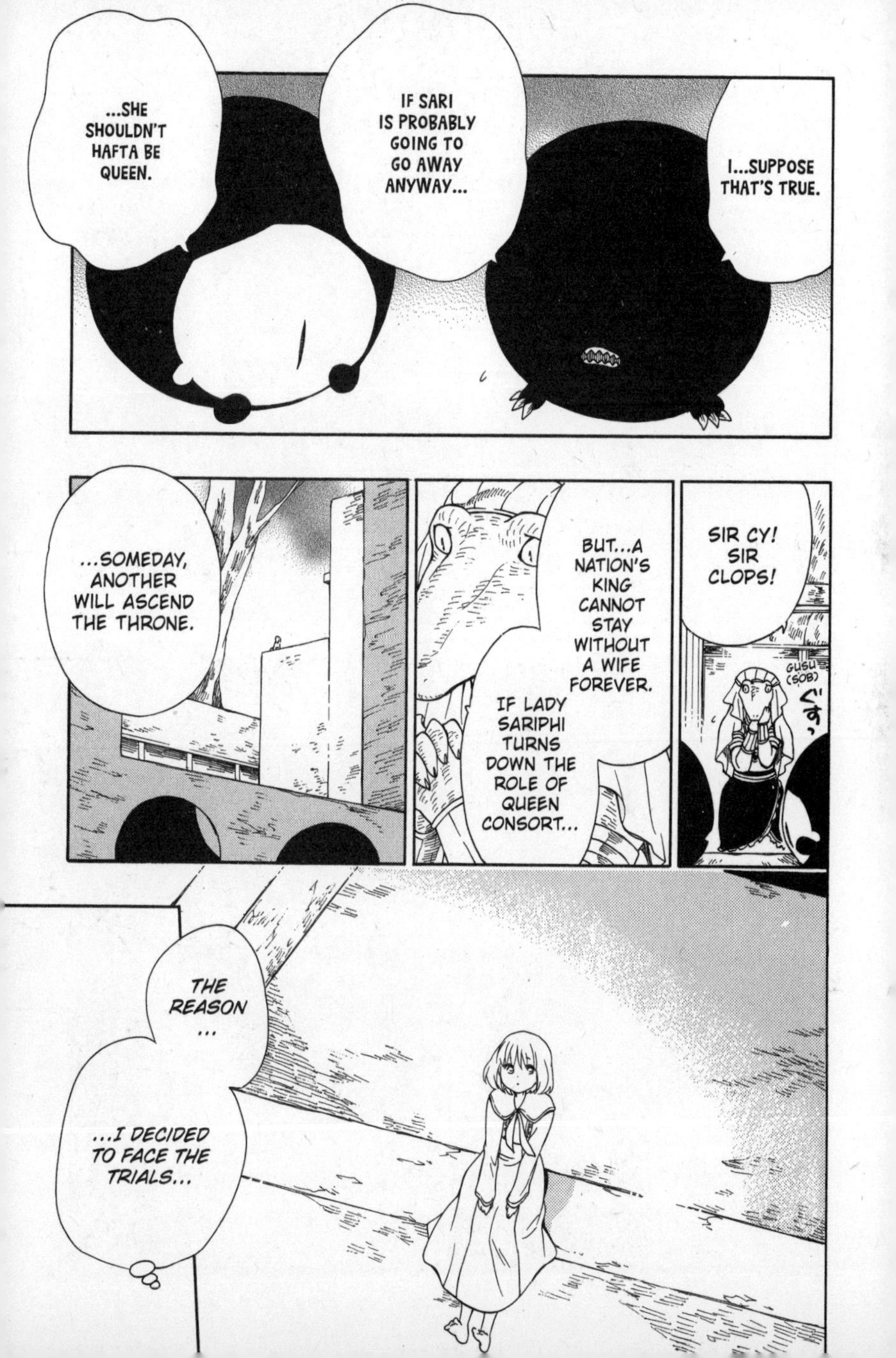
I...SUPPOSE THAT'S TRUE.
IF SARI IS PROBABLY GOING TO GO AWAY ANYWAY...
...SHE SHOULDN'T HAFTA BE QUEEN.
SIR CY! SIR CLOPS!
GUSU (SOB)
ぐす
BUT...A NATION'S KING CANNOT STAY WITHOUT A WIFE FOREVER.
IF LADY SARIPHI TURNS DOWN THE ROLE OF QUEEN CONSORT...
...SOMEDAY, ANOTHER WILL ASCEND THE THRONE.
THE REASON ...
...I DECIDED TO FACE THE TRIALS...

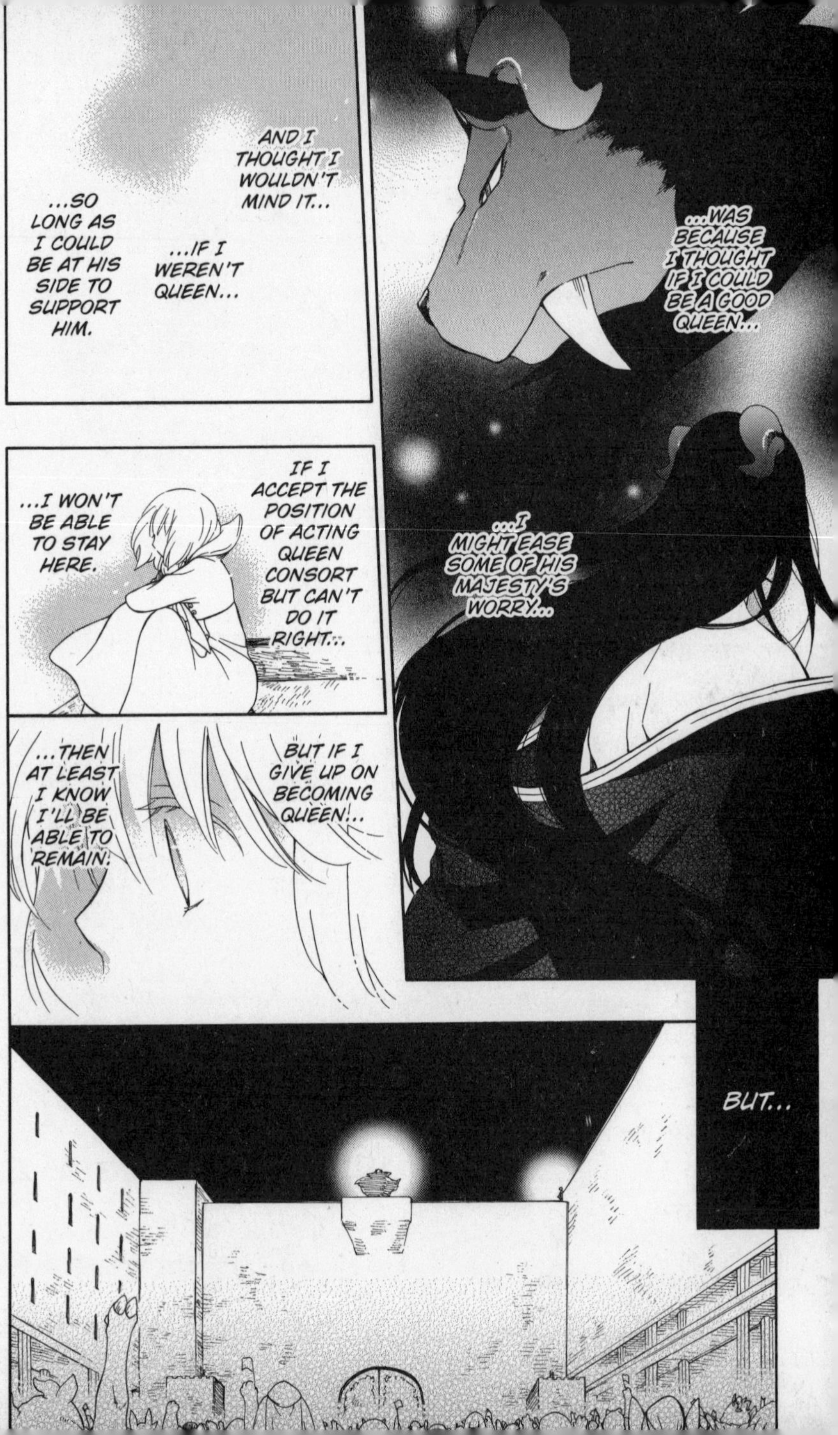
...WAS BECAUSE I THOUGHT IF I COULD BE A GOOD QUEEN...
...I MIGHT EASE SOME OF HIS MAJESTY'S WORRY...
AND I THOUGHT I WOULDN'T MIND IT...
...IF I WEREN'T QUEEN...
...SO LONG AS I COULD BE AT HIS SIDE TO SUPPORT HIM.
IF I ACCEPT THE POSITION OF ACTING QUEEN CONSORT BUT CAN'T DO IT RIGHT...
...I WON'T BE ABLE TO STAY HERE.
BUT IF I GIVE UP ON BECOMING QUEEN...
...THEN AT LEAST I KNOW I'LL BE ABLE TO REMAIN.
BUT...

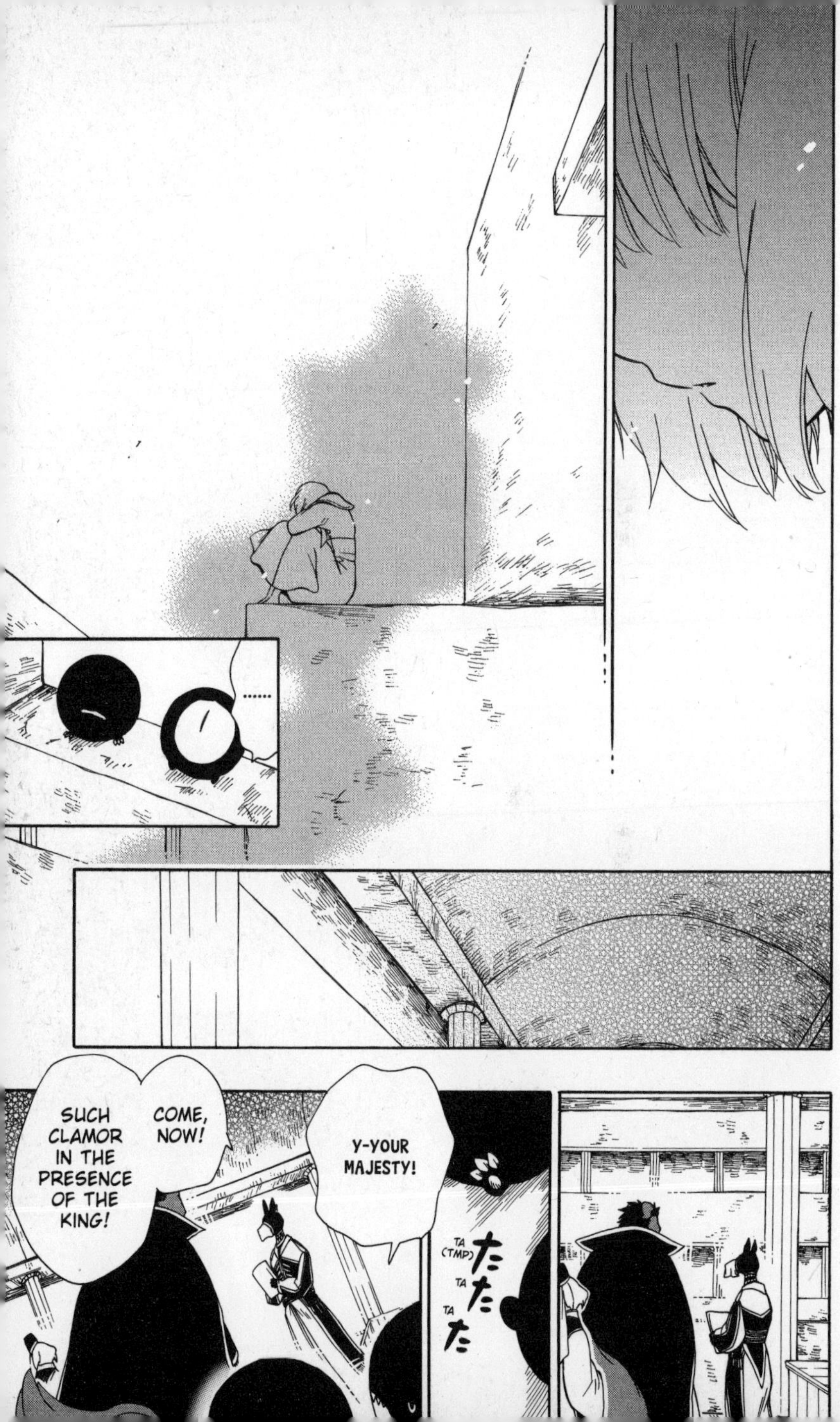
......
Y-YOUR MAJESTY!
COME, NOW!
SUCH CLAMOR IN THE PRESENCE OF THE KING!
TA (TMP) たTA たTA た

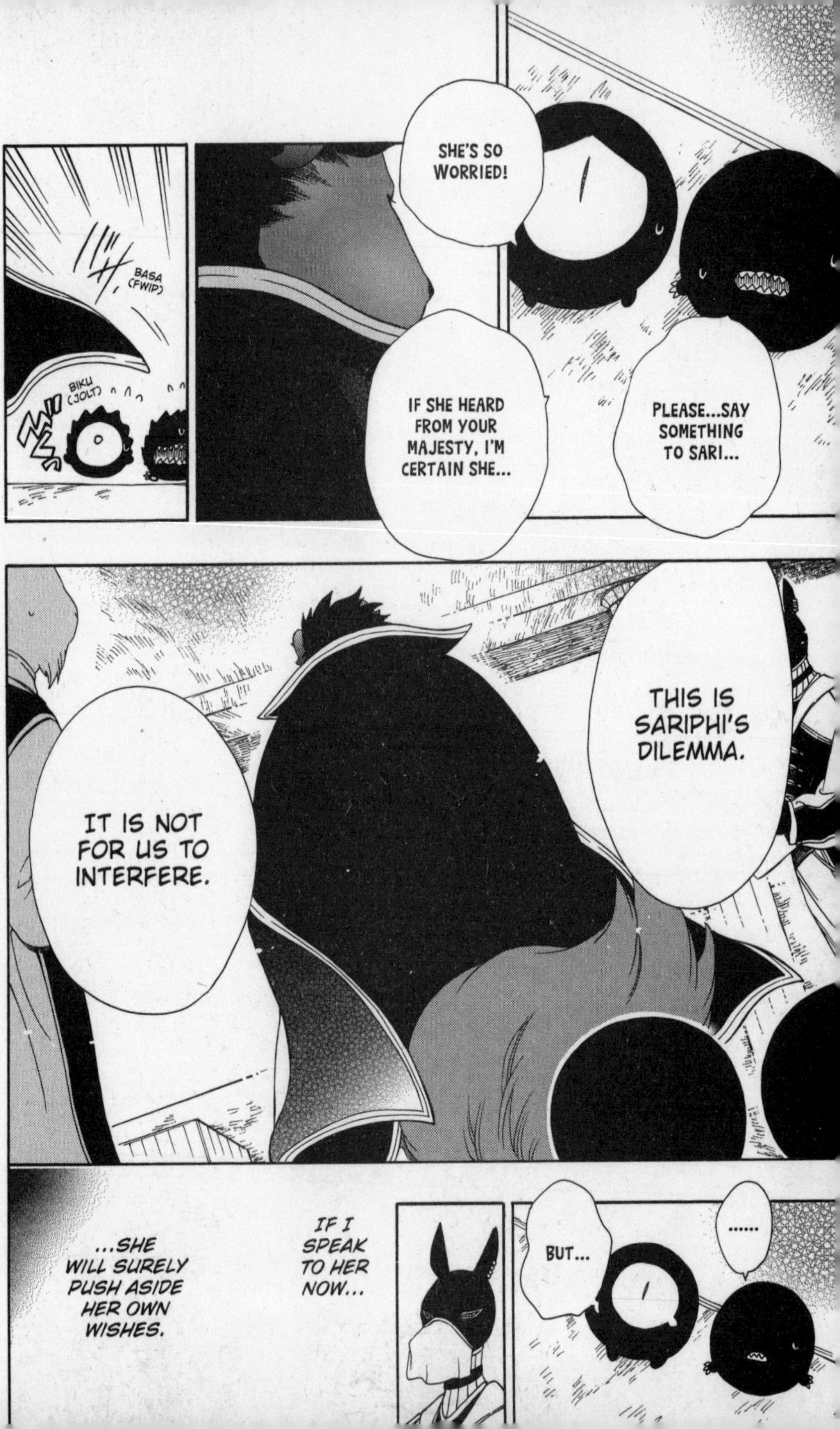
SHE'S SO WORRIED!
PLEASE...SAY SOMETHING TO SARI...
IF SHE HEARD FROM YOUR MAJESTY, I'M CERTAIN SHE...
BASA (FWIP)
BIKU (JOLT)
THIS IS SARIPHI'S DILEMMA.
IT IS NOT FOR US TO INTERFERE.
......
BUT...
IF I SPEAK TO HER NOW...
...SHE WILL SURELY PUSH ASIDE HER OWN WISHES.

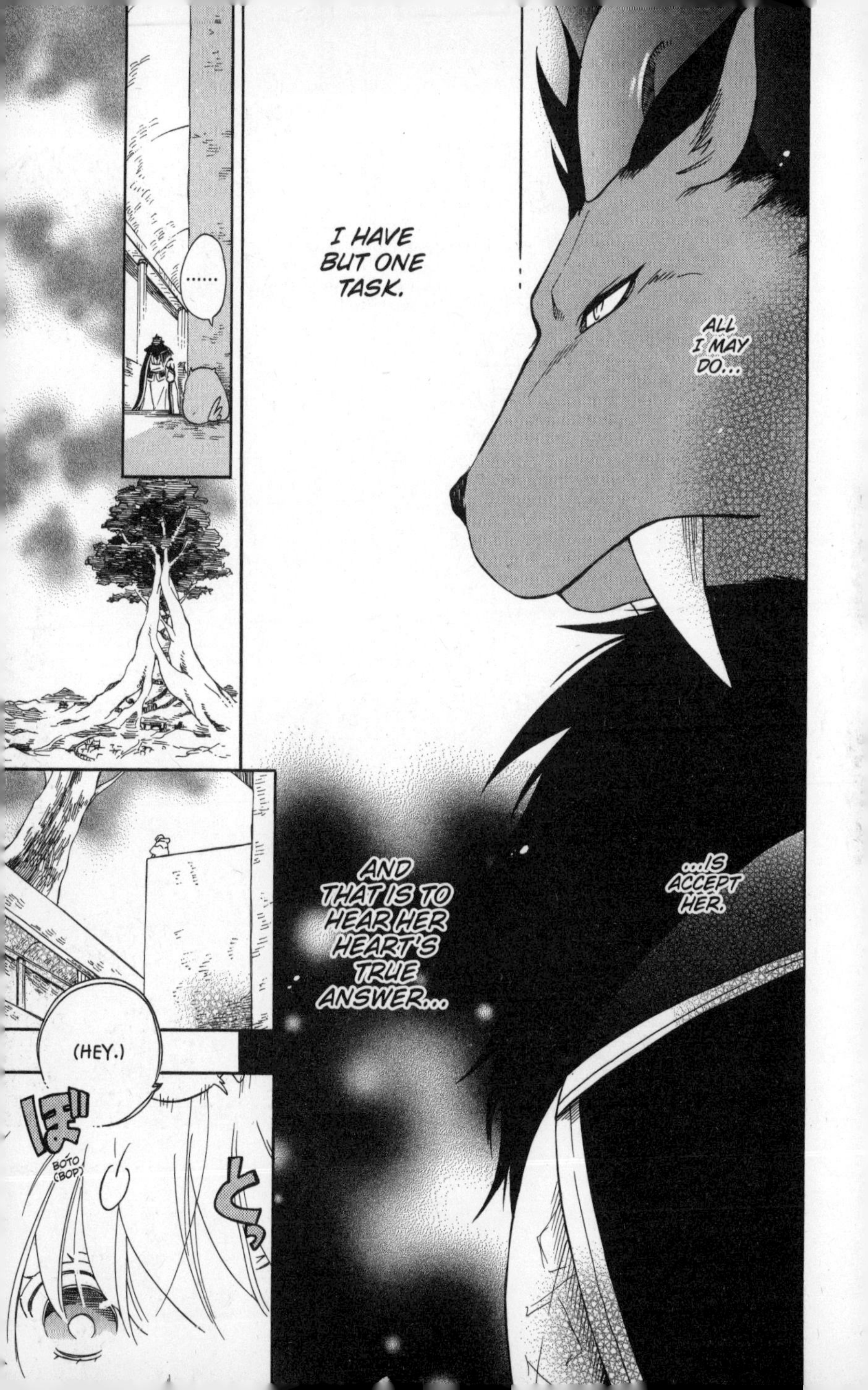

I HAVE BUT ONE TASK.
AND THAT IS TO HEAR HER HEART'S TRUE ANSWER...
ALL I MAY DO...
...IS ACCEPT HER.
......
(HEY.)
ぼ
BOTO (BOP)
と

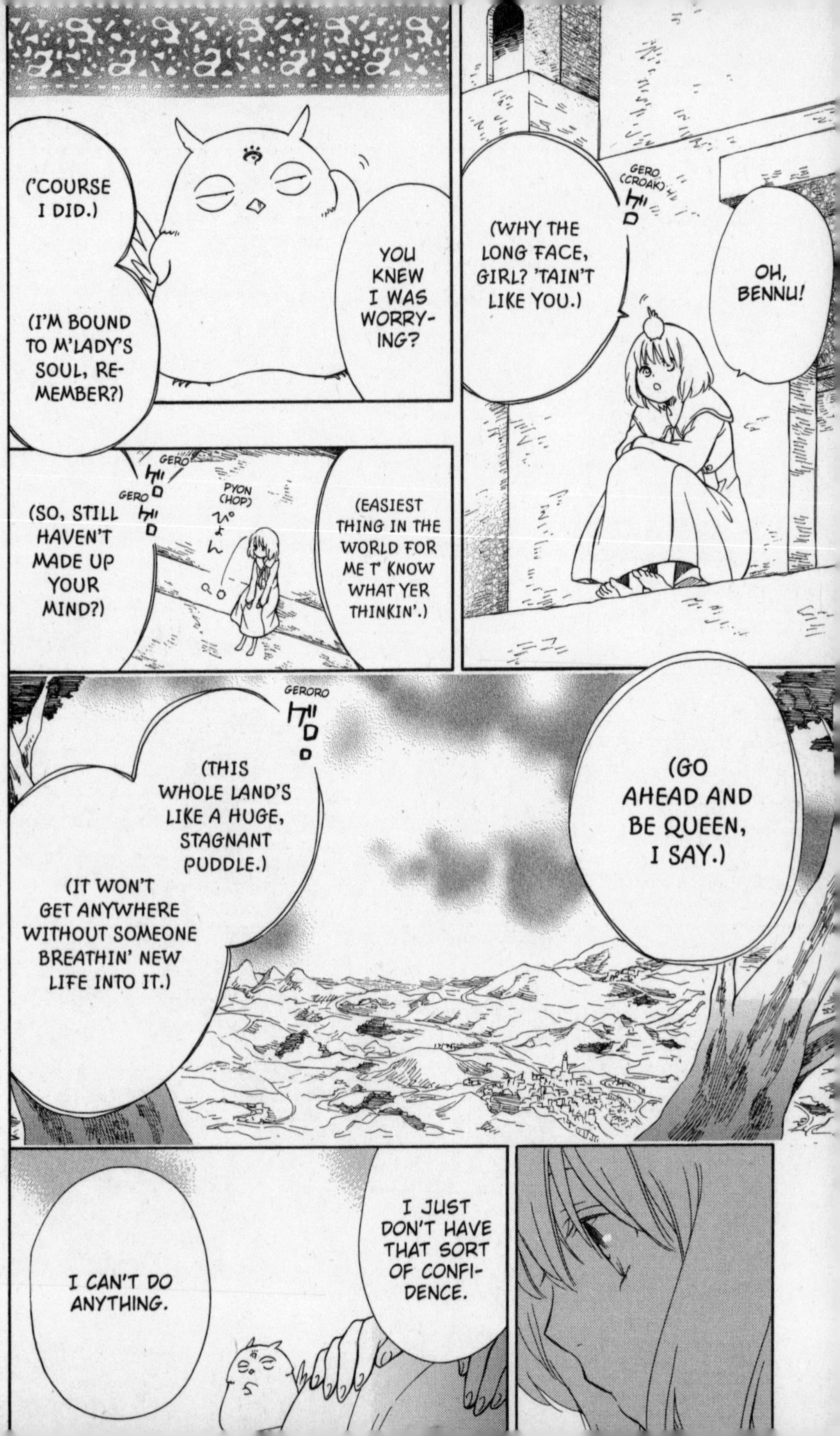
OH, BENNU!
GERO (CROAK)
ゲロ
(WHY THE LONG FACE, GIRL? 'TAIN'T LIKE YOU.)
YOU KNEW I WAS WORRYING?
('COURSE I DID.)
(I'M BOUND TO M'LADY'S SOUL, REMEMBER?)
(EASIEST THING IN THE WORLD FOR ME T' KNOW WHAT YER THINKIN'.)
PYON (HOP)
ぴょん
GERO
ゲロ
GERO
ゲロ
(SO, STILL HAVEN'T MADE UP YOUR MIND?)
(GO AHEAD AND BE QUEEN, I SAY.)
GERORO
ゲロロ
(THIS WHOLE LAND'S LIKE A HUGE, STAGNANT PUDDLE.)
(IT WON'T GET ANYWHERE WITHOUT SOMEONE BREATHIN' NEW LIFE INTO IT.)
I JUST DON'T HAVE THAT SORT OF CONFIDENCE.
I CAN'T DO ANYTHING.

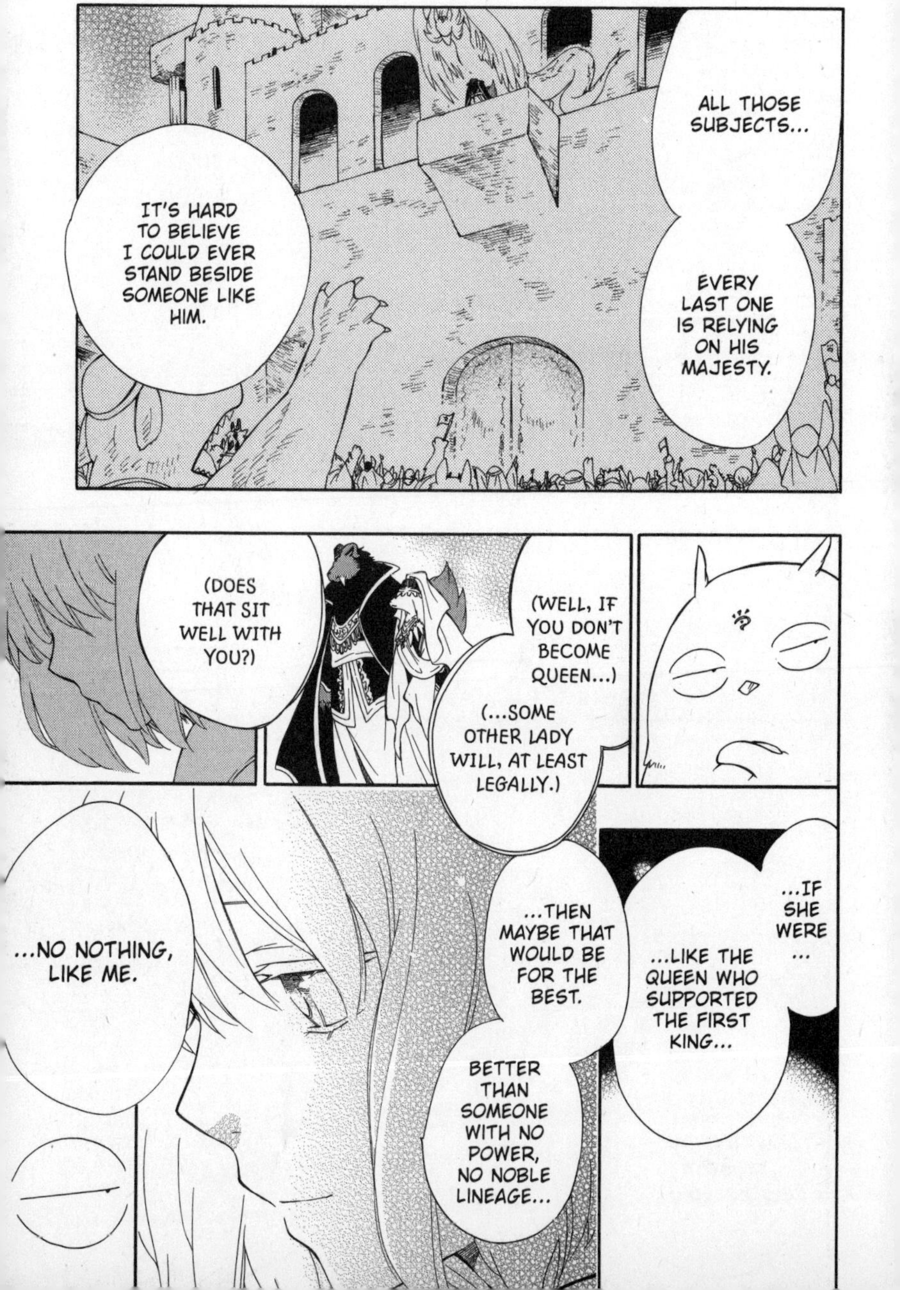
ALL THOSE SUBJECTS...
EVERY LAST ONE IS RELYING ON HIS MAJESTY.
IT'S HARD TO BELIEVE I COULD EVER STAND BESIDE SOMEONE LIKE HIM.
(WELL, IF YOU DON'T BECOME QUEEN...)
(...SOME OTHER LADY WILL, AT LEAST LEGALLY.)
(DOES THAT SIT WELL WITH YOU?)
...IF SHE WERE ...
...LIKE THE QUEEN WHO SUPPORTED THE FIRST KING...
...THEN MAYBE THAT WOULD BE FOR THE BEST.
BETTER THAN SOMEONE WITH NO POWER, NO NOBLE LINEAGE...
...NO NOTHING, LIKE ME.

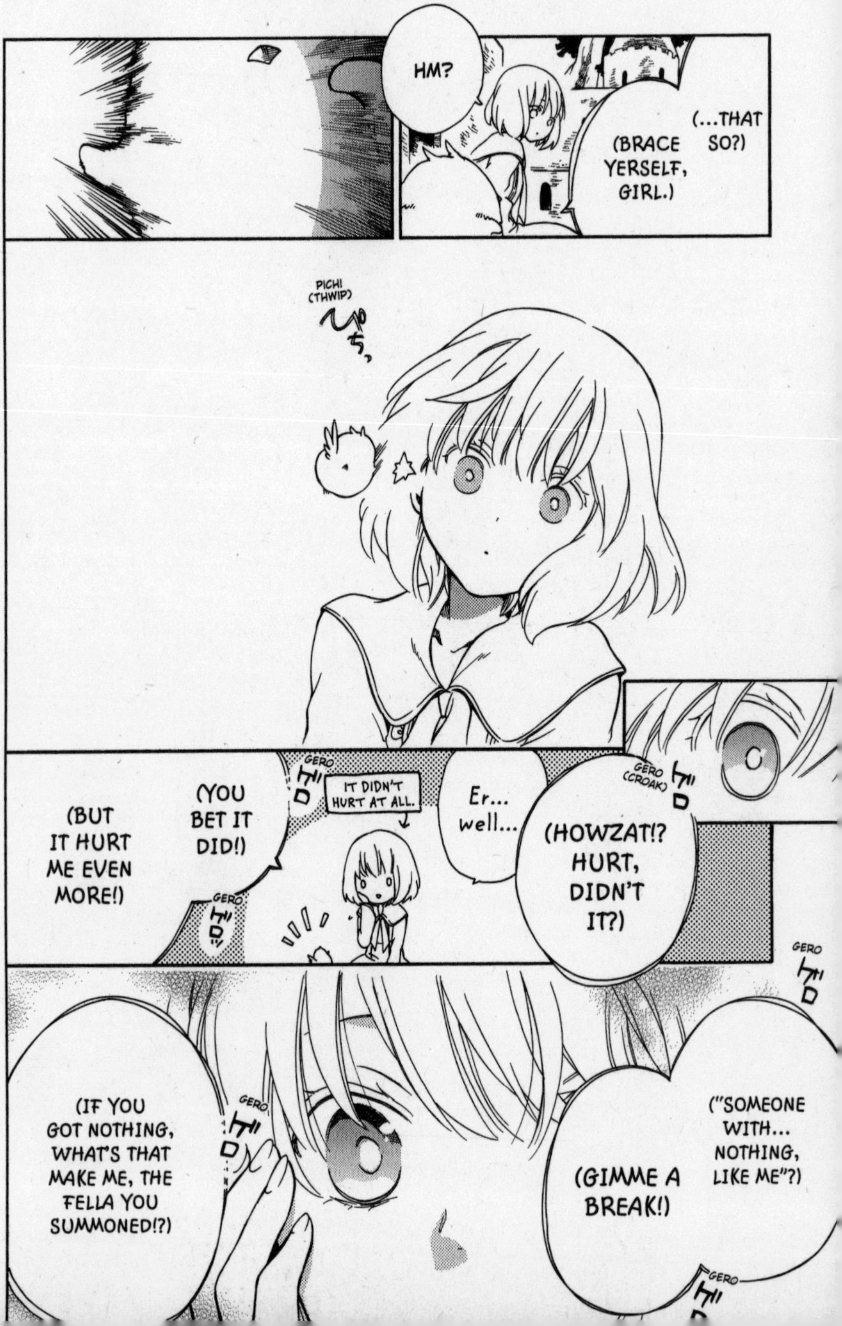
HM?
(BRACE YERSELF, GIRL.)
(...THAT SO?)
PICHI (THWIP)
ぴち
GERO (CROAK)
ゲロ
(HOWZAT!? HURT, DIDN'T IT?)
Er... well...
IT DIDN'T HURT AT ALL.
GERO
ゲロ
(YOU BET IT DID!)
(BUT IT HURT ME EVEN MORE!)
GERO
ゲロ
GERO
ゲロ
("SOMEONE WITH... NOTHING, LIKE ME"?)
(GIMME A BREAK!)
GERO
ゲロ
(IF YOU GOT NOTHING, WHAT'S THAT MAKE ME, THE FELLA YOU SUMMONED!?)
GERO
ゲロ

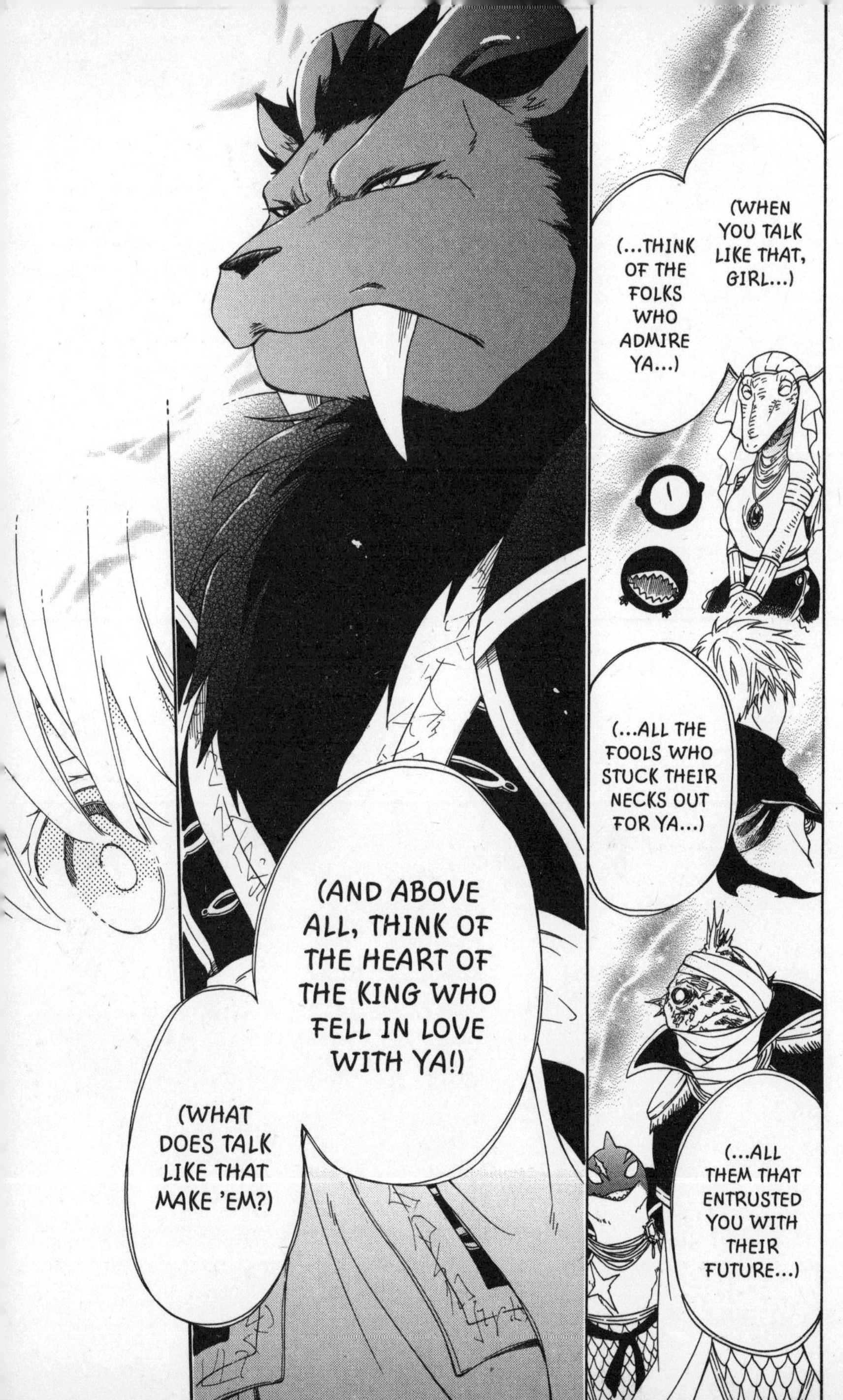
(WHEN YOU TALK LIKE THAT, GIRL...)
(...THINK OF THE FOLKS WHO ADMIRE YA...)
(...ALL THE FOOLS WHO STUCK THEIR NECKS OUT FOR YA...)
(...ALL THEM THAT ENTRUSTED YOU WITH THEIR FUTURE...)
(AND ABOVE ALL, THINK OF THE HEART OF THE KING WHO FELL IN LOVE WITH YA!)
(WHAT DOES TALK LIKE THAT MAKE 'EM?)

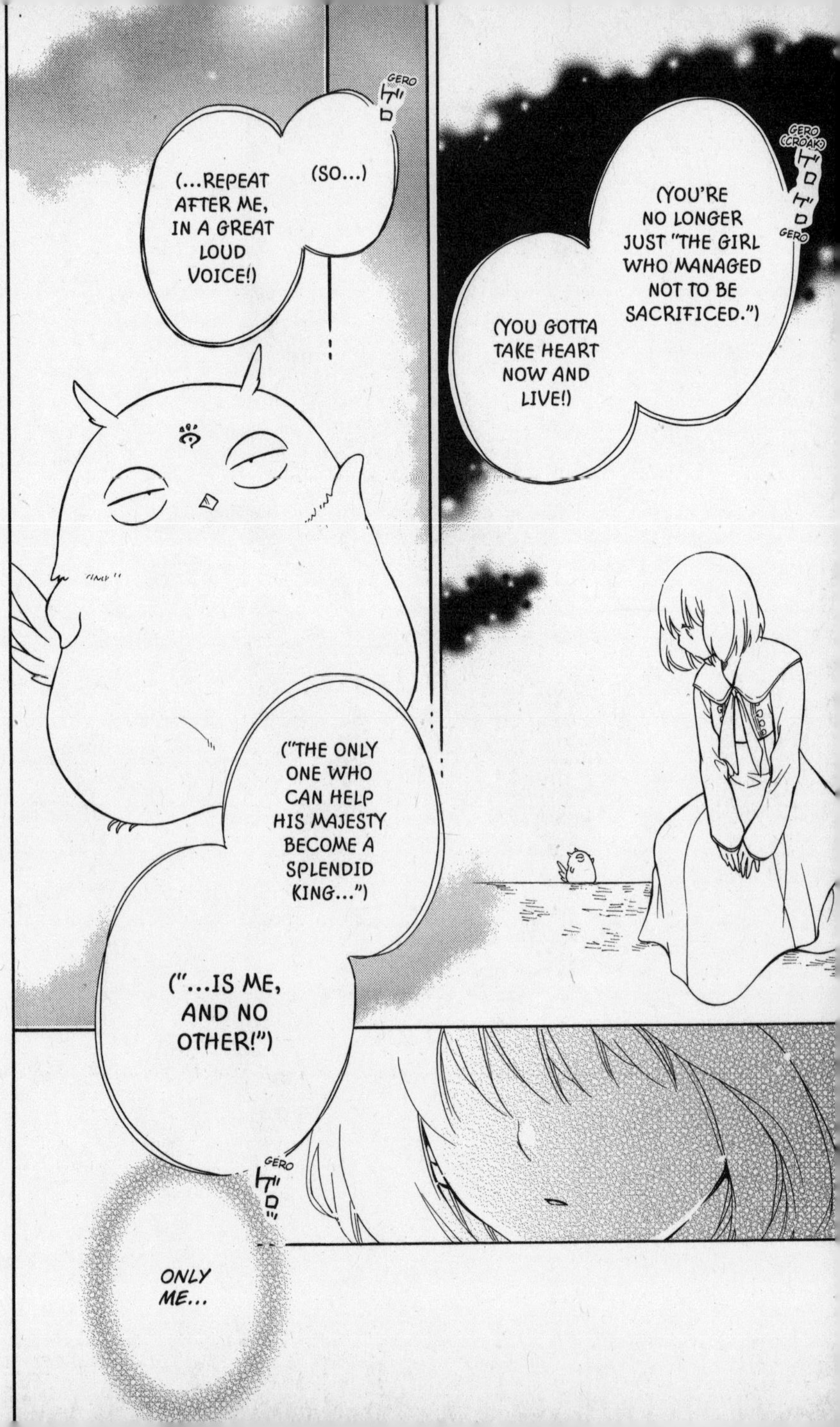
GERO (CROAK)
ゲロゲロ
GERO
(YOU'RE NO LONGER JUST "THE GIRL WHO MANAGED NOT TO BE SACRIFICED.")
(YOU GOTTA TAKE HEART NOW AND LIVE!)
GERO
ゲロ
(SO...)
(...REPEAT AFTER ME, IN A GREAT LOUD VOICE!)
("THE ONLY ONE WHO CAN HELP HIS MAJESTY BECOME A SPLENDID KING...")
("...IS ME, AND NO OTHER!")
GERO
ゲロ
ONLY ME...

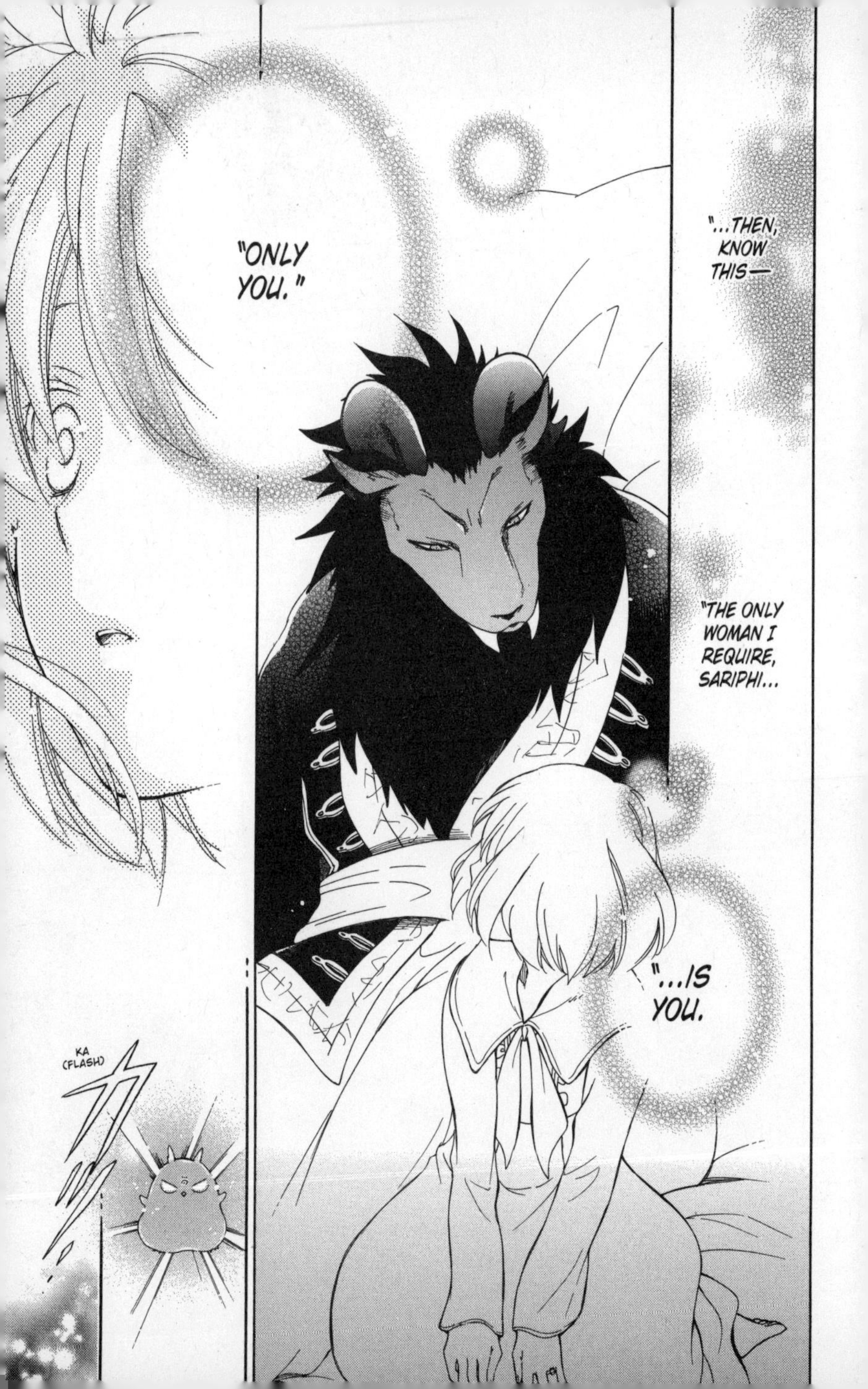
"...THEN, KNOW THIS—
"THE ONLY WOMAN I REQUIRE, SARIPHI...
"...IS YOU.
"ONLY YOU."
KA (FLASH)

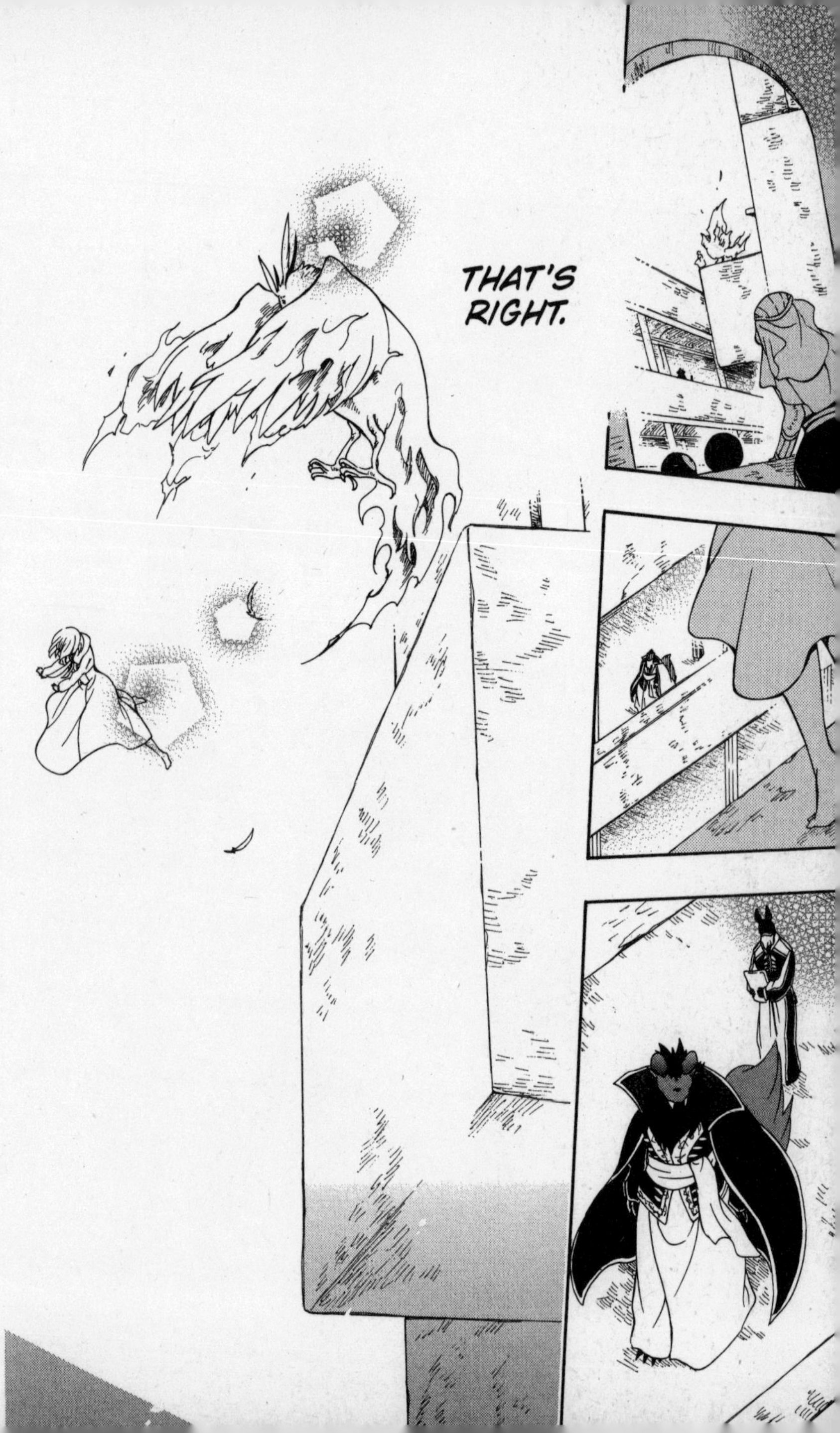
THAT'S RIGHT.

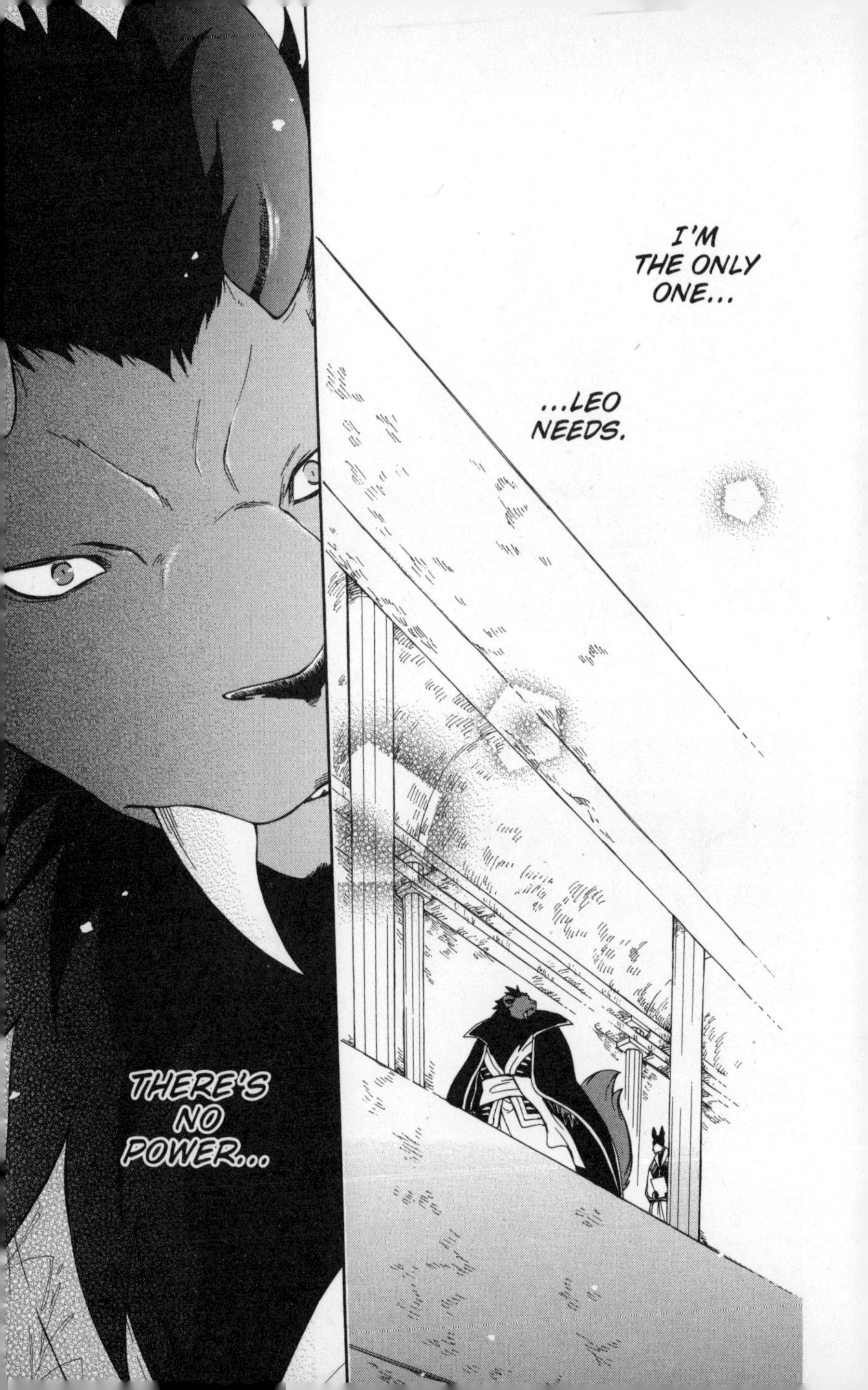
I'M THE ONLY ONE...
...LEO NEEDS.
THERE'S NO POWER...

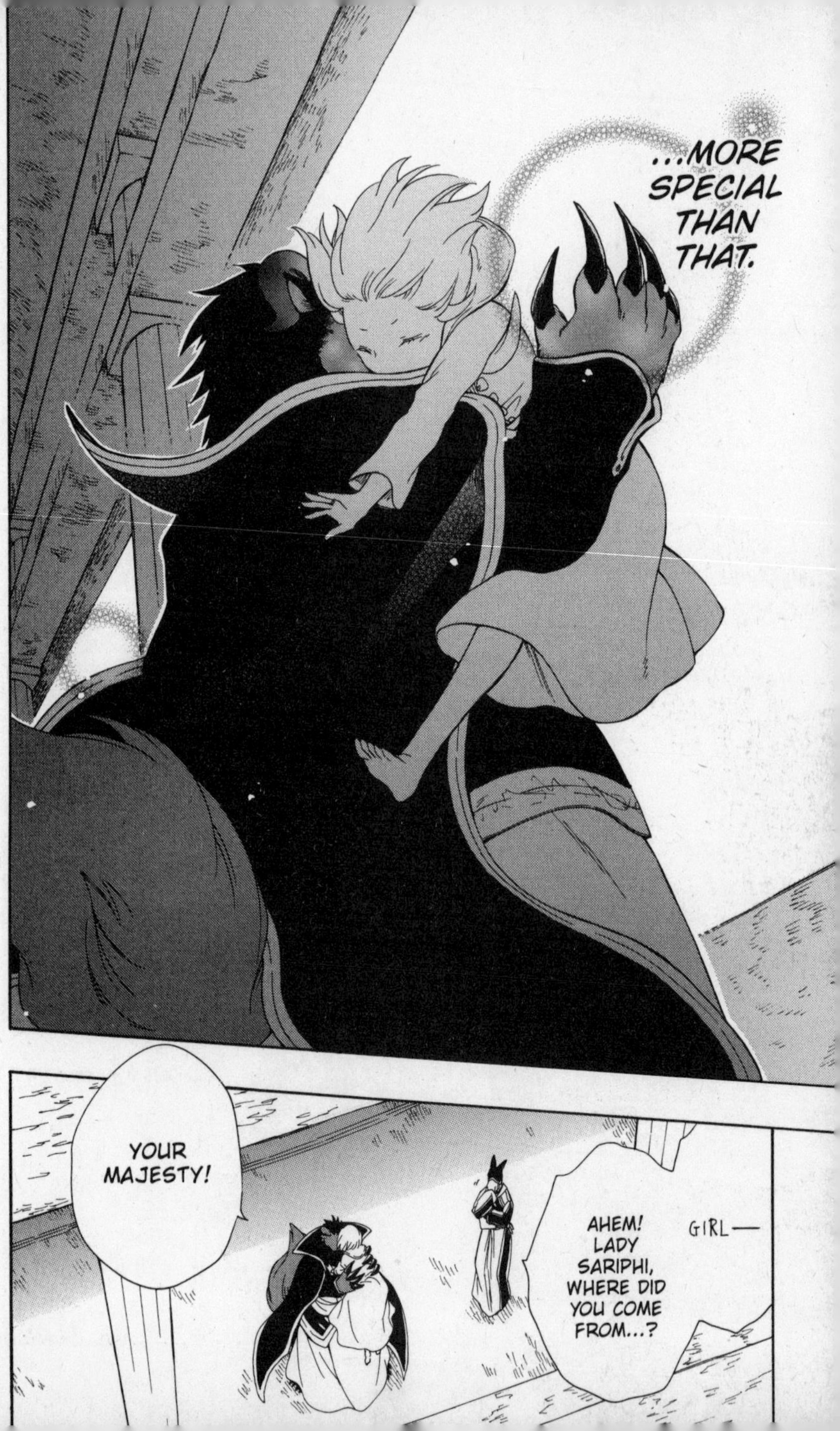
...MORE SPECIAL THAN THAT.
GIRL—
AHEM! LADY SARIPHI, WHERE DID YOU COME FROM...?
YOUR MAJESTY!

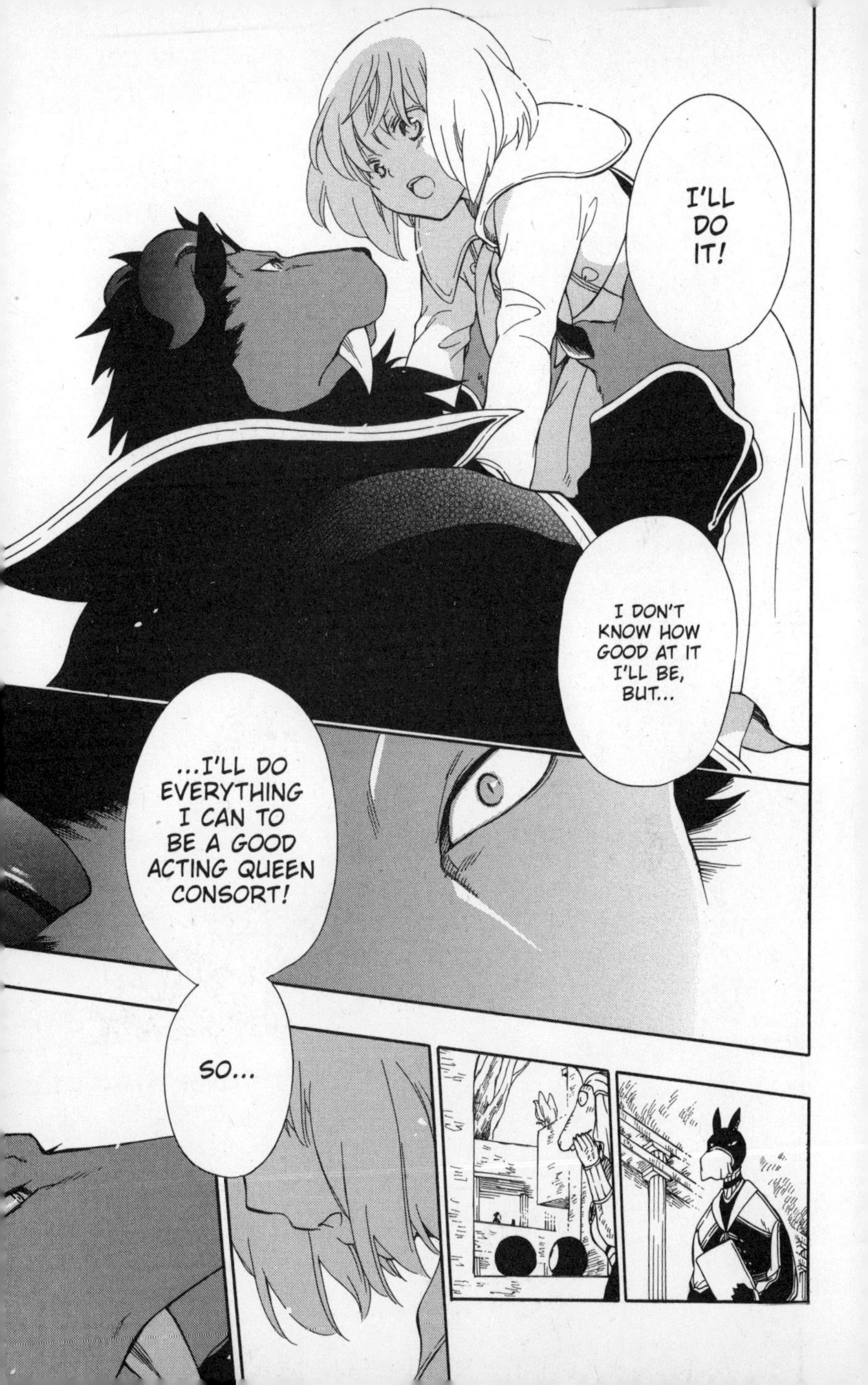
I'LL DO IT!
I DON'T KNOW HOW GOOD AT IT I'LL BE, BUT...
...I'LL DO EVERYTHING I CAN TO BE A GOOD ACTING QUEEN CONSORT!
SO...

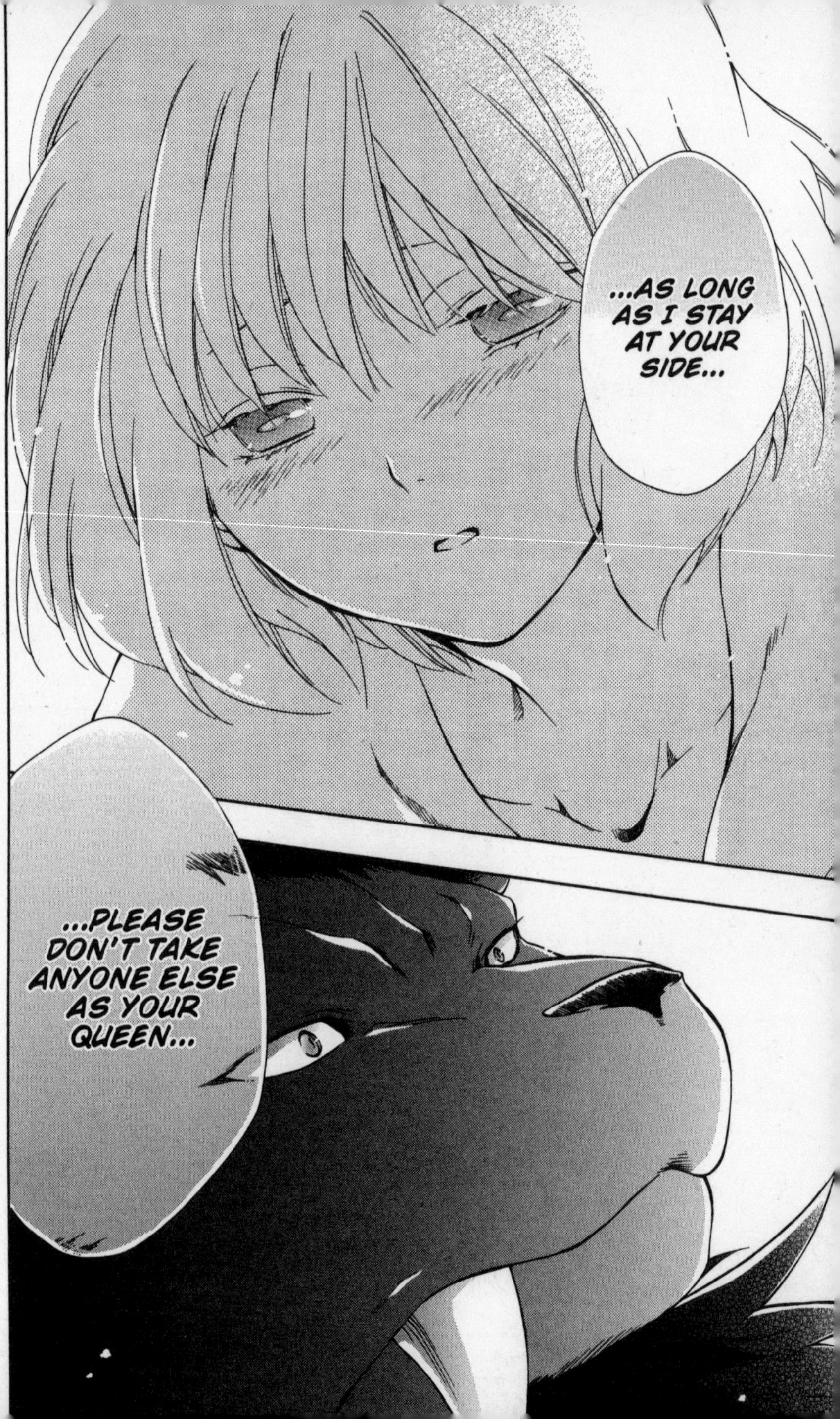
...AS LONG AS I STAY AT YOUR SIDE...
...PLEASE DON'T TAKE ANYONE ELSE AS YOUR QUEEN...

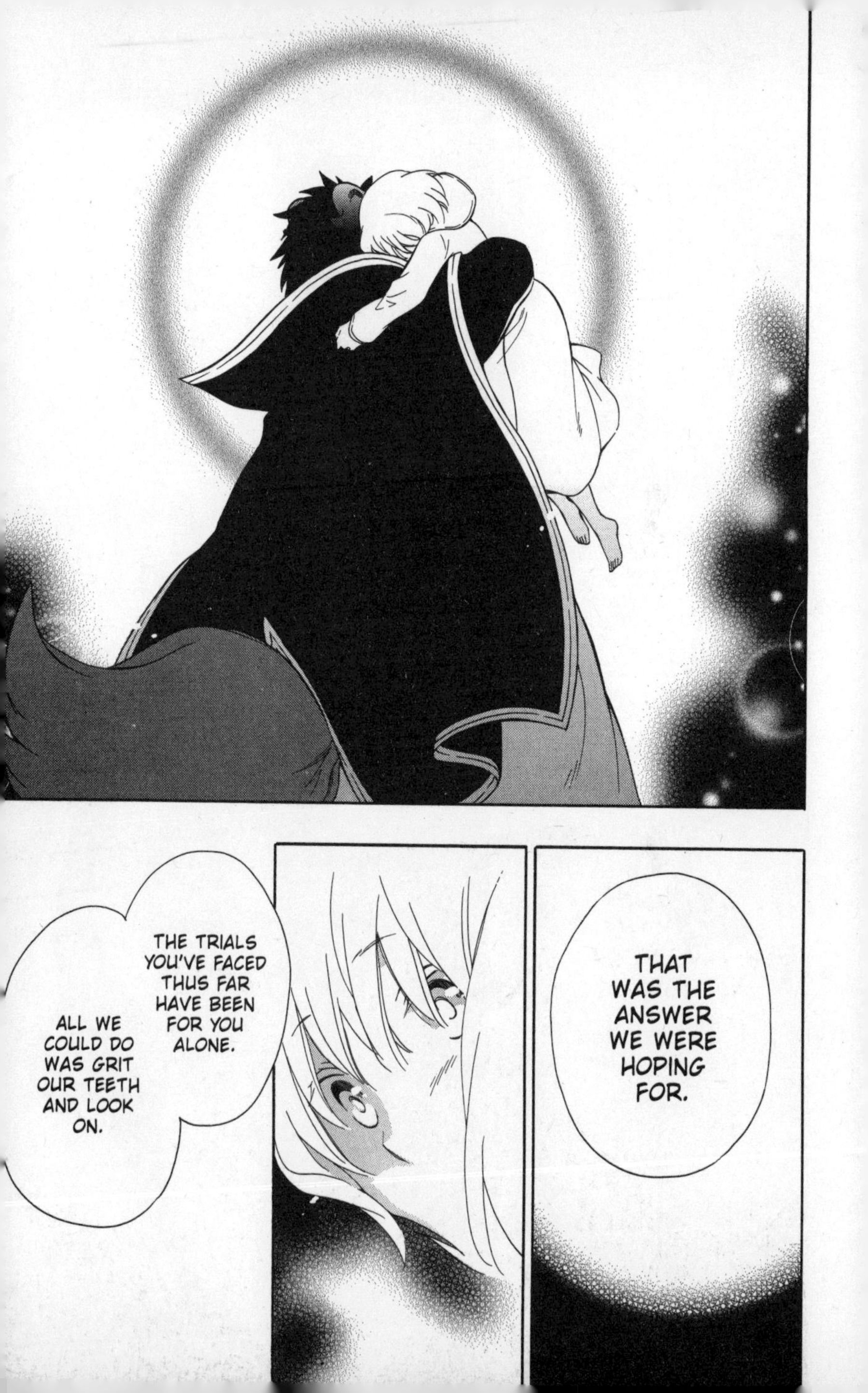
THAT WAS THE ANSWER WE WERE HOPING FOR.
THE TRIALS YOU'VE FACED THUS FAR HAVE BEEN FOR YOU ALONE.
ALL WE COULD DO WAS GRIT OUR TEETH AND LOOK ON.

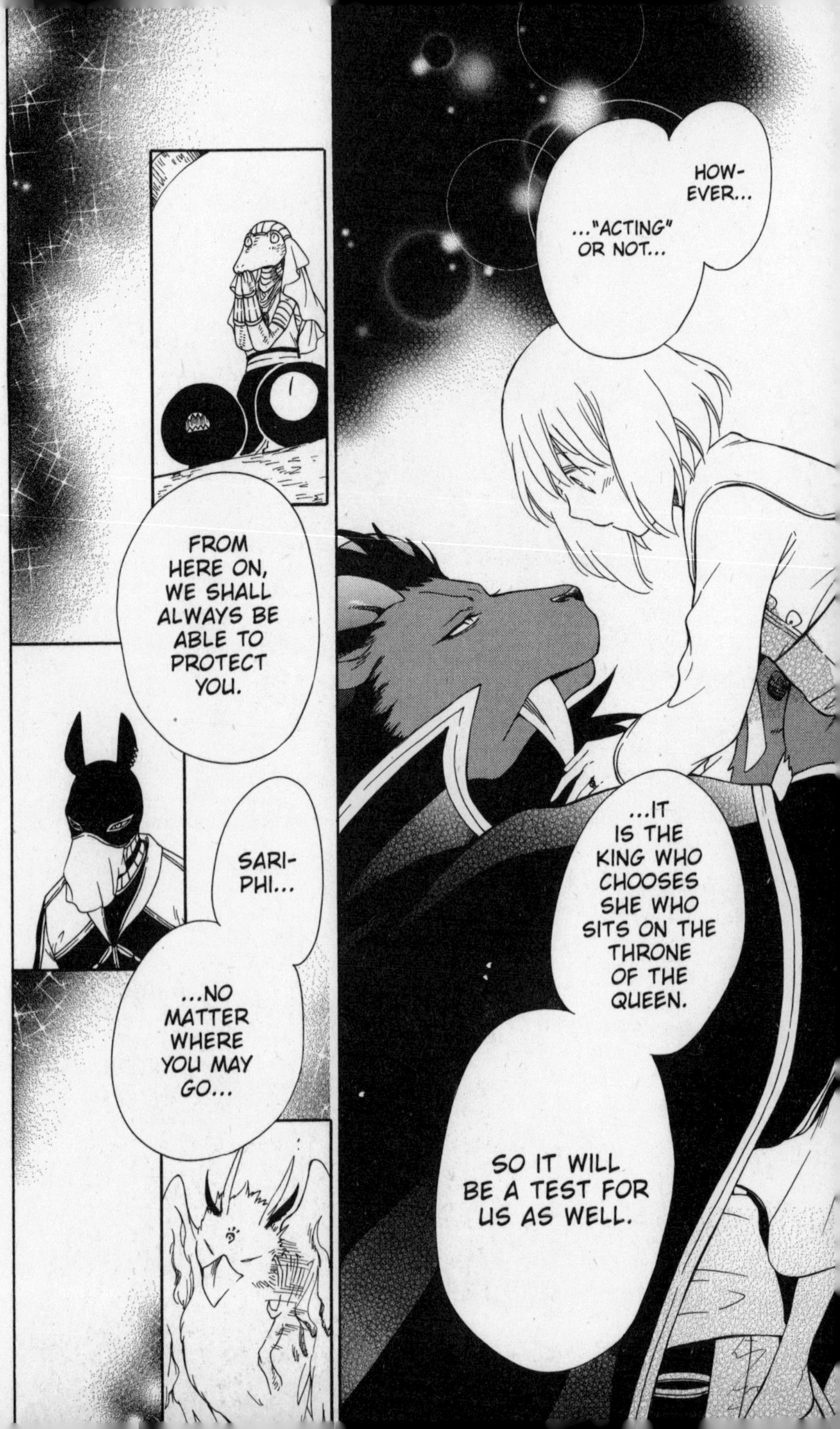
HOW-EVER...
..."ACTING" OR NOT...
...IT IS THE KING WHO CHOOSES SHE WHO SITS ON THE THRONE OF THE QUEEN.
SO IT WILL BE A TEST FOR US AS WELL.
FROM HERE ON, WE SHALL ALWAYS BE ABLE TO PROTECT YOU.
SARI-PHI...
...NO MATTER WHERE YOU MAY GO...

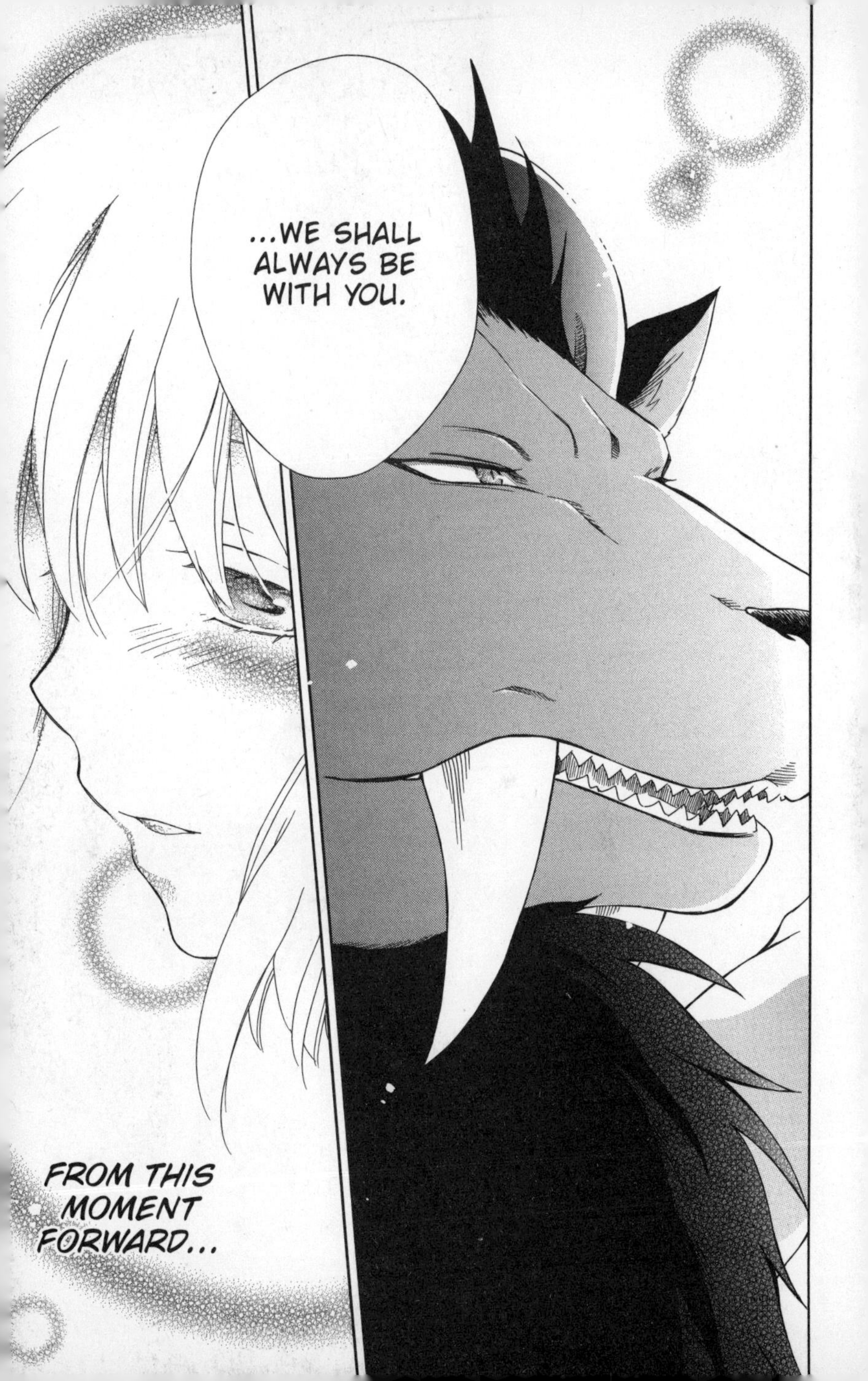
...WE SHALL ALWAYS BE WITH YOU.
FROM THIS MOMENT FORWARD...

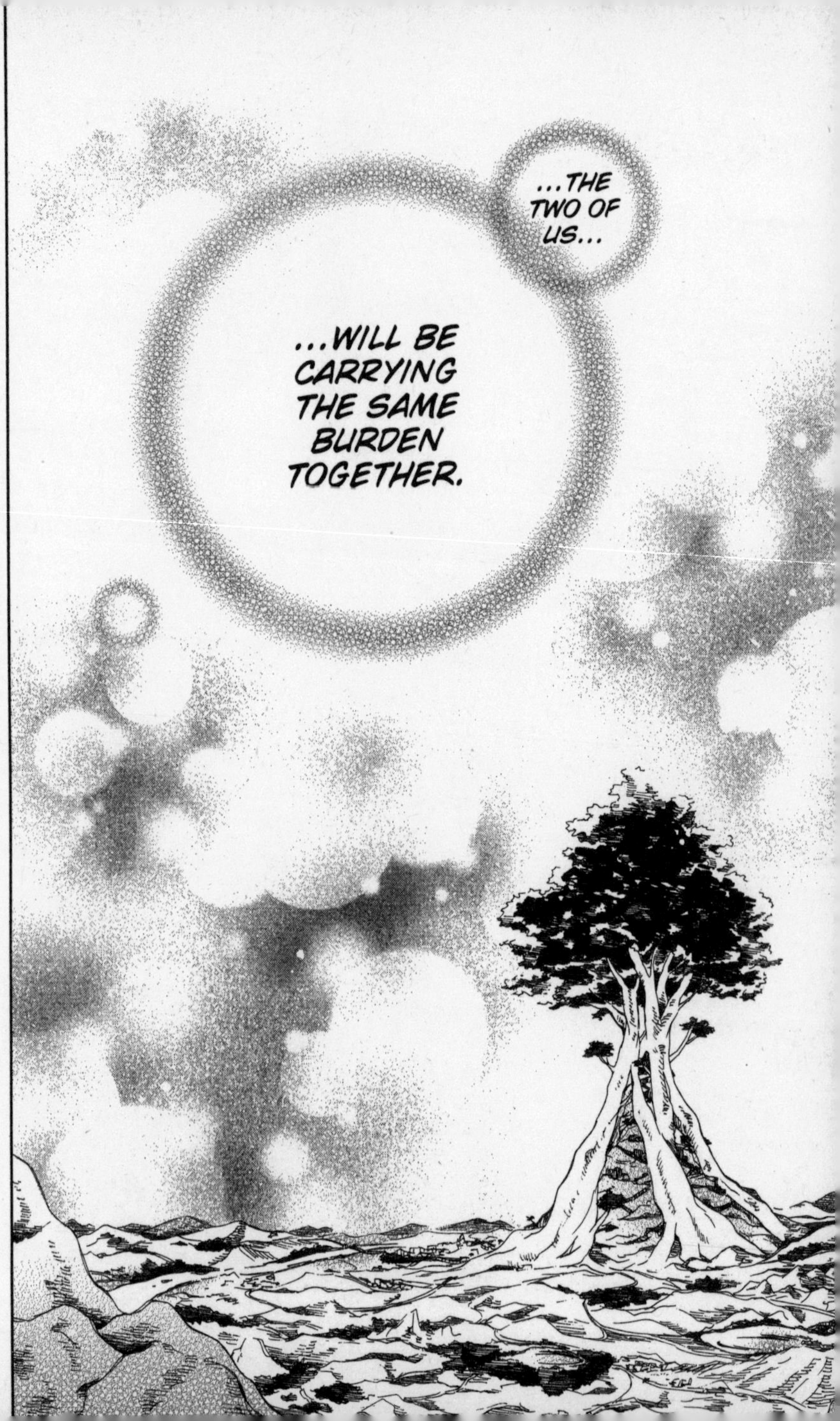
...THE TWO OF US...
...WILL BE CARRYING THE SAME BURDEN TOGETHER.

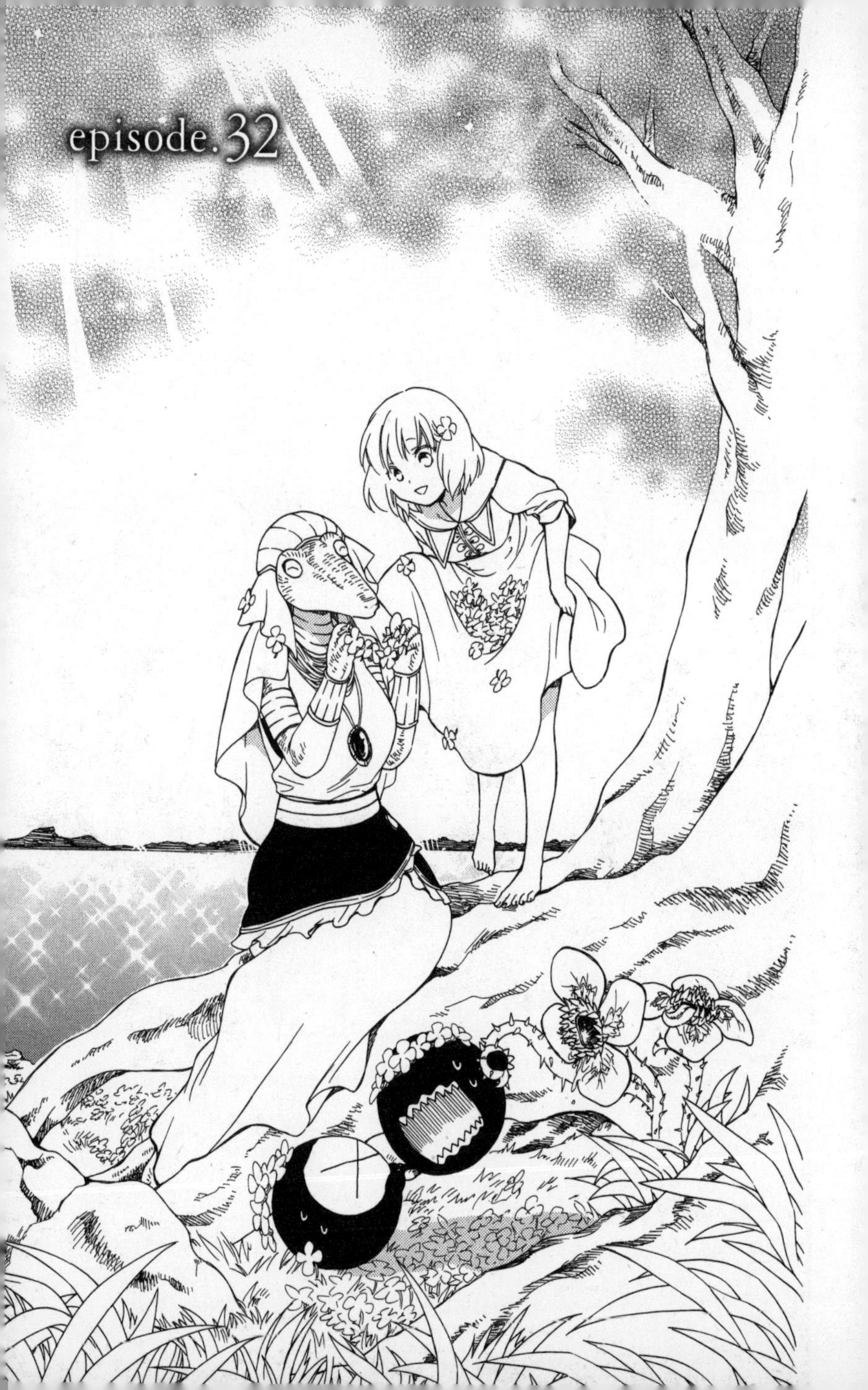
episode. 32

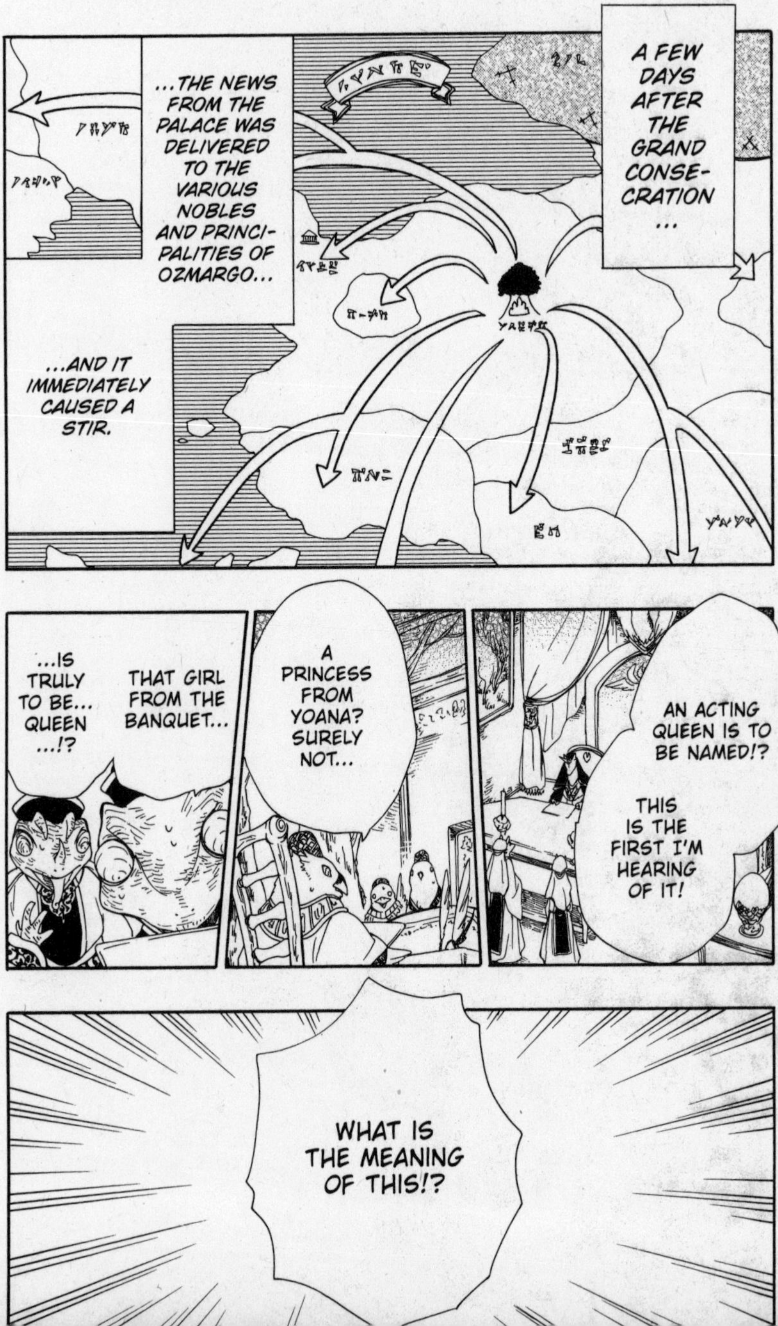
A FEW DAYS AFTER THE GRAND CONSECRATION...
...THE NEWS FROM THE PALACE WAS DELIVERED TO THE VARIOUS NOBLES AND PRINCIPALITIES OF OZMARGO...
...AND IT IMMEDIATELY CAUSED A STIR.
AN ACTING QUEEN IS TO BE NAMED!?
THIS IS THE FIRST I'M HEARING OF IT!
A PRINCESS FROM YOANA? SURELY NOT...
THAT GIRL FROM THE BANQUET...
...IS TRULY TO BE... QUEEN ...!?
WHAT IS THE MEANING OF THIS!?

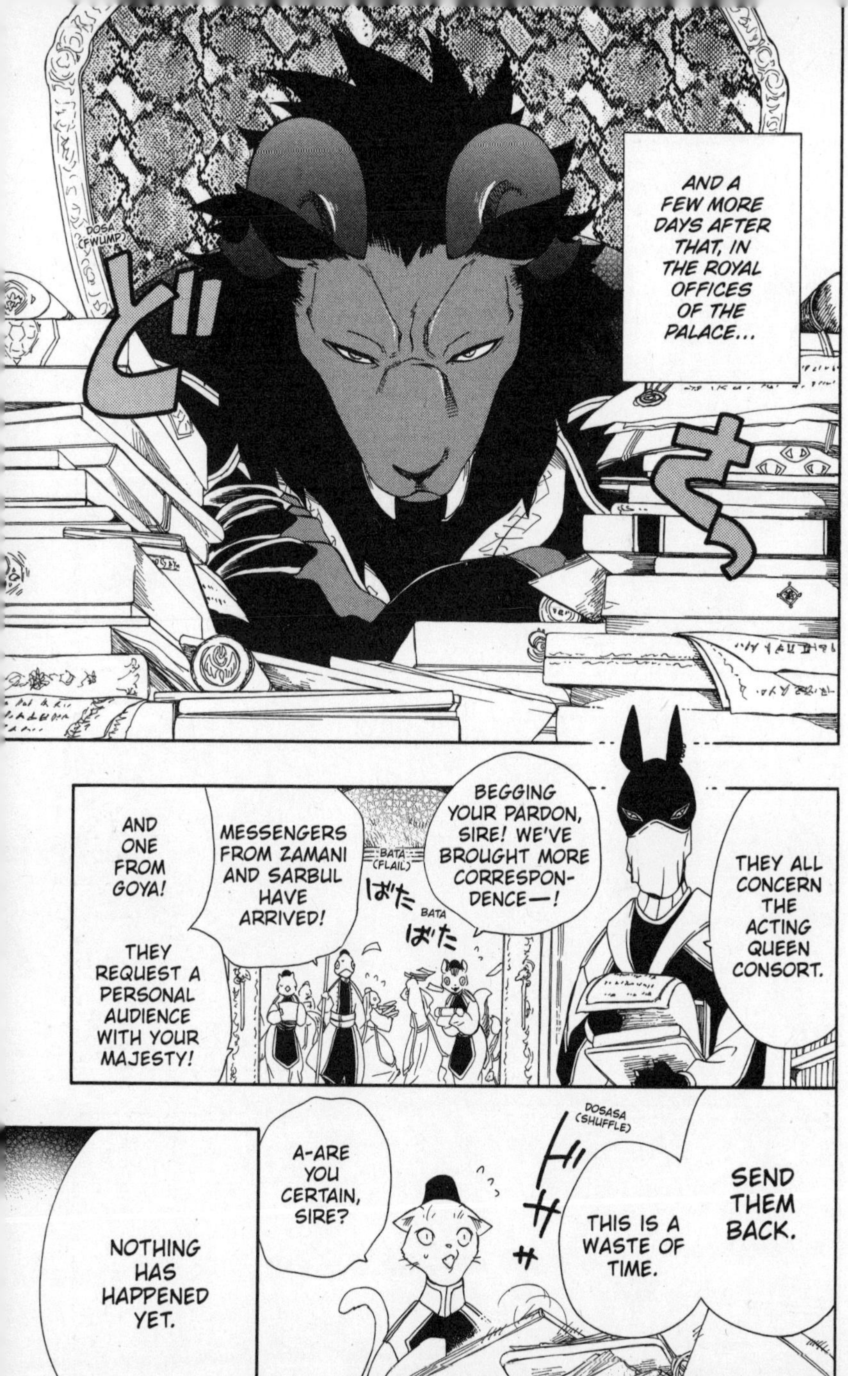
AND A FEW MORE DAYS AFTER THAT, IN THE ROYAL OFFICES OF THE PALACE...
DOSA (FWUMP)
THEY ALL CONCERN THE ACTING QUEEN CONSORT.
BEGGING YOUR PARDON, SIRE! WE'VE BROUGHT MORE CORRESPON-DENCE—!
BATA (FLAIL)
ばた
BATA
ばた
MESSENGERS FROM ZAMANI AND SARBUL HAVE ARRIVED!
AND ONE FROM GOYA!
THEY REQUEST A PERSONAL AUDIENCE WITH YOUR MAJESTY!
DOSASA (SHUFFLE)
SEND THEM BACK.
THIS IS A WASTE OF TIME.
A-ARE YOU CERTAIN, SIRE?
NOTHING HAS HAPPENED YET.

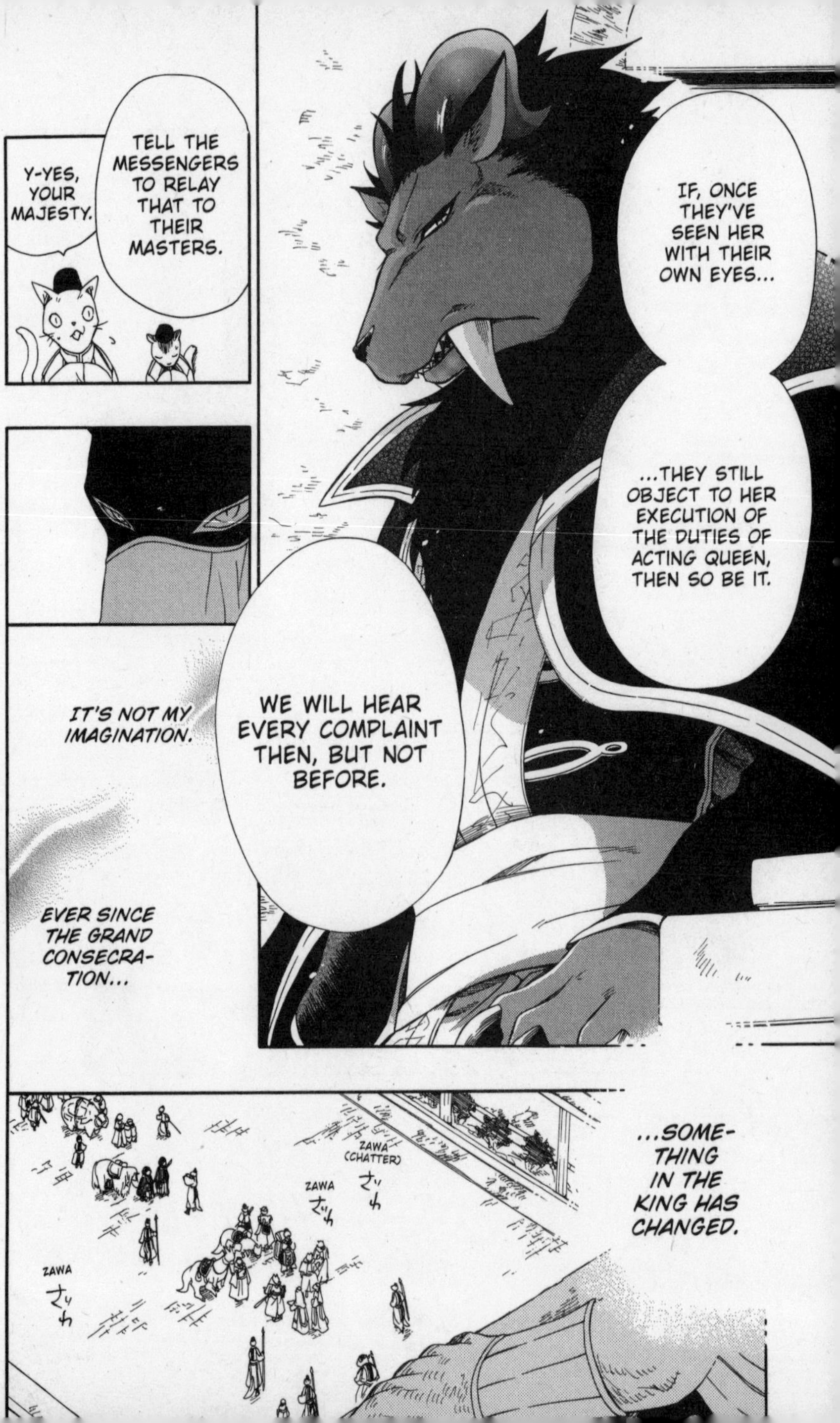
IF, ONCE THEY'VE SEEN HER WITH THEIR OWN EYES...
...THEY STILL OBJECT TO HER EXECUTION OF THE DUTIES OF ACTING QUEEN, THEN SO BE IT.
WE WILL HEAR EVERY COMPLAINT THEN, BUT NOT BEFORE.
TELL THE MESSENGERS TO RELAY THAT TO THEIR MASTERS.
Y-YES, YOUR MAJESTY.
IT'S NOT MY IMAGINATION.
EVER SINCE THE GRAND CONSECRA-TION...
...SOME-THING IN THE KING HAS CHANGED.
ZAWA (CHATTER) ざわ
ZAWA ざわ
ZAWA ざわ

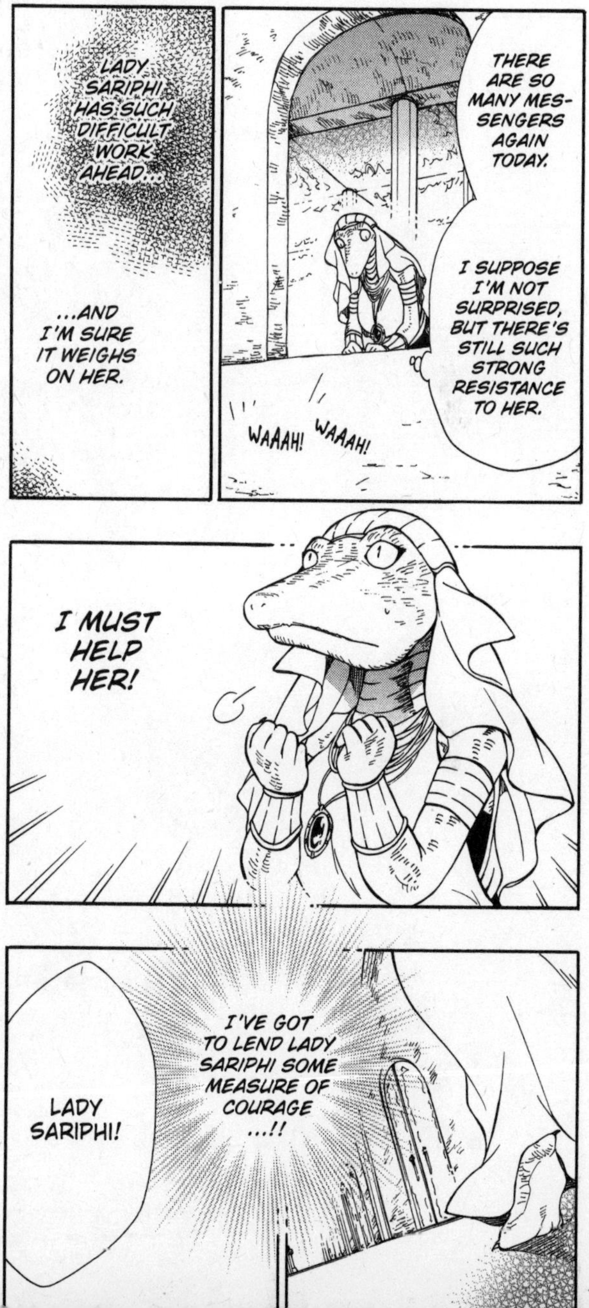
THERE ARE SO MANY MES-SENGERS AGAIN TODAY.
I SUPPOSE I'M NOT SURPRISED, BUT THERE'S STILL SUCH STRONG RESISTANCE TO HER.
WAAAH!
WAAAH!
LADY SARIPHI HAS SUCH DIFFICULT WORK AHEAD...
...AND I'M SURE IT WEIGHS ON HER.
I MUST HELP HER!
I'VE GOT TO LEND LADY SARIPHI SOME MEASURE OF COURAGE ...!!
LADY SARIPHI!

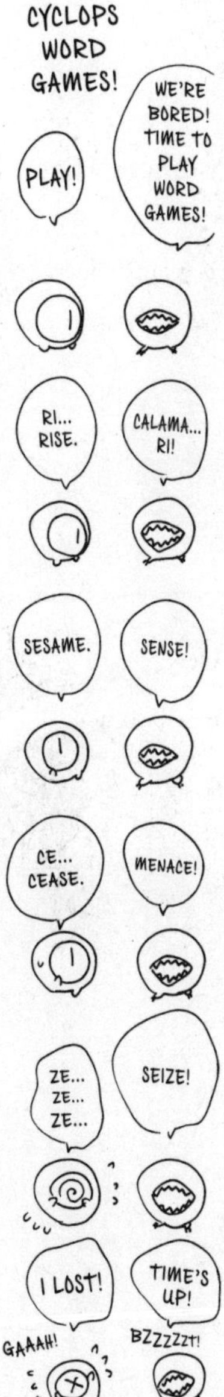
CYCLOPS WORD GAMES!
WE'RE BORED! TIME TO PLAY WORD GAMES!
PLAY!
CALAMA... RI!
RI... RISE.
SENSE!
SESAME.
MENACE!
CE... CEASE.
SEIZE!
ZE... ZE... ZE...
TIME'S UP!
I LOST!
BZZZZZT!
GAAAH!

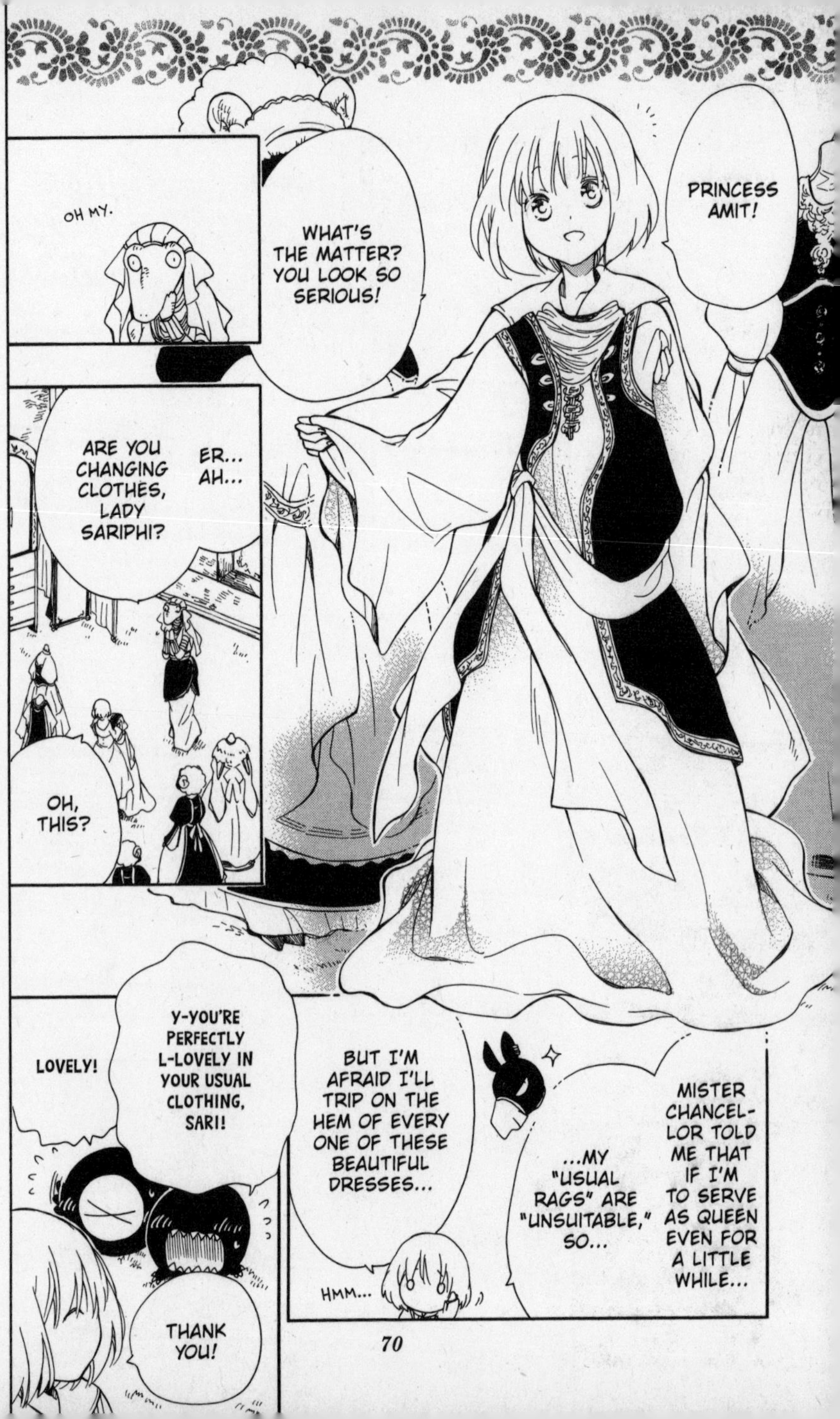
PRINCESS AMIT!
WHAT'S THE MATTER? YOU LOOK SO SERIOUS!
OH MY.
ARE YOU CHANGING CLOTHES, LADY SARIPHI?
ER... AH...
OH, THIS?
MISTER CHANCEL-LOR TOLD ME THAT IF I'M TO SERVE AS QUEEN EVEN FOR A LITTLE WHILE...
...MY "USUAL RAGS" ARE "UNSUITABLE," SO...
BUT I'M AFRAID I'LL TRIP ON THE HEM OF EVERY ONE OF THESE BEAUTIFUL DRESSES...
HMM...
Y-YOU'RE PERFECTLY L-LOVELY IN YOUR USUAL CLOTHING, SARI!
LOVELY!
THANK YOU!

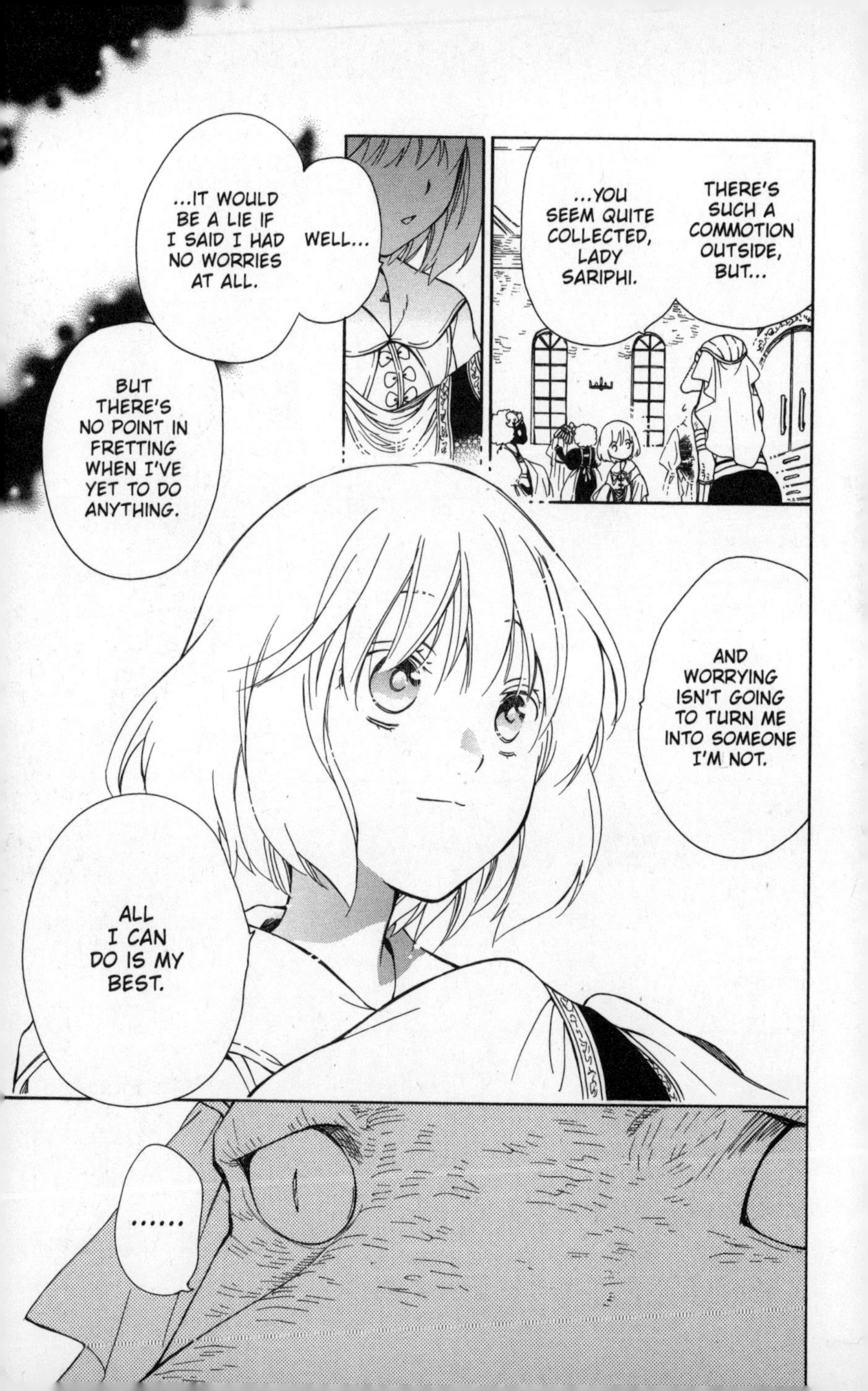
THERE'S SUCH A COMMOTION OUTSIDE, BUT...
...YOU SEEM QUITE COLLECTED, LADY SARIPHI.
WELL...
...IT WOULD BE A LIE IF I SAID I HAD NO WORRIES AT ALL.
BUT THERE'S NO POINT IN FRETTING WHEN I'VE YET TO DO ANYTHING.
AND WORRYING ISN'T GOING TO TURN ME INTO SOMEONE I'M NOT.
ALL I CAN DO IS MY BEST.
......

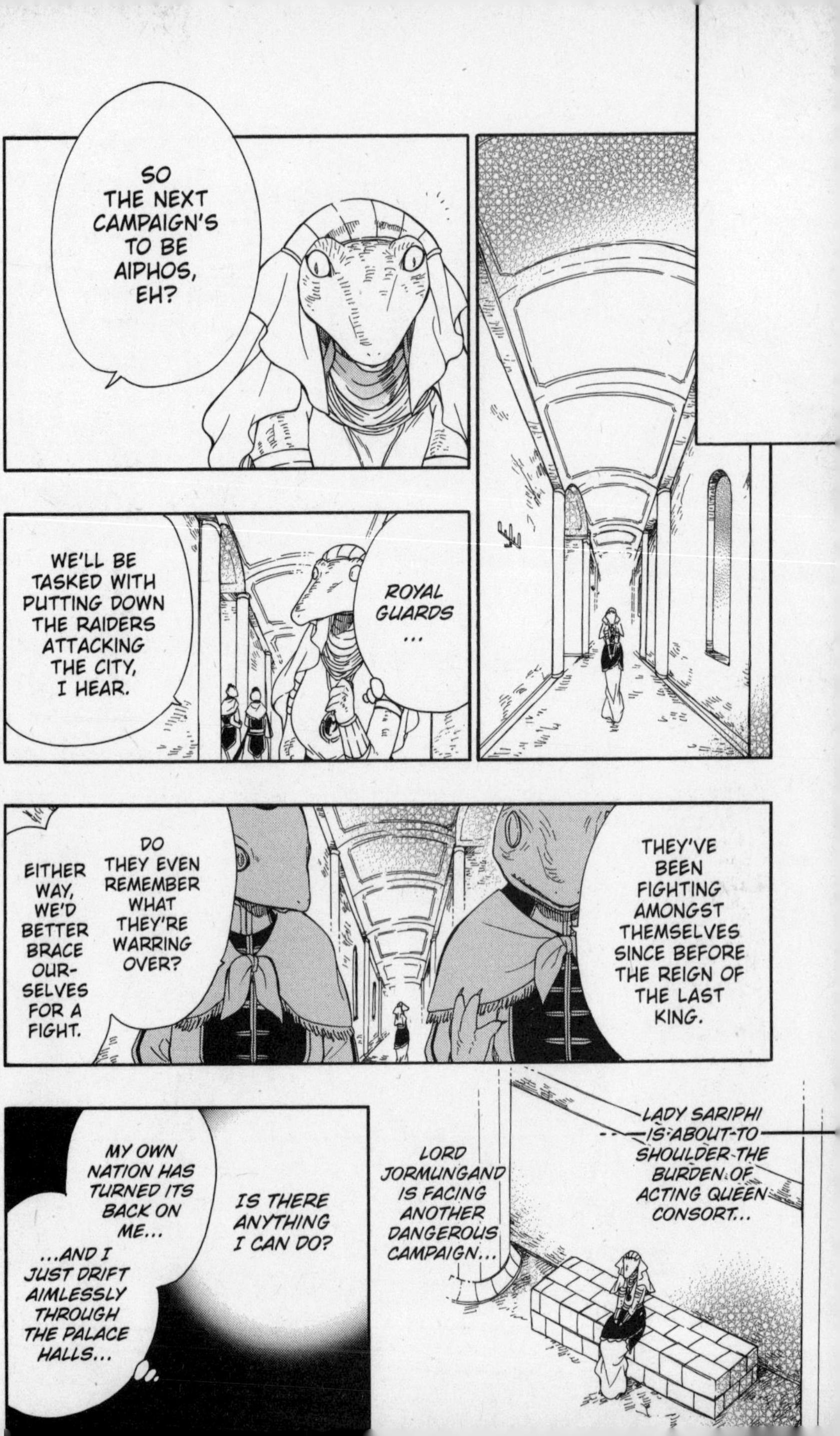
SO THE NEXT CAMPAIGN'S TO BE AIPHOS, EH?
ROYAL GUARDS ...
WE'LL BE TASKED WITH PUTTING DOWN THE RAIDERS ATTACKING THE CITY, I HEAR.
THEY'VE BEEN FIGHTING AMONGST THEMSELVES SINCE BEFORE THE REIGN OF THE LAST KING.
DO THEY EVEN REMEMBER WHAT THEY'RE WARRING OVER?
EITHER WAY, WE'D BETTER BRACE OUR-SELVES FOR A FIGHT.
LADY SARIPHI IS ABOUT TO SHOULDER THE BURDEN OF ACTING QUEEN CONSORT...
LORD JORMUNGAND IS FACING ANOTHER DANGEROUS CAMPAIGN...
IS THERE ANYTHING I CAN DO?
MY OWN NATION HAS TURNED ITS BACK ON ME...
...AND I JUST DRIFT AIMLESSLY THROUGH THE PALACE HALLS...

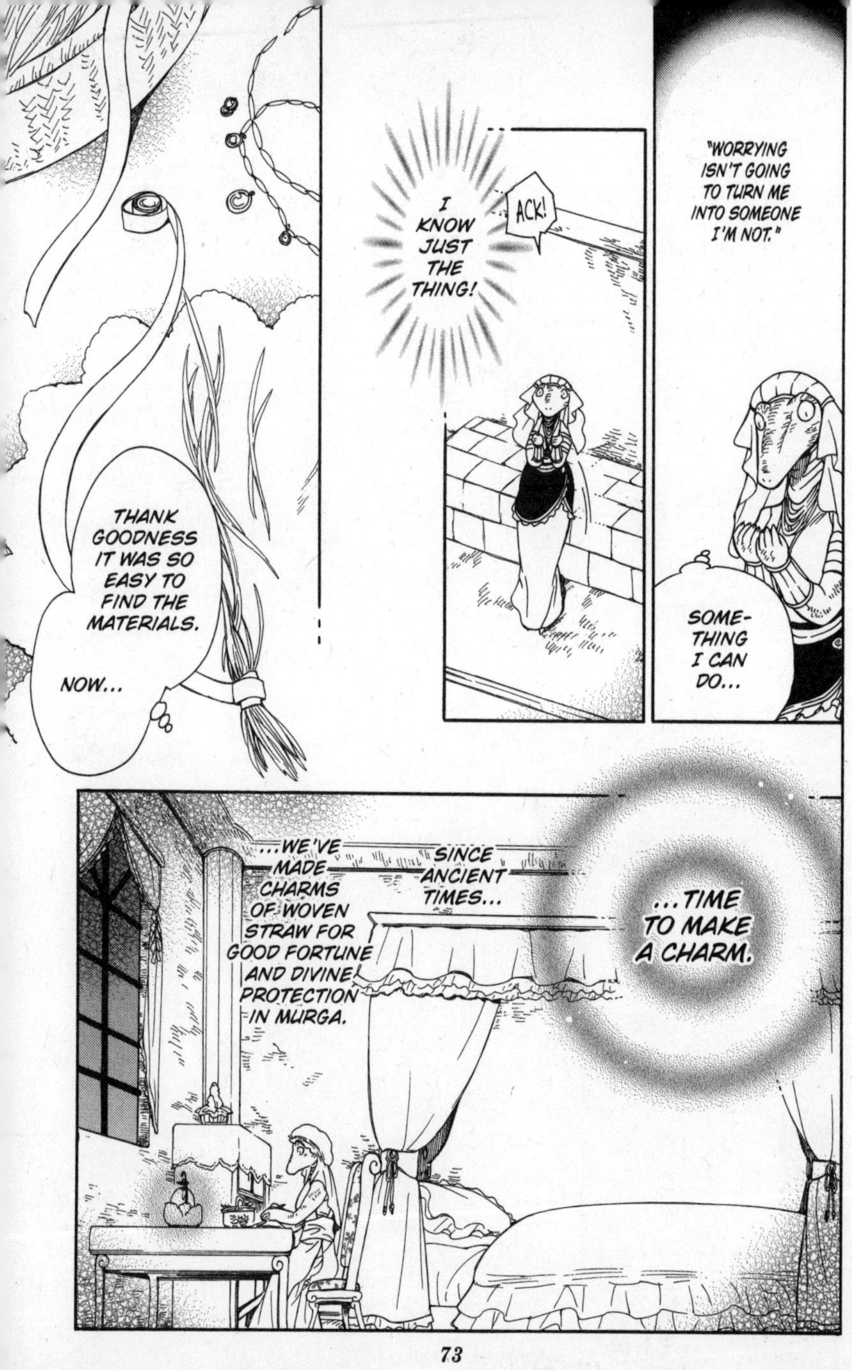
"WORRYING ISN'T GOING TO TURN ME INTO SOMEONE I'M NOT."
SOME-THING I CAN DO...
I KNOW JUST THE THING!
ACK!
THANK GOODNESS IT WAS SO EASY TO FIND THE MATERIALS.
NOW...
...TIME TO MAKE A CHARM.
SINCE ANCIENT TIMES...
...WE'VE MADE CHARMS OF WOVEN STRAW FOR GOOD FORTUNE AND DIVINE PROTECTION IN MURGA.

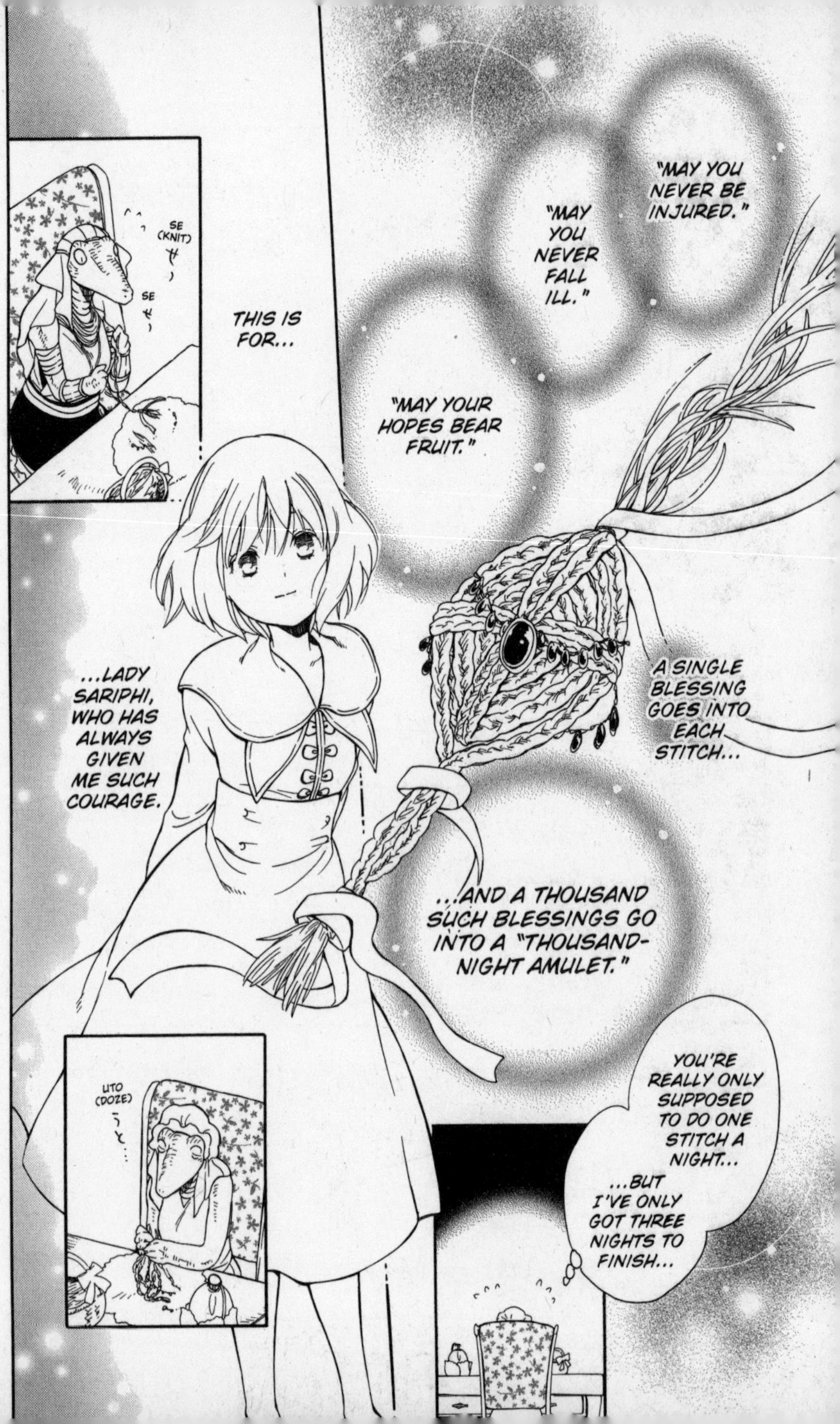
"MAY YOU NEVER BE INJURED."
"MAY YOU NEVER FALL ILL."
"MAY YOUR HOPES BEAR FRUIT."
SE (KNIT) せ
SE せ
THIS IS FOR...
A SINGLE BLESSING GOES INTO EACH STITCH...
...LADY SARIPHI, WHO HAS ALWAYS GIVEN ME SUCH COURAGE.
...AND A THOUSAND SUCH BLESSINGS GO INTO A "THOUSAND-NIGHT AMULET."
YOU'RE REALLY ONLY SUPPOSED TO DO ONE STITCH A NIGHT...
...BUT I'VE ONLY GOT THREE NIGHTS TO FINISH...
UTO (DOZE) うと...

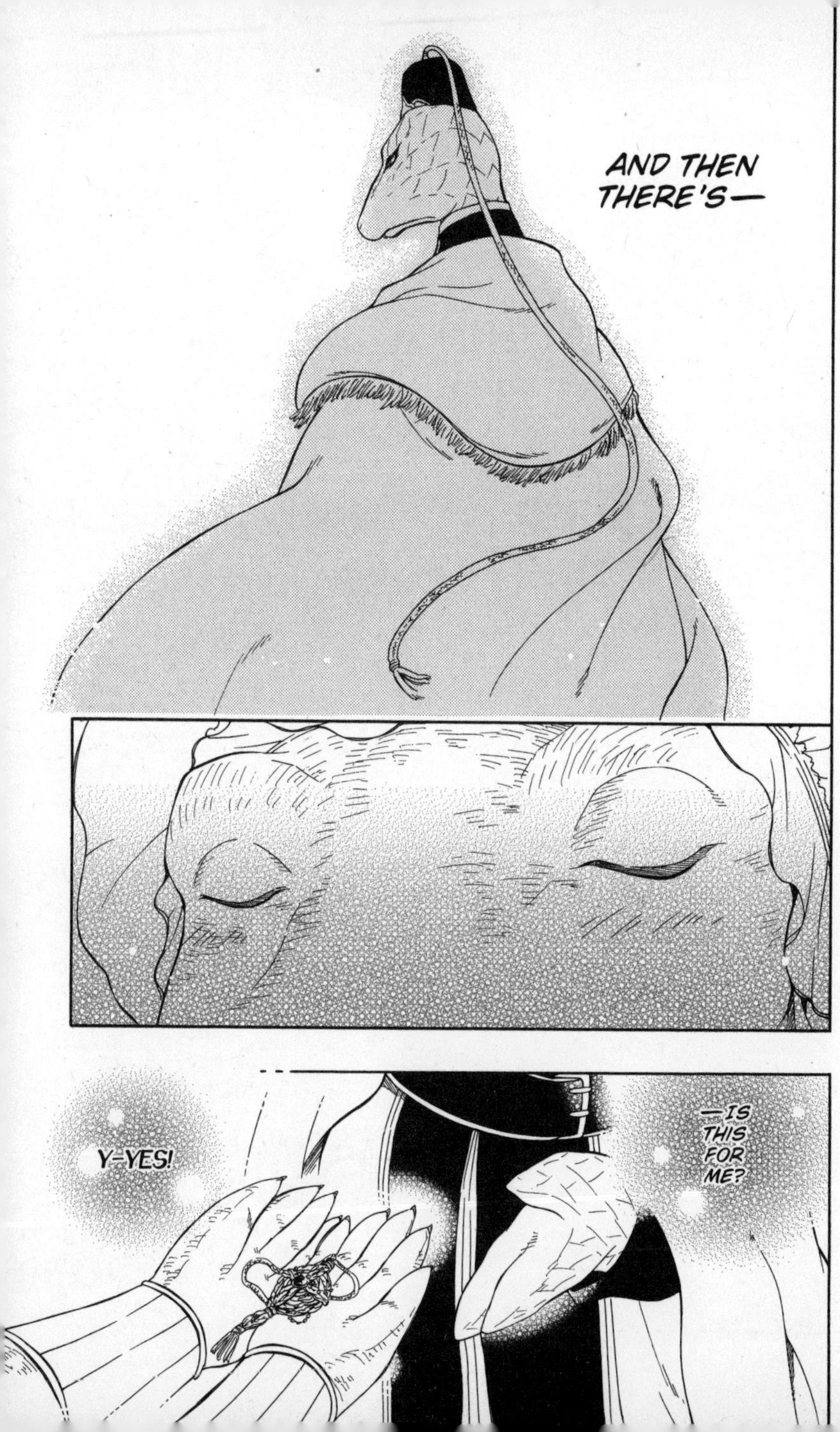
AND THEN THERE'S—
—IS THIS FOR ME?
Y-YES!

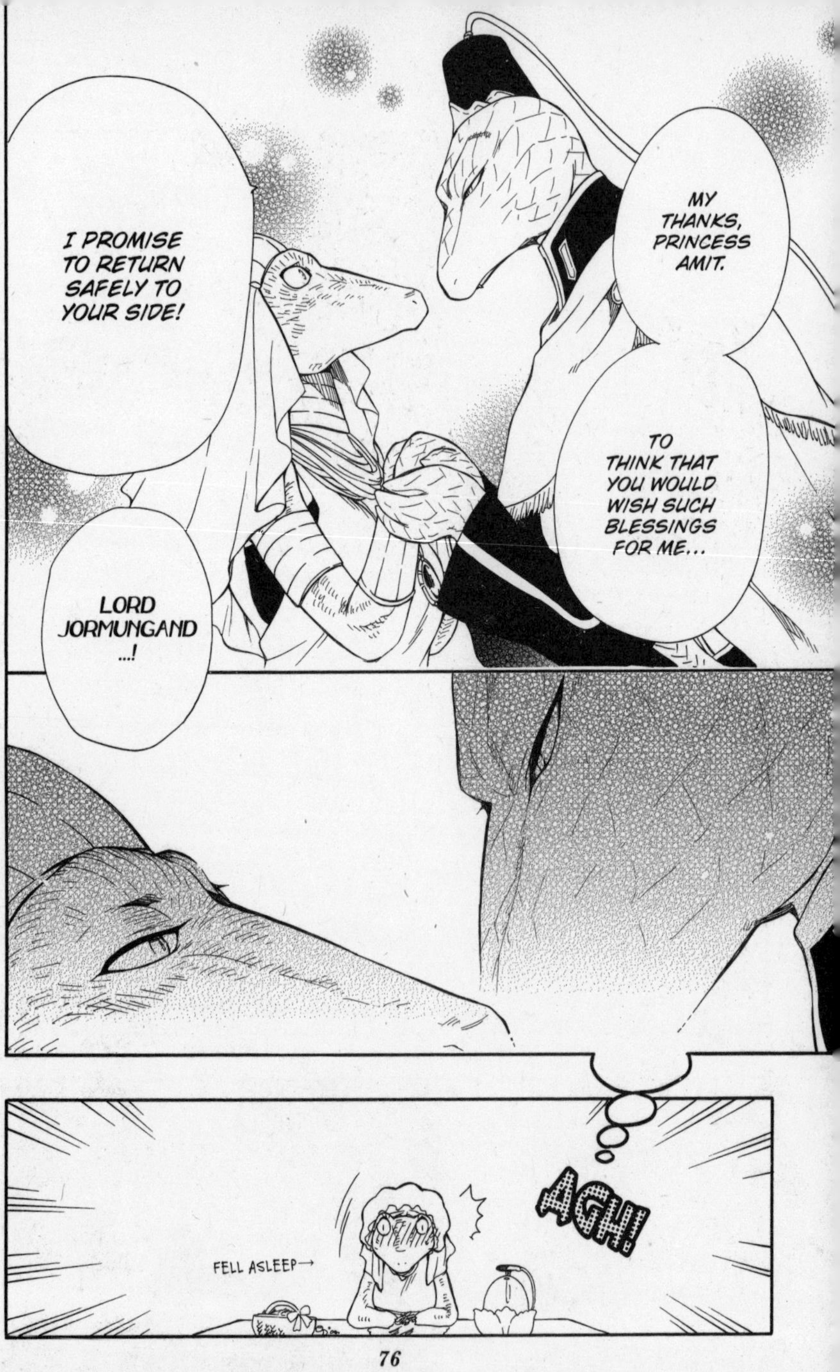
MY THANKS, PRINCESS AMIT.
TO THINK THAT YOU WOULD WISH SUCH BLESSINGS FOR ME...
I PROMISE TO RETURN SAFELY TO YOUR SIDE!
LORD JORMUNGAND ...!
AGH!
FELL ASLEEP→

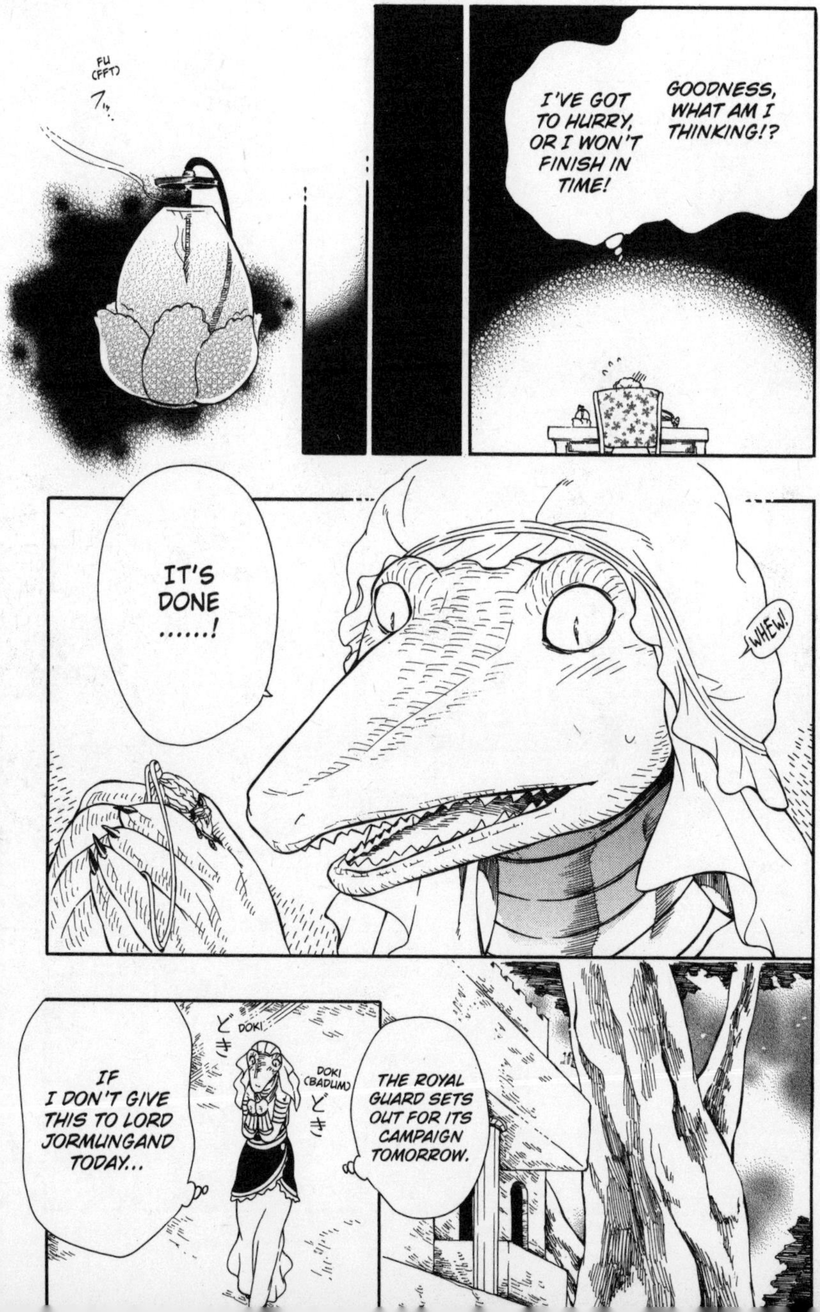
GOODNESS, WHAT AM I THINKING!?
I'VE GOT TO HURRY, OR I WON'T FINISH IN TIME!
FU (FFT)
フッ
WHEW!
IT'S DONE ......!
THE ROYAL GUARD SETS OUT FOR ITS CAMPAIGN TOMORROW.
DOKI (BADUM)
どき
DOKI
どき
IF I DON'T GIVE THIS TO LORD JORMUNGAND TODAY...

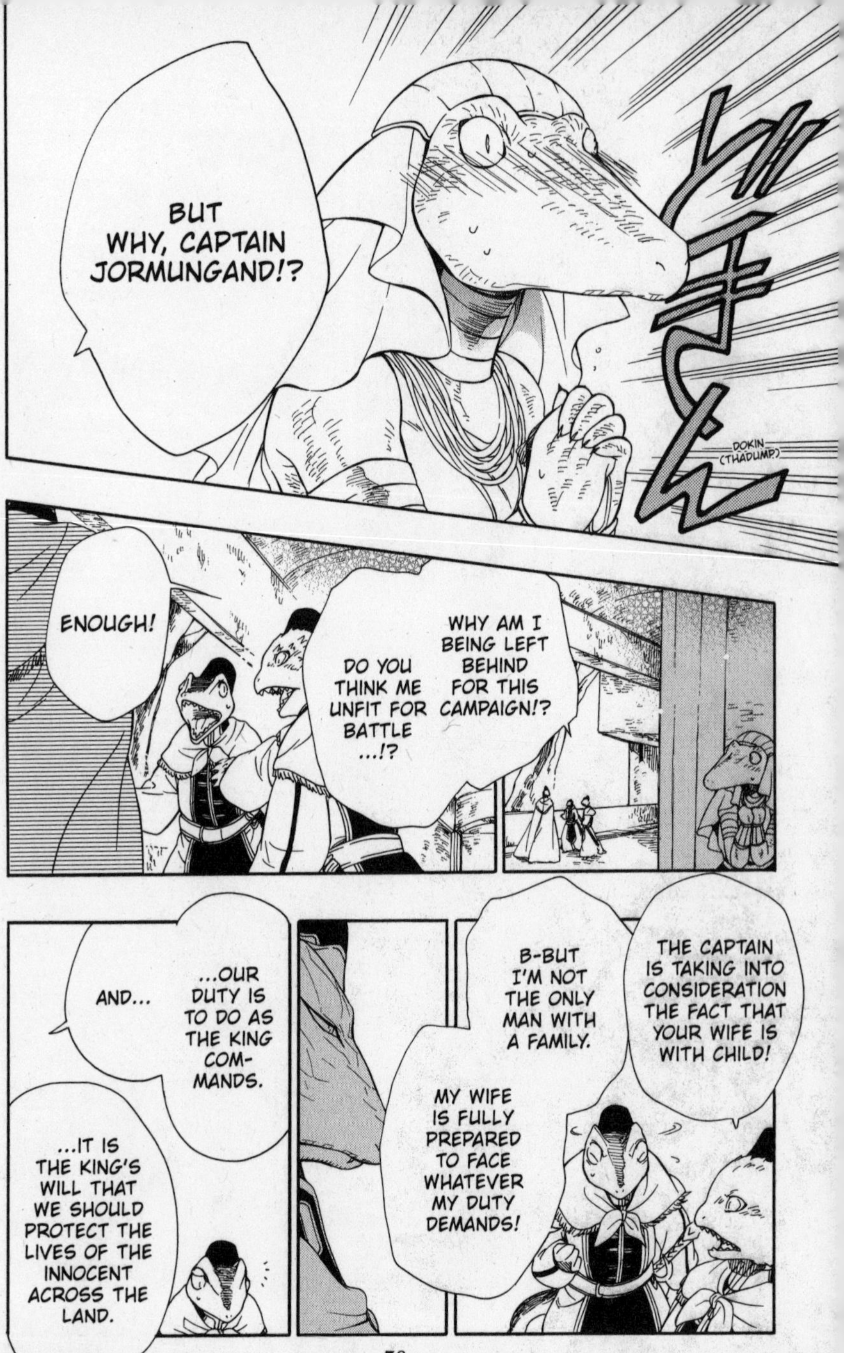
BUT WHY, CAPTAIN JORMUNGAND!?
DOKIN (THADUMP)
WHY AM I BEING LEFT BEHIND FOR THIS CAMPAIGN!? DO YOU THINK ME UNFIT FOR BATTLE ...!?
ENOUGH!
THE CAPTAIN IS TAKING INTO CONSIDERATION THE FACT THAT YOUR WIFE IS WITH CHILD!
B-BUT I'M NOT THE ONLY MAN WITH A FAMILY.
MY WIFE IS FULLY PREPARED TO FACE WHATEVER MY DUTY DEMANDS!
...OUR DUTY IS TO DO AS THE KING COM-MANDS.
AND...
...IT IS THE KING'S WILL THAT WE SHOULD PROTECT THE LIVES OF THE INNOCENT ACROSS THE LAND.

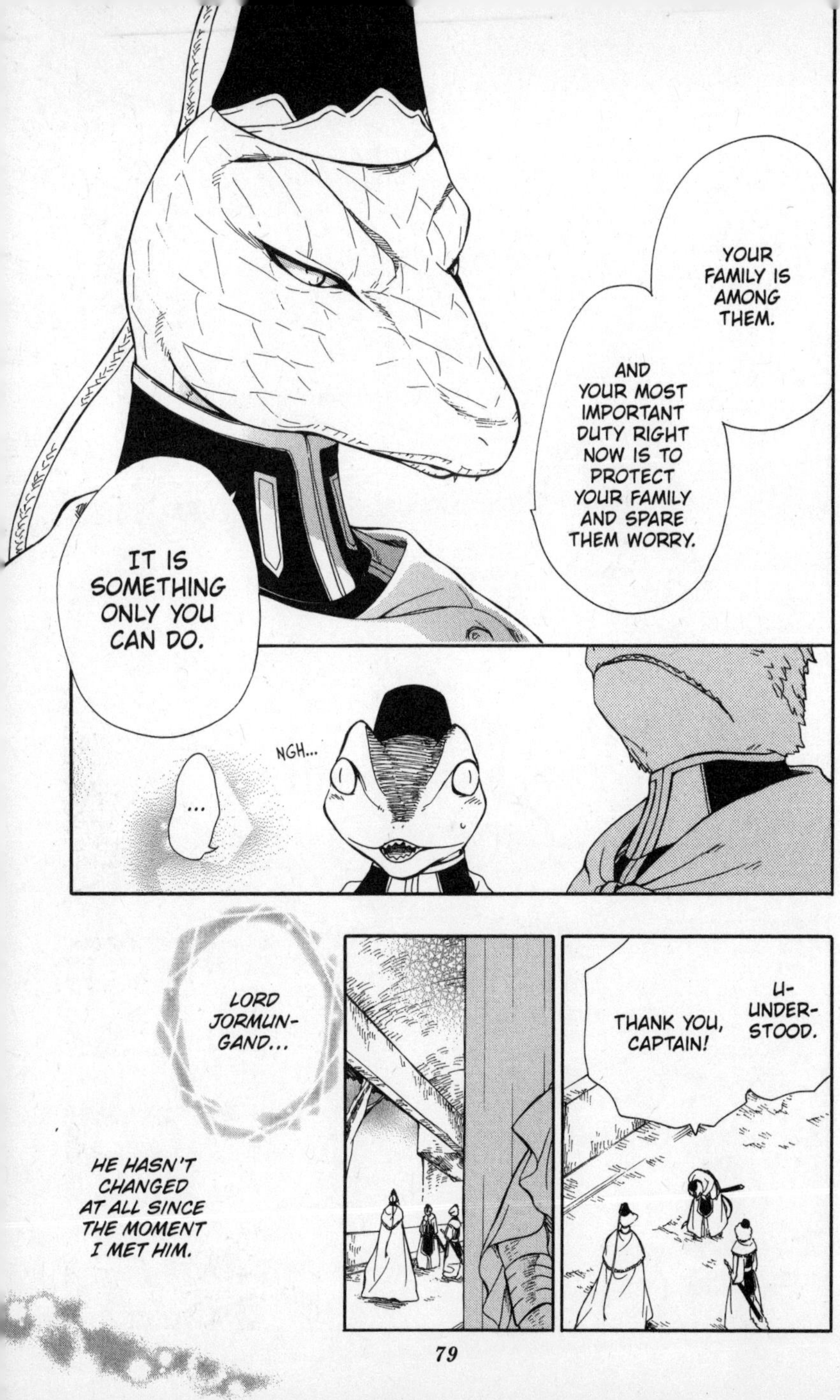
YOUR FAMILY IS AMONG THEM.
AND YOUR MOST IMPORTANT DUTY RIGHT NOW IS TO PROTECT YOUR FAMILY AND SPARE THEM WORRY.
IT IS SOMETHING ONLY YOU CAN DO.
NGH...
...
U-UNDER-STOOD.
THANK YOU, CAPTAIN!
LORD JORMUN-GAND...
HE HASN'T CHANGED AT ALL SINCE THE MOMENT I MET HIM.

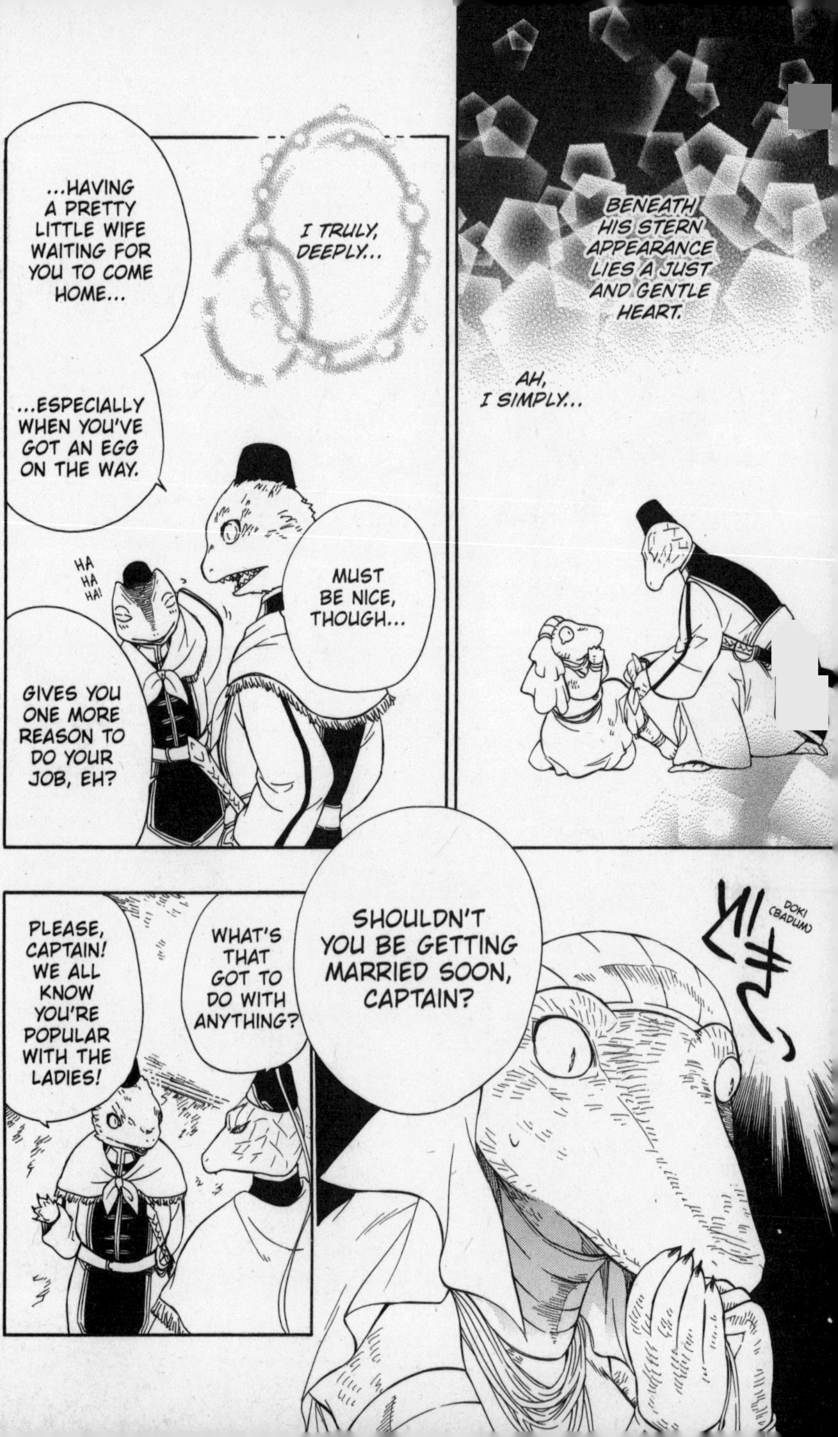
BENEATH HIS STERN APPEARANCE LIES A JUST AND GENTLE HEART.
AH, I SIMPLY...
I TRULY, DEEPLY...
...HAVING A PRETTY LITTLE WIFE WAITING FOR YOU TO COME HOME...
...ESPECIALLY WHEN YOU'VE GOT AN EGG ON THE WAY.
MUST BE NICE, THOUGH...
HA HA HA!
GIVES YOU ONE MORE REASON TO DO YOUR JOB, EH?
DOKI (BADUM)
SHOULDN'T YOU BE GETTING MARRIED SOON, CAPTAIN?
WHAT'S THAT GOT TO DO WITH ANYTHING?
PLEASE, CAPTAIN! WE ALL KNOW YOU'RE POPULAR WITH THE LADIES!

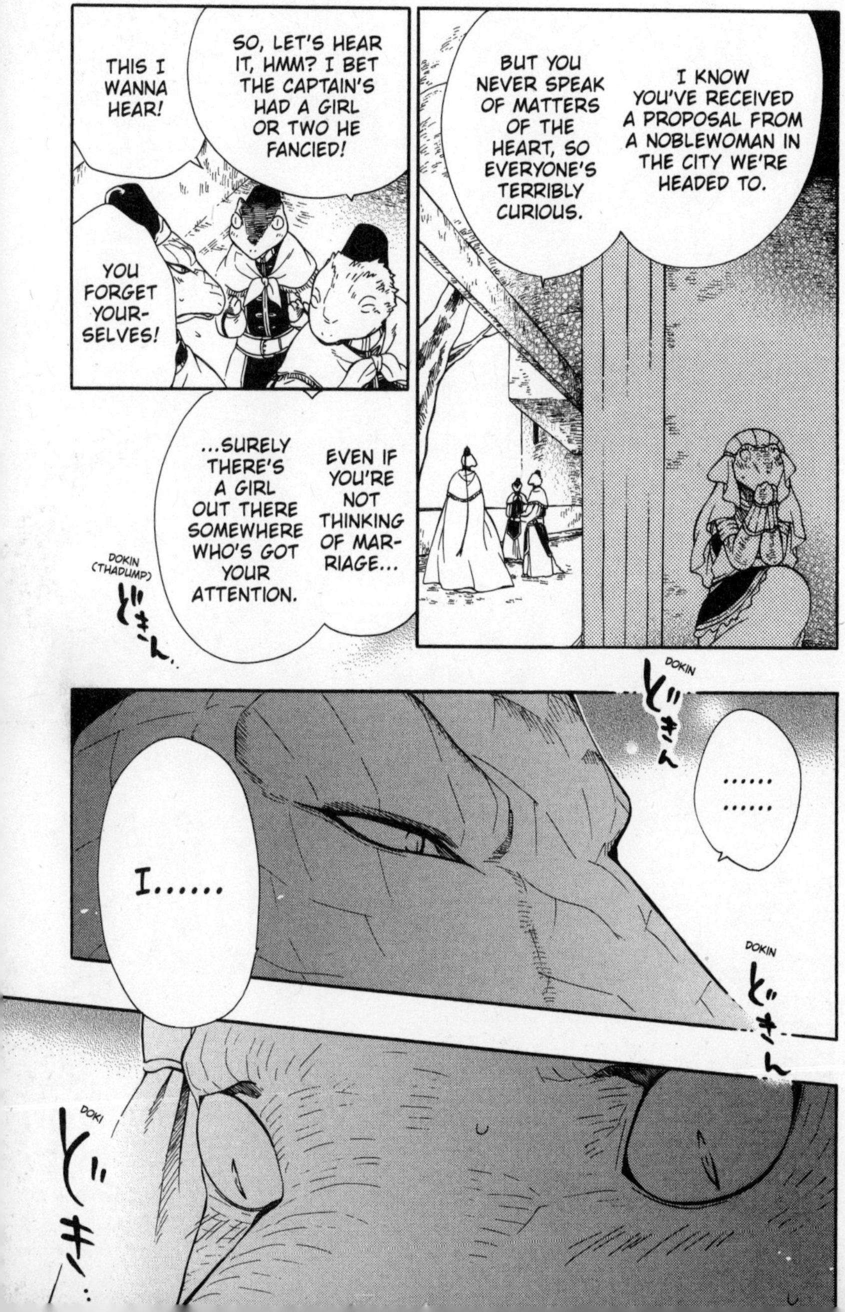
I KNOW YOU'VE RECEIVED A PROPOSAL FROM A NOBLEWOMAN IN THE CITY WE'RE HEADED TO.
BUT YOU NEVER SPEAK OF MATTERS OF THE HEART, SO EVERYONE'S TERRIBLY CURIOUS.
SO, LET'S HEAR IT, HMM? I BET THE CAPTAIN'S HAD A GIRL OR TWO HE FANCIED!
THIS I WANNA HEAR!
YOU FORGET YOUR-SELVES!
EVEN IF YOU'RE NOT THINKING OF MAR-RIAGE...
...SURELY THERE'S A GIRL OUT THERE SOMEWHERE WHO'S GOT YOUR ATTENTION.
DOKIN (THADUMP)
どきん
DOKIN
どきん
......
......
I......
DOKIN
どきん
DOKI
どキ

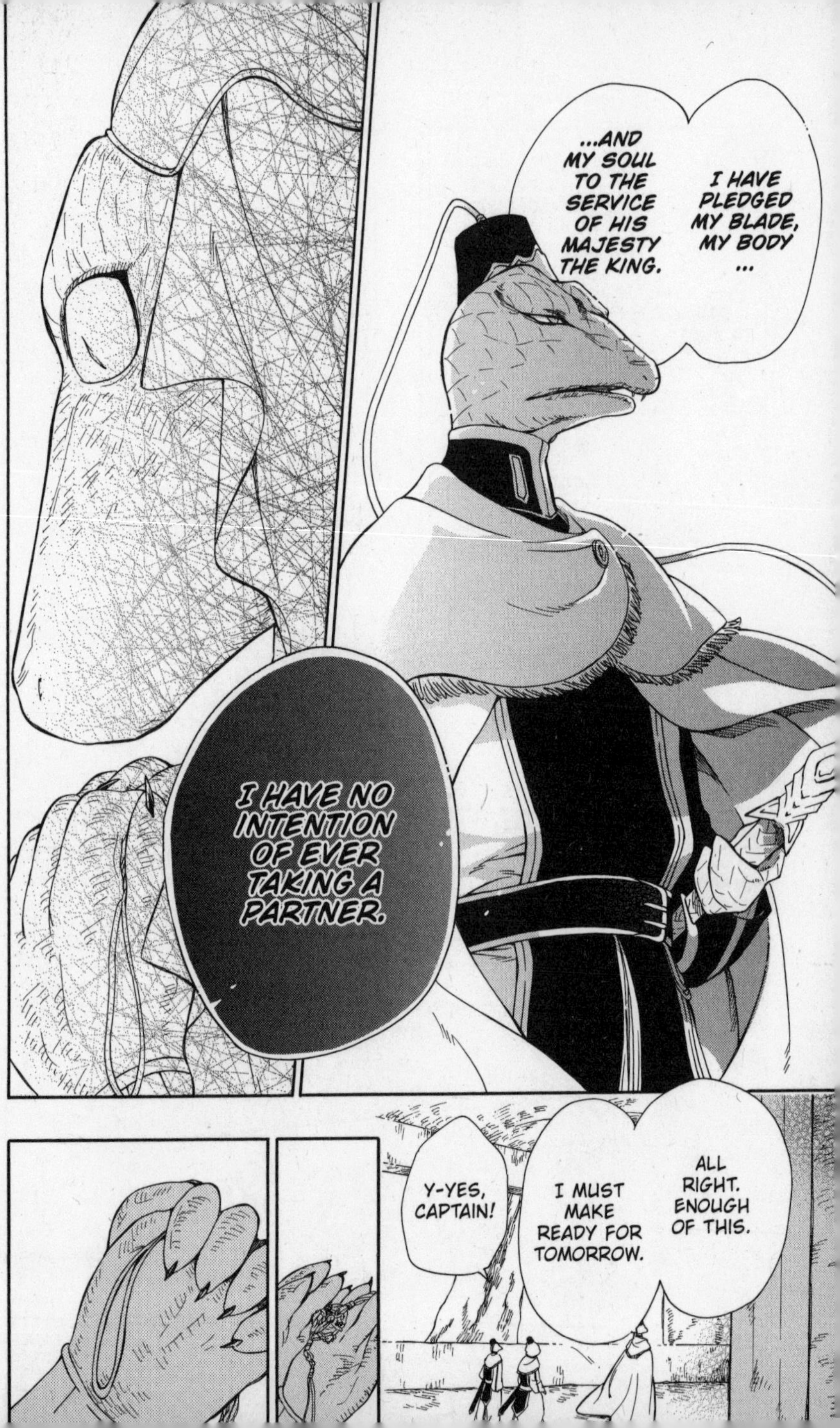
I HAVE PLEDGED MY BLADE, MY BODY ...
...AND MY SOUL TO THE SERVICE OF HIS MAJESTY THE KING.
I HAVE NO INTENTION OF EVER TAKING A PARTNER.
ALL RIGHT. ENOUGH OF THIS.
I MUST MAKE READY FOR TOMORROW.
Y-YES, CAPTAIN!

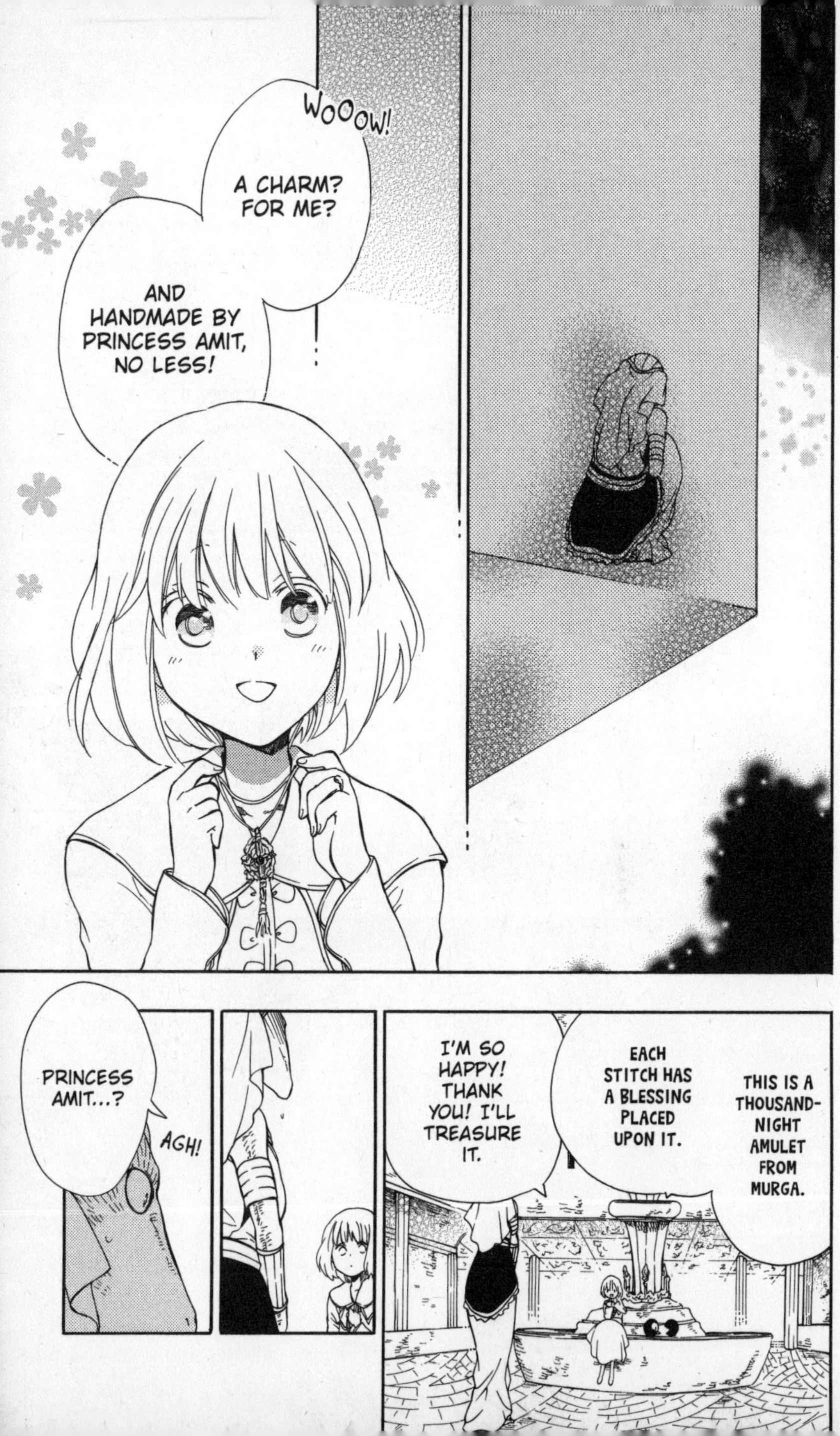
WOOOW!
A CHARM? FOR ME?
AND HANDMADE BY PRINCESS AMIT, NO LESS!
THIS IS A THOUSAND-NIGHT AMULET FROM MURGA.
EACH STITCH HAS A BLESSING PLACED UPON IT.
I'M SO HAPPY! THANK YOU! I'LL TREASURE IT.
PRINCESS AMIT...?
AGH!

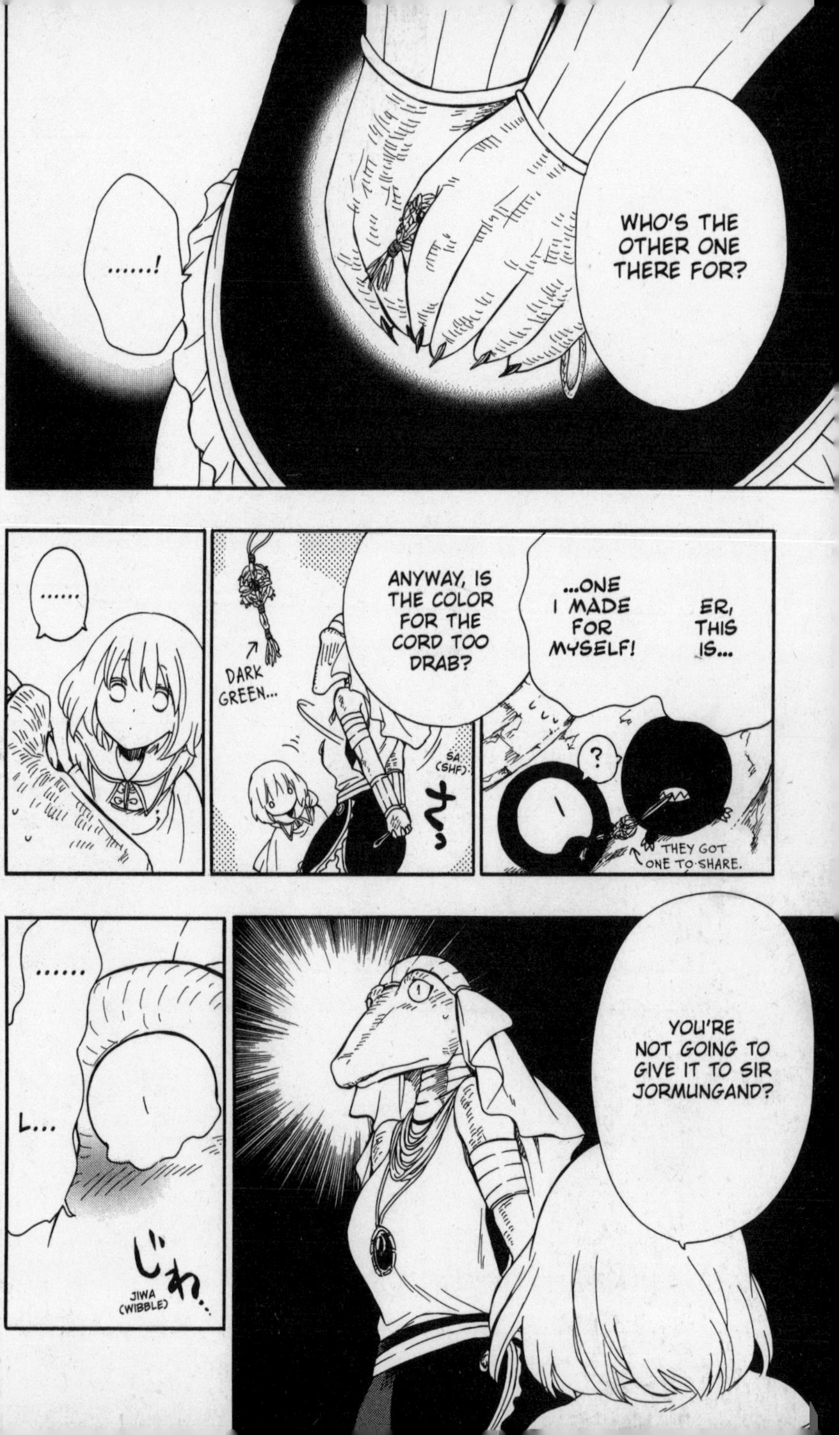
WHO'S THE OTHER ONE THERE FOR?
......!
ER, THIS IS...
...ONE I MADE FOR MYSELF!
?
THEY GOT ONE TO SHARE.
ANYWAY, IS THE COLOR FOR THE CORD TOO DRAB?
DARK GREEN...
さっ
SA (SHF)
......
YOU'RE NOT GOING TO GIVE IT TO SIR JORMUNGAND?
......
L...
じわ…
JIWA (WIBBLE)

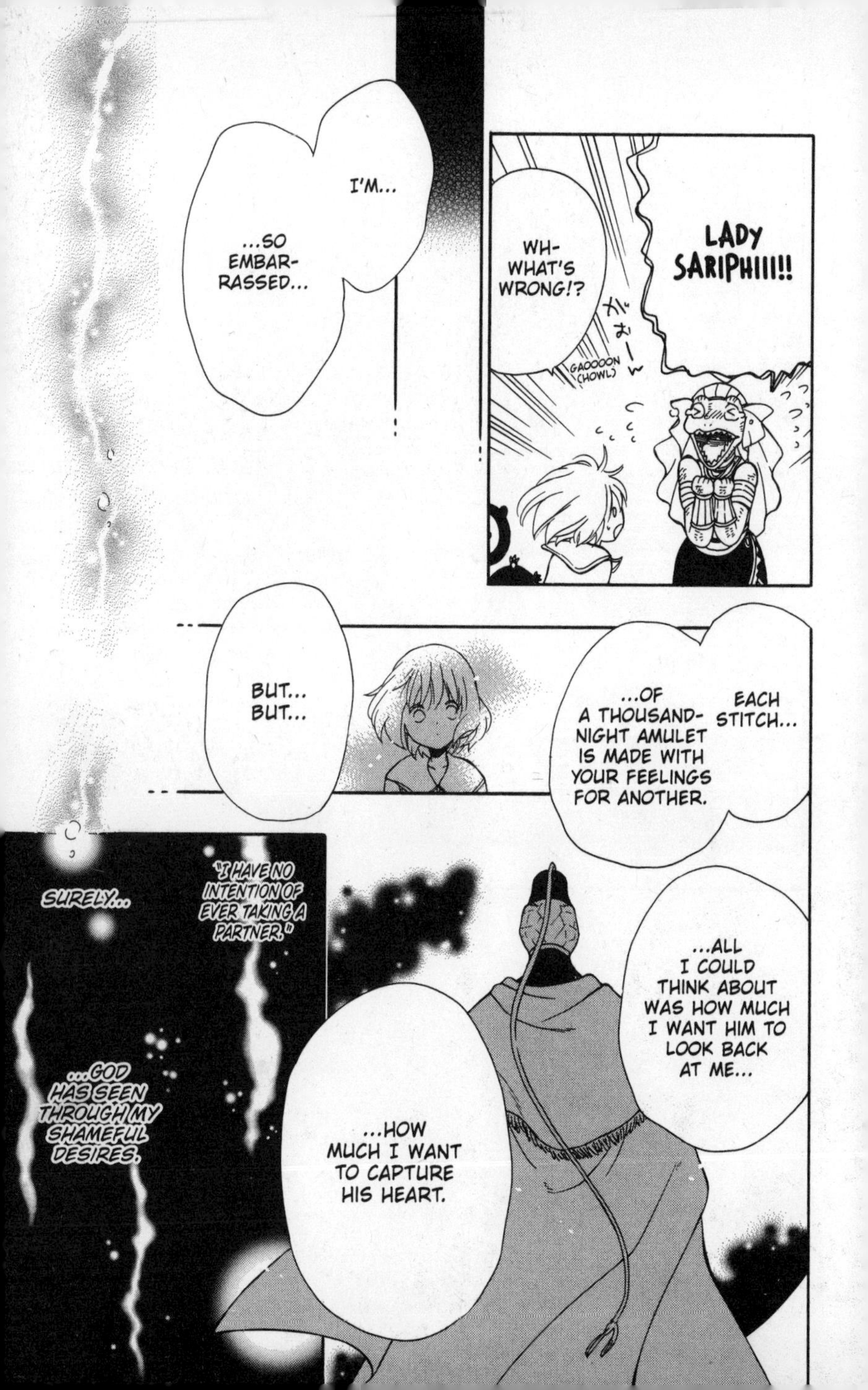
LADY SARIPHIIII!!
WH- WHAT'S WRONG!?
がおーん
GAOOOON (HOWL)
I'M...
...SO EMBARRASSED...
EACH STITCH...
...OF A THOUSAND-NIGHT AMULET IS MADE WITH YOUR FEELINGS FOR ANOTHER.
BUT... BUT...
...ALL I COULD THINK ABOUT WAS HOW MUCH I WANT HIM TO LOOK BACK AT ME...
...HOW MUCH I WANT TO CAPTURE HIS HEART.
"I HAVE NO INTENTION OF EVER TAKING A PARTNER."
SURELY...
...GOD HAS SEEN THROUGH MY SHAMEFUL DESIRES.

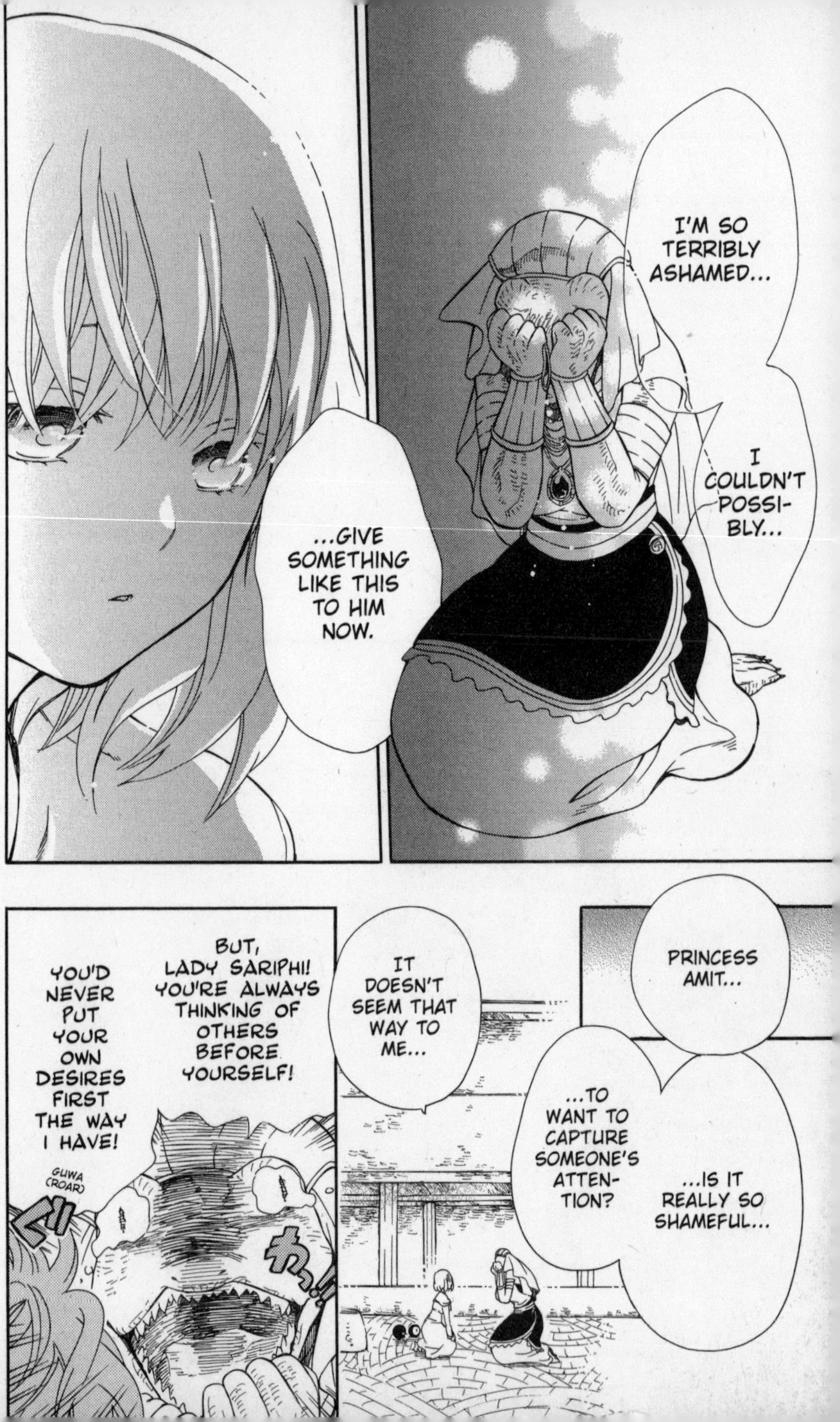
I'M SO TERRIBLY ASHAMED...
I COULDN'T POSSIBLY...
...GIVE SOMETHING LIKE THIS TO HIM NOW.
PRINCESS AMIT...
...IS IT REALLY SO SHAMEFUL...
...TO WANT TO CAPTURE SOMEONE'S ATTENTION?
IT DOESN'T SEEM THAT WAY TO ME...
BUT, LADY SARIPHI! YOU'RE ALWAYS THINKING OF OTHERS BEFORE YOURSELF!
YOU'D NEVER PUT YOUR OWN DESIRES FIRST THE WAY I HAVE!
GUWA (ROAR)

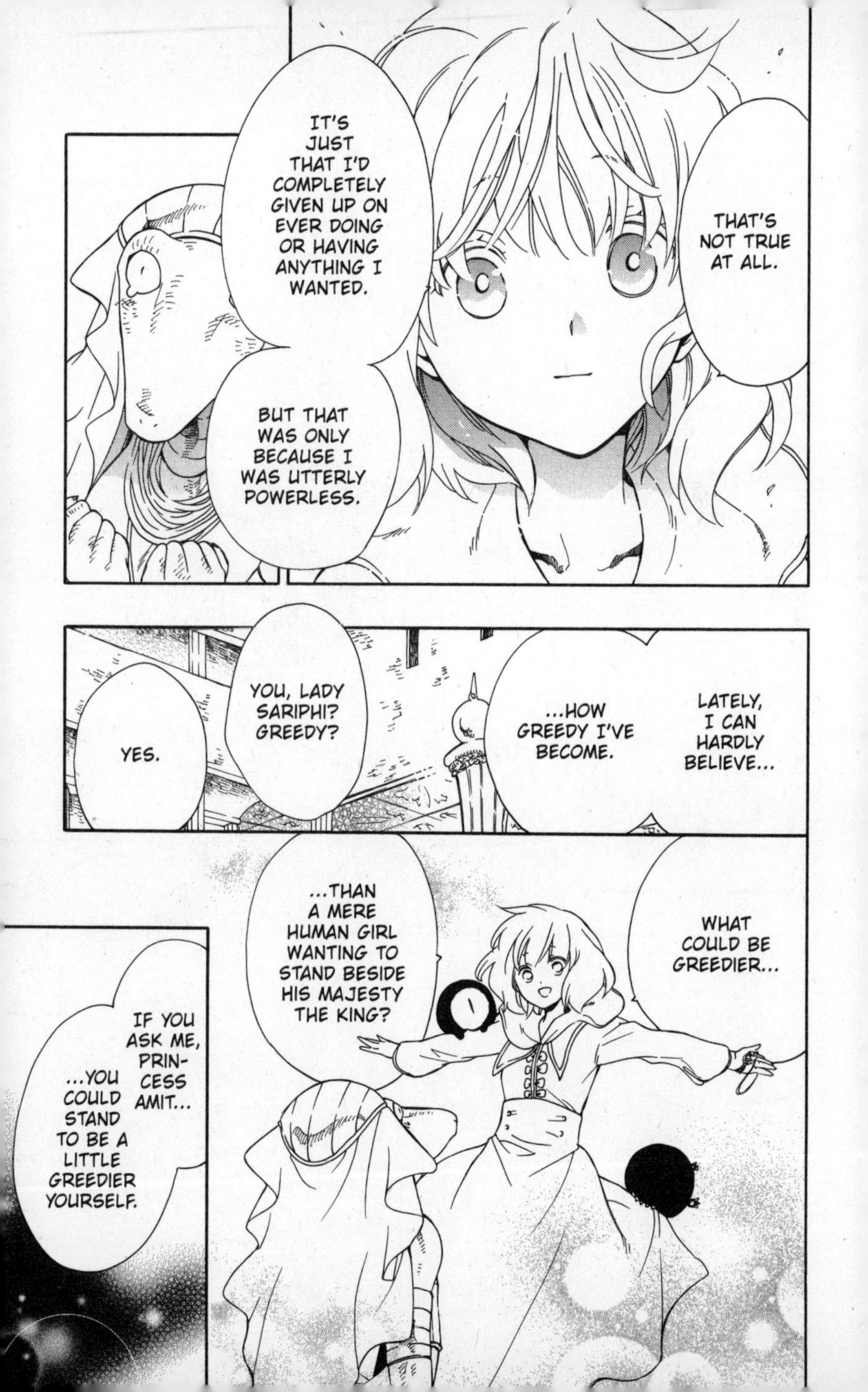
THAT'S NOT TRUE AT ALL.
IT'S JUST THAT I'D COMPLETELY GIVEN UP ON EVER DOING OR HAVING ANYTHING I WANTED.
BUT THAT WAS ONLY BECAUSE I WAS UTTERLY POWERLESS.
LATELY, I CAN HARDLY BELIEVE...
...HOW GREEDY I'VE BECOME.
YOU, LADY SARIPHI? GREEDY?
YES.
WHAT COULD BE GREEDIER...
...THAN A MERE HUMAN GIRL WANTING TO STAND BESIDE HIS MAJESTY THE KING?
IF YOU ASK ME, PRIN-CESS AMIT...
...YOU COULD STAND TO BE A LITTLE GREEDIER YOURSELF.

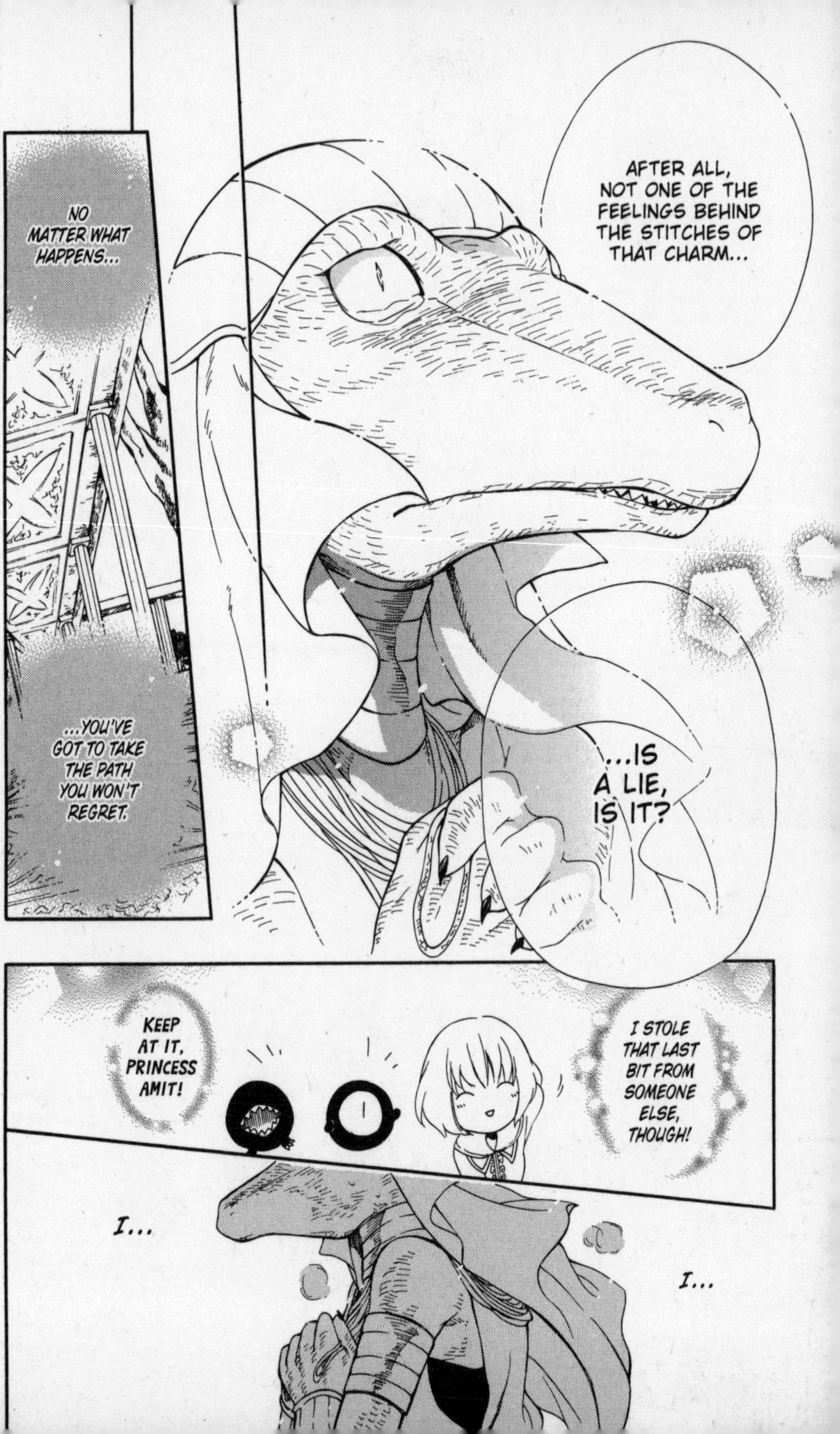
AFTER ALL, NOT ONE OF THE FEELINGS BEHIND THE STITCHES OF THAT CHARM...
...IS A LIE, IS IT?
NO MATTER WHAT HAPPENS...
...YOU'VE GOT TO TAKE THE PATH YOU WON'T REGRET.
I STOLE THAT LAST BIT FROM SOMEONE ELSE, THOUGH!
KEEP AT IT, PRINCESS AMIT!
I...
I...

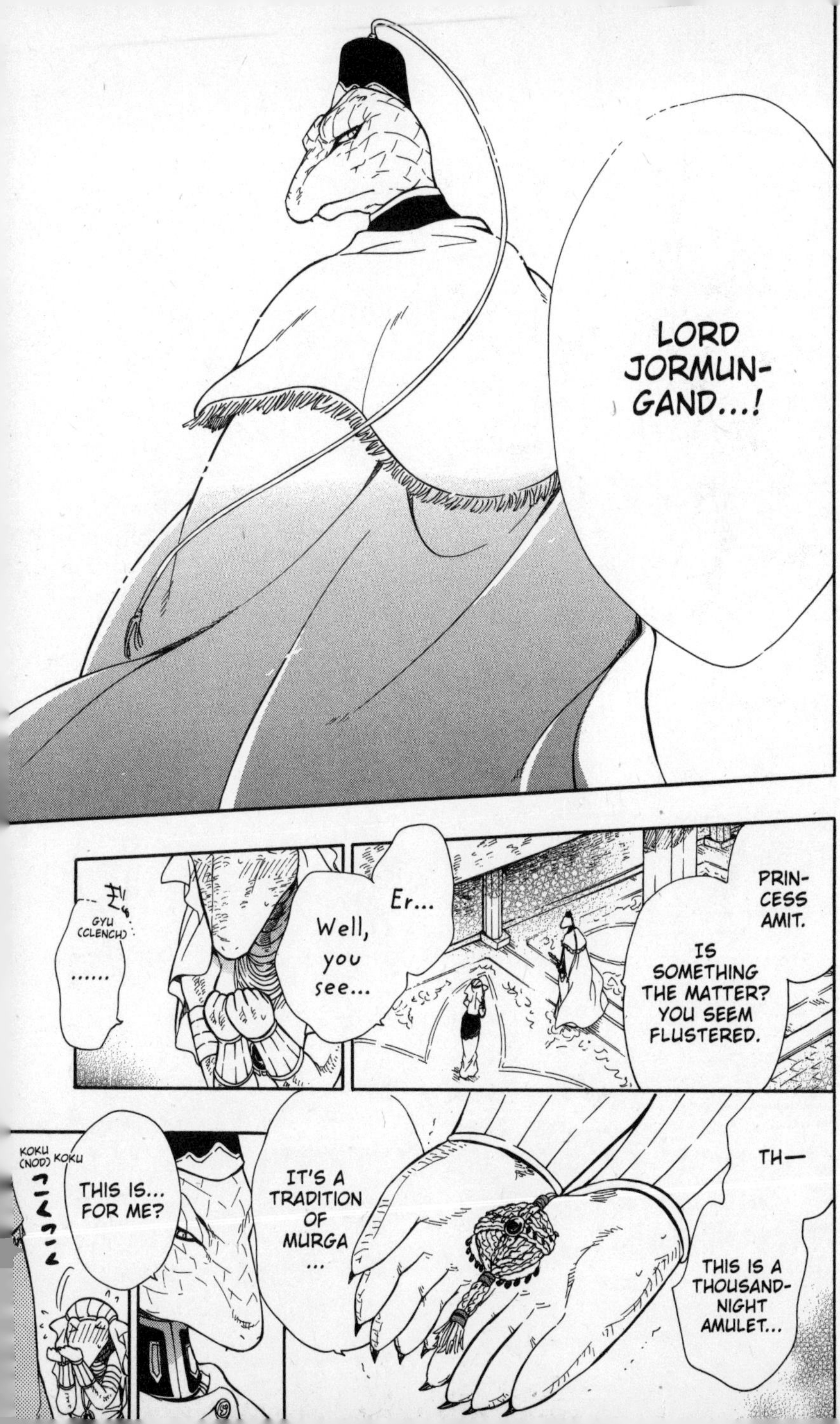
LORD JORMUN-GAND...!
PRIN-CESS AMIT.
IS SOMETHING THE MATTER? YOU SEEM FLUSTERED.
Er...
Well, you see...
GYU (CLENCH)
......
TH—
THIS IS A THOUSAND-NIGHT AMULET...
IT'S A TRADITION OF MURGA...
THIS IS... FOR ME?
KOKU KOKU (NOD)

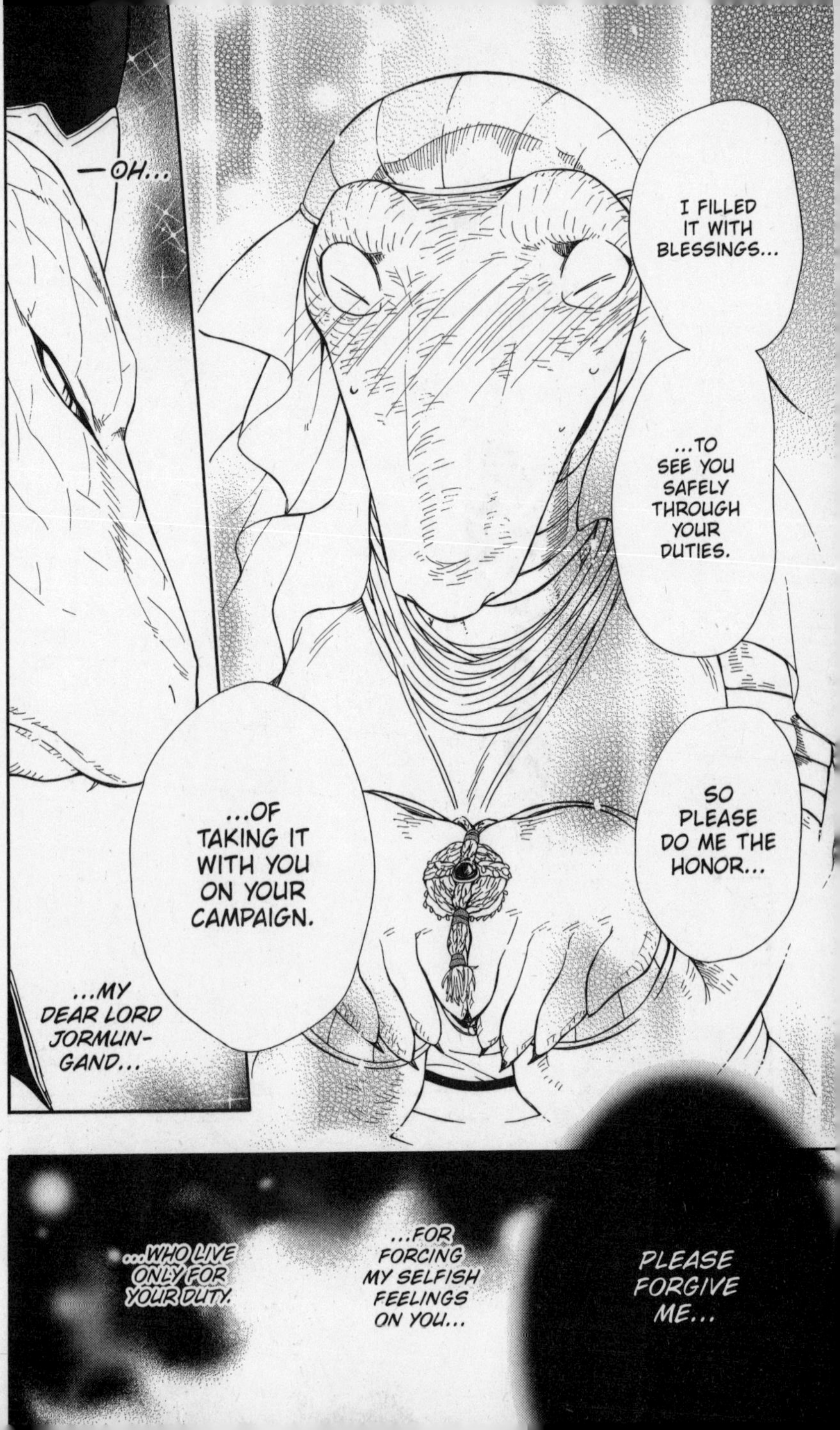
I FILLED IT WITH BLESSINGS...
...TO SEE YOU SAFELY THROUGH YOUR DUTIES.
SO PLEASE DO ME THE HONOR...
...OF TAKING IT WITH YOU ON YOUR CAMPAIGN.
—OH...
...MY DEAR LORD JORMUN-GAND...
PLEASE FORGIVE ME...
...FOR FORCING MY SELFISH FEELINGS ON YOU...
...WHO LIVE ONLY FOR YOUR DUTY.

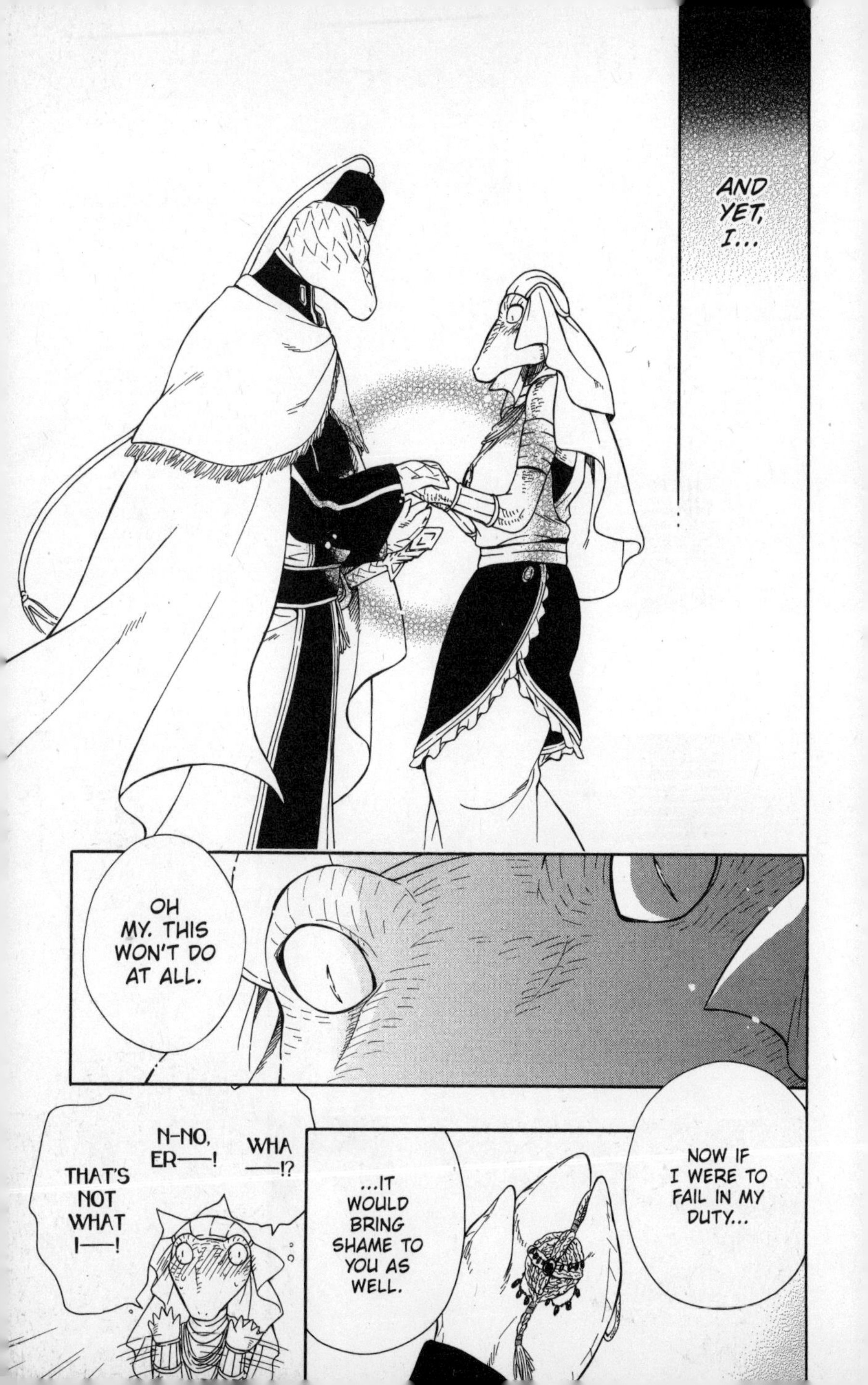
AND YET, I...
OH MY. THIS WON'T DO AT ALL.
NOW IF I WERE TO FAIL IN MY DUTY...
...IT WOULD BRING SHAME TO YOU AS WELL.
WHA—!?
N-NO, ER—!
THAT'S NOT WHAT I—!

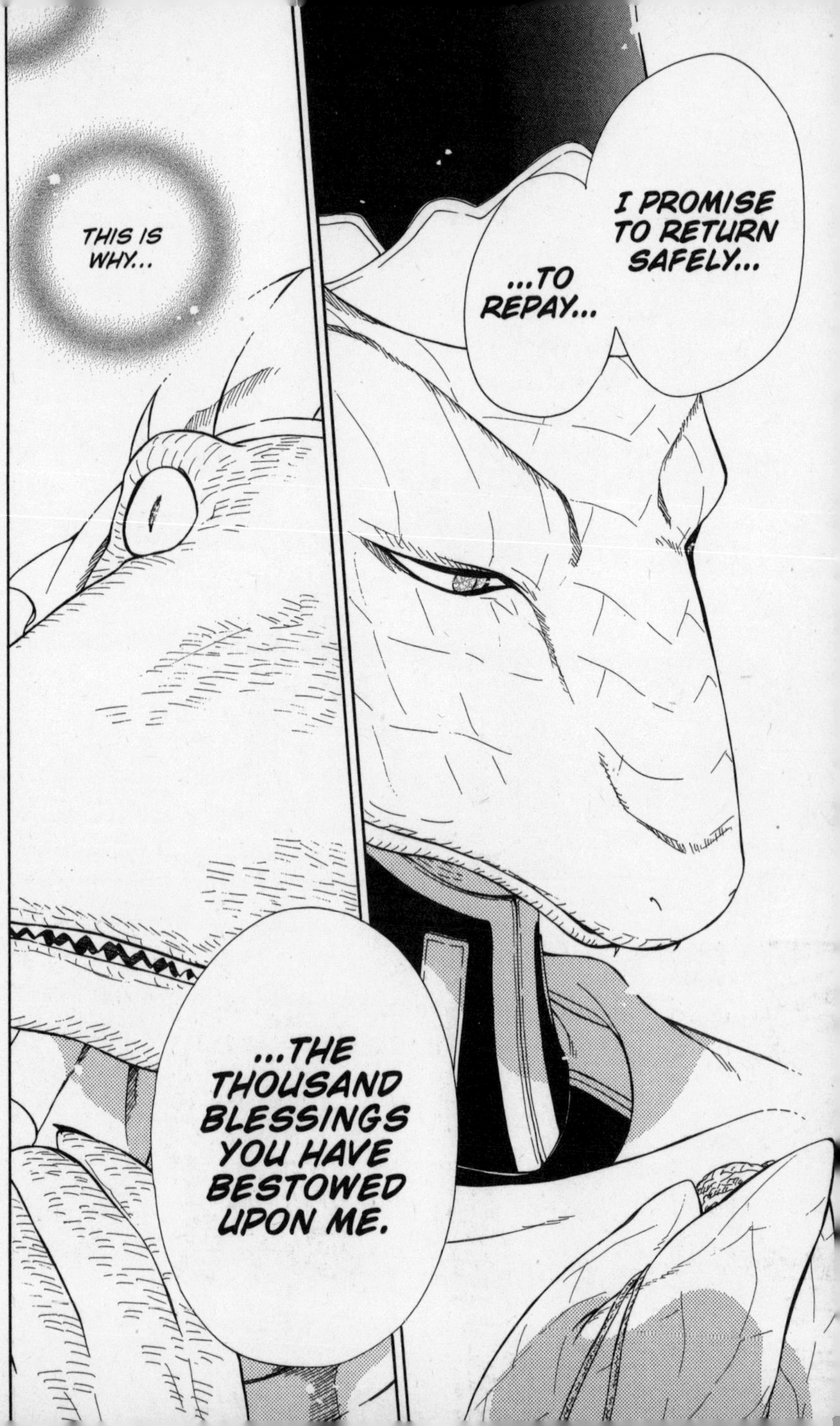
I PROMISE TO RETURN SAFELY...
...TO REPAY...
THIS IS WHY...
...THE THOUSAND BLESSINGS YOU HAVE BESTOWED UPON ME.

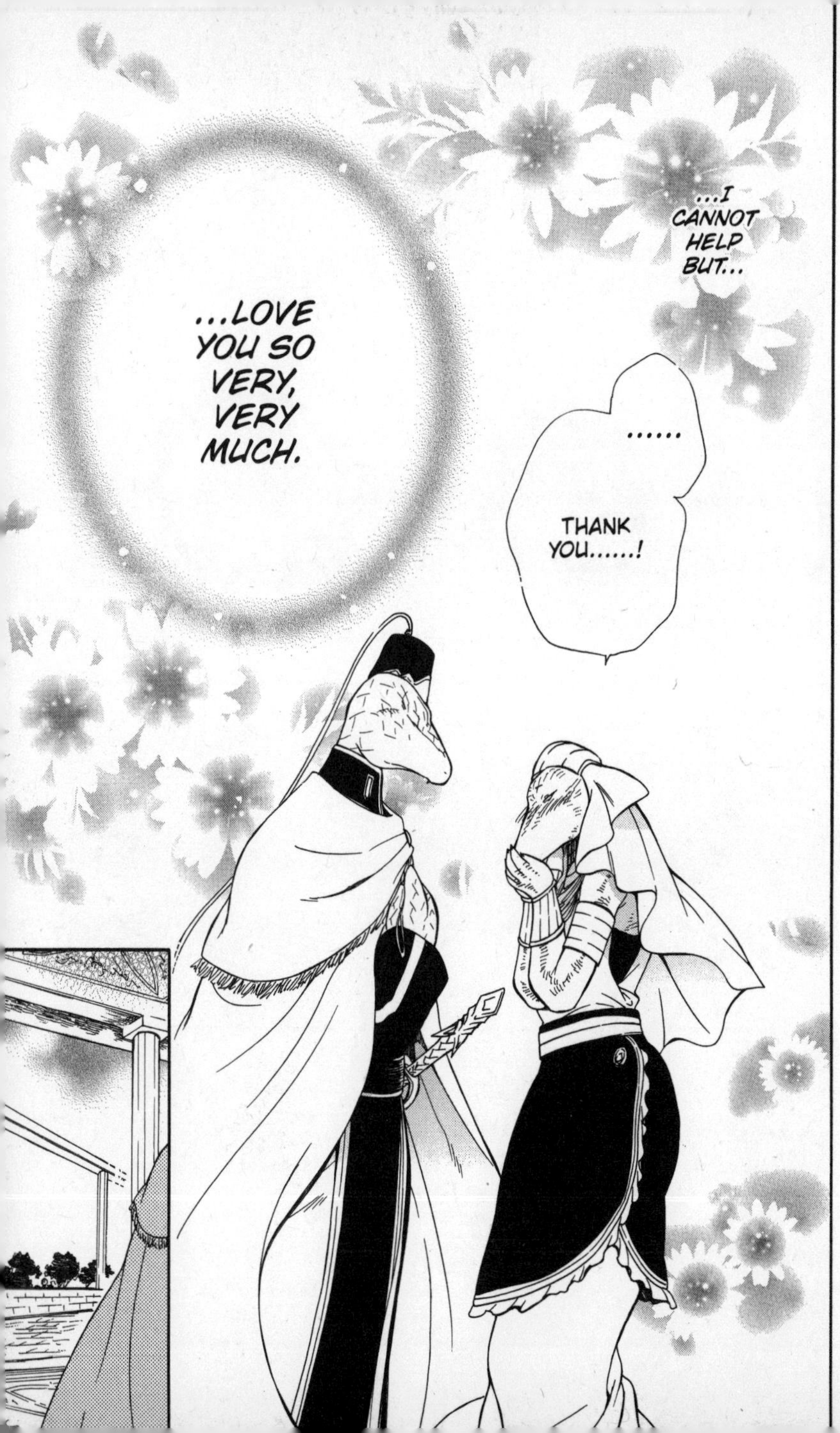
...I CANNOT HELP BUT...
...LOVE YOU SO VERY, VERY MUCH.
......
THANK YOU......!

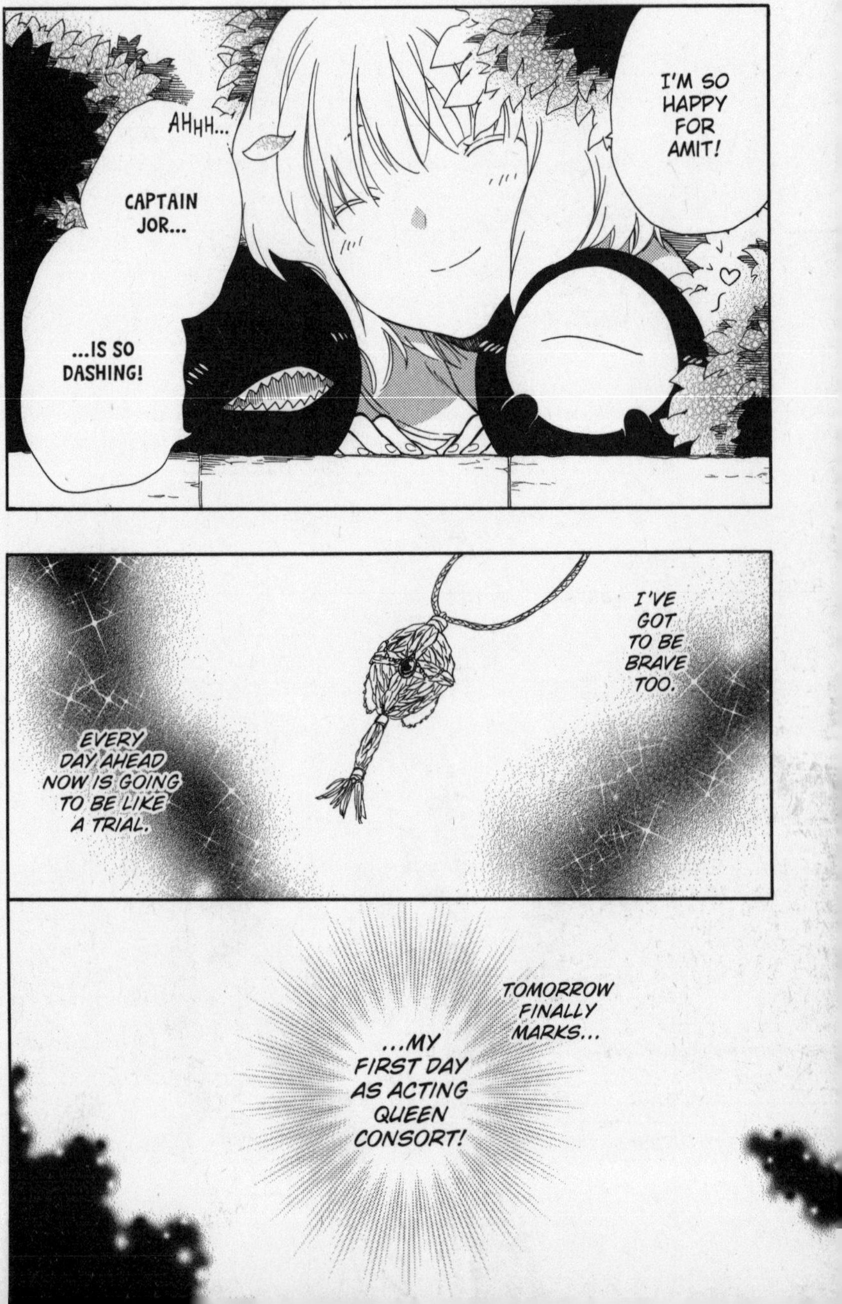
I'M SO HAPPY FOR AMIT!
AHHH...
CAPTAIN JOR...
...IS SO DASHING!
I'VE GOT TO BE BRAVE TOO.
EVERY DAY AHEAD NOW IS GOING TO BE LIKE A TRIAL.
TOMORROW FINALLY MARKS...
...MY FIRST DAY AS ACTING QUEEN CONSORT!

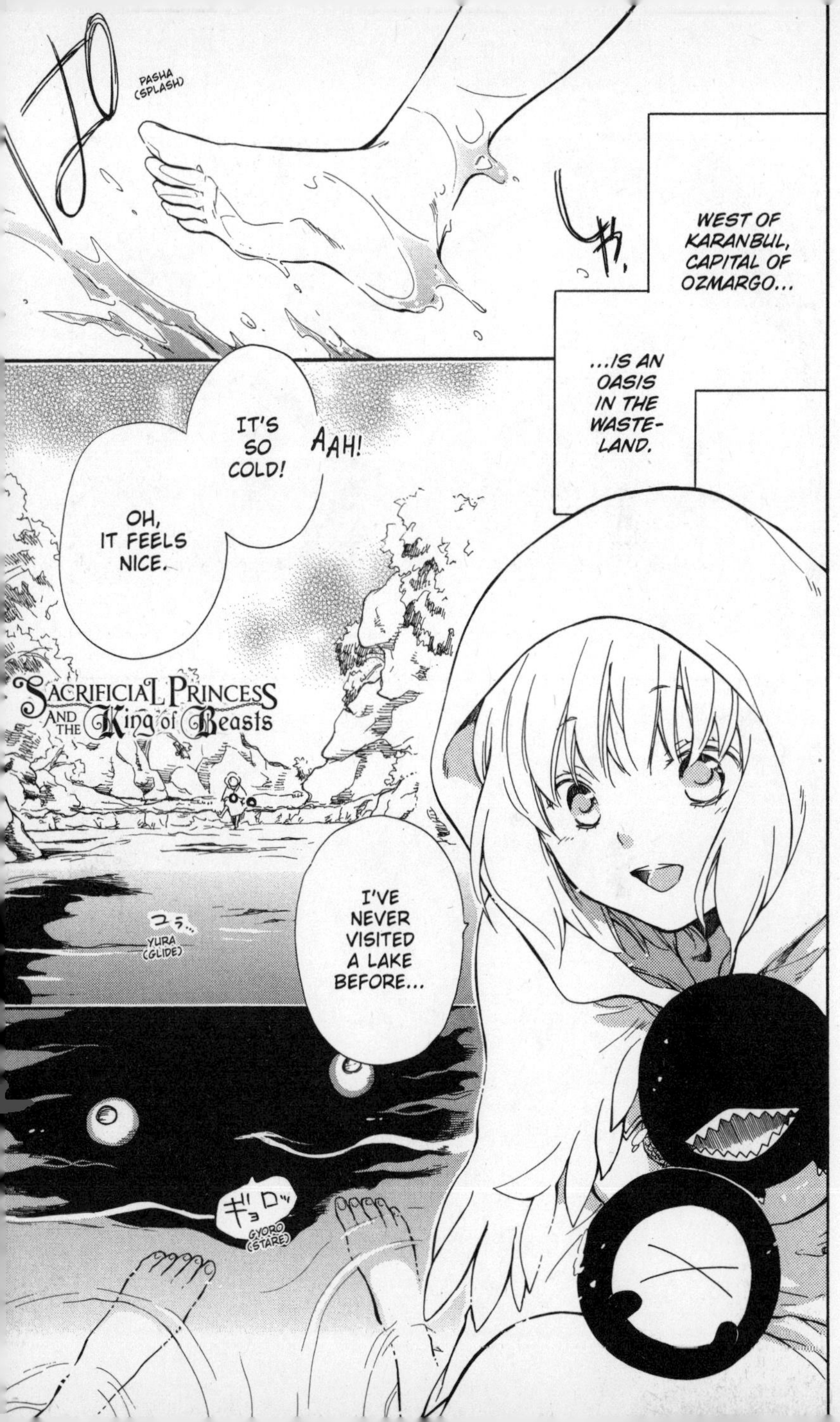
WEST OF KARANBUL, CAPITAL OF OZMARGO...
...IS AN OASIS IN THE WASTE-LAND.
PASHA (SPLASH)
AAH!
IT'S SO COLD!
OH, IT FEELS NICE.
SACRIFICIAL PRINCESS AND THE KING of BEASTS
I'VE NEVER VISITED A LAKE BEFORE...
ユラ...
YURA (GLIDE)
ギョロッ
GYORO (STARE)

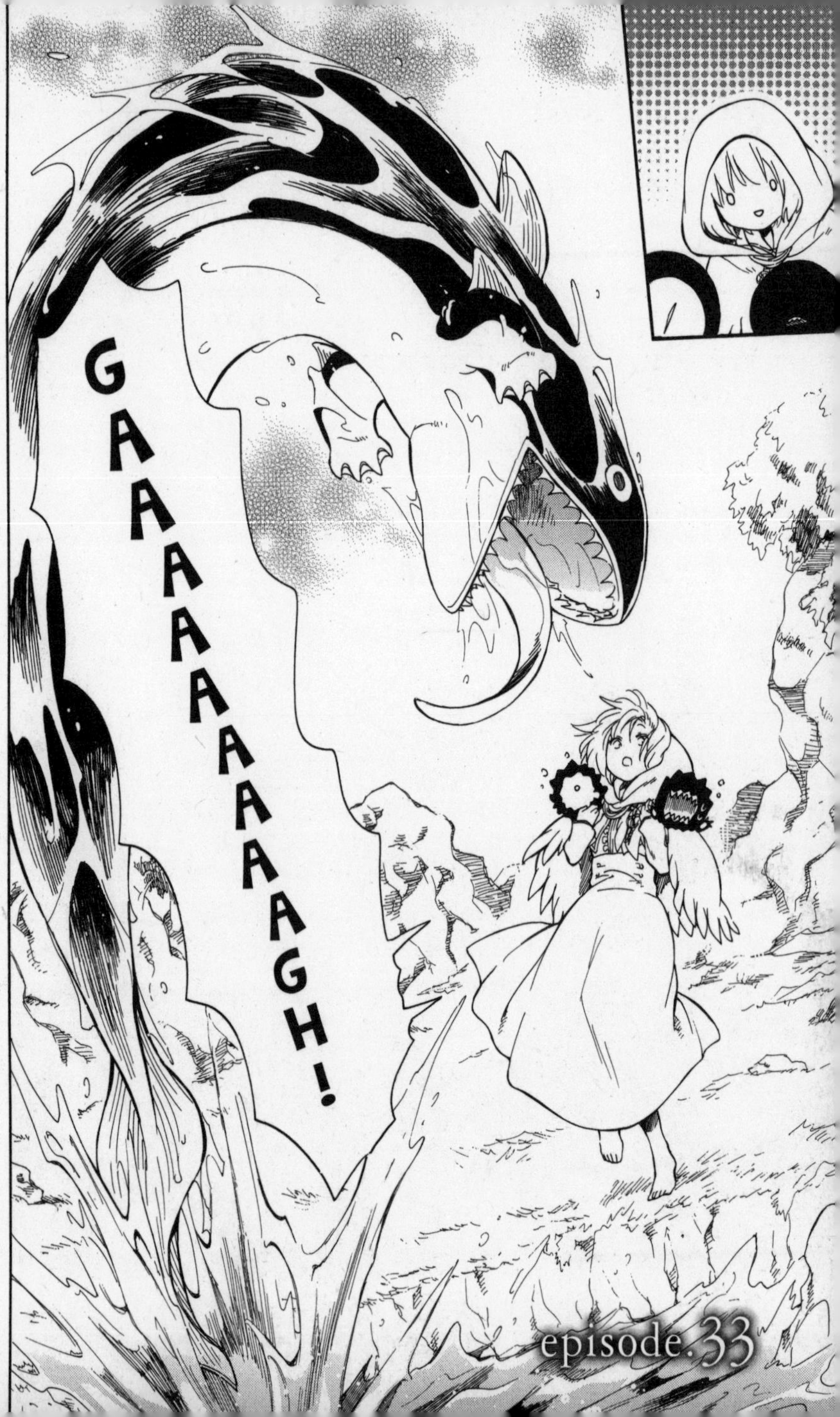
GAAAAAAAAAGH!
episode. 33

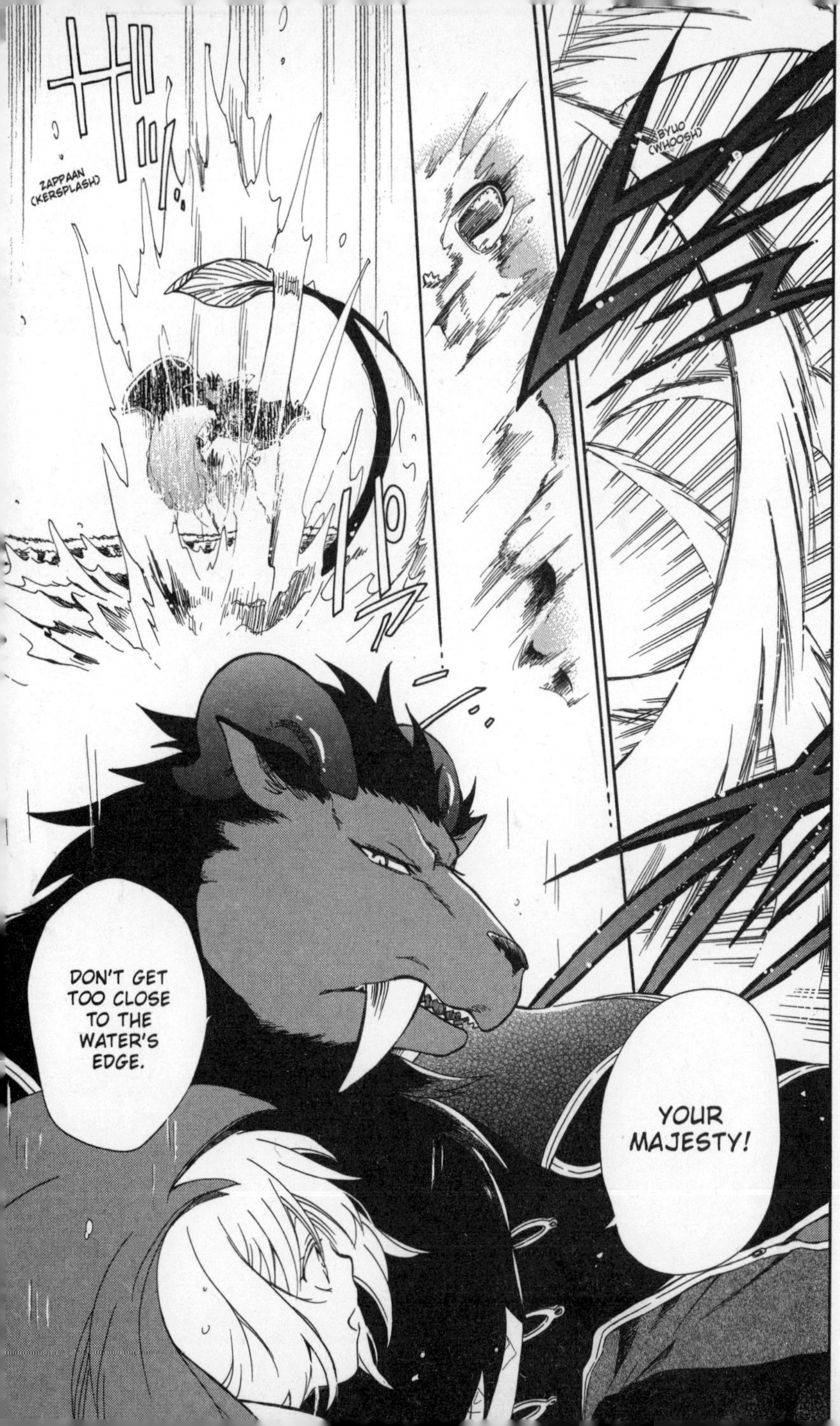
BYUO (WHOOSH)
ZAPPAAN (KERSPLASH)
YOUR MAJESTY!
DON'T GET TOO CLOSE TO THE WATER'S EDGE.

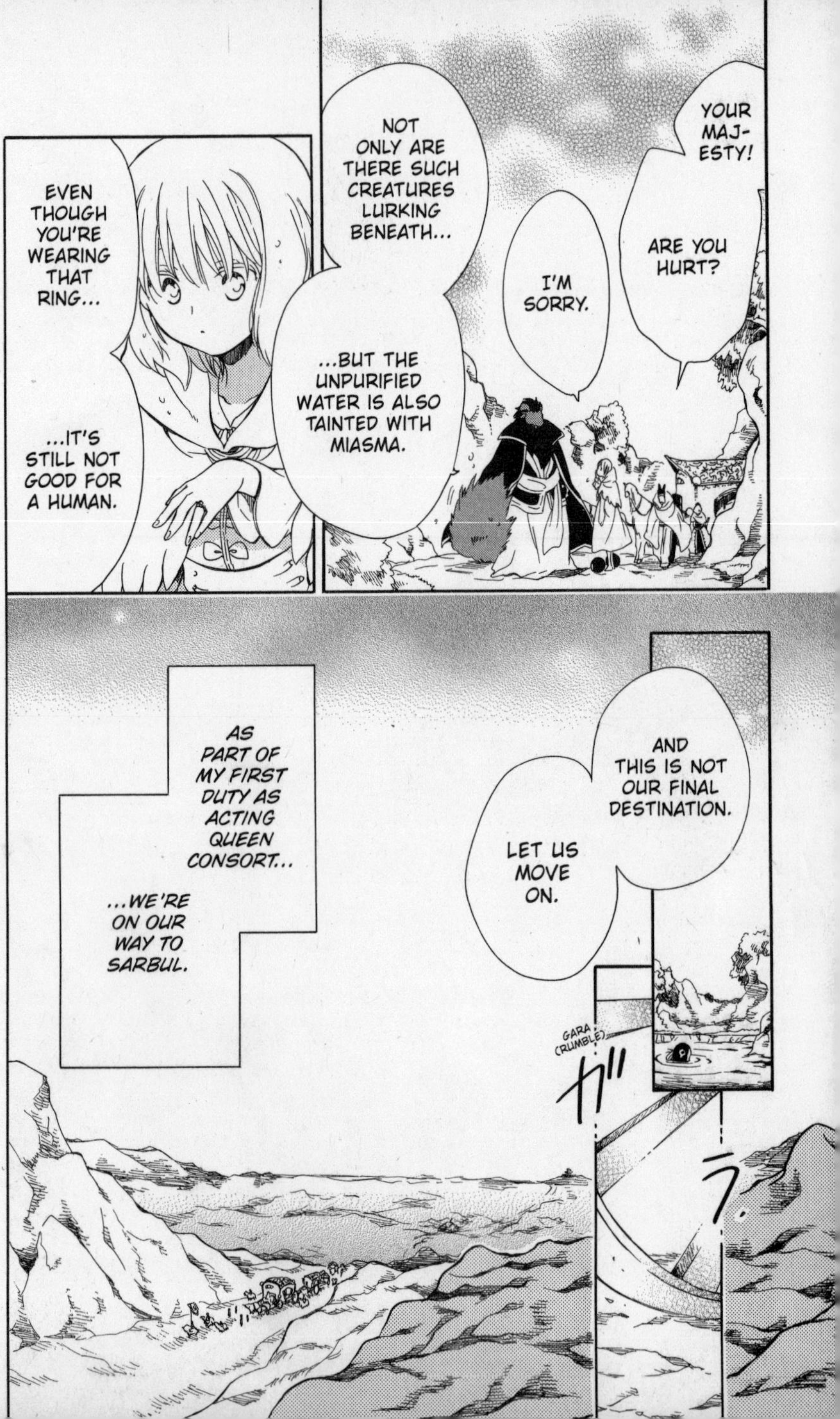
YOUR MAJ-ESTY!
ARE YOU HURT?
I'M SORRY.
NOT ONLY ARE THERE SUCH CREATURES LURKING BENEATH...
...BUT THE UNPURIFIED WATER IS ALSO TAINTED WITH MIASMA.
EVEN THOUGH YOU'RE WEARING THAT RING...
...IT'S STILL NOT GOOD FOR A HUMAN.
AND THIS IS NOT OUR FINAL DESTINATION.
LET US MOVE ON.
GARA (RUMBLE)
AS PART OF MY FIRST DUTY AS ACTING QUEEN CONSORT...
...WE'RE ON OUR WAY TO SARBUL.

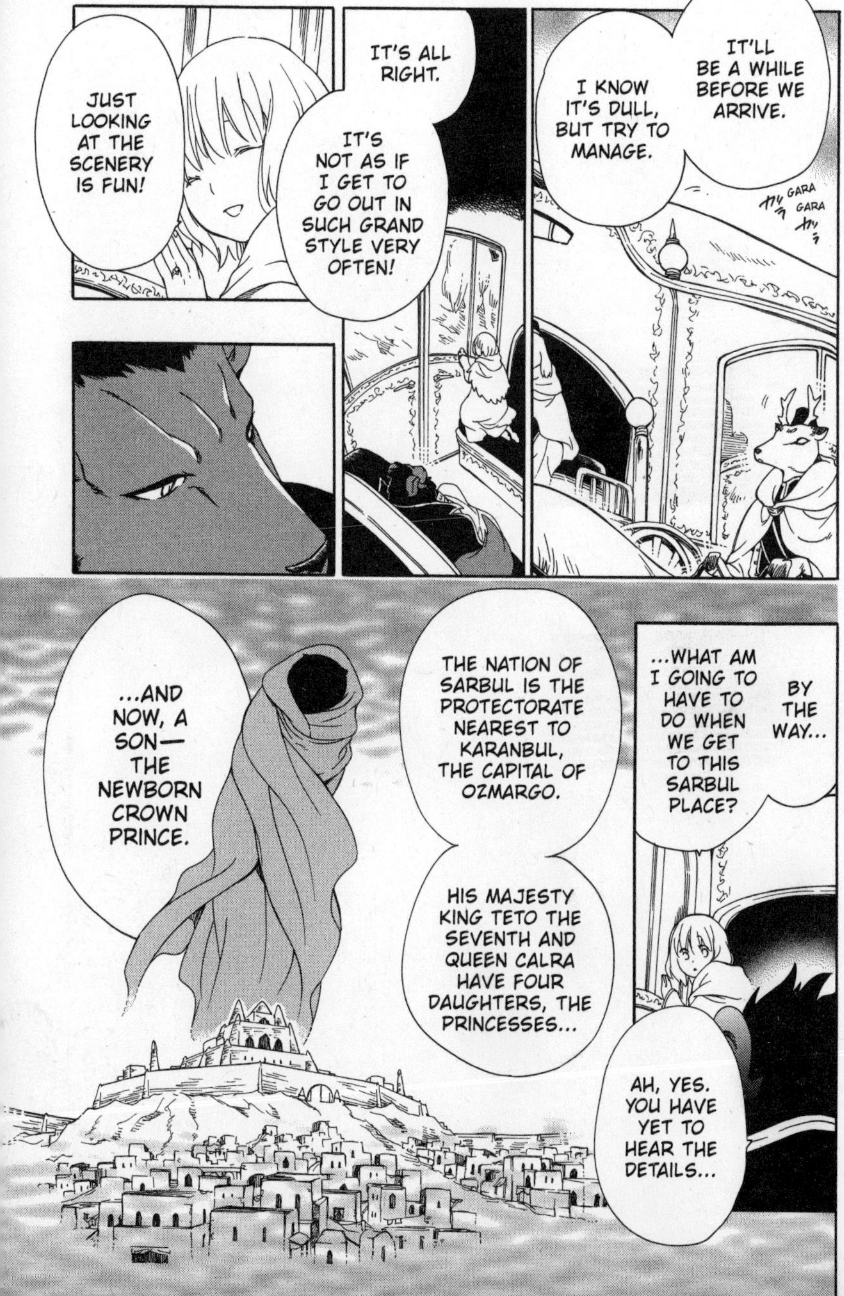
IT'LL BE A WHILE BEFORE WE ARRIVE.
I KNOW IT'S DULL, BUT TRY TO MANAGE.
GARA GARA
IT'S ALL RIGHT.
IT'S NOT AS IF I GET TO GO OUT IN SUCH GRAND STYLE VERY OFTEN!
JUST LOOKING AT THE SCENERY IS FUN!
BY THE WAY...
...WHAT AM I GOING TO HAVE TO DO WHEN WE GET TO THIS SARBUL PLACE?
AH, YES. YOU HAVE YET TO HEAR THE DETAILS...
THE NATION OF SARBUL IS THE PROTECTORATE NEAREST TO KARANBUL, THE CAPITAL OF OZMARGO.
HIS MAJESTY KING TETO THE SEVENTH AND QUEEN CALRA HAVE FOUR DAUGHTERS, THE PRINCESSES...
...AND NOW, A SON—THE NEWBORN CROWN PRINCE.

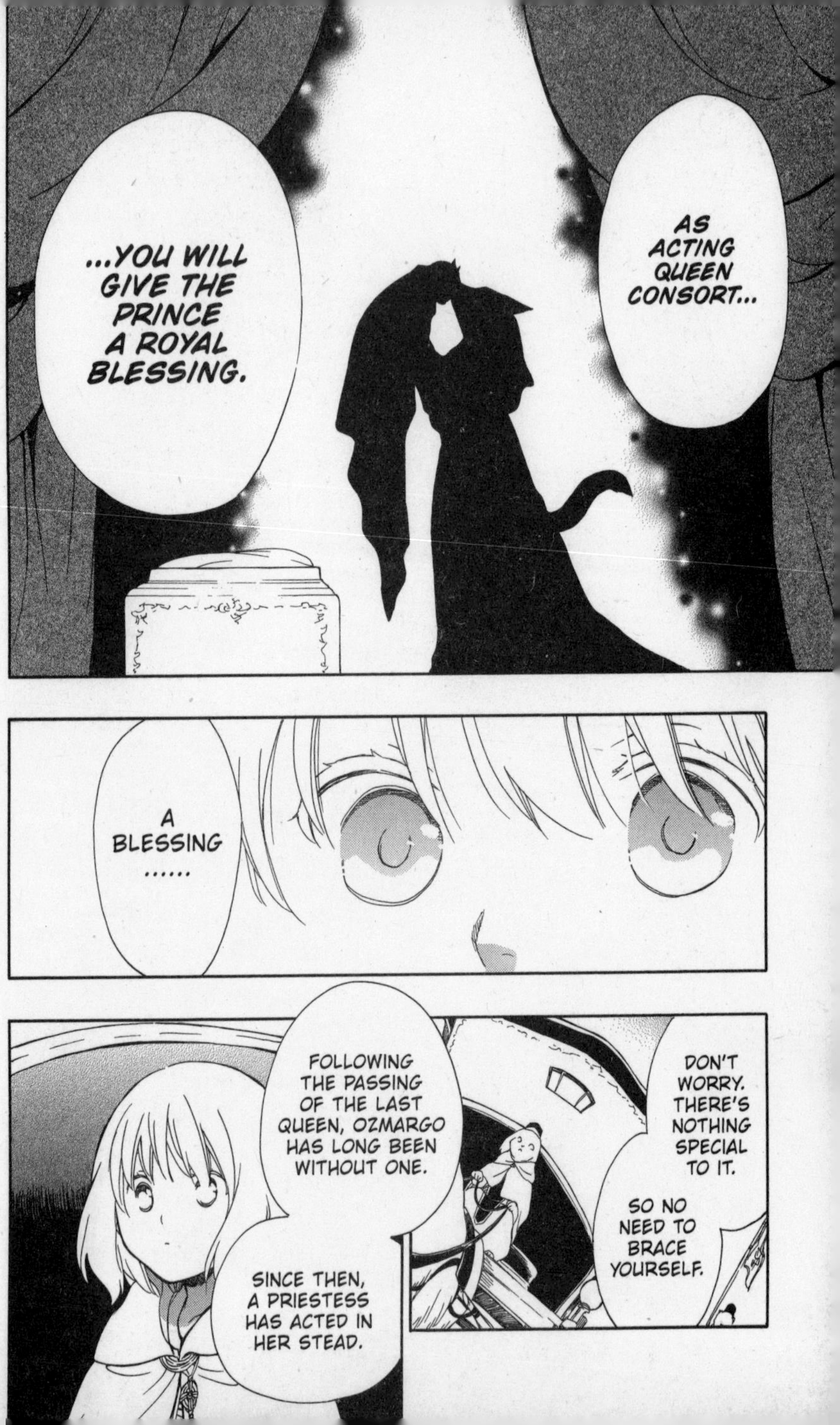
AS ACTING QUEEN CONSORT...
...YOU WILL GIVE THE PRINCE A ROYAL BLESSING.
A BLESSING ......
DON'T WORRY. THERE'S NOTHING SPECIAL TO IT.
SO NO NEED TO BRACE YOURSELF.
FOLLOWING THE PASSING OF THE LAST QUEEN, OZMARGO HAS LONG BEEN WITHOUT ONE.
SINCE THEN, A PRIESTESS HAS ACTED IN HER STEAD.

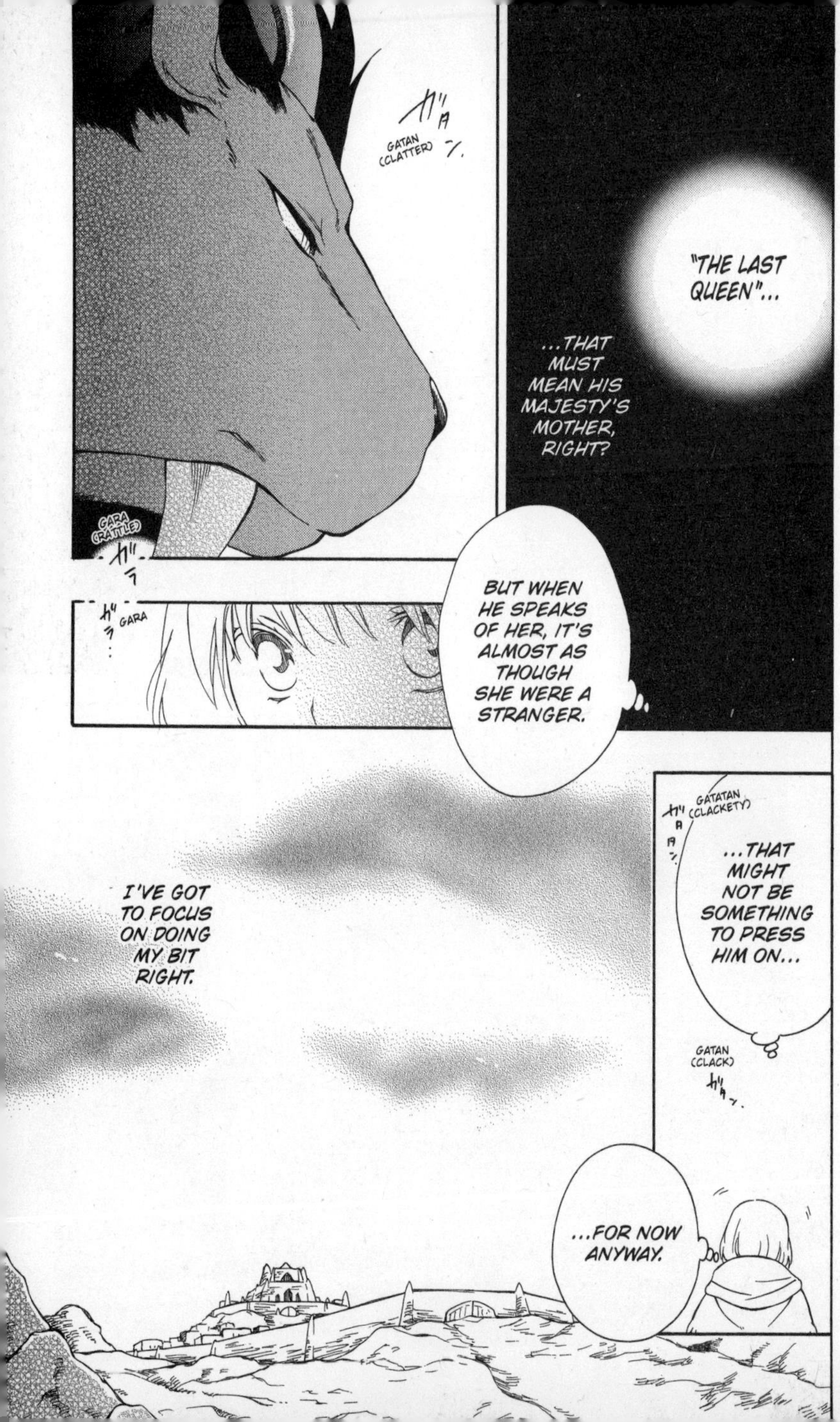
"THE LAST QUEEN"...
...THAT MUST MEAN HIS MAJESTY'S MOTHER, RIGHT?
GATAN (CLATTER)
GARA (RATTLE)
GARA
BUT WHEN HE SPEAKS OF HER, IT'S ALMOST AS THOUGH SHE WERE A STRANGER.
GATATAN (CLACKETY)
...THAT MIGHT NOT BE SOMETHING TO PRESS HIM ON...
GATAN (CLACK)
...FOR NOW ANYWAY.
I'VE GOT TO FOCUS ON DOING MY BIT RIGHT.

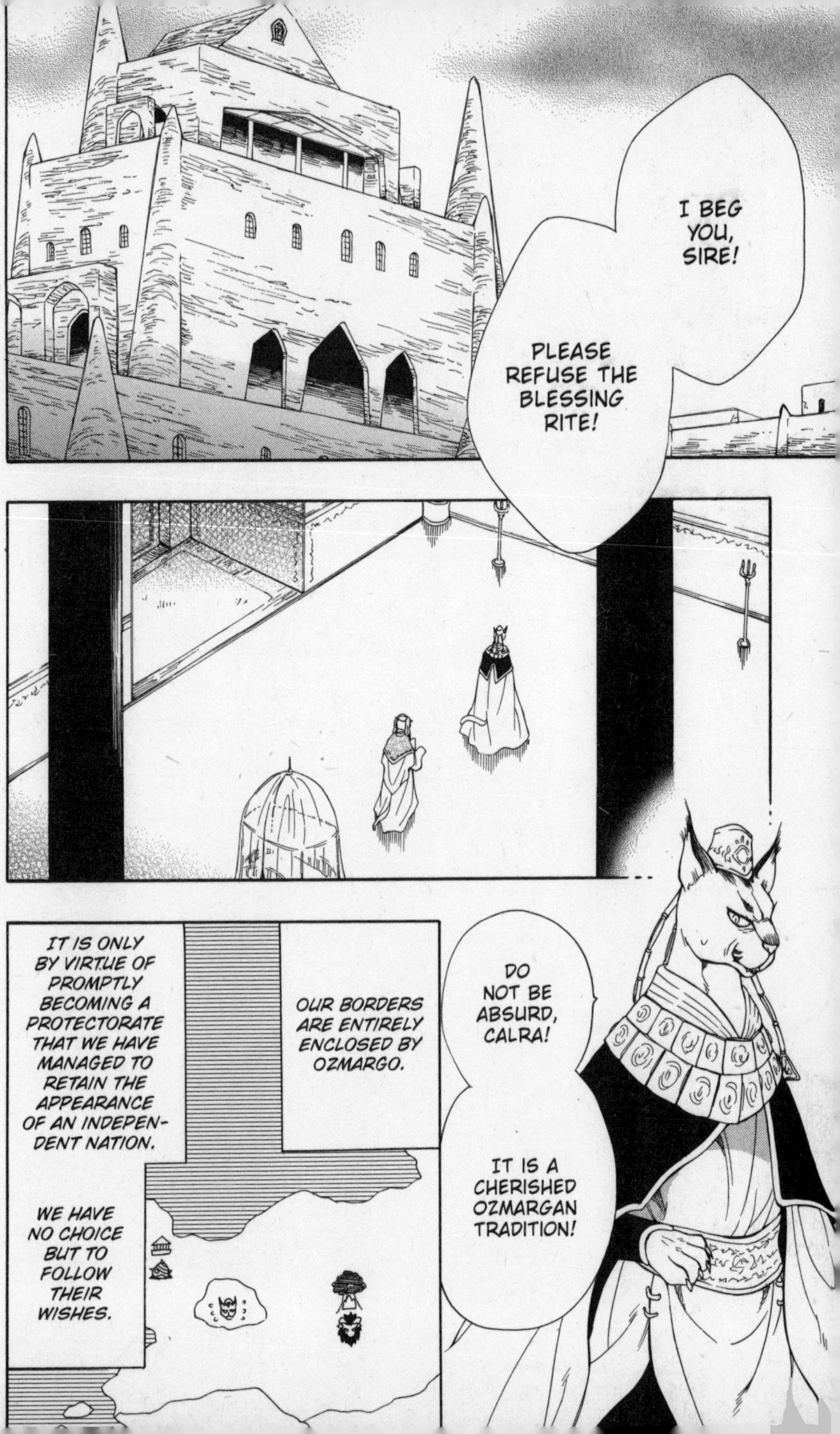
I BEG YOU, SIRE!
PLEASE REFUSE THE BLESSING RITE!
DO NOT BE ABSURD, CALRA!
IT IS A CHERISHED OZMARGAN TRADITION!
OUR BORDERS ARE ENTIRELY ENCLOSED BY OZMARGO.
IT IS ONLY BY VIRTUE OF PROMPTLY BECOMING A PROTECTORATE THAT WE HAVE MANAGED TO RETAIN THE APPEARANCE OF AN INDEPENDENT NATION.
WE HAVE NO CHOICE BUT TO FOLLOW THEIR WISHES.

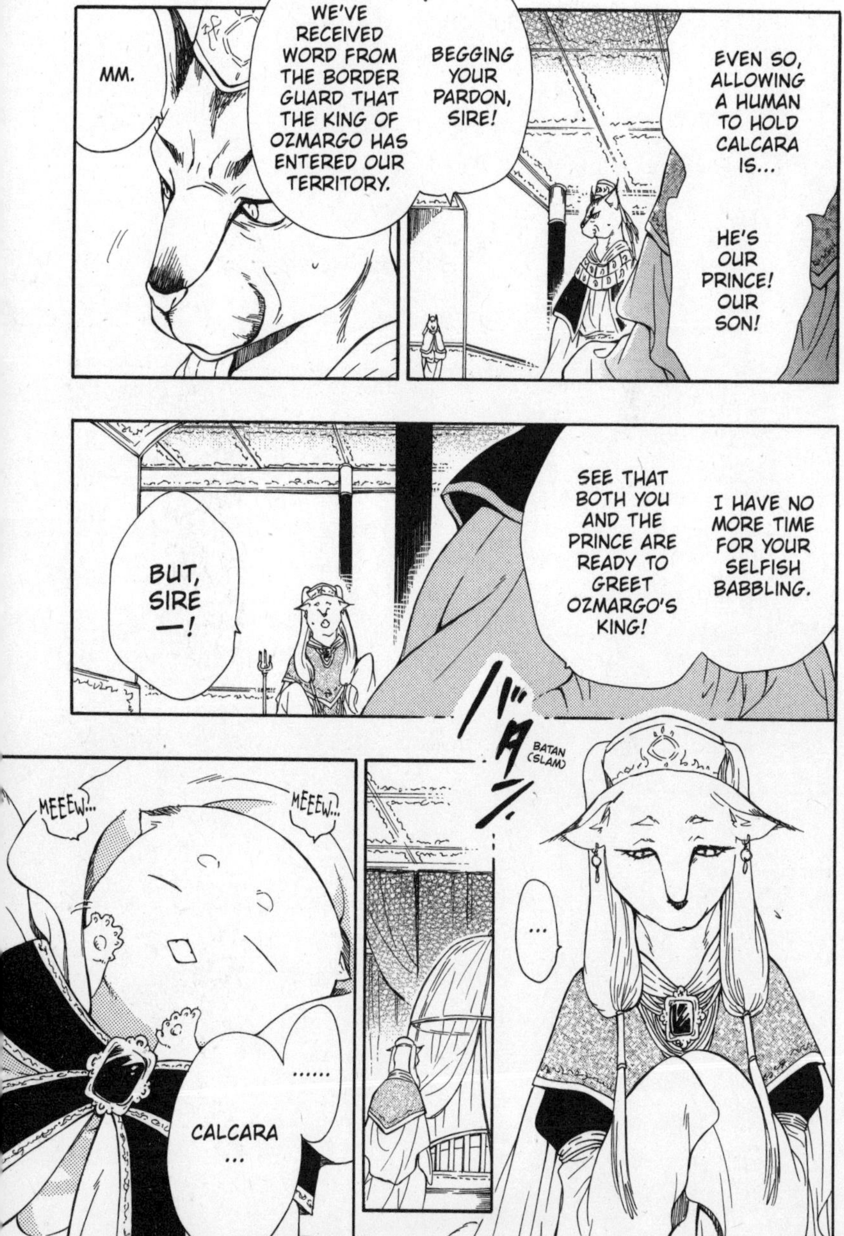

EVEN SO, ALLOWING A HUMAN TO HOLD CALCARA IS...
HE'S OUR PRINCE! OUR SON!
BEGGING YOUR PARDON, SIRE!
WE'VE RECEIVED WORD FROM THE BORDER GUARD THAT THE KING OF OZMARGO HAS ENTERED OUR TERRITORY.
MM.
I HAVE NO MORE TIME FOR YOUR SELFISH BABBLING.
SEE THAT BOTH YOU AND THE PRINCE ARE READY TO GREET OZMARGO'S KING!
BUT, SIRE—!
BATAN (SLAM)
...
MEEEW...
MEEEW...
......
CALCARA ...

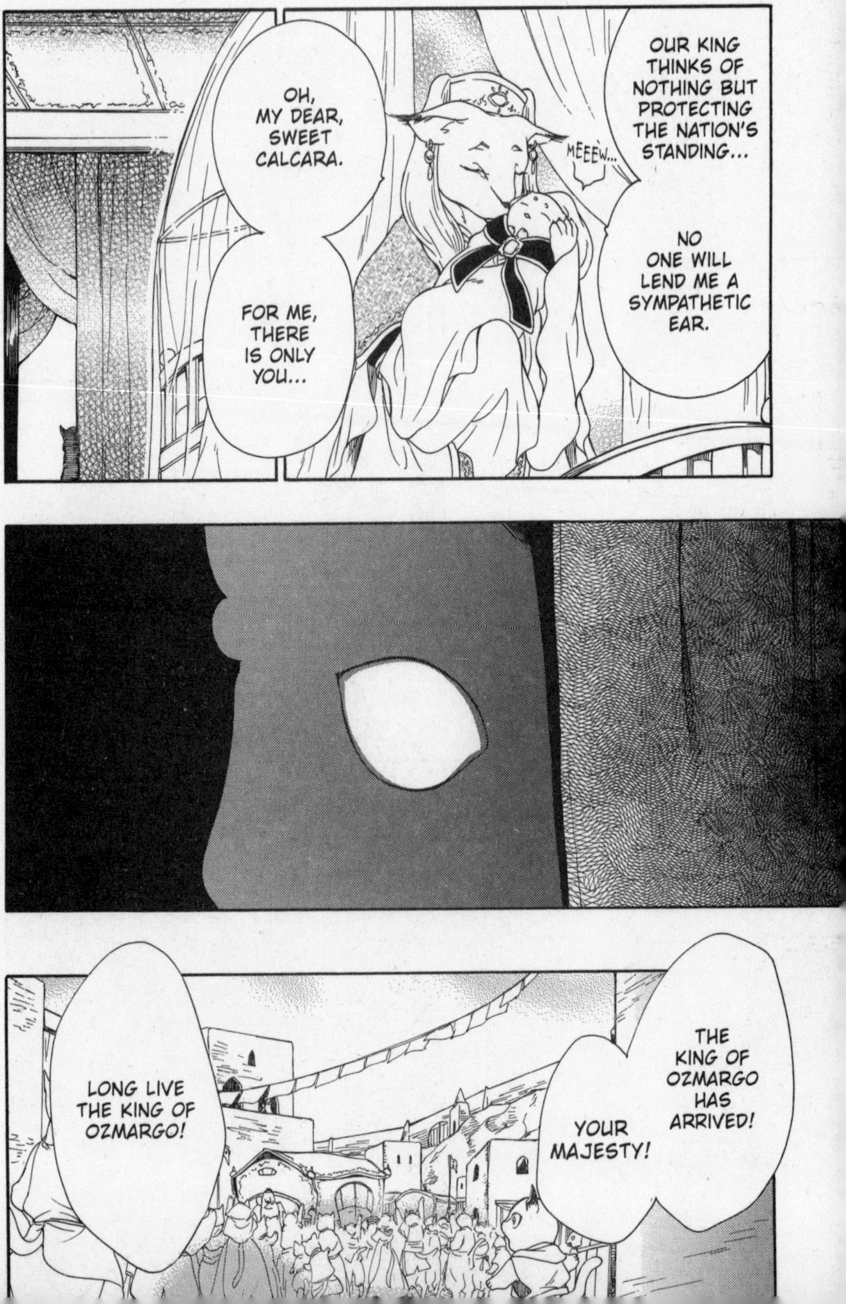
OUR KING THINKS OF NOTHING BUT PROTECTING THE NATION'S STANDING...
MEEEW...
NO ONE WILL LEND ME A SYMPATHETIC EAR.
OH, MY DEAR, SWEET CALCARA.
FOR ME, THERE IS ONLY YOU...
THE KING OF OZMARGO HAS ARRIVED!
YOUR MAJESTY!
LONG LIVE THE KING OF OZMARGO!

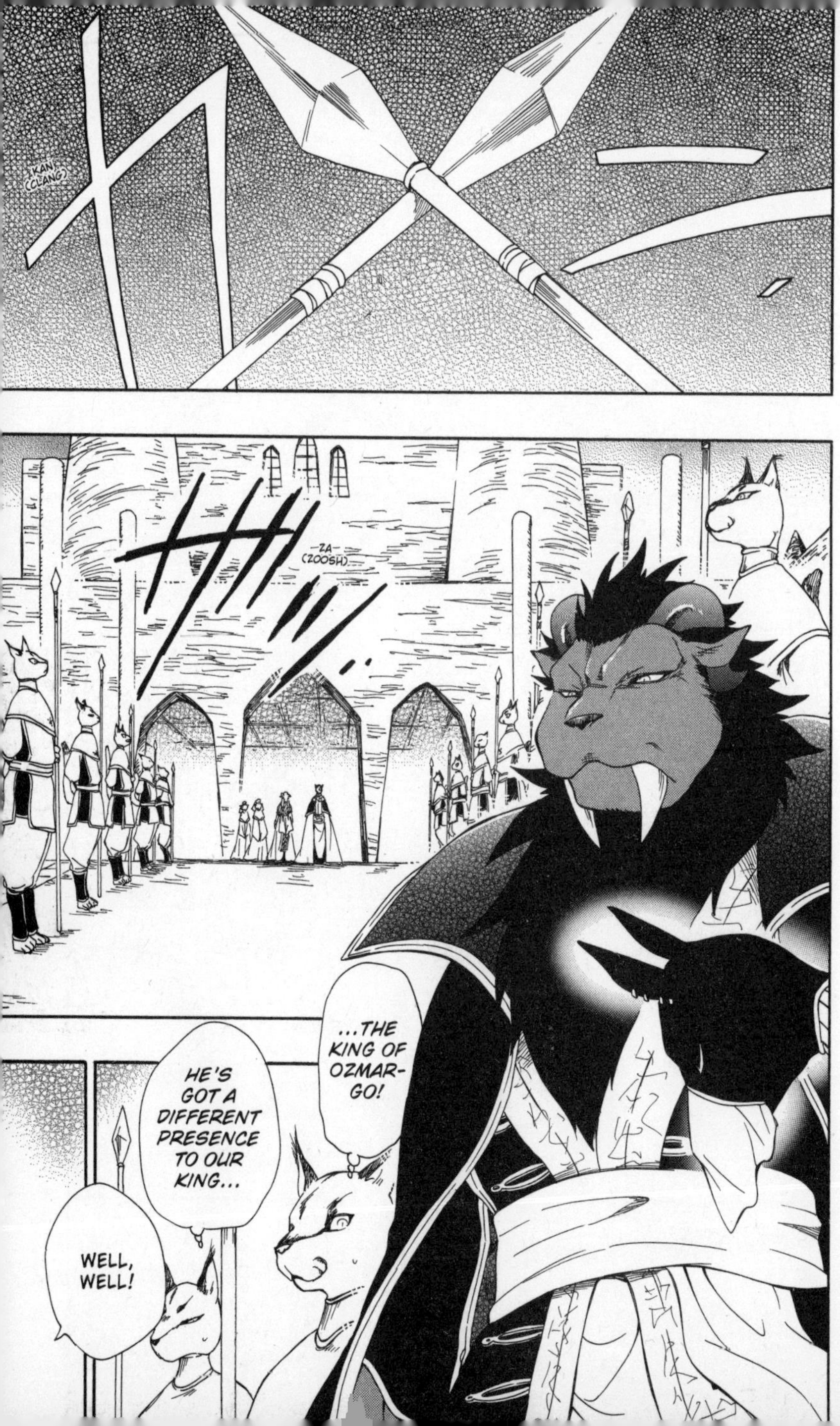
KAN (CLANG)
ZA (ZOOSH)
...THE KING OF OZMAR-GO!
HE'S GOT A DIFFERENT PRESENCE TO OUR KING...
WELL, WELL!

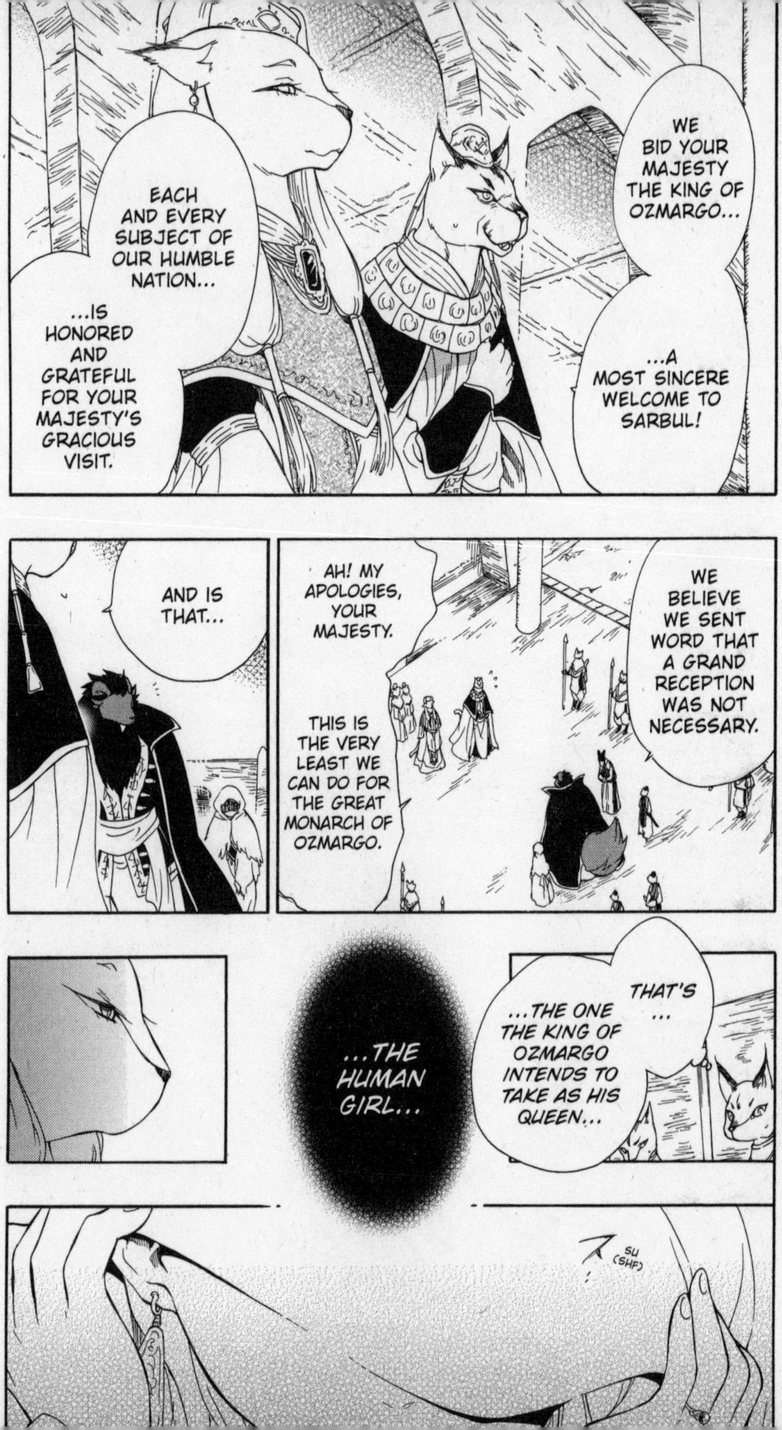
WE BID YOUR MAJESTY THE KING OF OZMARGO...
...A MOST SINCERE WELCOME TO SARBUL!
EACH AND EVERY SUBJECT OF OUR HUMBLE NATION...
...IS HONORED AND GRATEFUL FOR YOUR MAJESTY'S GRACIOUS VISIT.
WE BELIEVE WE SENT WORD THAT A GRAND RECEPTION WAS NOT NECESSARY.
AH! MY APOLOGIES, YOUR MAJESTY.
THIS IS THE VERY LEAST WE CAN DO FOR THE GREAT MONARCH OF OZMARGO.
AND IS THAT...
THAT'S ...
...THE ONE THE KING OF OZMARGO INTENDS TO TAKE AS HIS QUEEN...
...THE HUMAN GIRL...
SU (SHF)

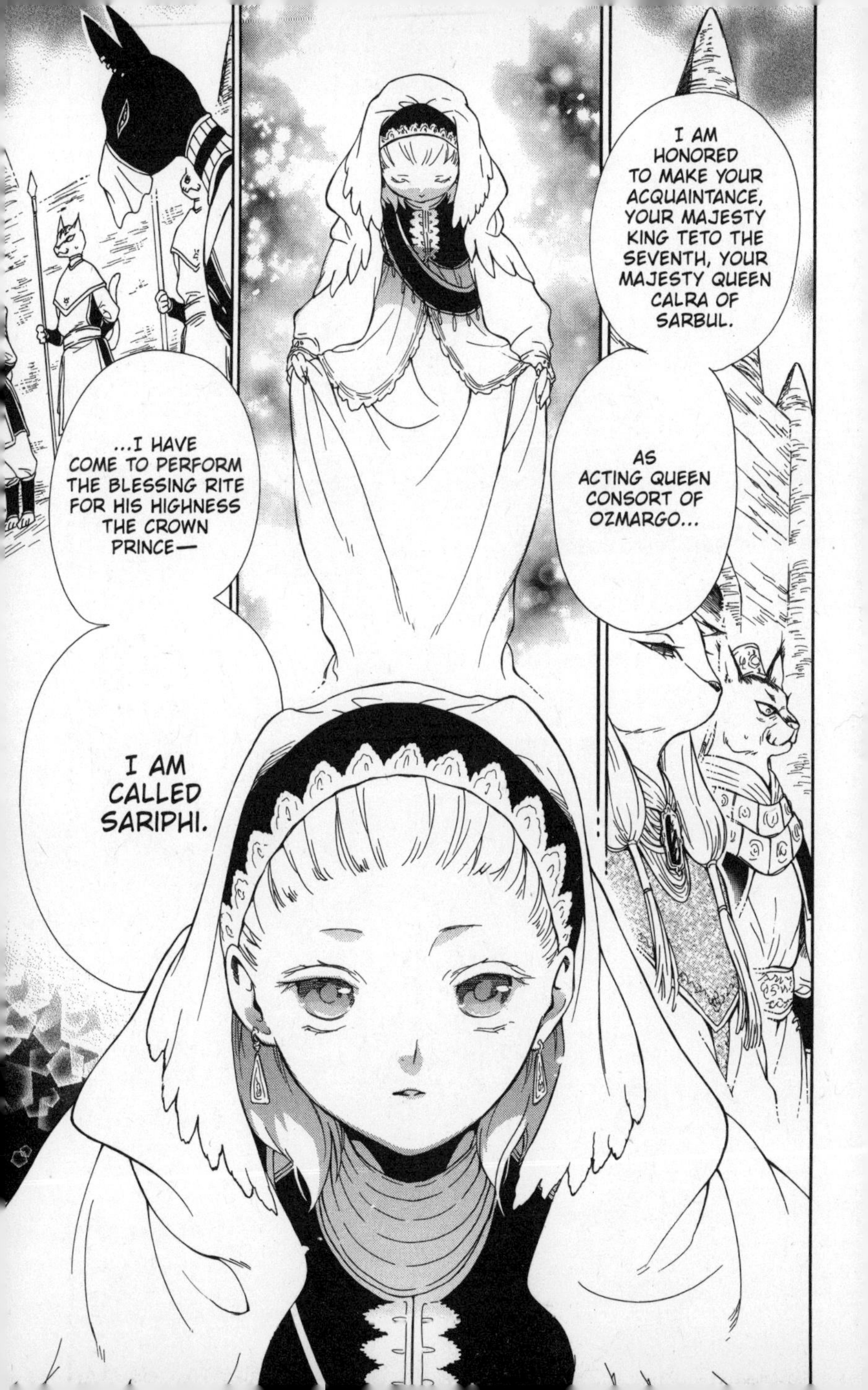
I AM HONORED TO MAKE YOUR ACQUAINTANCE, YOUR MAJESTY KING TETO THE SEVENTH, YOUR MAJESTY QUEEN CALRA OF SARBUL.
AS ACTING QUEEN CONSORT OF OZMARGO...
...I HAVE COME TO PERFORM THE BLESSING RITE FOR HIS HIGHNESS THE CROWN PRINCE—
I AM CALLED SARIPHI.

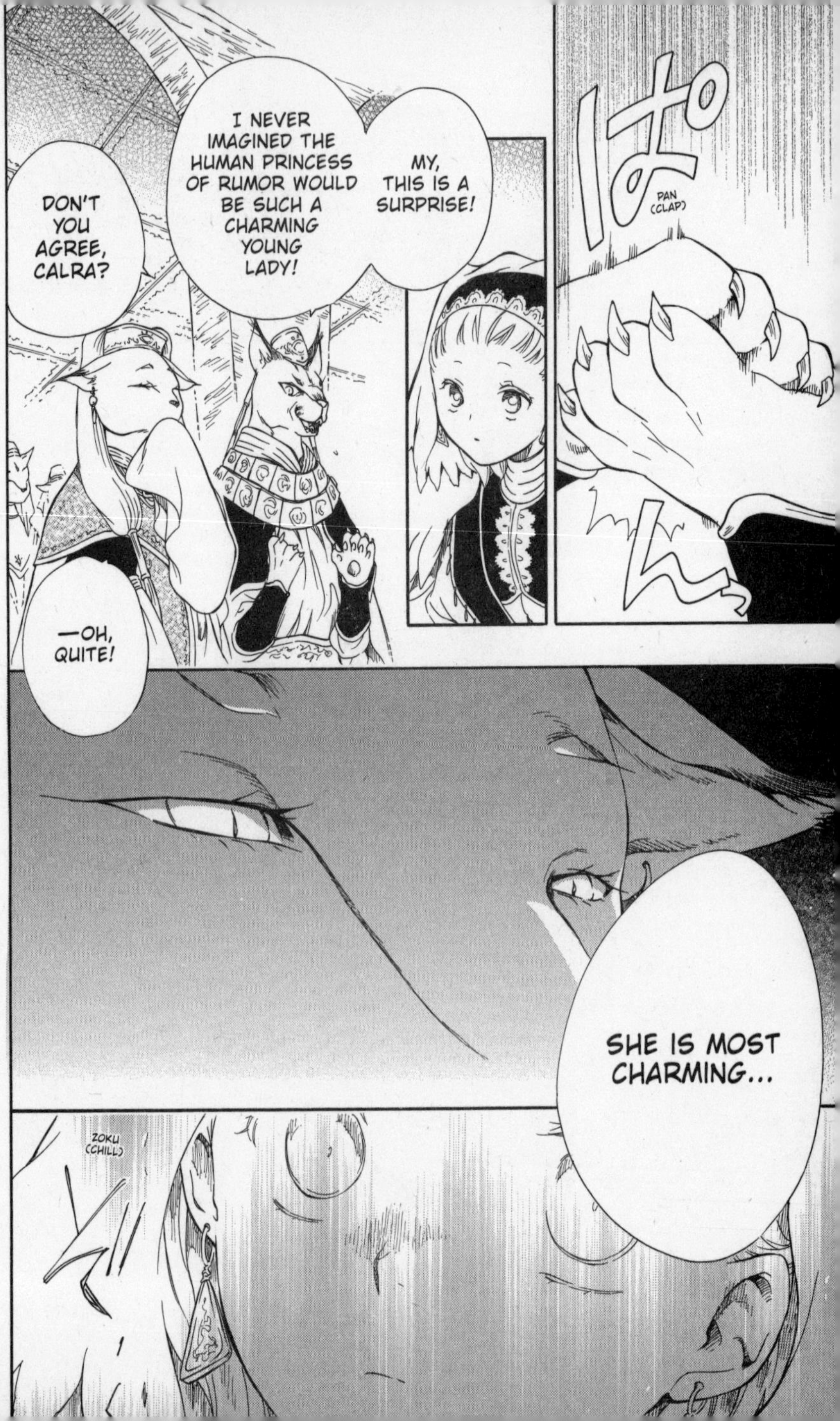
ぱん
PAN (CLAP)
MY, THIS IS A SURPRISE!
I NEVER IMAGINED THE HUMAN PRINCESS OF RUMOR WOULD BE SUCH A CHARMING YOUNG LADY!
DON'T YOU AGREE, CALRA?
—OH, QUITE!
SHE IS MOST CHARMING...
ZOKU (CHILL)

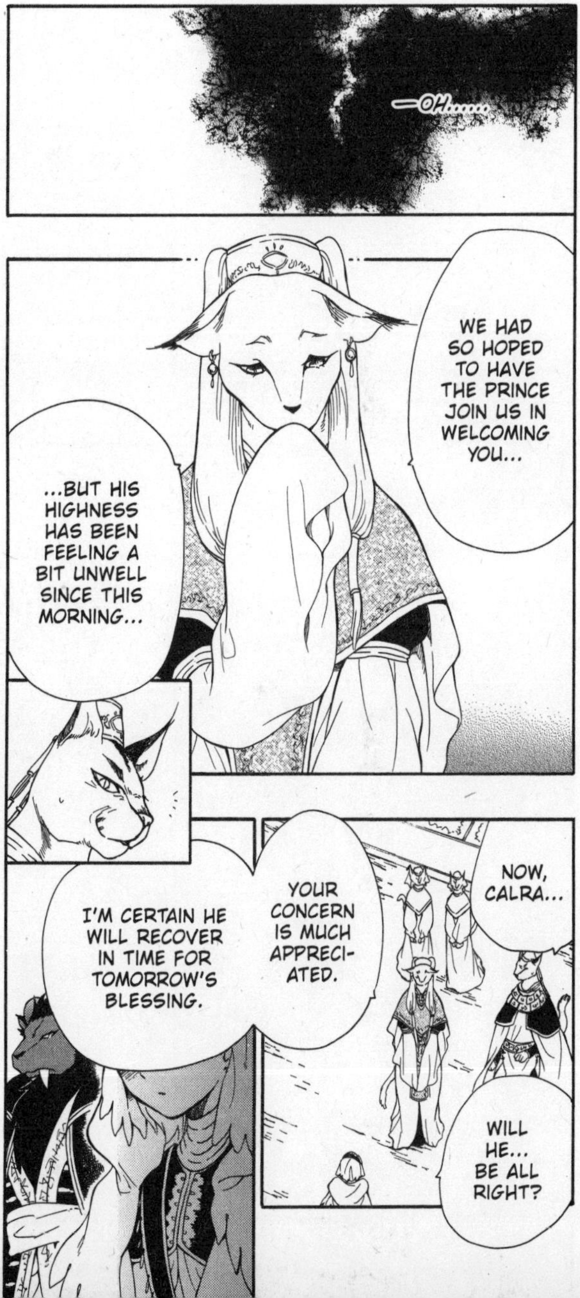
—OH......
WE HAD SO HOPED TO HAVE THE PRINCE JOIN US IN WELCOMING YOU...
...BUT HIS HIGHNESS HAS BEEN FEELING A BIT UNWELL SINCE THIS MORNING...
NOW, CALRA...
WILL HE... BE ALL RIGHT?
YOUR CONCERN IS MUCH APPRECI-ATED.
I'M CERTAIN HE WILL RECOVER IN TIME FOR TOMORROW'S BLESSING.

CY & CLOPS COLORING PAGE

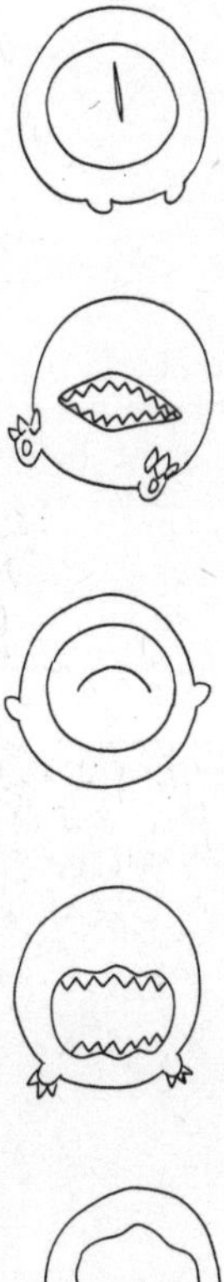

WHEN YOU'RE BORED TO DEATH, GO AHEAD AND COLOR THEM IN!

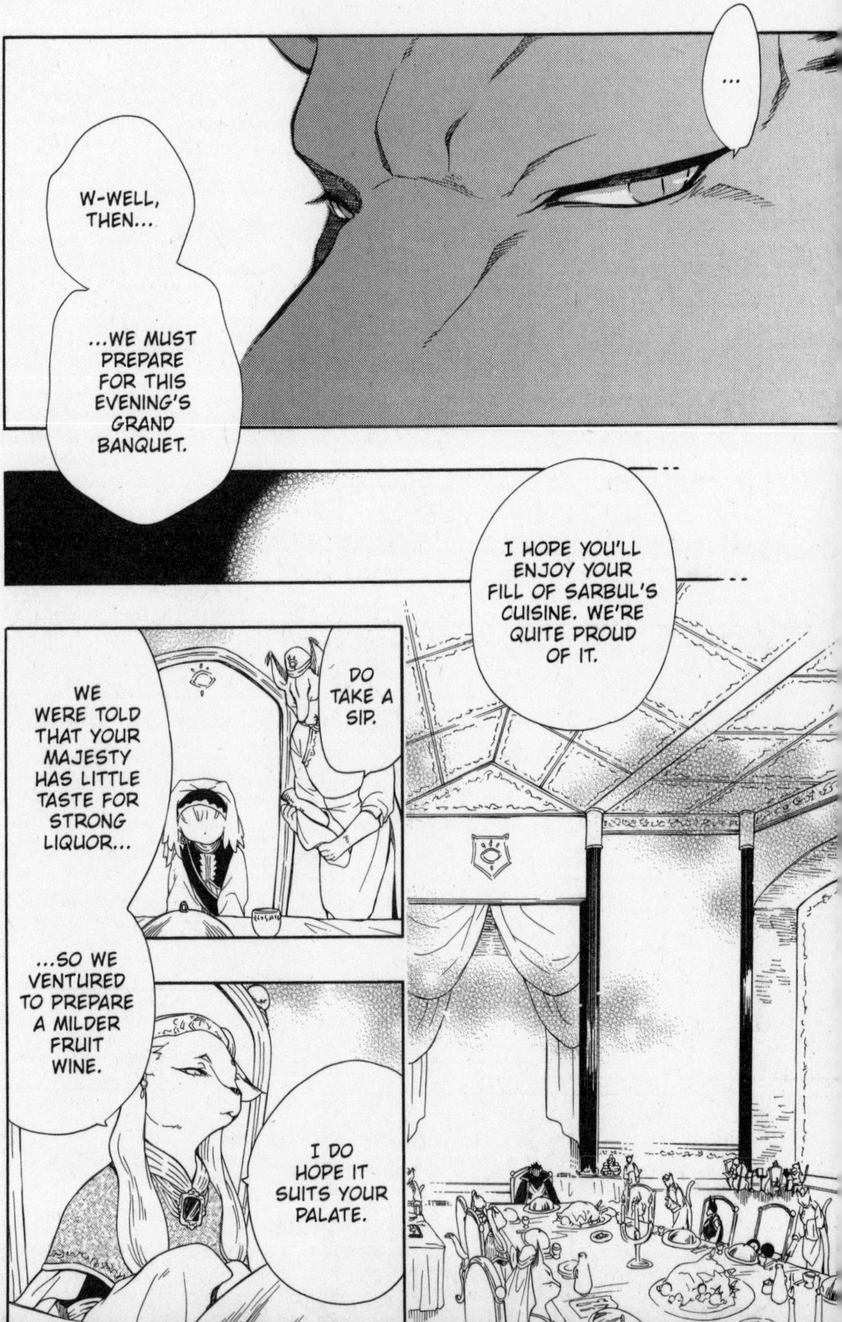
...
W-WELL, THEN...
...WE MUST PREPARE FOR THIS EVENING'S GRAND BANQUET.
I HOPE YOU'LL ENJOY YOUR FILL OF SARBUL'S CUISINE. WE'RE QUITE PROUD OF IT.
DO TAKE A SIP.
WE WERE TOLD THAT YOUR MAJESTY HAS LITTLE TASTE FOR STRONG LIQUOR...
...SO WE VENTURED TO PREPARE A MILDER FRUIT WINE.
I DO HOPE IT SUITS YOUR PALATE.

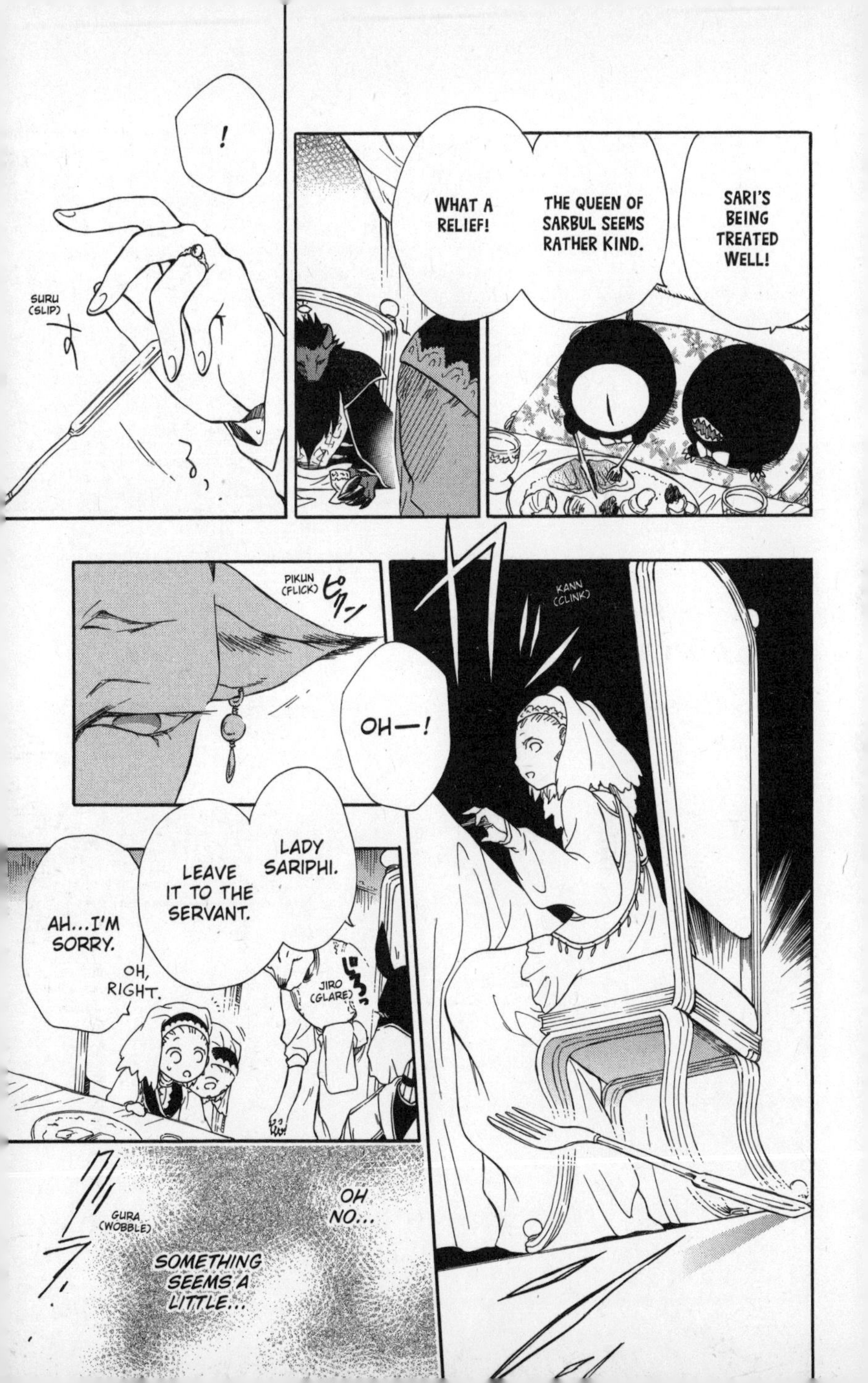
SARI'S BEING TREATED WELL!
THE QUEEN OF SARBUL SEEMS RATHER KIND.
WHAT A RELIEF!
!
SURU (SLIP)
KANN (CLINK)
OH—!
PIKUN (FLICK)
LADY SARIPHI.
LEAVE IT TO THE SERVANT.
JIRO (GLARE)
AH...I'M SORRY.
OH, RIGHT.
OH NO...
GURA (WOBBLE)
SOMETHING SEEMS A LITTLE...

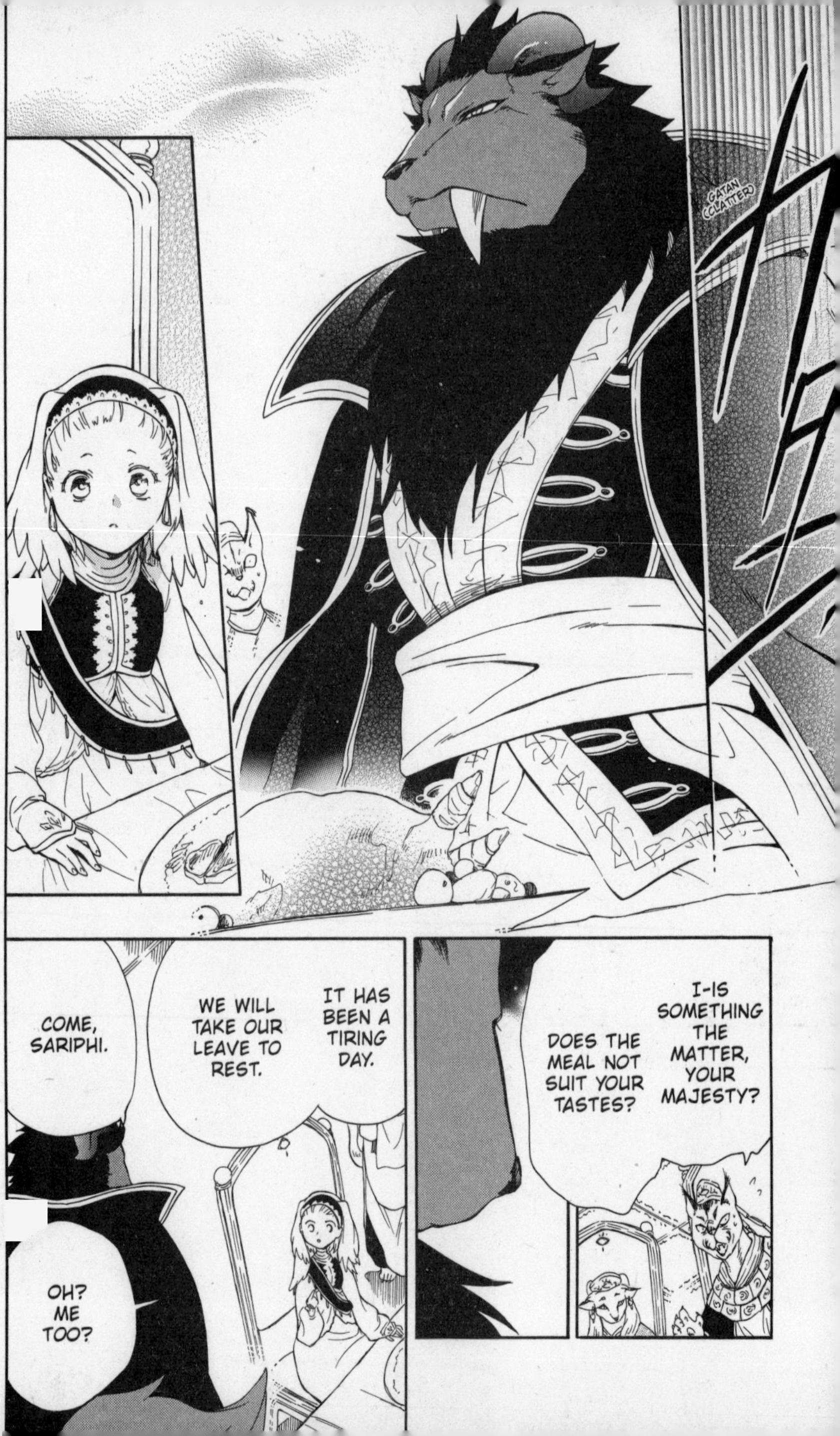
GATAN (CLATTER)
I-IS SOMETHING THE MATTER, YOUR MAJESTY?
DOES THE MEAL NOT SUIT YOUR TASTES?
IT HAS BEEN A TIRING DAY.
WE WILL TAKE OUR LEAVE TO REST.
COME, SARIPHI.
OH? ME TOO?

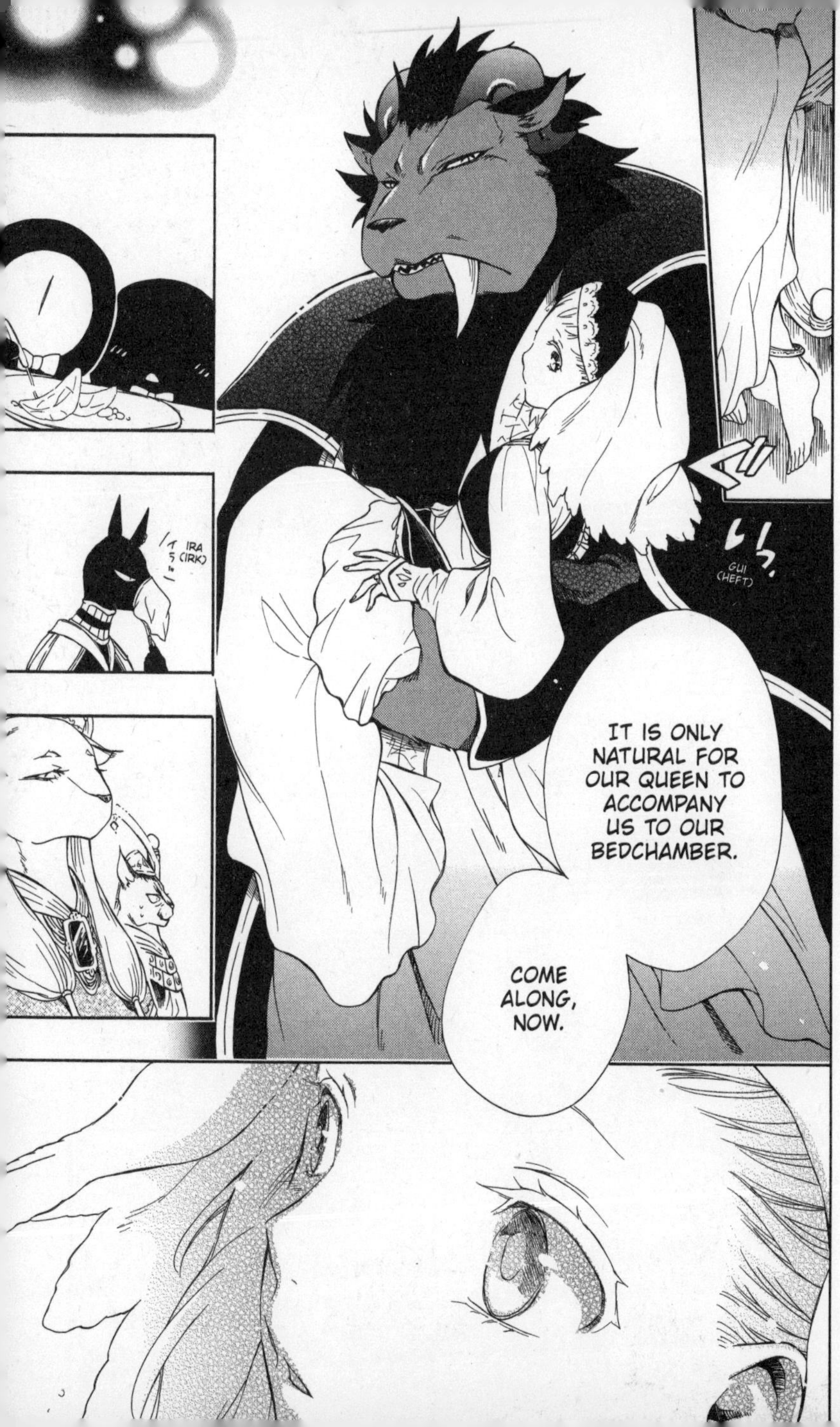
GUI (HEFT)
IT IS ONLY NATURAL FOR OUR QUEEN TO ACCOMPANY US TO OUR BEDCHAMBER.
COME ALONG, NOW.
IRA (IRK)

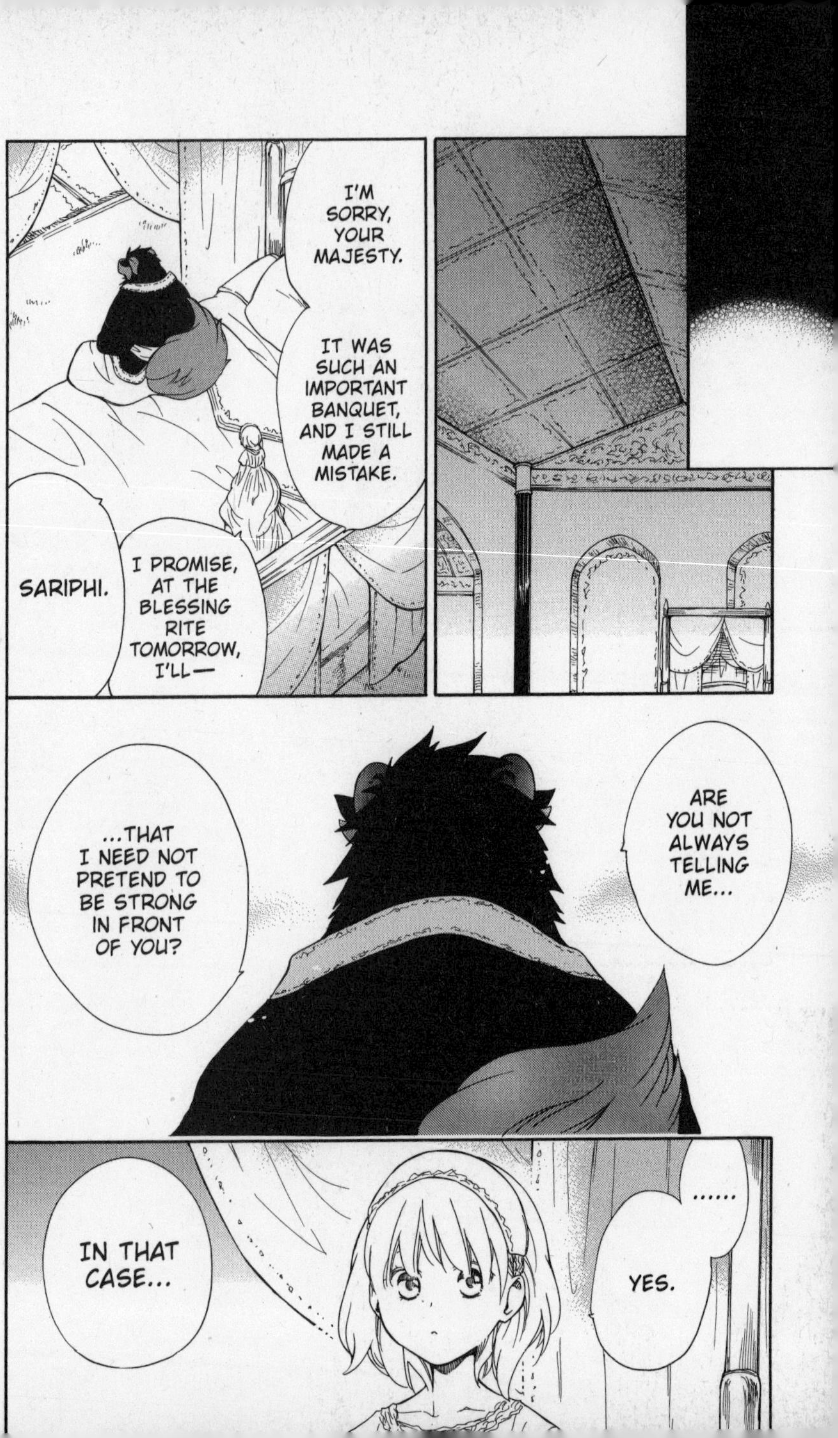
I'M SORRY, YOUR MAJESTY.
IT WAS SUCH AN IMPORTANT BANQUET, AND I STILL MADE A MISTAKE.
I PROMISE, AT THE BLESSING RITE TOMORROW, I'LL—
SARIPHI.
ARE YOU NOT ALWAYS TELLING ME...
...THAT I NEED NOT PRETEND TO BE STRONG IN FRONT OF YOU?
......
YES.
IN THAT CASE...

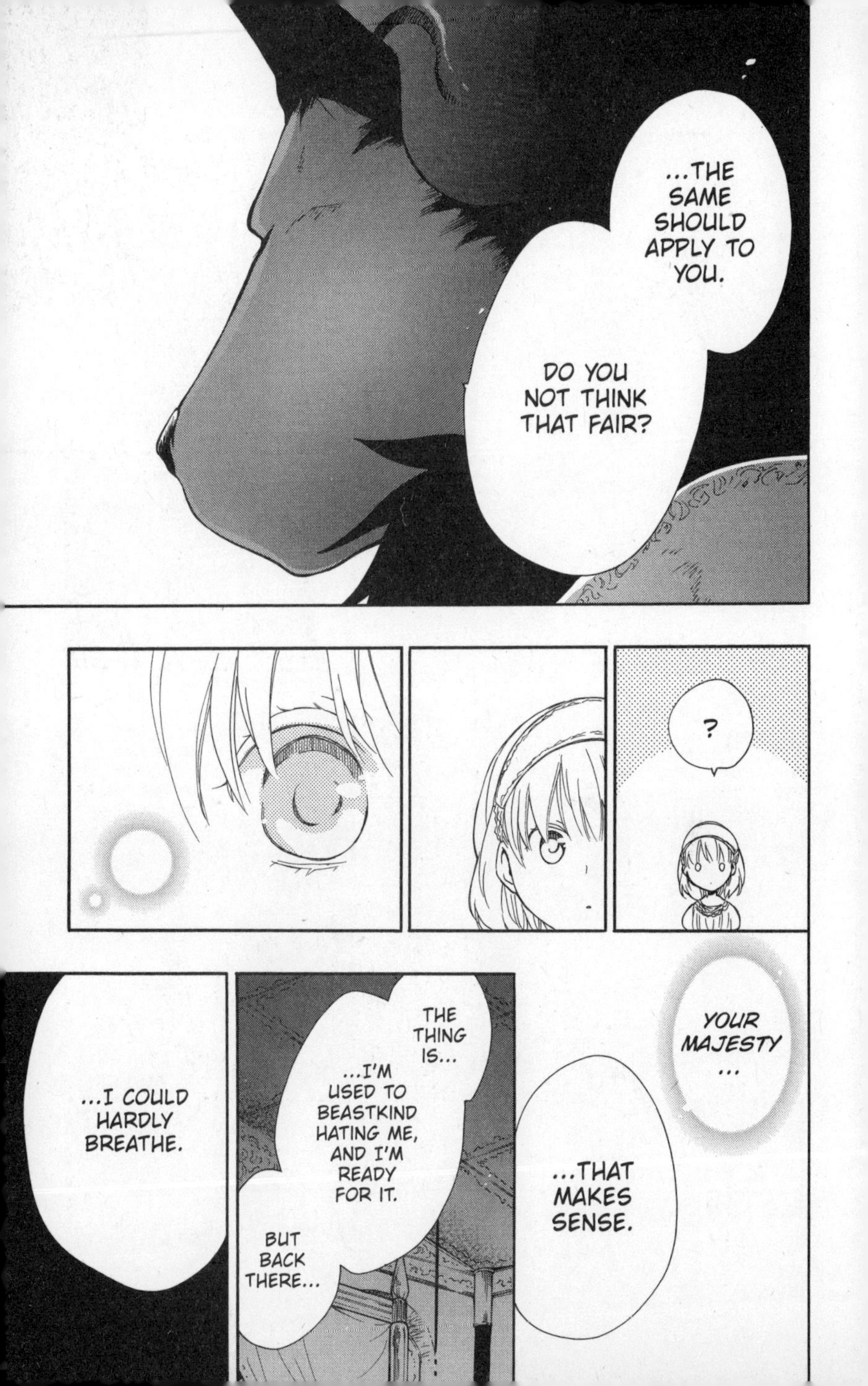
...THE SAME SHOULD APPLY TO YOU.
DO YOU NOT THINK THAT FAIR?
?
YOUR MAJESTY...
...THAT MAKES SENSE.
THE THING IS...
...I'M USED TO BEASTKIND HATING ME, AND I'M READY FOR IT.
BUT BACK THERE...
...I COULD HARDLY BREATHE.

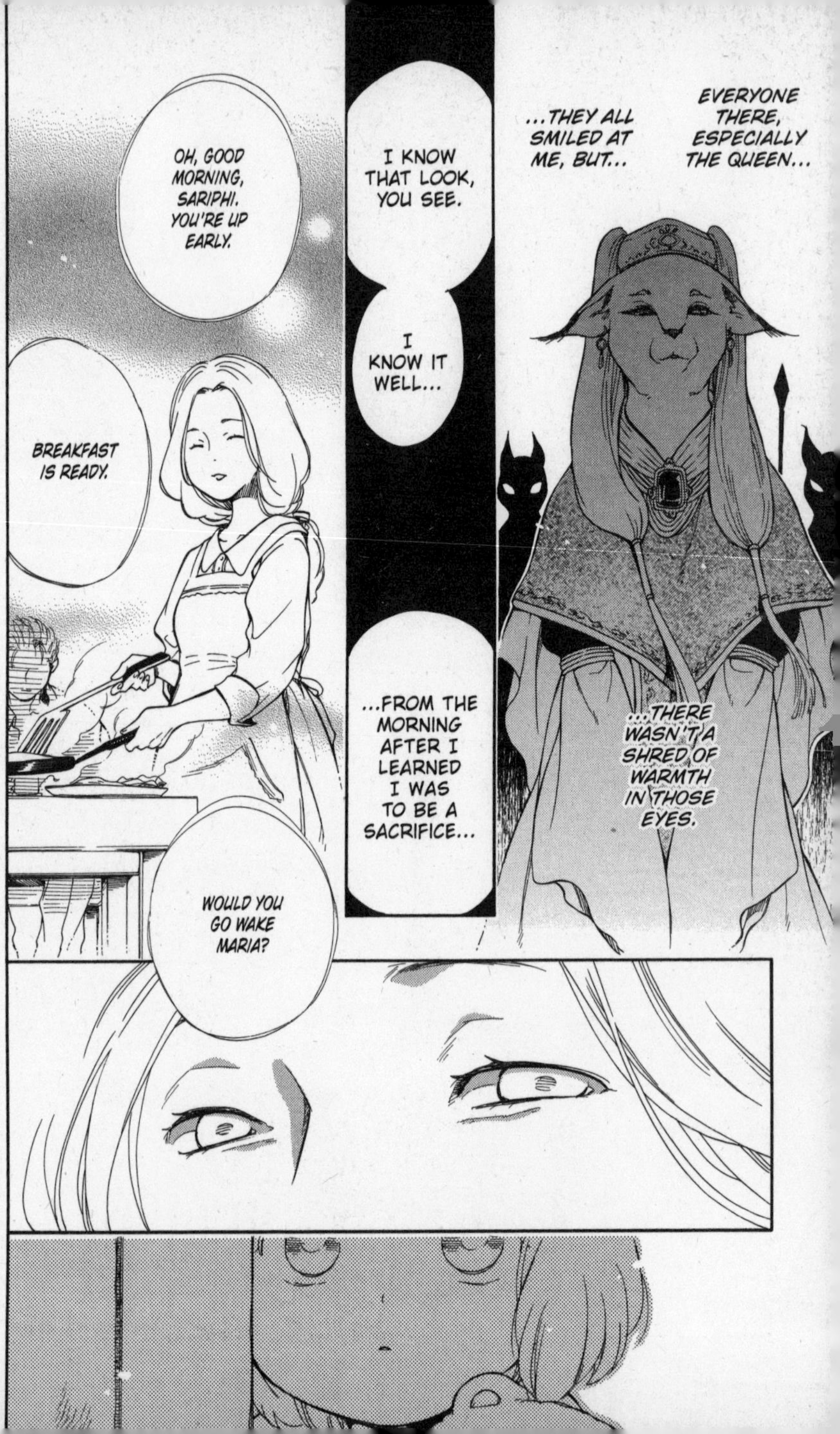
EVERYONE THERE, ESPECIALLY THE QUEEN...
...THEY ALL SMILED AT ME, BUT...
...THERE WASN'T A SHRED OF WARMTH IN THOSE EYES.
I KNOW THAT LOOK, YOU SEE.
I KNOW IT WELL...
...FROM THE MORNING AFTER I LEARNED I WAS TO BE A SACRIFICE...
OH, GOOD MORNING, SARIPHI. YOU'RE UP EARLY.
BREAKFAST IS READY.
WOULD YOU GO WAKE MARIA?

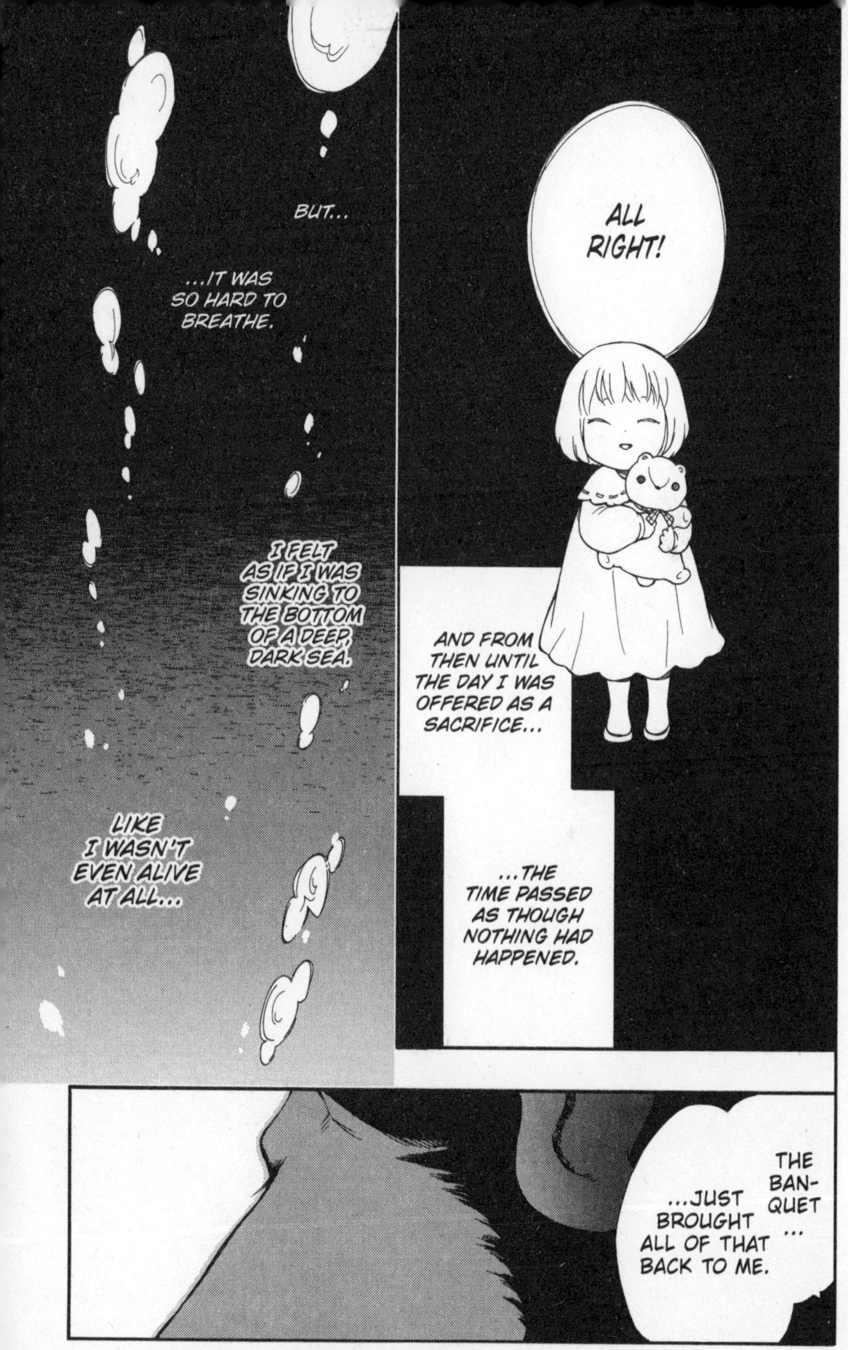
ALL RIGHT!
AND FROM THEN UNTIL THE DAY I WAS OFFERED AS A SACRIFICE...
...THE TIME PASSED AS THOUGH NOTHING HAD HAPPENED.
BUT...
...IT WAS SO HARD TO BREATHE.
I FELT AS IF I WAS SINKING TO THE BOTTOM OF A DEEP, DARK SEA.
LIKE I WASN'T EVEN ALIVE AT ALL...
THE BAN-QUET...
...JUST BROUGHT ALL OF THAT BACK TO ME.

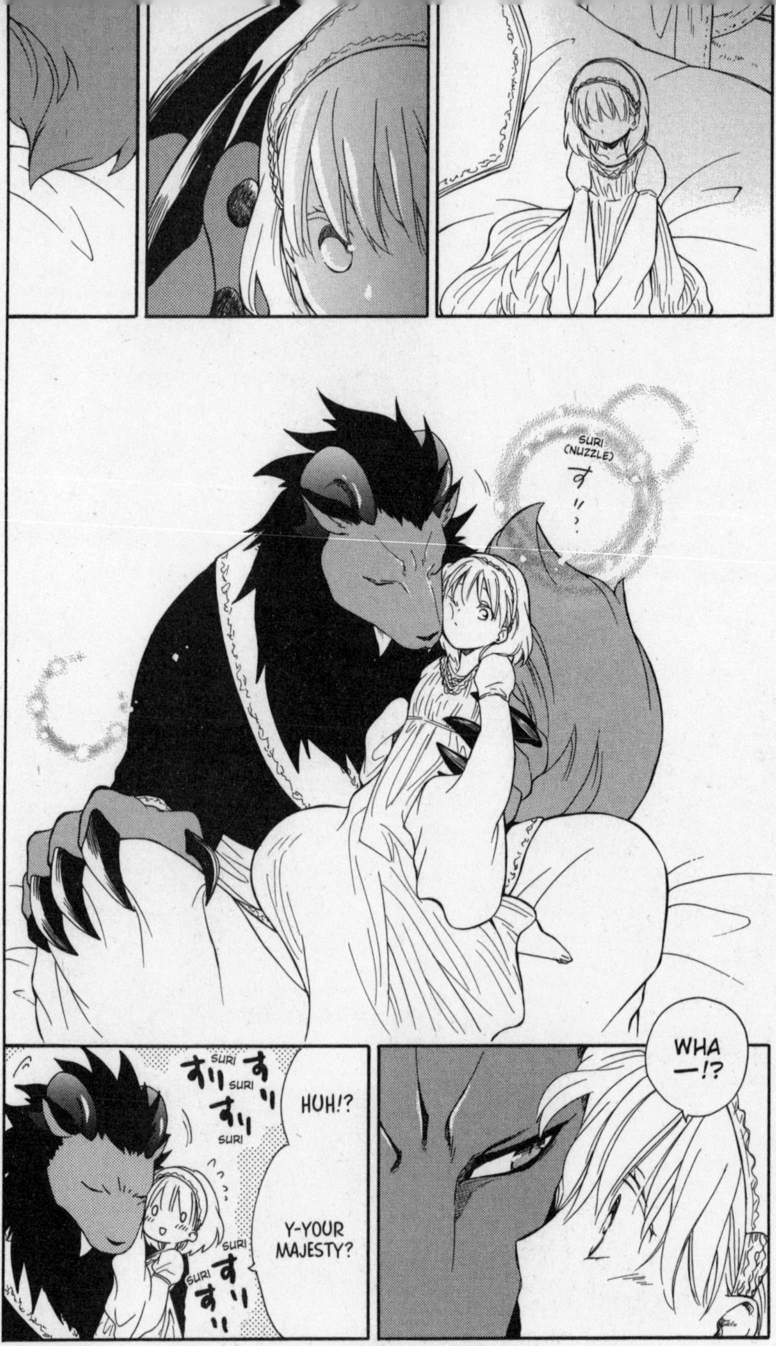
SURI (NUZZLE)
す
WHA—!?
HUH!?
すり SURI
すり SURI
すり SURI
Y-YOUR MAJESTY?
すり SURI
すり SURI

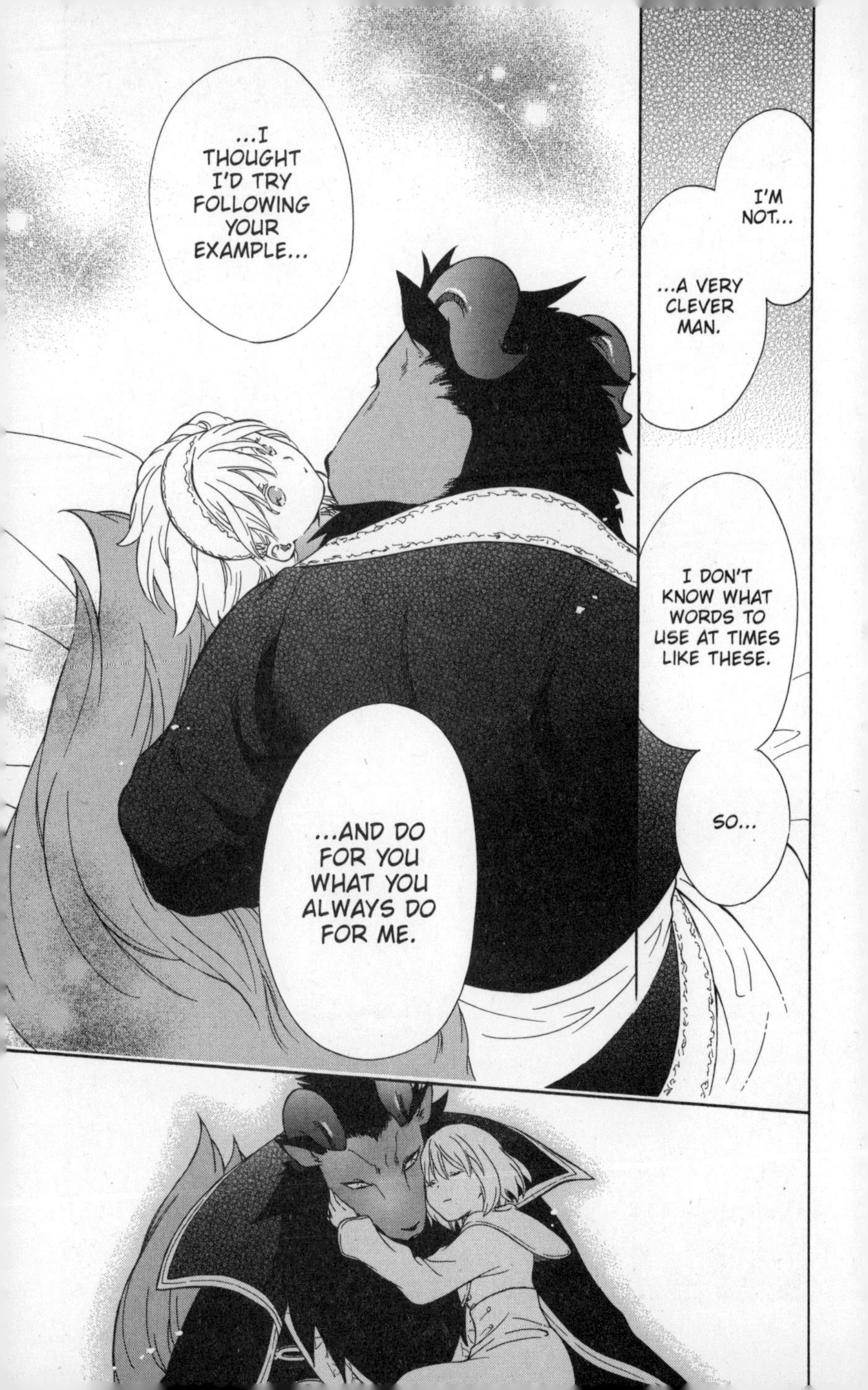
I'M NOT...
...A VERY CLEVER MAN.
I DON'T KNOW WHAT WORDS TO USE AT TIMES LIKE THESE.
SO...
...I THOUGHT I'D TRY FOLLOWING YOUR EXAMPLE...
...AND DO FOR YOU WHAT YOU ALWAYS DO FOR ME.

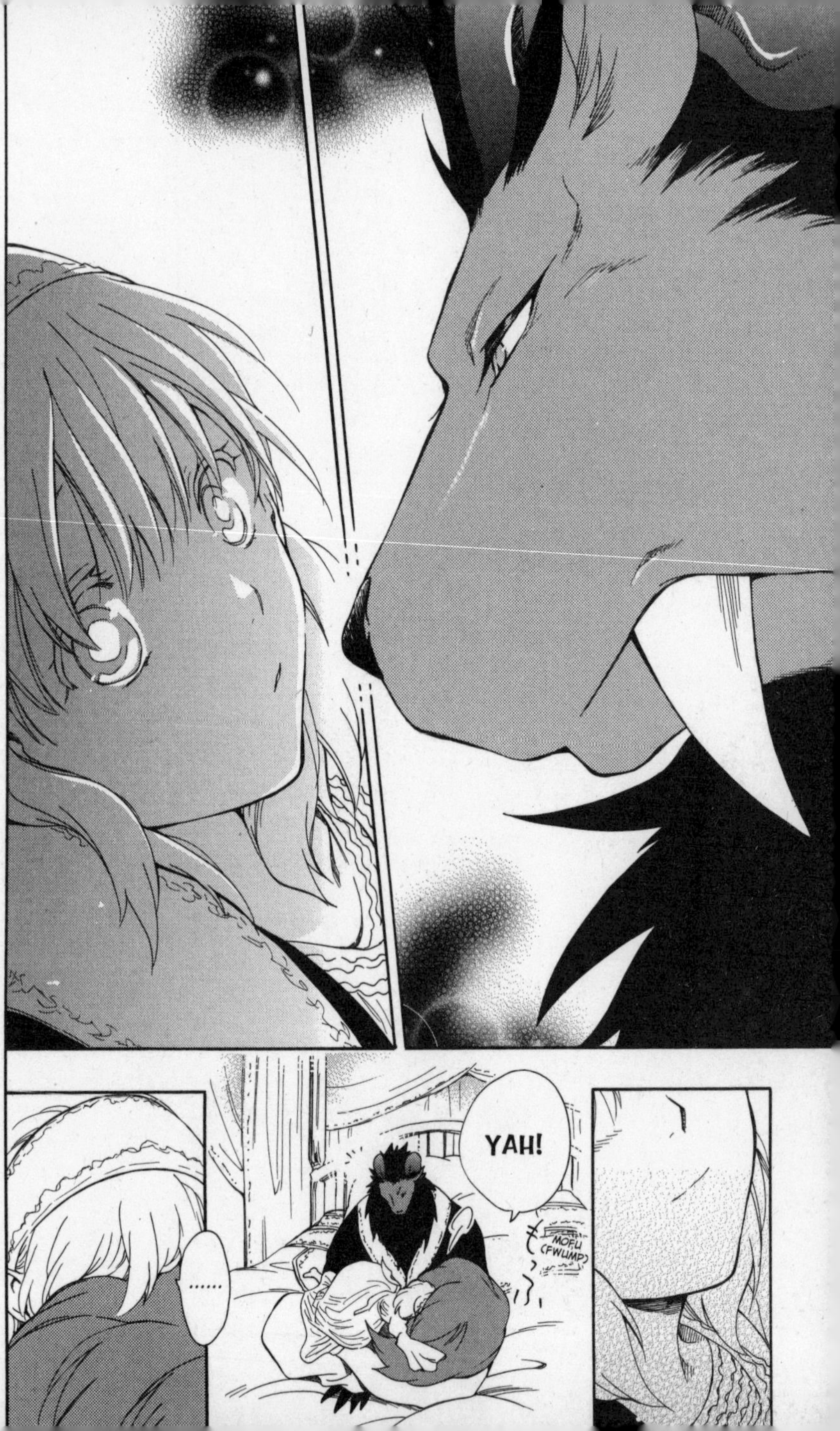
YAH!
MOFU (FWUMP)
......

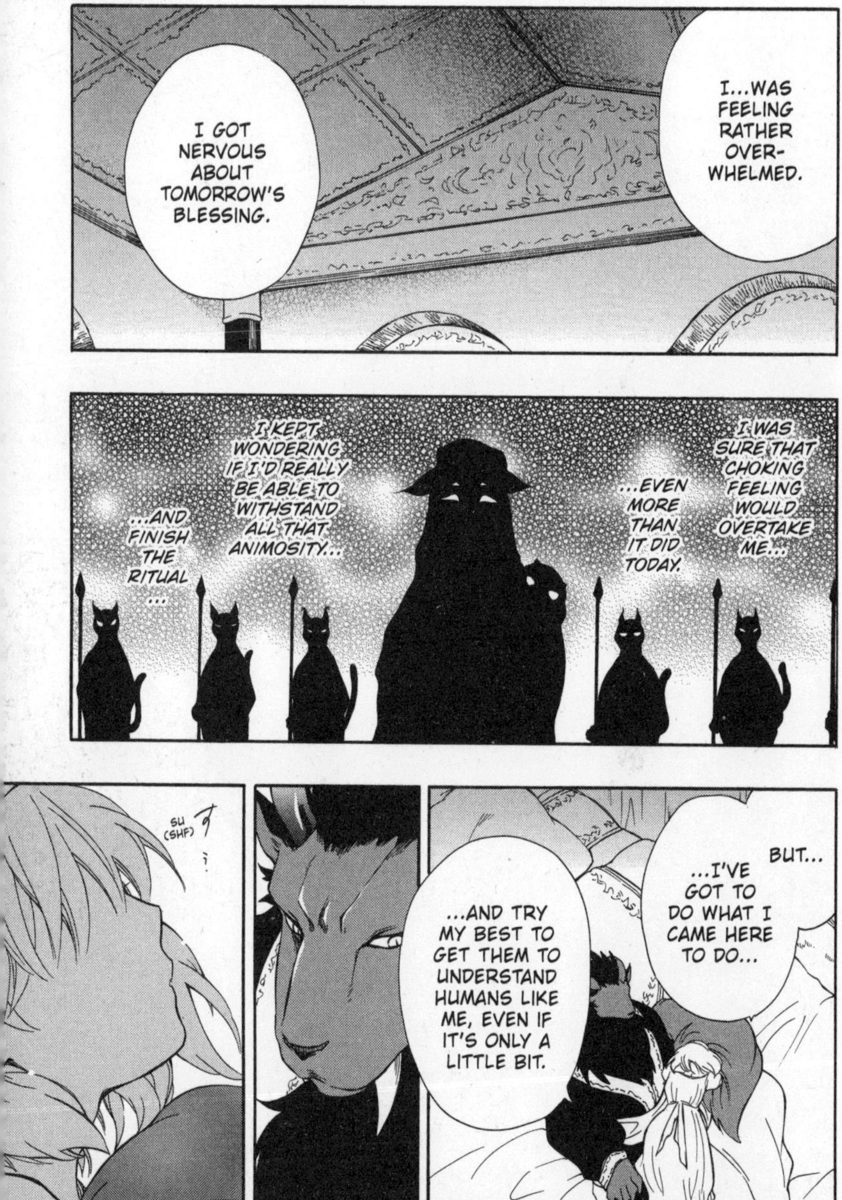
I...WAS FEELING RATHER OVER-WHELMED.
I GOT NERVOUS ABOUT TOMORROW'S BLESSING.
I WAS SURE THAT CHOKING FEELING WOULD OVERTAKE ME...
...EVEN MORE THAN IT DID TODAY.
I KEPT WONDERING IF I'D REALLY BE ABLE TO WITHSTAND ALL THAT ANIMOSITY...
...AND FINISH THE RITUAL...
BUT...
...I'VE GOT TO DO WHAT I CAME HERE TO DO...
...AND TRY MY BEST TO GET THEM TO UNDERSTAND HUMANS LIKE ME, EVEN IF IT'S ONLY A LITTLE BIT.
SU (SHF)

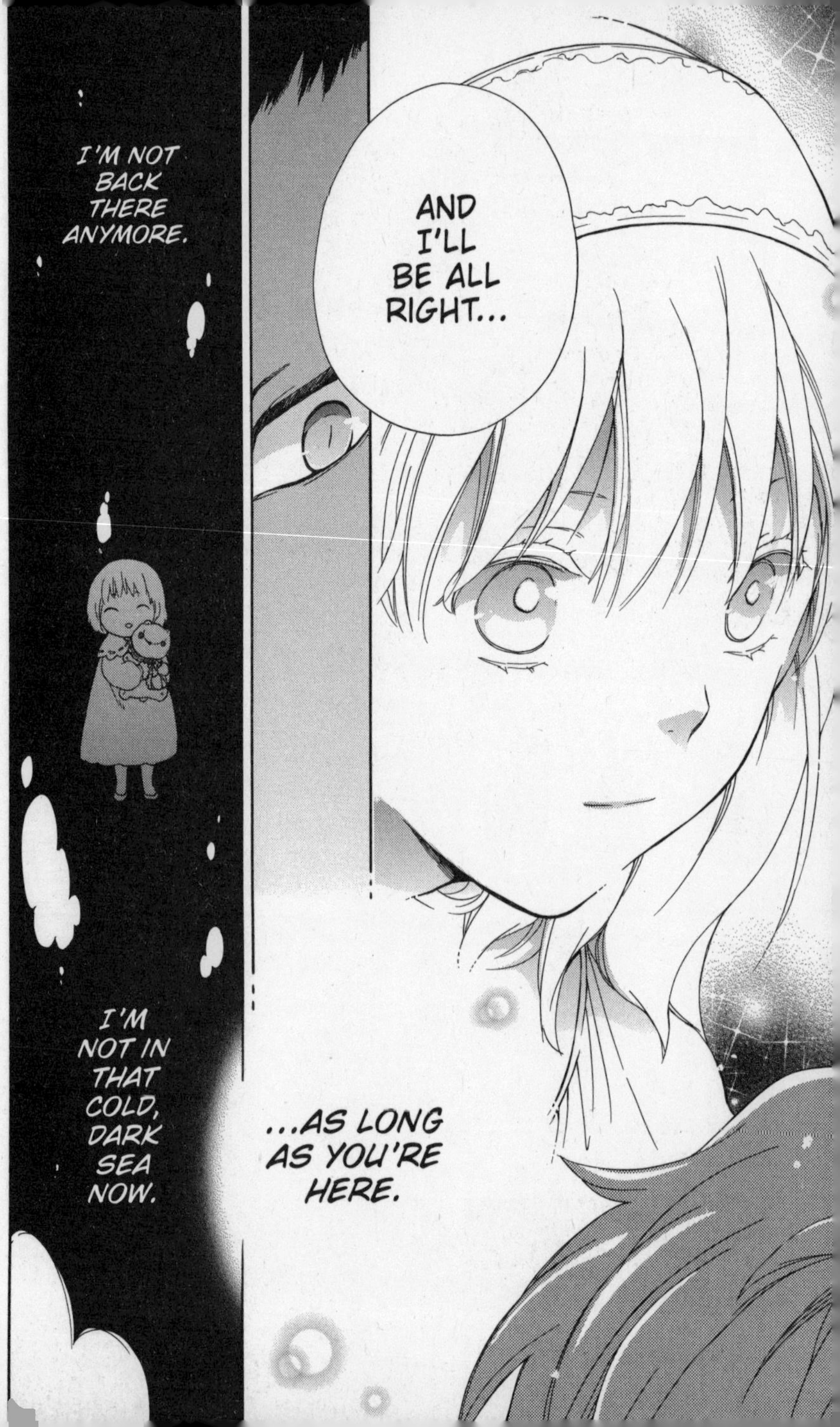
AND I'LL BE ALL RIGHT...
...AS LONG AS YOU'RE HERE.
I'M NOT BACK THERE ANYMORE.
I'M NOT IN THAT COLD, DARK SEA NOW.

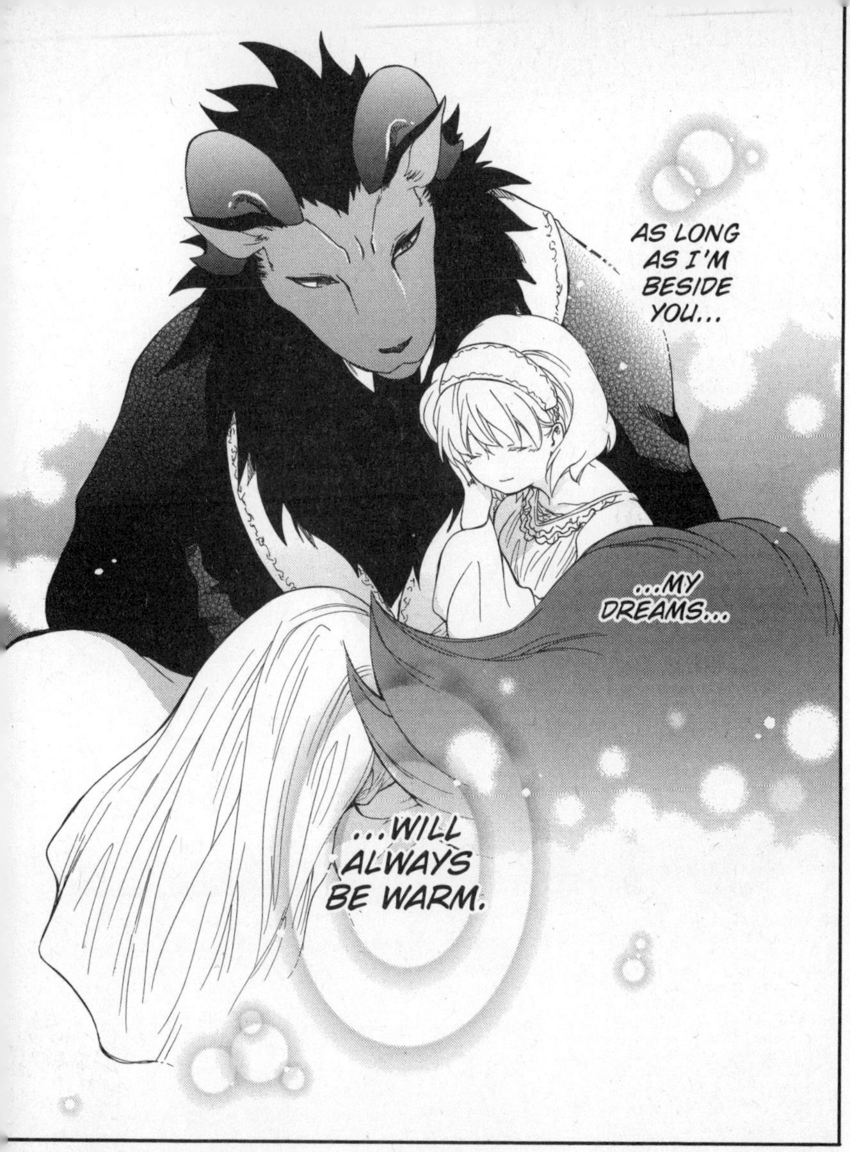
AS LONG AS I'M BESIDE YOU...
...MY DREAMS...
...WILL ALWAYS BE WARM.
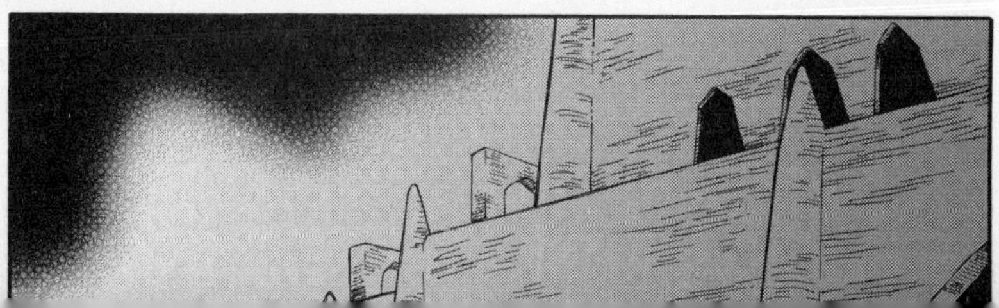

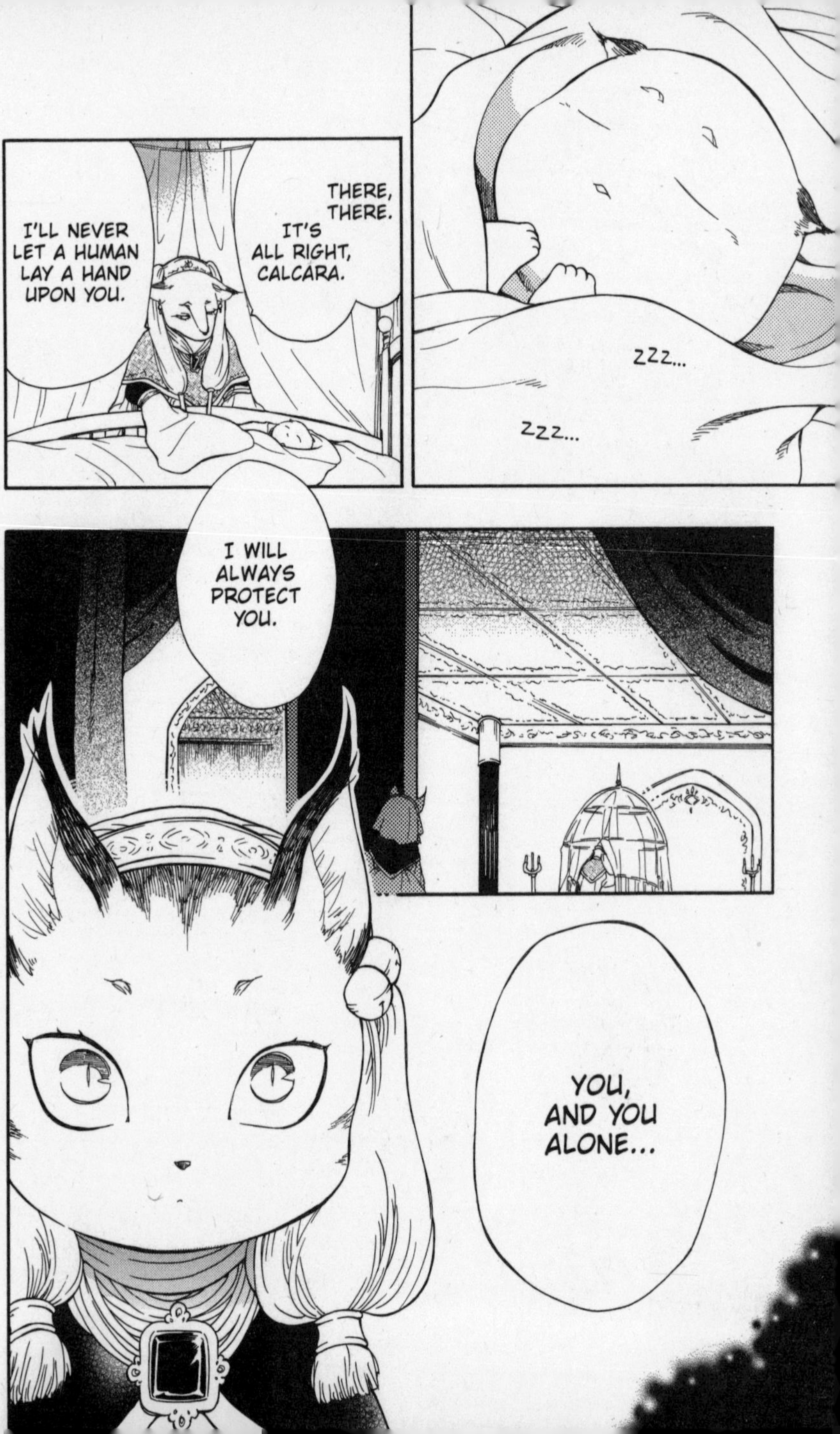
ZZZ...
ZZZ...
THERE, THERE. IT'S ALL RIGHT, CALCARA.
I'LL NEVER LET A HUMAN LAY A HAND UPON YOU.
I WILL ALWAYS PROTECT YOU.
YOU, AND YOU ALONE...

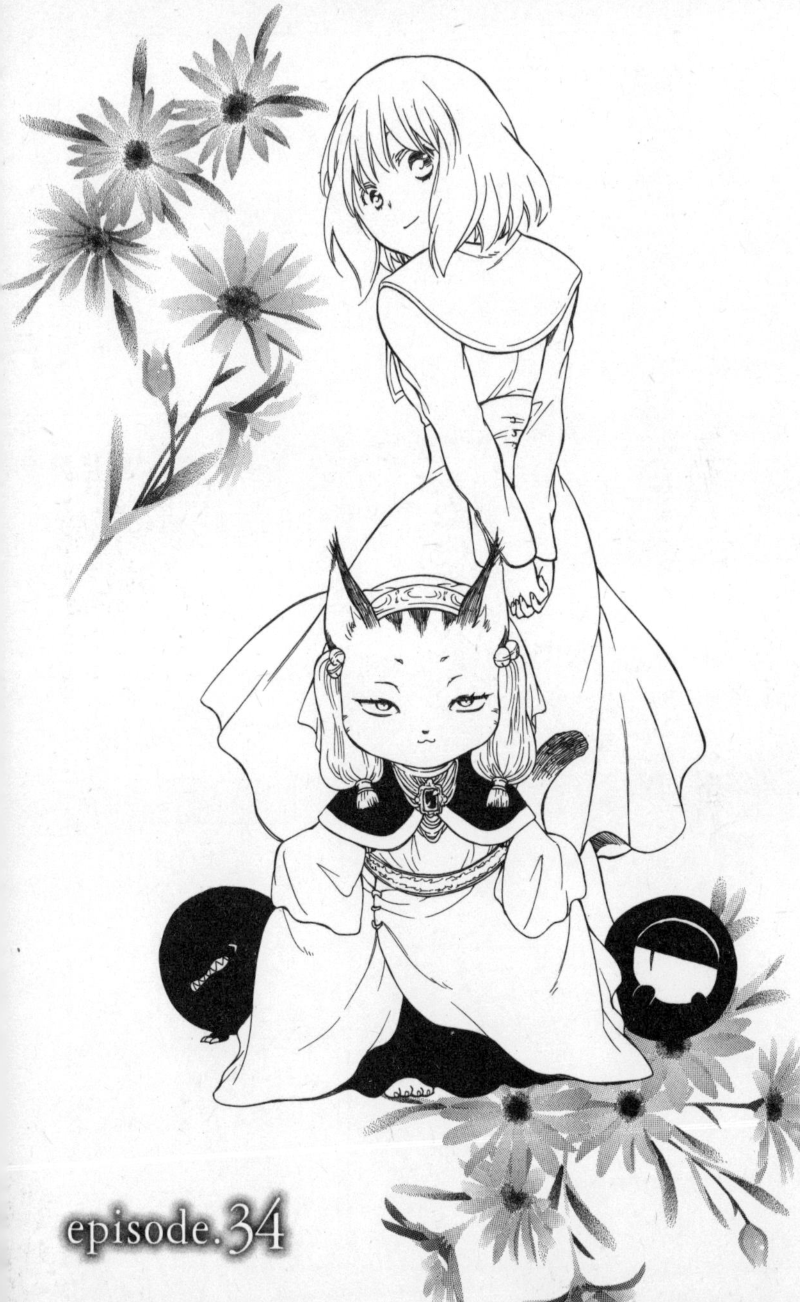
episode. 34

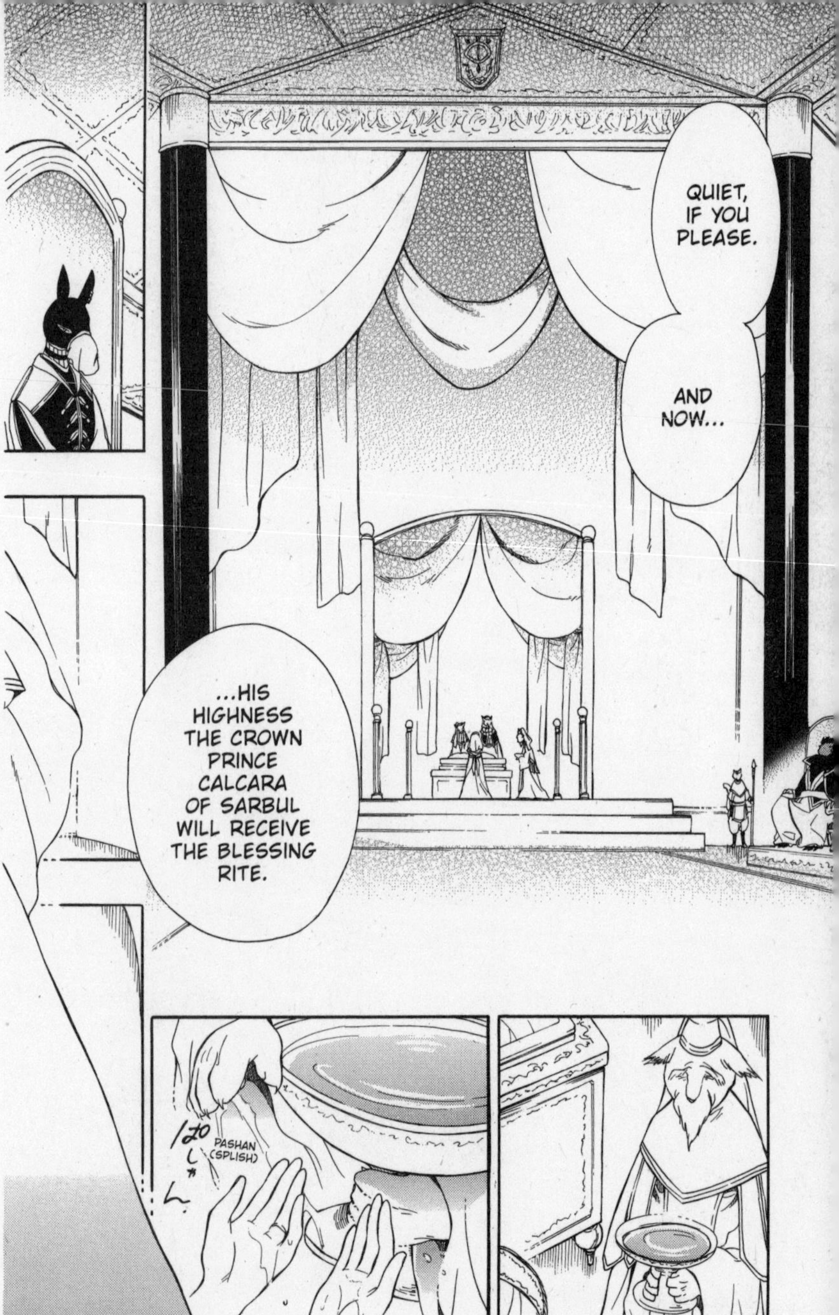
QUIET, IF YOU PLEASE.
AND NOW...
...HIS HIGHNESS THE CROWN PRINCE CALCARA OF SARBUL WILL RECEIVE THE BLESSING RITE.
PASHAN (SPLISH)

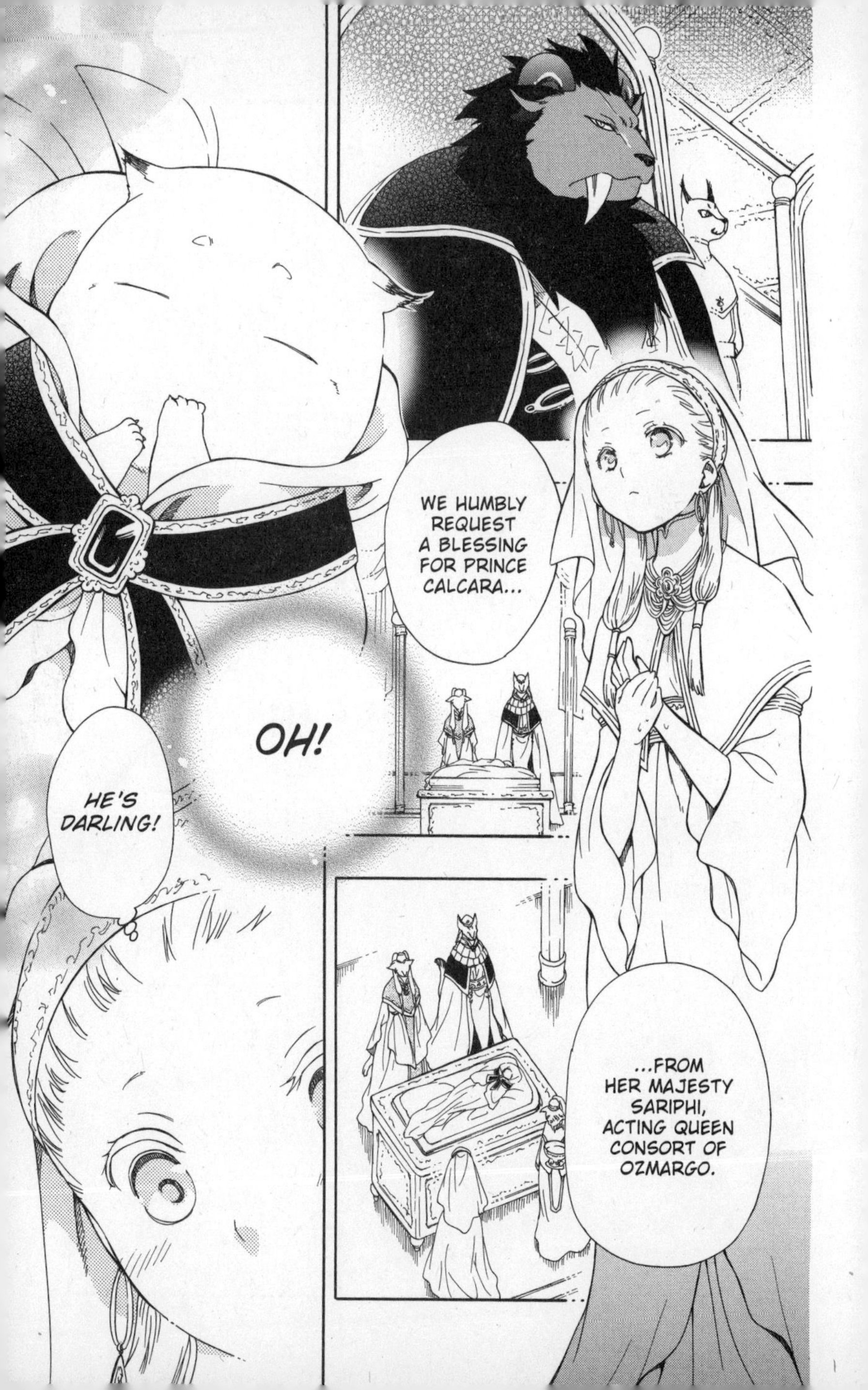
WE HUMBLY REQUEST A BLESSING FOR PRINCE CALCARA...
...FROM HER MAJESTY SARIPHI, ACTING QUEEN CONSORT OF OZMARGO.
OH!
HE'S DARLING!

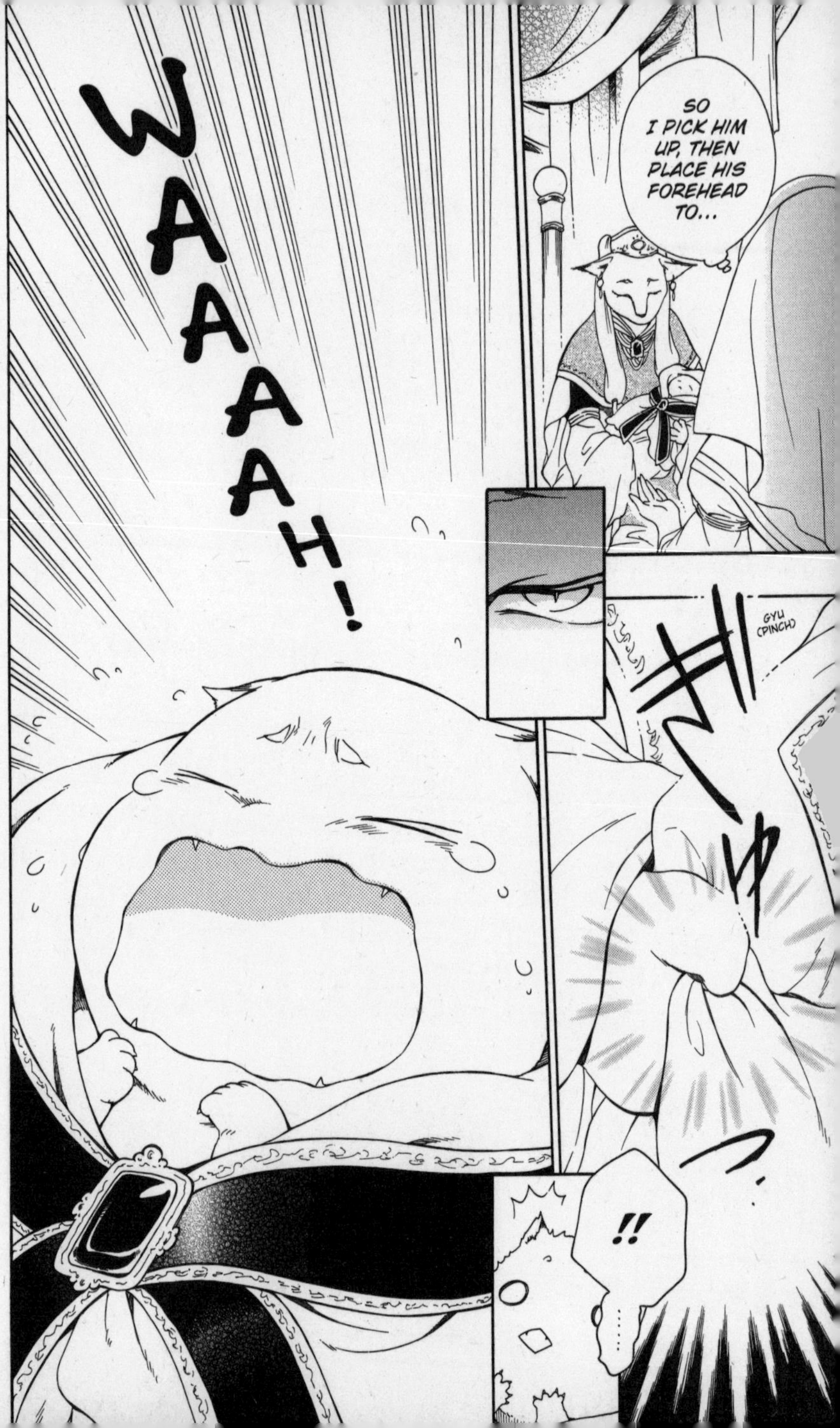
SO I PICK HIM UP, THEN PLACE HIS FOREHEAD TO...
GYU (PINCH)
ぎゅ
!!
WAAAAAH!

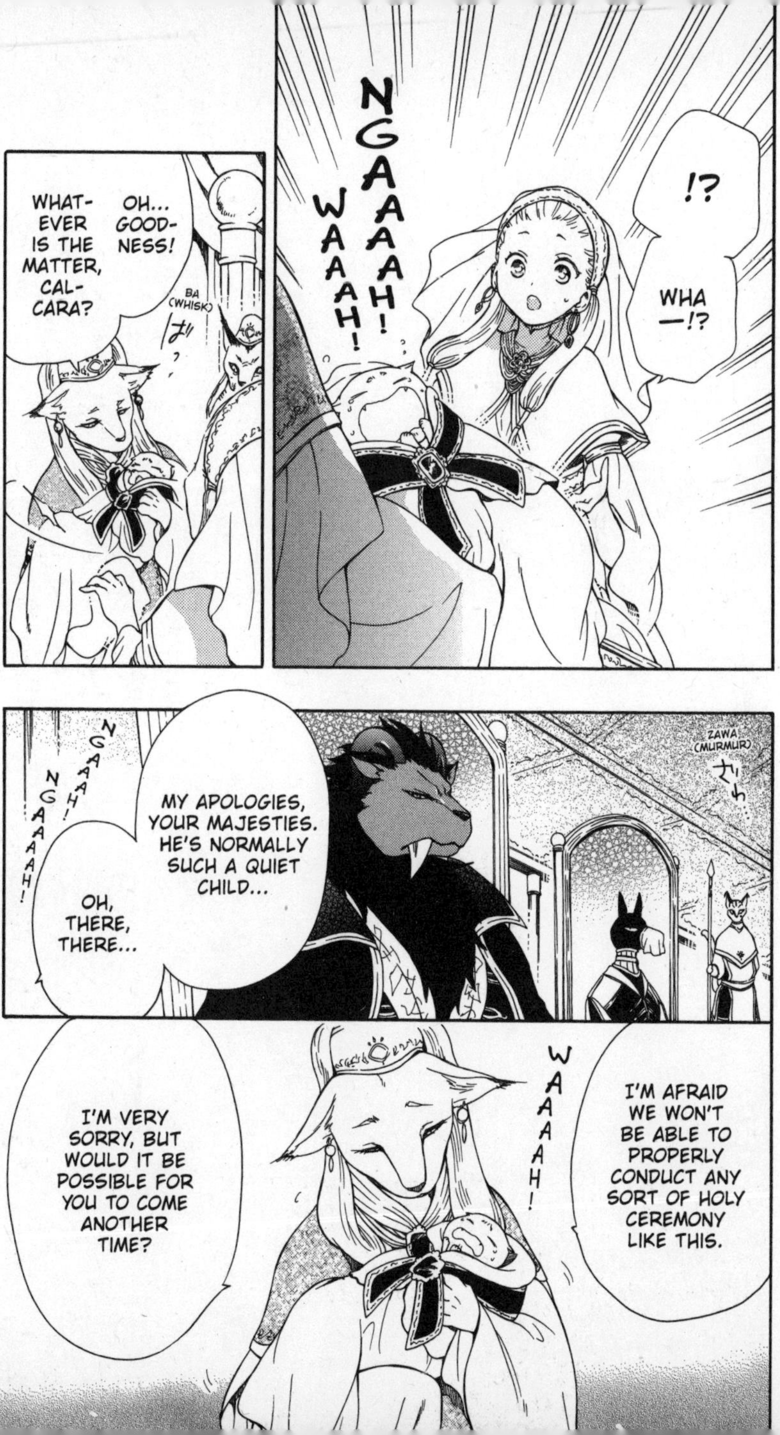
!?
NGAAAAAH!
WAAAAH!
WHA—!?
OH... GOODNESS!
WHATEVER IS THE MATTER, CALCARA?
BA (WHISK)
ZAWA (MURMUR)
MY APOLOGIES, YOUR MAJESTIES. HE'S NORMALLY SUCH A QUIET CHILD...
NGAAAH!
NGAAAAAH!
OH, THERE, THERE...
I'M AFRAID WE WON'T BE ABLE TO PROPERLY CONDUCT ANY SORT OF HOLY CEREMONY LIKE THIS.
WAAAAAH!
I'M VERY SORRY, BUT WOULD IT BE POSSIBLE FOR YOU TO COME ANOTHER TIME?

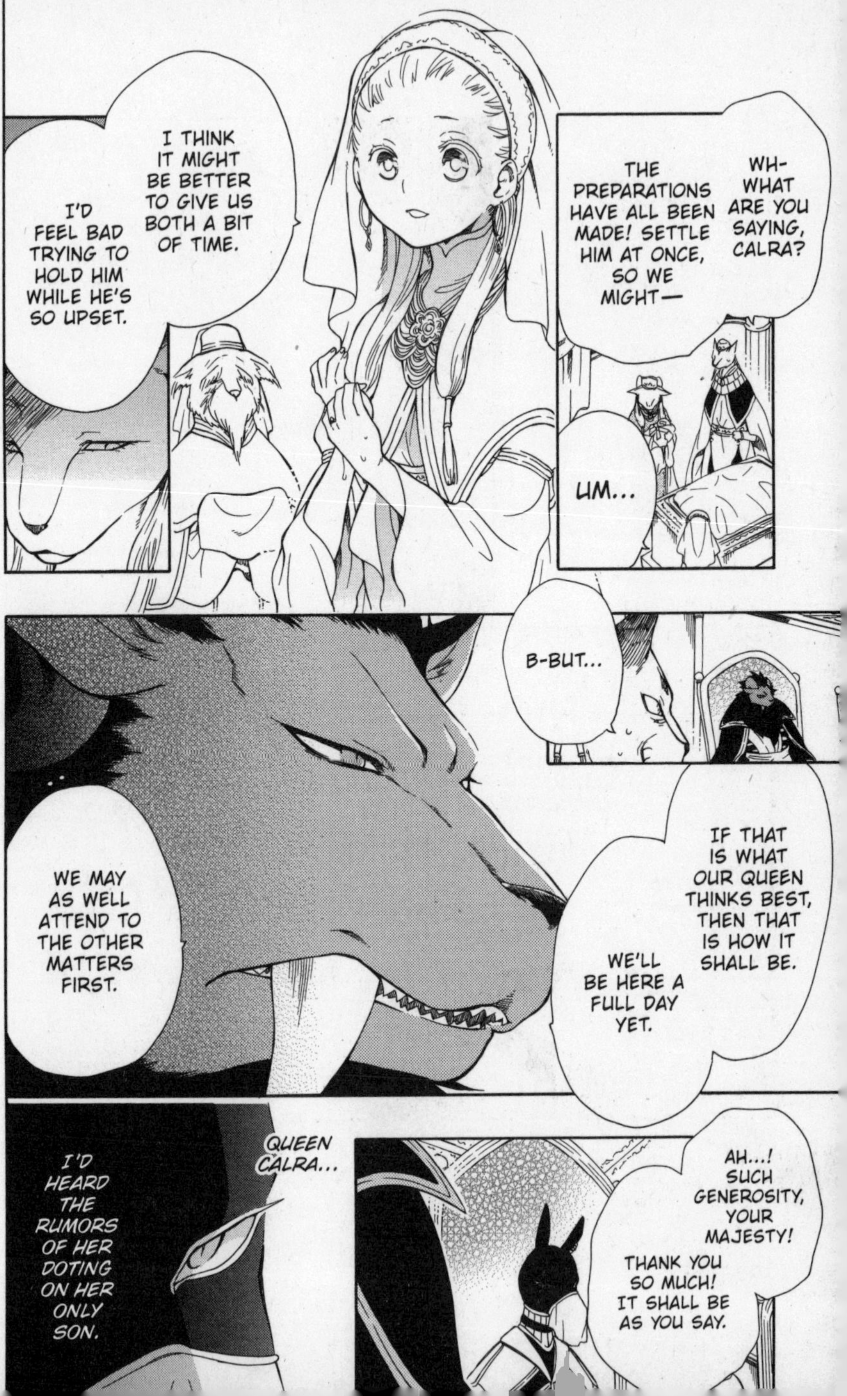
WH-WHAT ARE YOU SAYING, CALRA?
THE PREPARATIONS HAVE ALL BEEN MADE! SETTLE HIM AT ONCE, SO WE MIGHT—
UM...
I THINK IT MIGHT BE BETTER TO GIVE US BOTH A BIT OF TIME.
I'D FEEL BAD TRYING TO HOLD HIM WHILE HE'S SO UPSET.
B-BUT...
IF THAT IS WHAT OUR QUEEN THINKS BEST, THEN THAT IS HOW IT SHALL BE.
WE'LL BE HERE A FULL DAY YET.
WE MAY AS WELL ATTEND TO THE OTHER MATTERS FIRST.
AH...! SUCH GENEROSITY, YOUR MAJESTY!
THANK YOU SO MUCH! IT SHALL BE AS YOU SAY.
QUEEN CALRA...
I'D HEARD THE RUMORS OF HER DOTING ON HER ONLY SON.

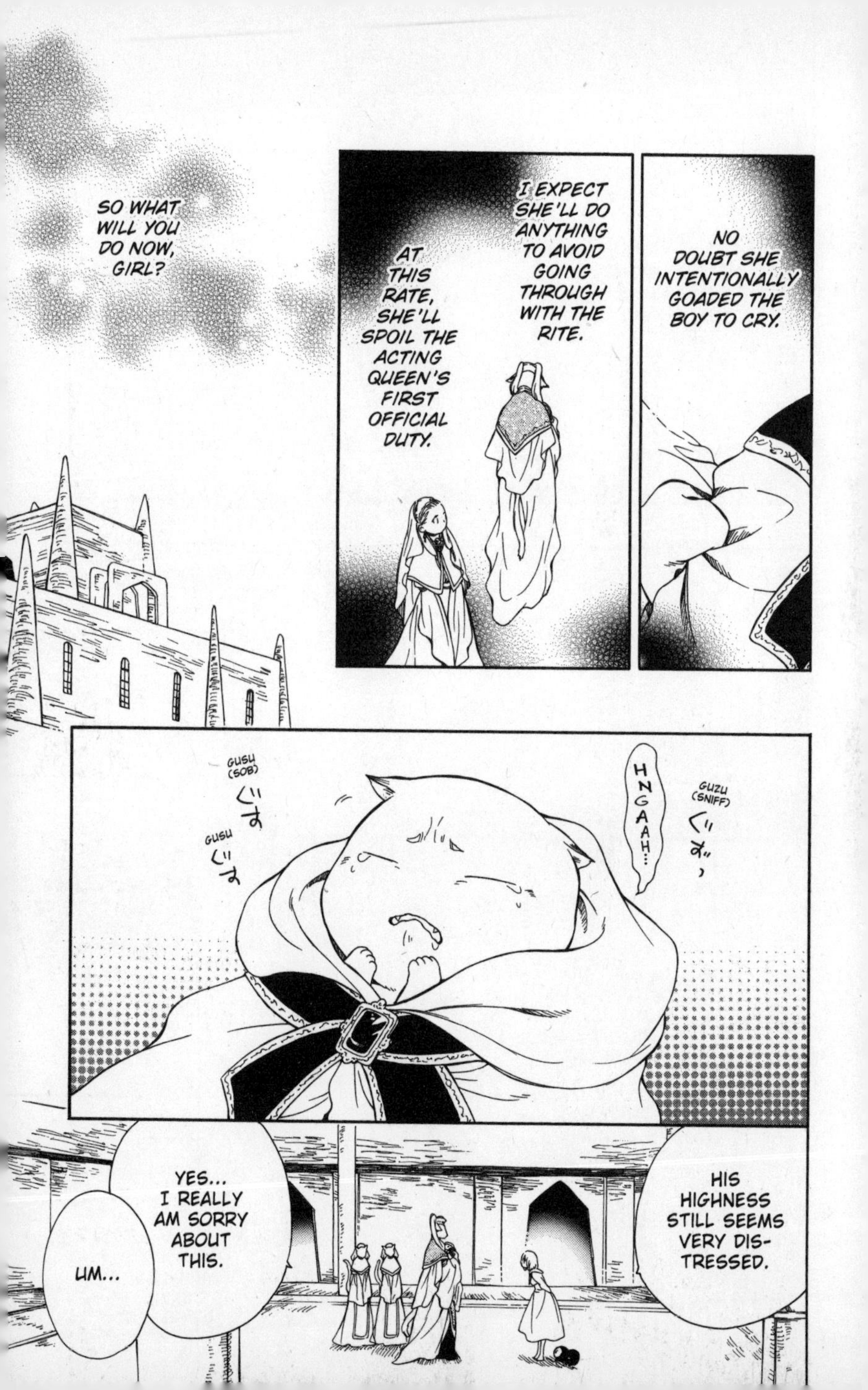
NO DOUBT SHE INTENTIONALLY GOADED THE BOY TO CRY.
I EXPECT SHE'LL DO ANYTHING TO AVOID GOING THROUGH WITH THE RITE.
AT THIS RATE, SHE'LL SPOIL THE ACTING QUEEN'S FIRST OFFICIAL DUTY.
SO WHAT WILL YOU DO NOW, GIRL?
GUZU (SNIFF) ぐず,
HNGAAH...
GUSU (SOB) ぐす
GUSU ぐす
HIS HIGHNESS STILL SEEMS VERY DIS-TRESSED.
YES... I REALLY AM SORRY ABOUT THIS.
UM...

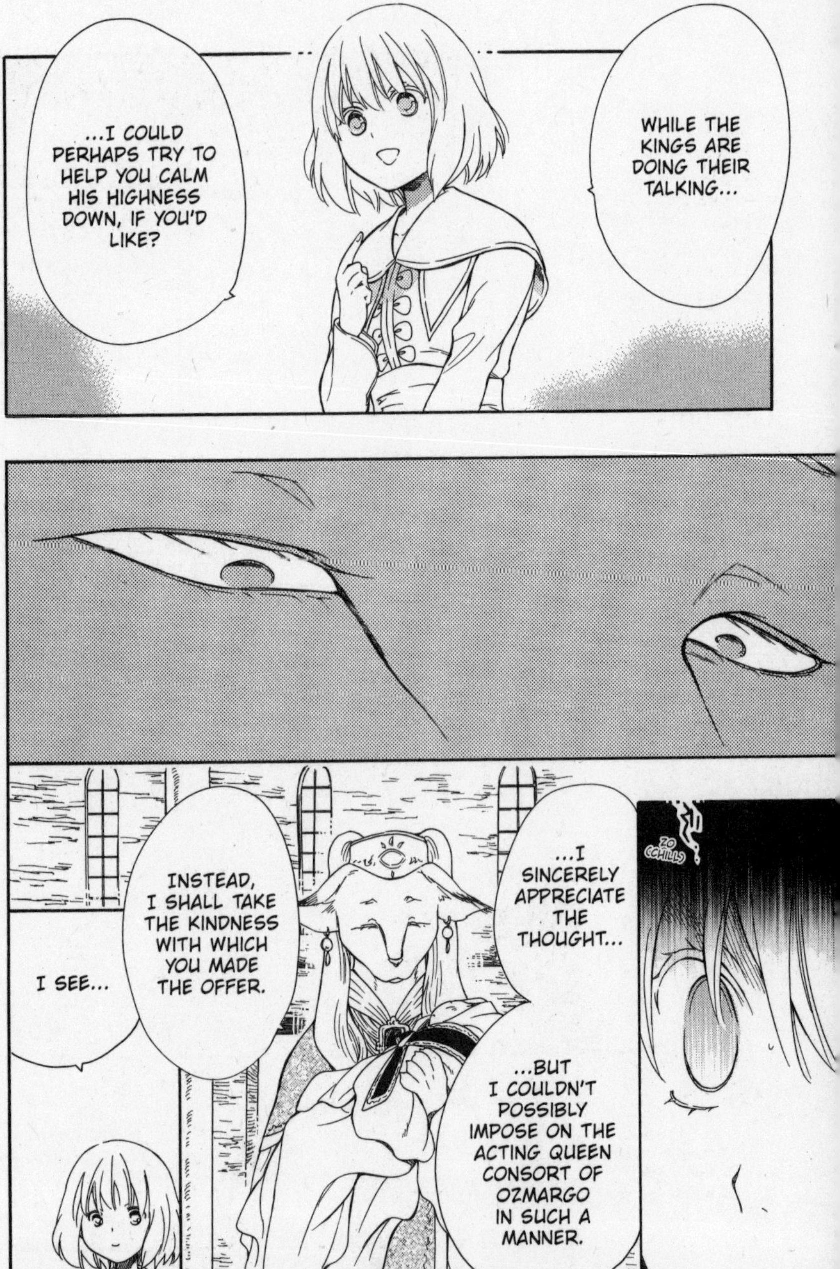
WHILE THE KINGS ARE DOING THEIR TALKING...
...I COULD PERHAPS TRY TO HELP YOU CALM HIS HIGHNESS DOWN, IF YOU'D LIKE?
ZO (CHILL)
...I SINCERELY APPRECIATE THE THOUGHT...
...BUT I COULDN'T POSSIBLY IMPOSE ON THE ACTING QUEEN CONSORT OF OZMARGO IN SUCH A MANNER.
INSTEAD, I SHALL TAKE THE KINDNESS WITH WHICH YOU MADE THE OFFER.
I SEE...

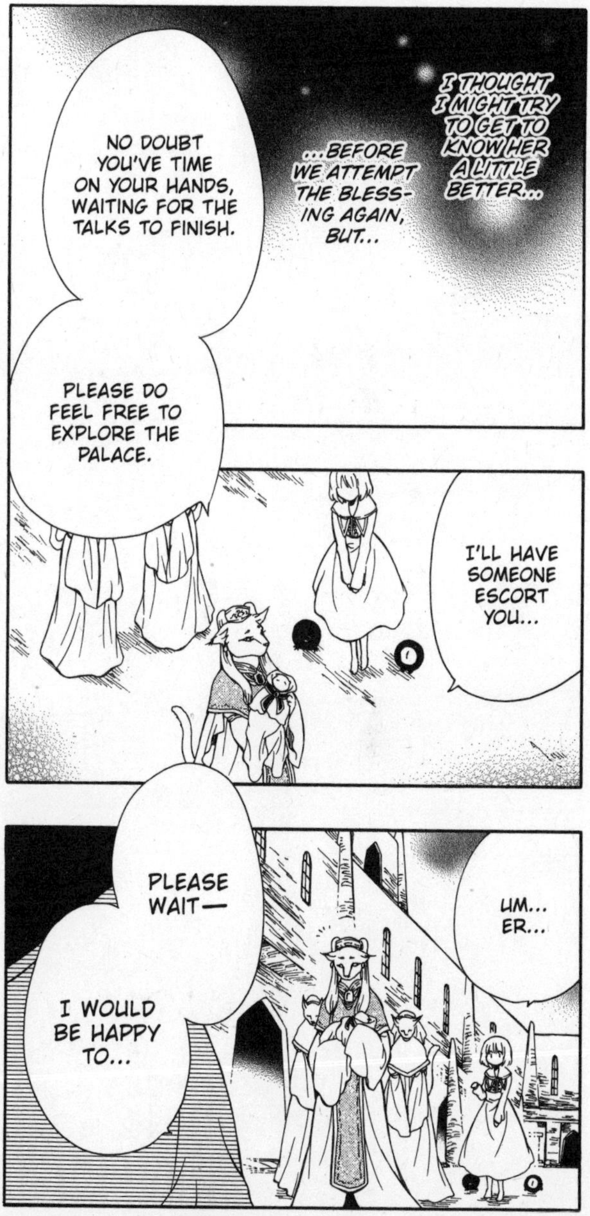
I THOUGHT I MIGHT TRY TO GET TO KNOW HER A LITTLE BETTER...
...BEFORE WE ATTEMPT THE BLESS-ING AGAIN, BUT...
NO DOUBT YOU'VE TIME ON YOUR HANDS, WAITING FOR THE TALKS TO FINISH.
PLEASE DO FEEL FREE TO EXPLORE THE PALACE.
I'LL HAVE SOMEONE ESCORT YOU...
UM... ER...
PLEASE WAIT—
I WOULD BE HAPPY TO...

AND THAT BRINGS VOLUME 6 TO A CLOSE. THERE'S STILL A CHAPTER OF THE BOOK LEFT, BUT I MADE THE ROOKIE MISTAKE OF FORGETTING TO LEAVE SPACE IN THE NEXT CHAPTER WHEN I WAS DRAWING IT FOR SERIALIZATION, SO I HAVE TO SAY MY GOOD-BYES HERE.

I HOPE WE'LL MEET AGAIN IN VOLUME 7!

THANKS THIS TIME TO MY ASSISTANTS A-SAN AND O-SAN.

SO WITH THANKS TO ALL OF YOU, MY DEAR READERS, I BID YOU FAREWELL!

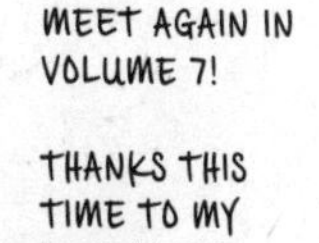

THE MOST BORING COLORING PAGE IN THE WORLD...

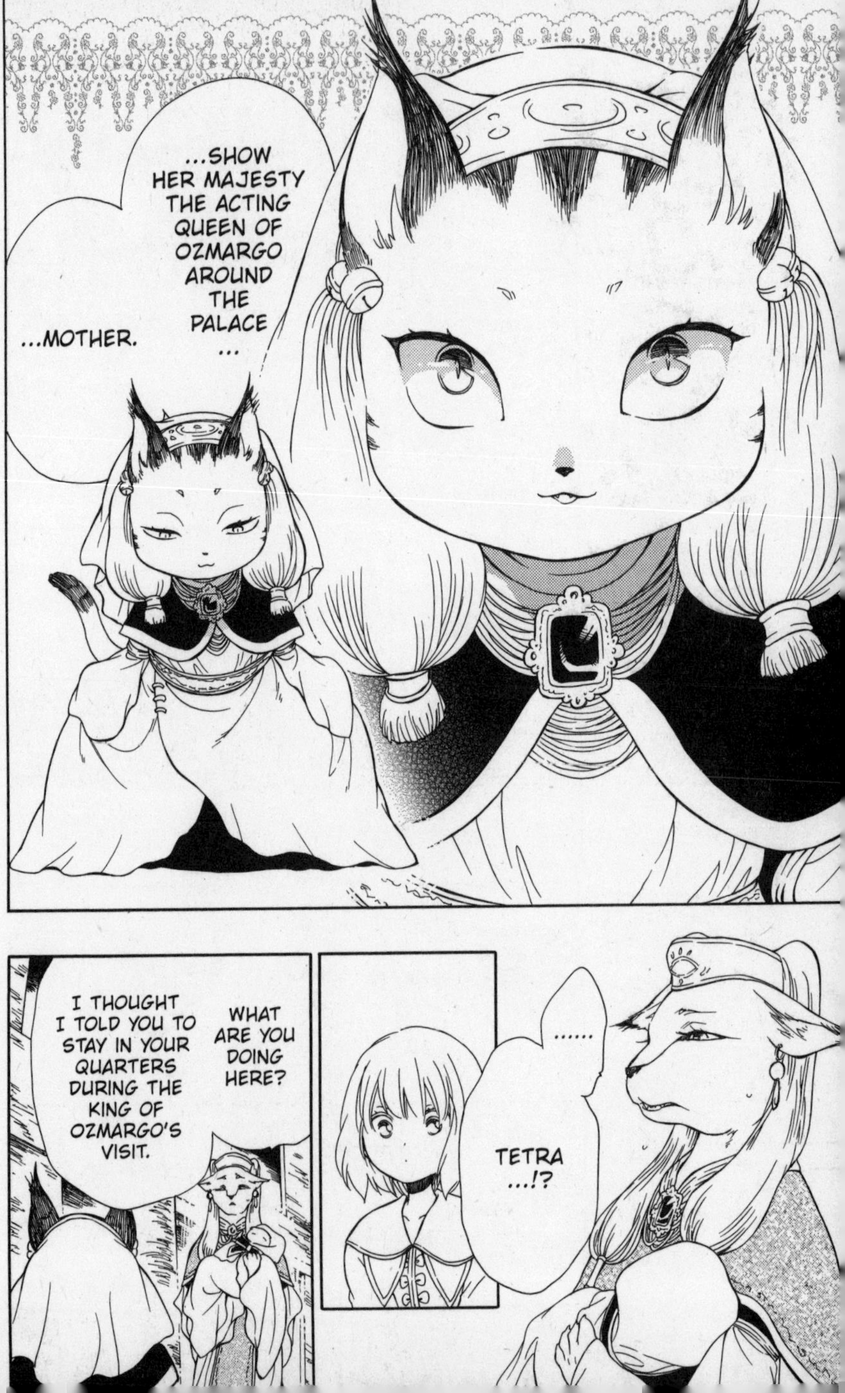
...SHOW HER MAJESTY THE ACTING QUEEN OF OZMARGO AROUND THE PALACE...
...MOTHER.
......
TETRA ...!?
WHAT ARE YOU DOING HERE?
I THOUGHT I TOLD YOU TO STAY IN YOUR QUARTERS DURING THE KING OF OZMARGO'S VISIT.

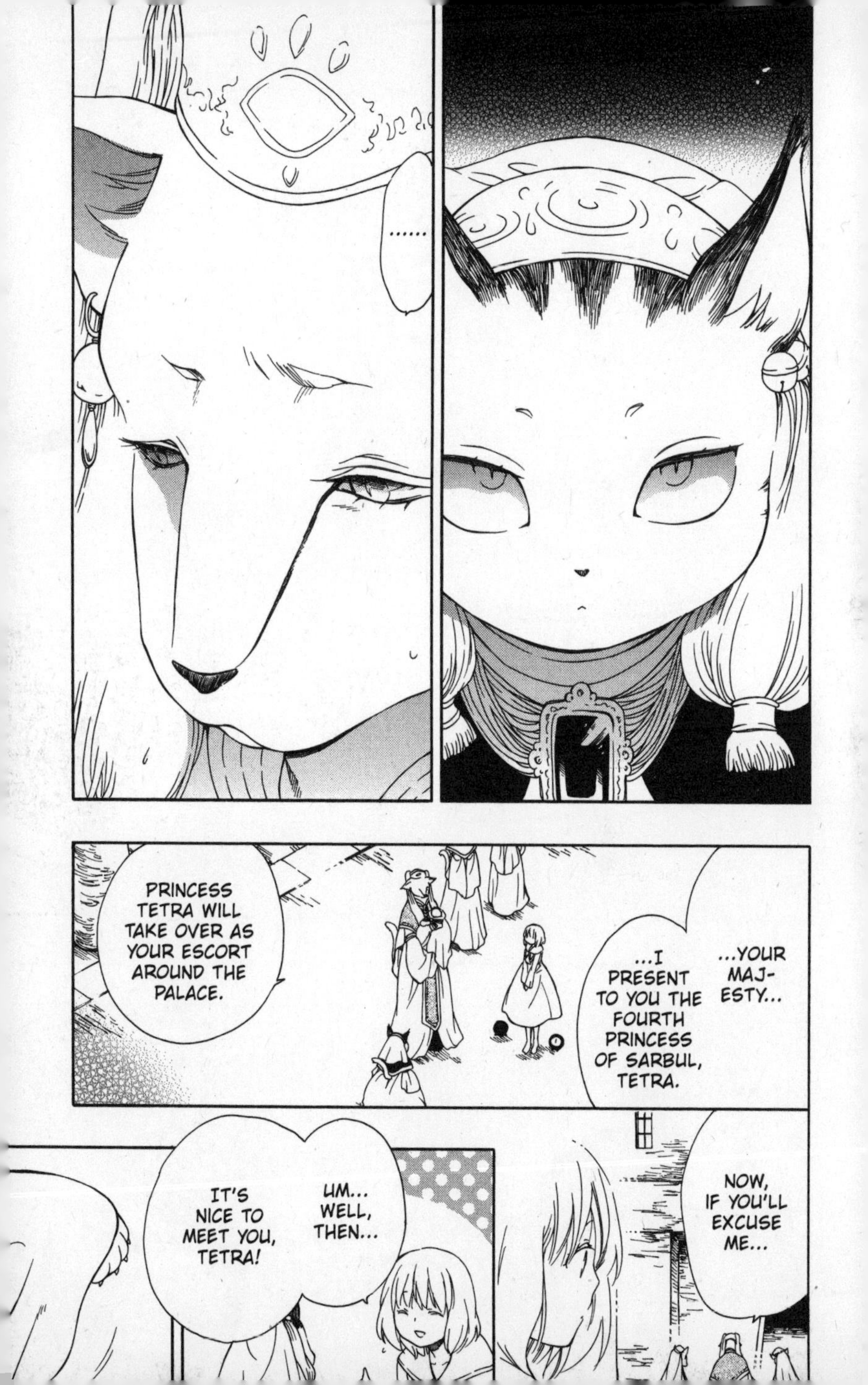
......
...YOUR MAJ-ESTY...
...I PRESENT TO YOU THE FOURTH PRINCESS OF SARBUL, TETRA.
PRINCESS TETRA WILL TAKE OVER AS YOUR ESCORT AROUND THE PALACE.
NOW, IF YOU'LL EXCUSE ME...
UM... WELL, THEN...
IT'S NICE TO MEET YOU, TETRA!

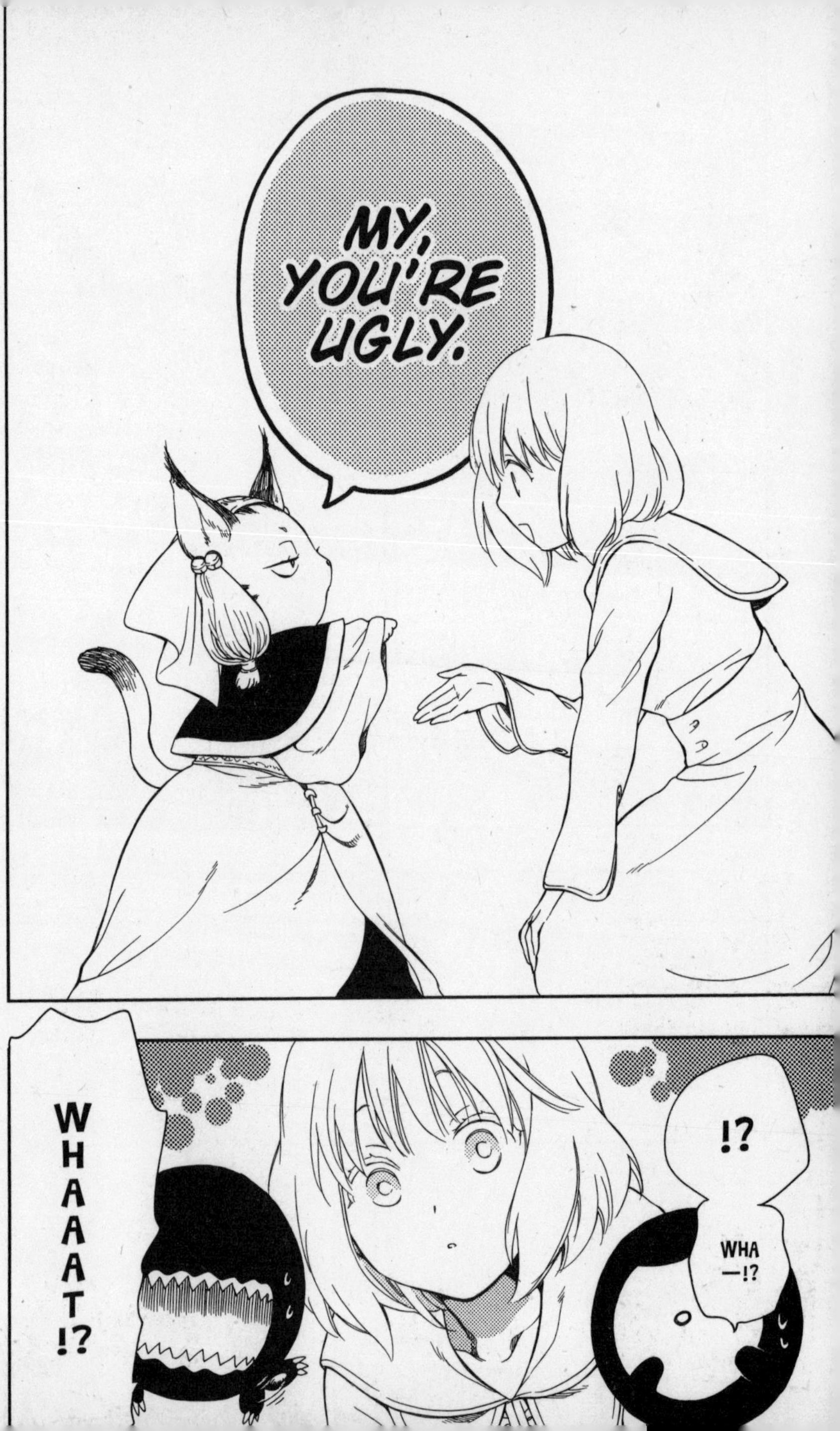
MY, YOU'RE UGLY.
!?
WHA—!?
WHAAAT!?

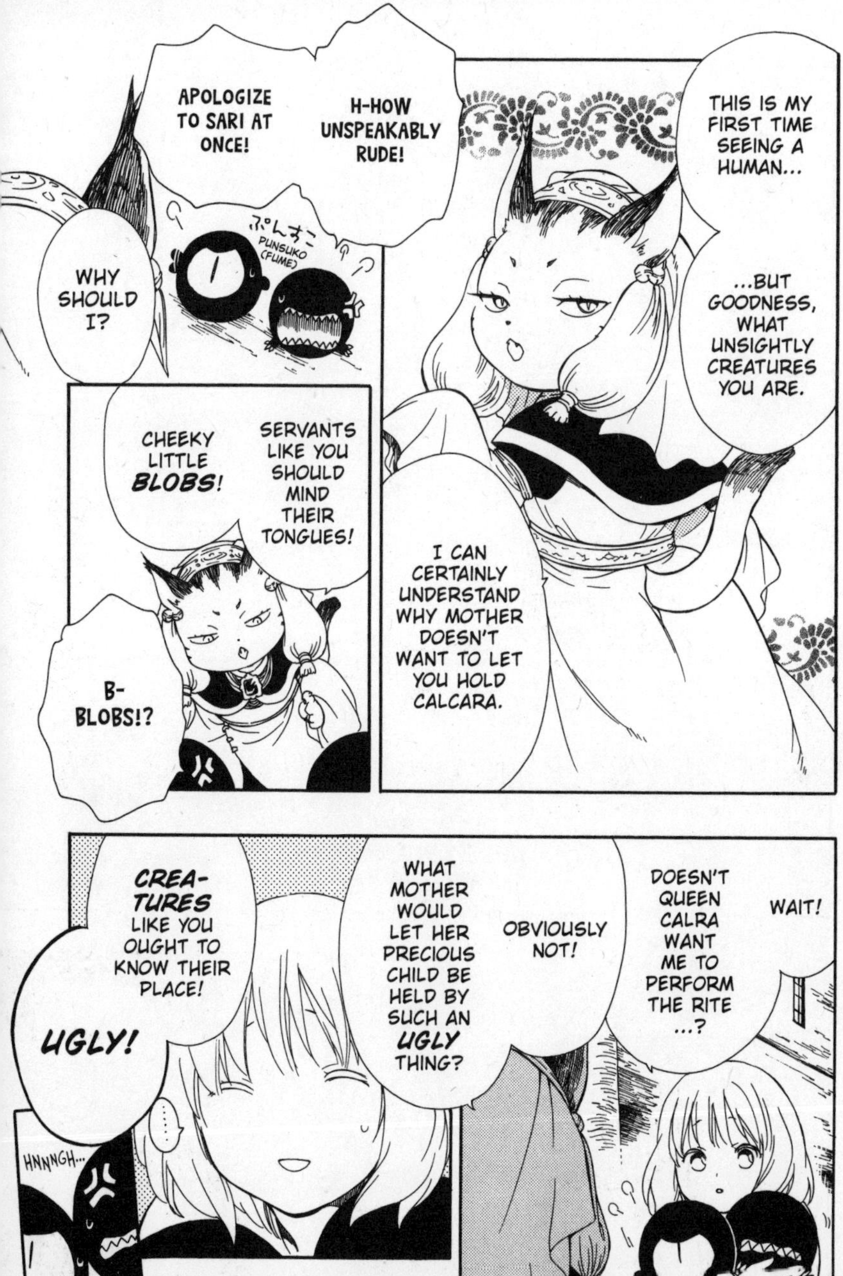
THIS IS MY FIRST TIME SEEING A HUMAN...
...BUT GOODNESS, WHAT UNSIGHTLY CREATURES YOU ARE.
I CAN CERTAINLY UNDERSTAND WHY MOTHER DOESN'T WANT TO LET YOU HOLD CALCARA.
H-HOW UNSPEAKABLY RUDE!
APOLOGIZE TO SARI AT ONCE!
ぷんすこ
PUNSUKO (FUME)
WHY SHOULD I?
SERVANTS LIKE YOU SHOULD MIND THEIR TONGUES!
CHEEKY LITTLE **BLOBS**!
B-BLOBS!?
WAIT!
DOESN'T QUEEN CALRA WANT ME TO PERFORM THE RITE ...?
OBVIOUSLY NOT!
WHAT MOTHER WOULD LET HER PRECIOUS CHILD BE HELD BY SUCH AN **UGLY** THING?
CREATURES LIKE YOU OUGHT TO KNOW THEIR PLACE!
UGLY!
...
HNNNGH...

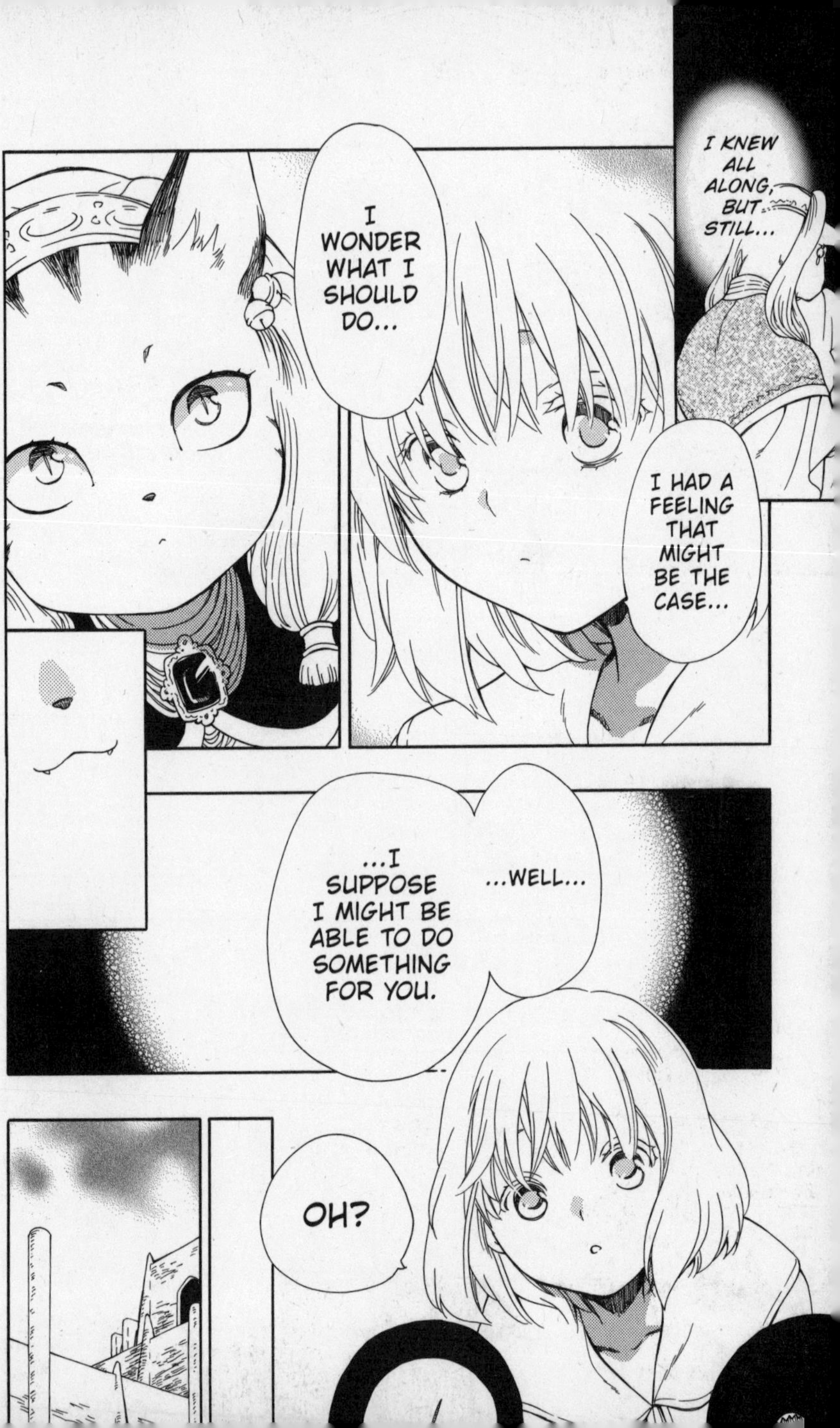
I KNEW ALL ALONG, BUT STILL...
I WONDER WHAT I SHOULD DO...
I HAD A FEELING THAT MIGHT BE THE CASE...
...WELL...
...I SUPPOSE I MIGHT BE ABLE TO DO SOMETHING FOR YOU.
OH?

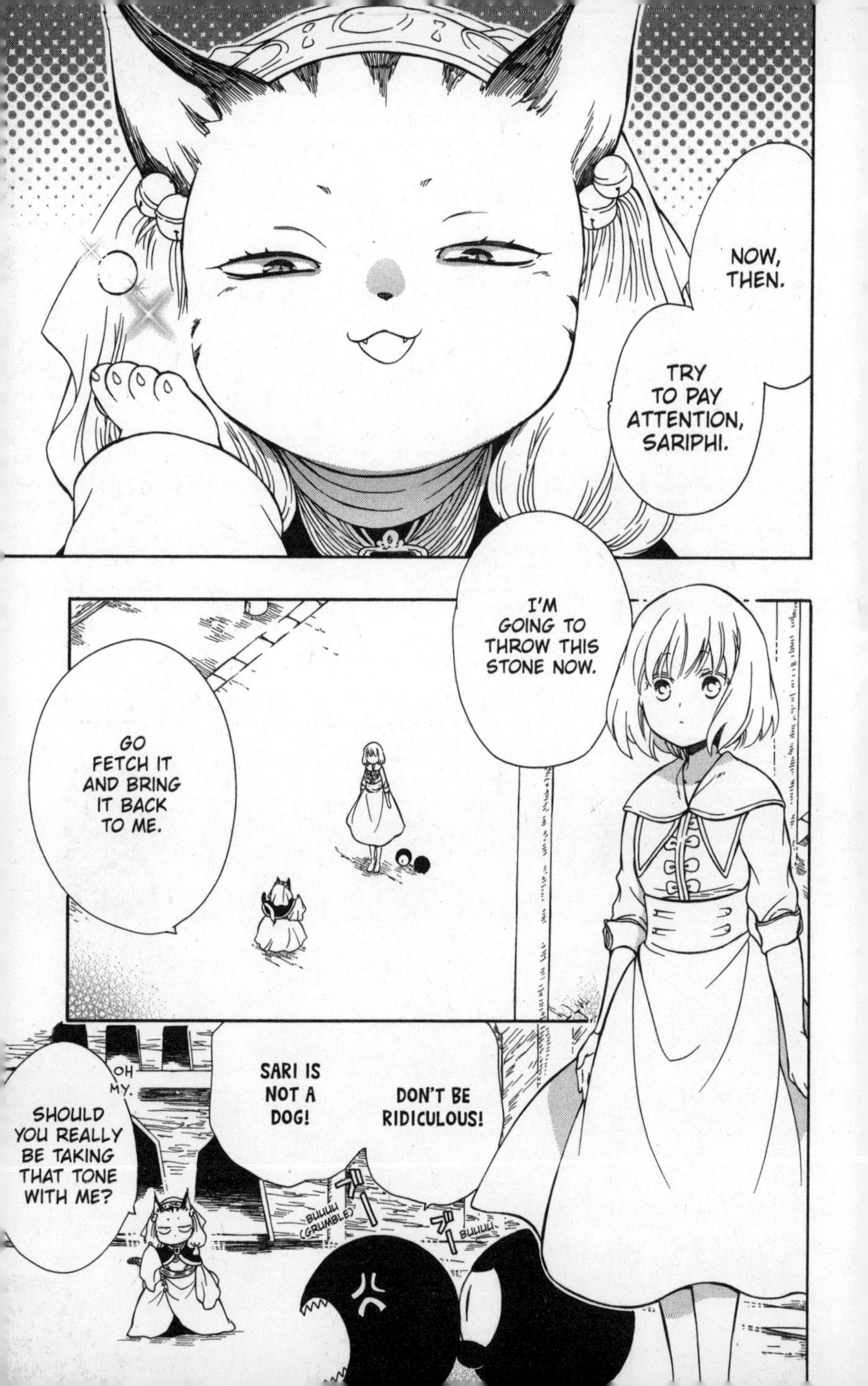
NOW, THEN.
TRY TO PAY ATTENTION, SARIPHI.
I'M GOING TO THROW THIS STONE NOW.
GO FETCH IT AND BRING IT BACK TO ME.
DON'T BE RIDICULOUS!
SARI IS NOT A DOG!
BULULU
BULULU (GRUMBLE)
OH MY.
SHOULD YOU REALLY BE TAKING THAT TONE WITH ME?

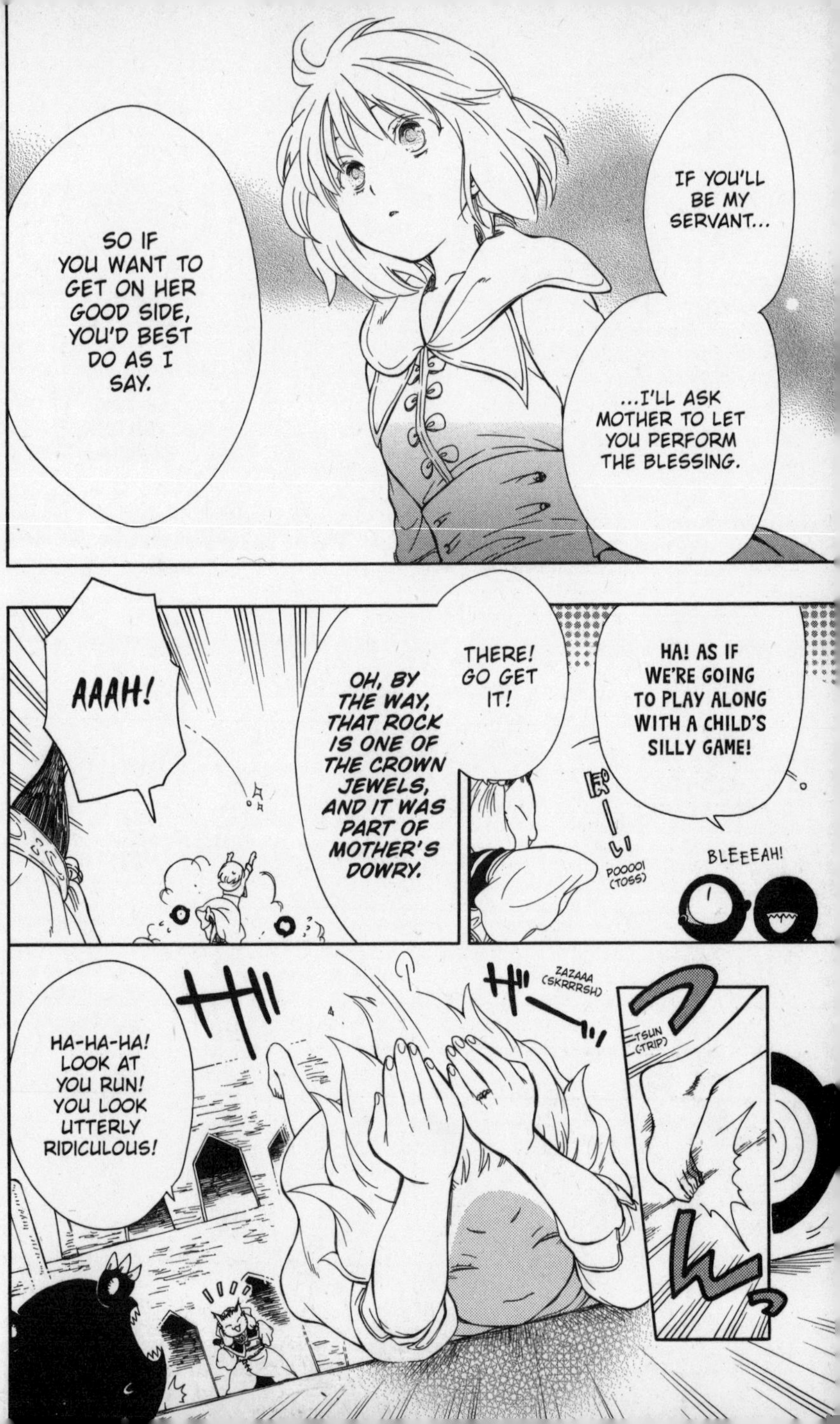
IF YOU'LL BE MY SERVANT...
...I'LL ASK MOTHER TO LET YOU PERFORM THE BLESSING.
SO IF YOU WANT TO GET ON HER GOOD SIDE, YOU'D BEST DO AS I SAY.
HA! AS IF WE'RE GOING TO PLAY ALONG WITH A CHILD'S SILLY GAME!
BLEEEAH!
ぽーい
POOOOI (TOSS)
THERE! GO GET IT!
OH, BY THE WAY, THAT ROCK IS ONE OF THE CROWN JEWELS, AND IT WAS PART OF MOTHER'S DOWRY.
AAAH!
TSUN (TRIP)
ZAZAAA (SKRRRSH)
HA-HA-HA! LOOK AT YOU RUN! YOU LOOK UTTERLY RIDICULOUS!

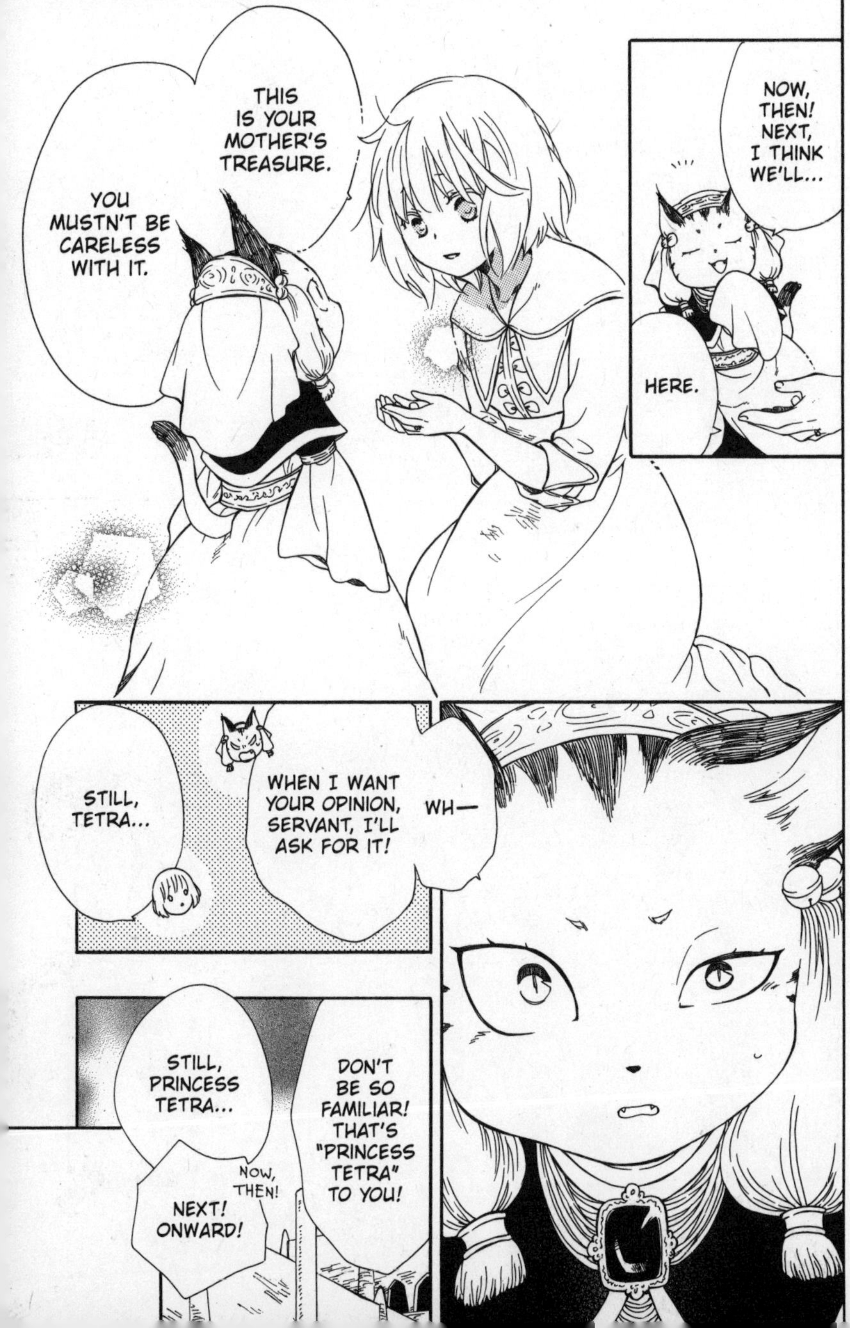
NOW, THEN! NEXT, I THINK WE'LL...
HERE.
THIS IS YOUR MOTHER'S TREASURE.
YOU MUSTN'T BE CARELESS WITH IT.
WH—
STILL, TETRA...
WHEN I WANT YOUR OPINION, SERVANT, I'LL ASK FOR IT!
STILL, PRINCESS TETRA...
DON'T BE SO FAMILIAR! THAT'S "PRINCESS TETRA" TO YOU!
NOW, THEN!
NEXT! ONWARD!

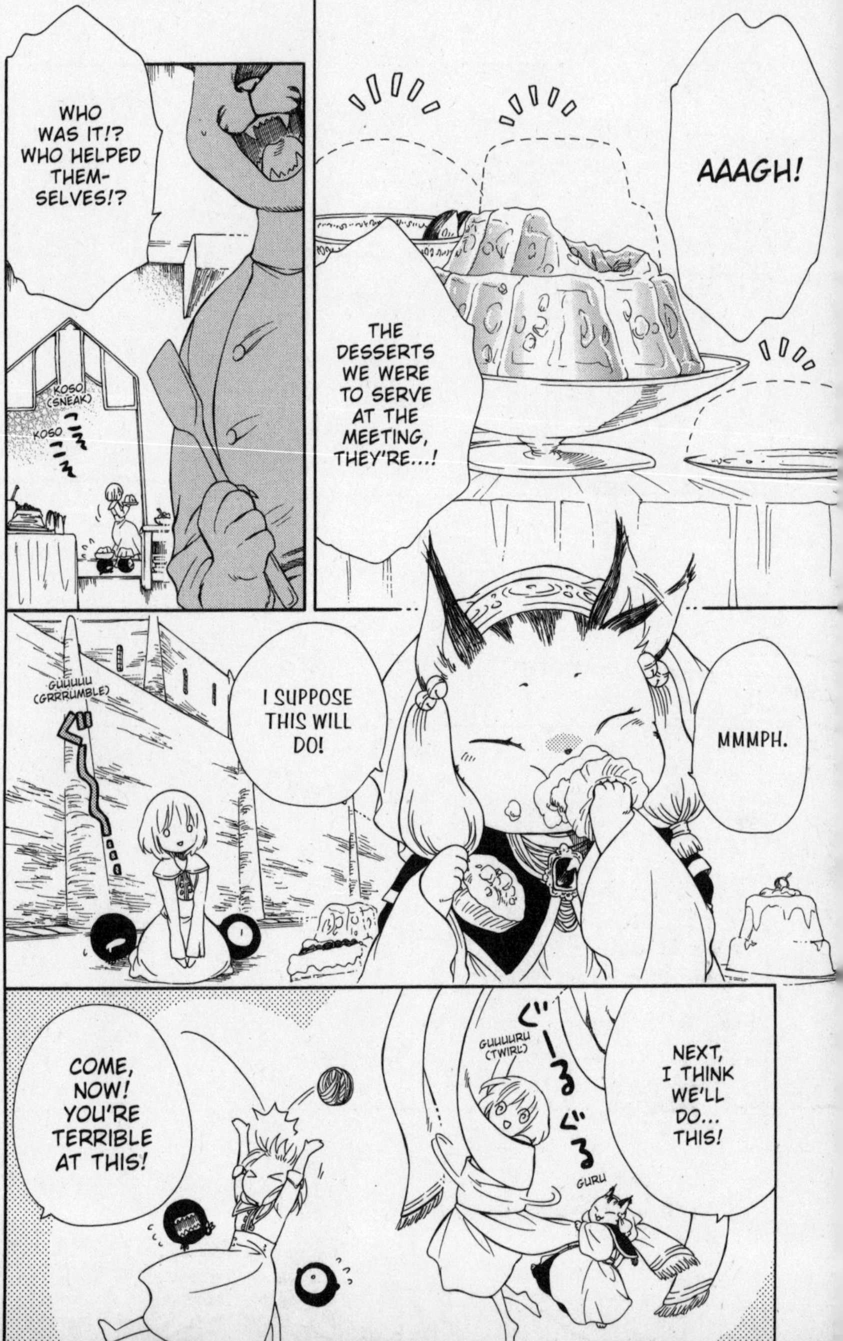
AAAGH!
THE DESSERTS WE WERE TO SERVE AT THE MEETING, THEY'RE...!
WHO WAS IT!? WHO HELPED THEM-SELVES!?
KOSO (SNEAK)
KOSO
MMMPH.
I SUPPOSE THIS WILL DO!
GUUUUU (GRRRUMBLE)
NEXT, I THINK WE'LL DO... THIS!
ぐーるぐる
GUUUURU (TWIRL)
GURU
COME, NOW! YOU'RE TERRIBLE AT THIS!

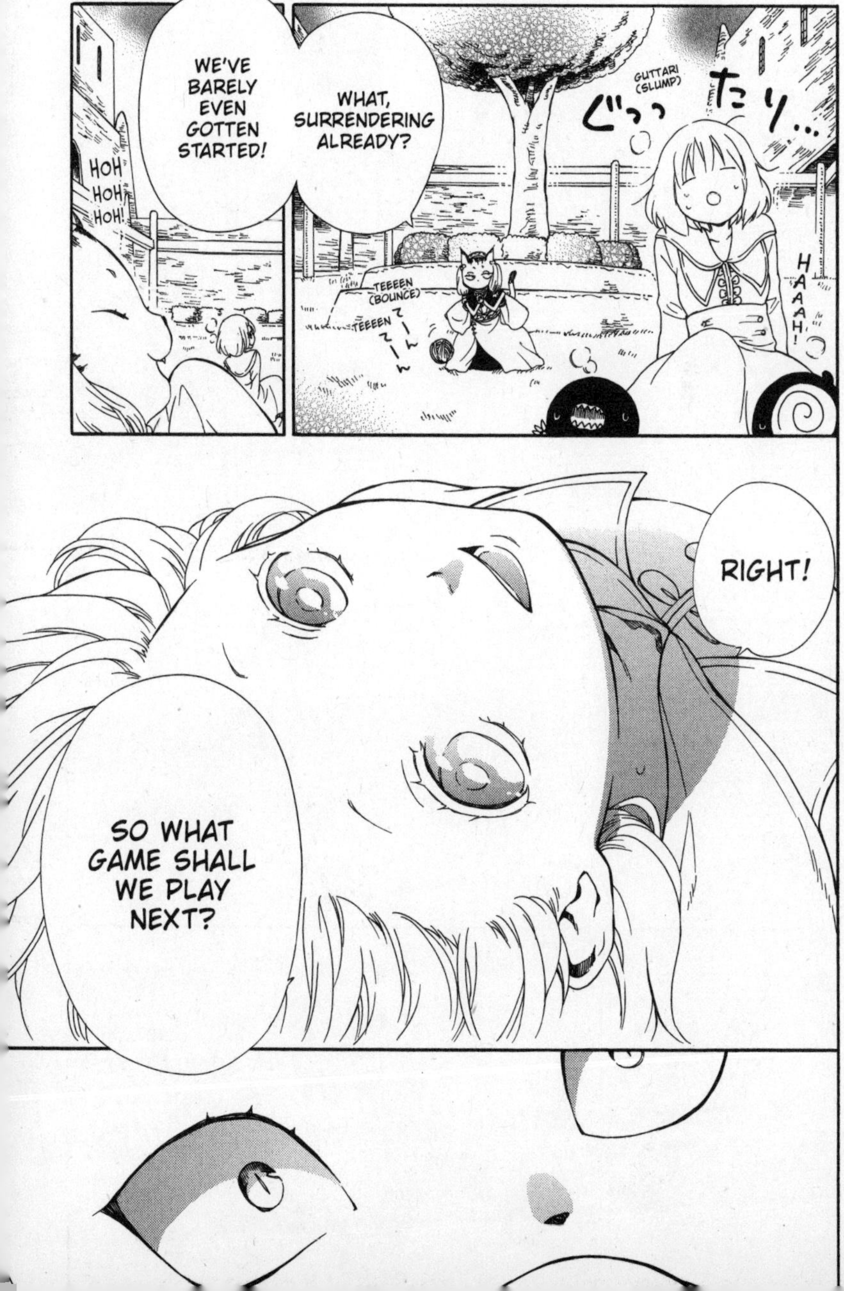
GUTTARI (SLUMP)
ぐったり…
HAAAAH!
WHAT, SURRENDERING ALREADY?
TEEEEN (BOUNCE)
TEEEEN
てーんてーん
WE'VE BARELY EVEN GOTTEN STARTED!
HOH HOH HOH!
RIGHT!
SO WHAT GAME SHALL WE PLAY NEXT?

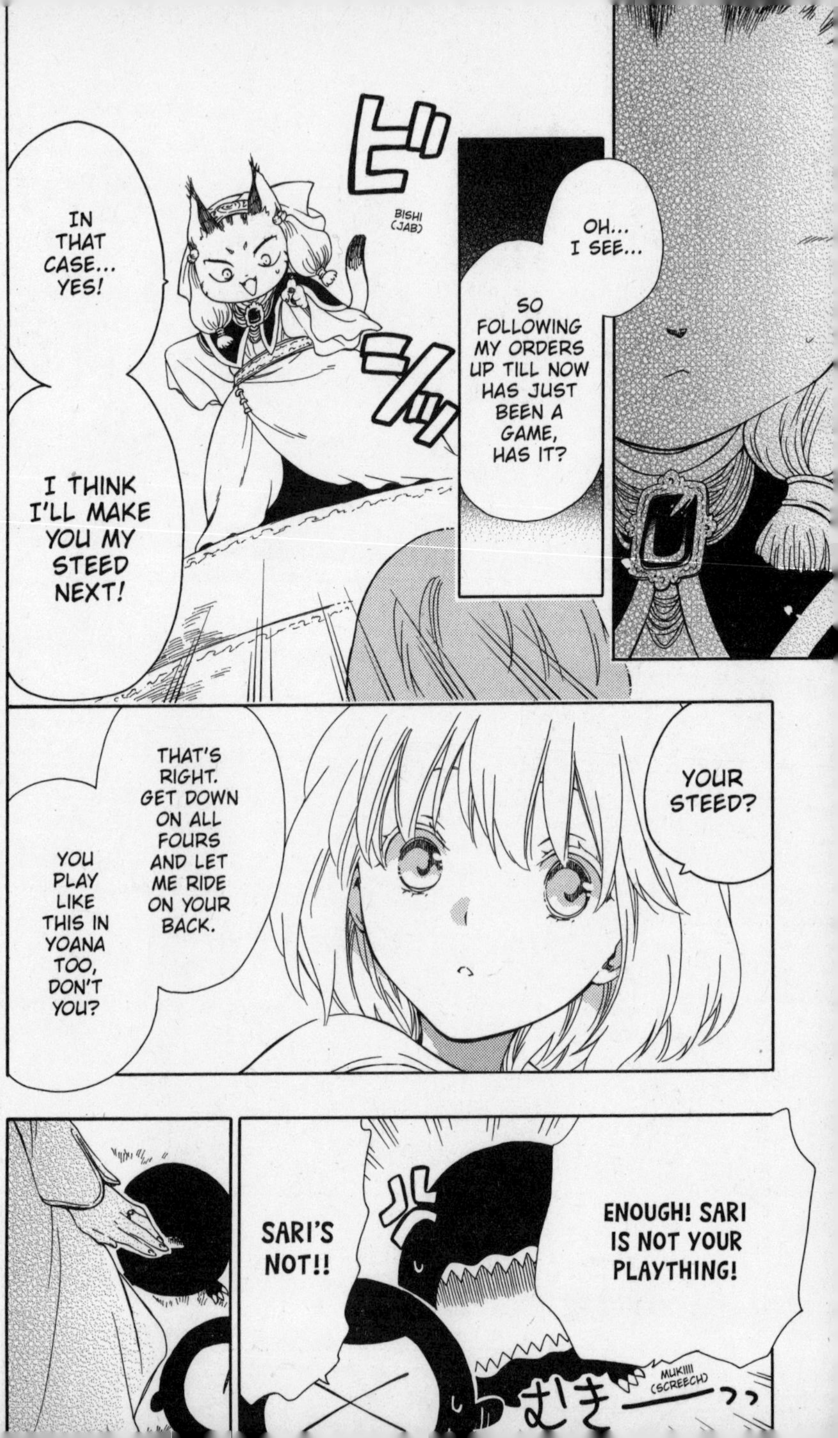
OH... I SEE...
SO FOLLOWING MY ORDERS UP TILL NOW HAS JUST BEEN A GAME, HAS IT?
BISHI (JAB)
IN THAT CASE... YES!
I THINK I'LL MAKE YOU MY STEED NEXT!
YOUR STEED?
THAT'S RIGHT. GET DOWN ON ALL FOURS AND LET ME RIDE ON YOUR BACK.
YOU PLAY LIKE THIS IN YOANA TOO, DON'T YOU?
ENOUGH! SARI IS NOT YOUR PLAYTHING!
SARI'S NOT!!
MUKIIII (SCREECH)

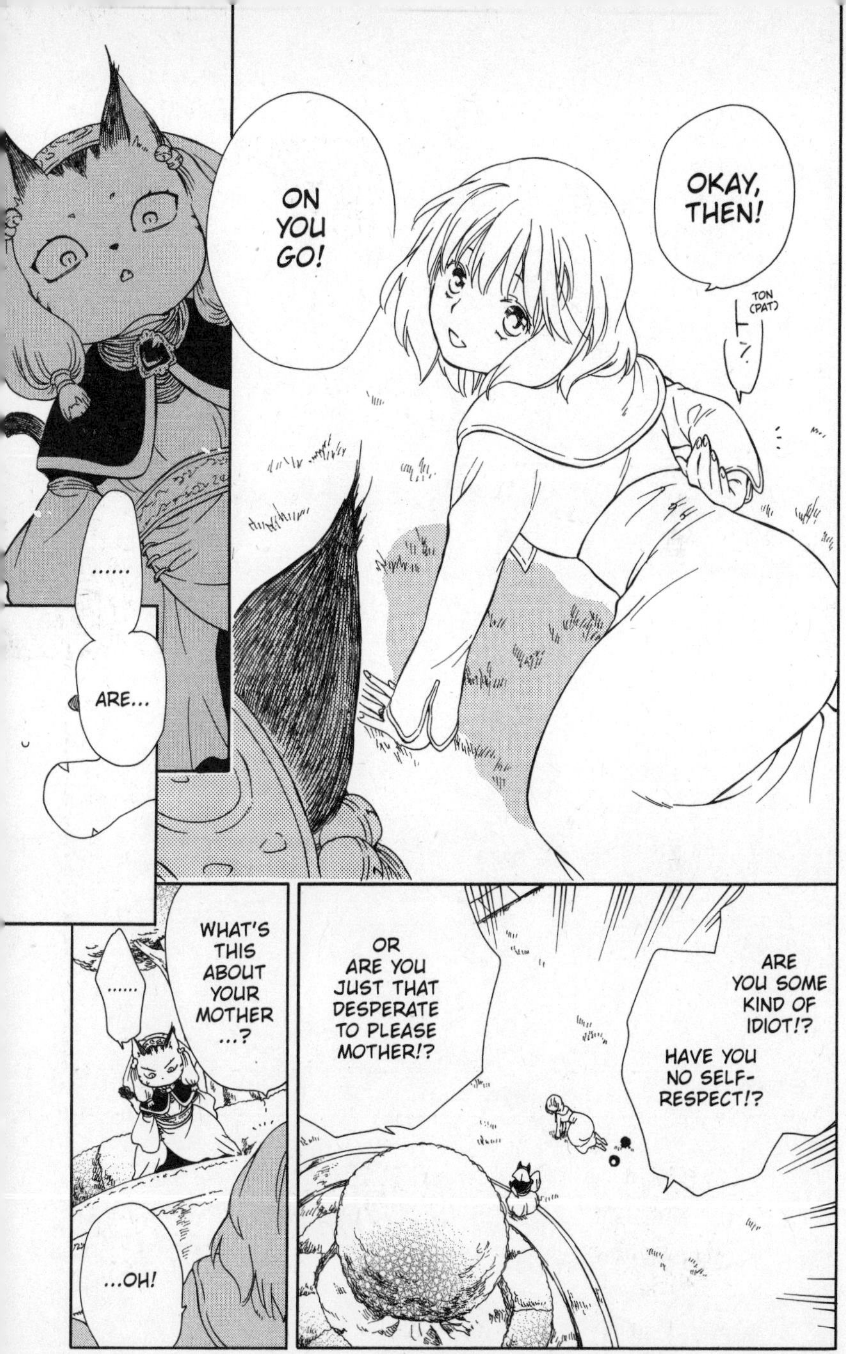
OKAY, THEN!
TON (PAT)
ON YOU GO!
......
ARE...
ARE YOU SOME KIND OF IDIOT!?
HAVE YOU NO SELF-RESPECT!?
OR ARE YOU JUST THAT DESPERATE TO PLEASE MOTHER!?
WHAT'S THIS ABOUT YOUR MOTHER ...?
......
...OH!

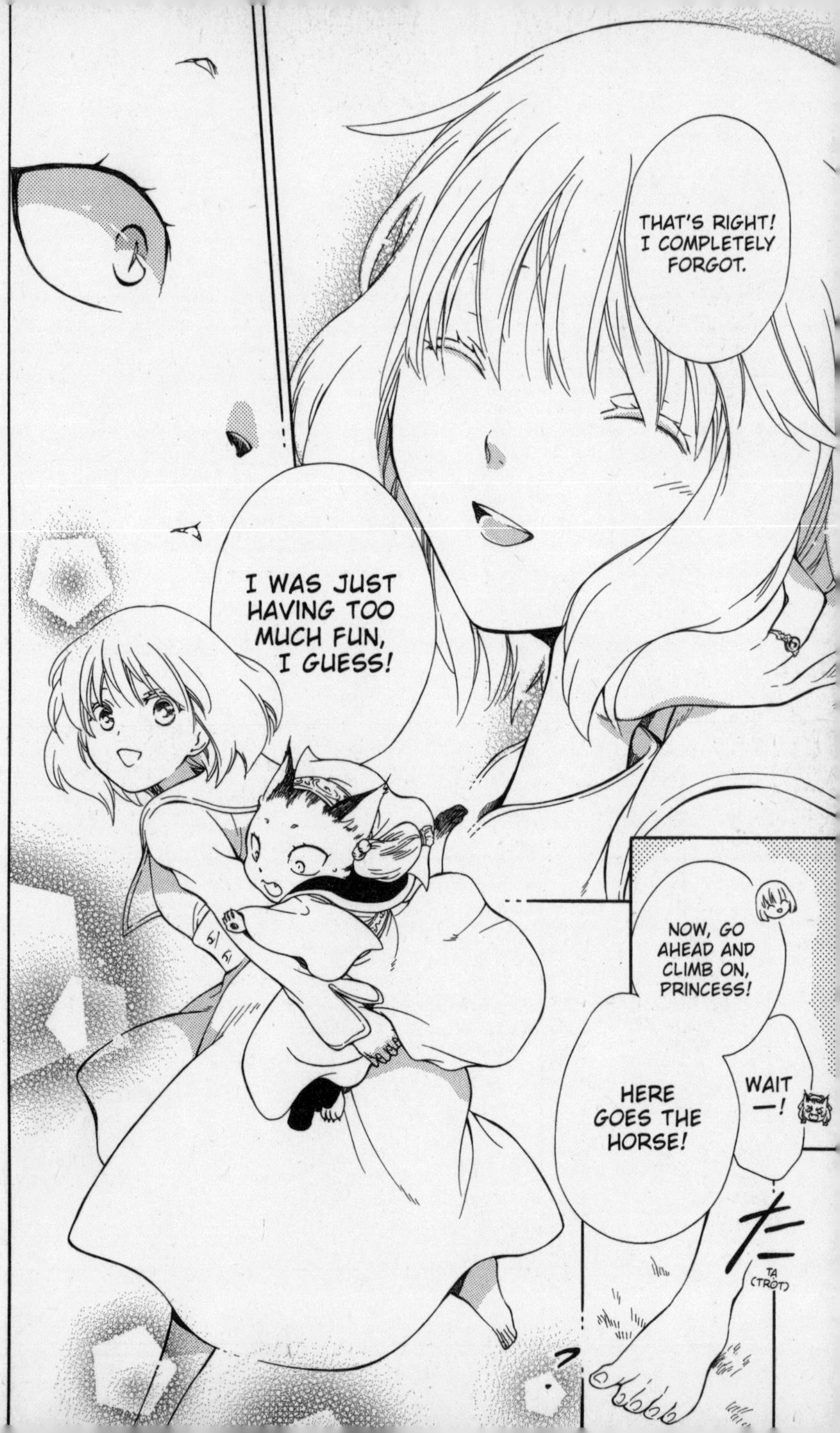
THAT'S RIGHT! I COMPLETELY FORGOT.
I WAS JUST HAVING TOO MUCH FUN, I GUESS!
NOW, GO AHEAD AND CLIMB ON, PRINCESS!
WAIT—!
HERE GOES THE HORSE!
TA (TROT)

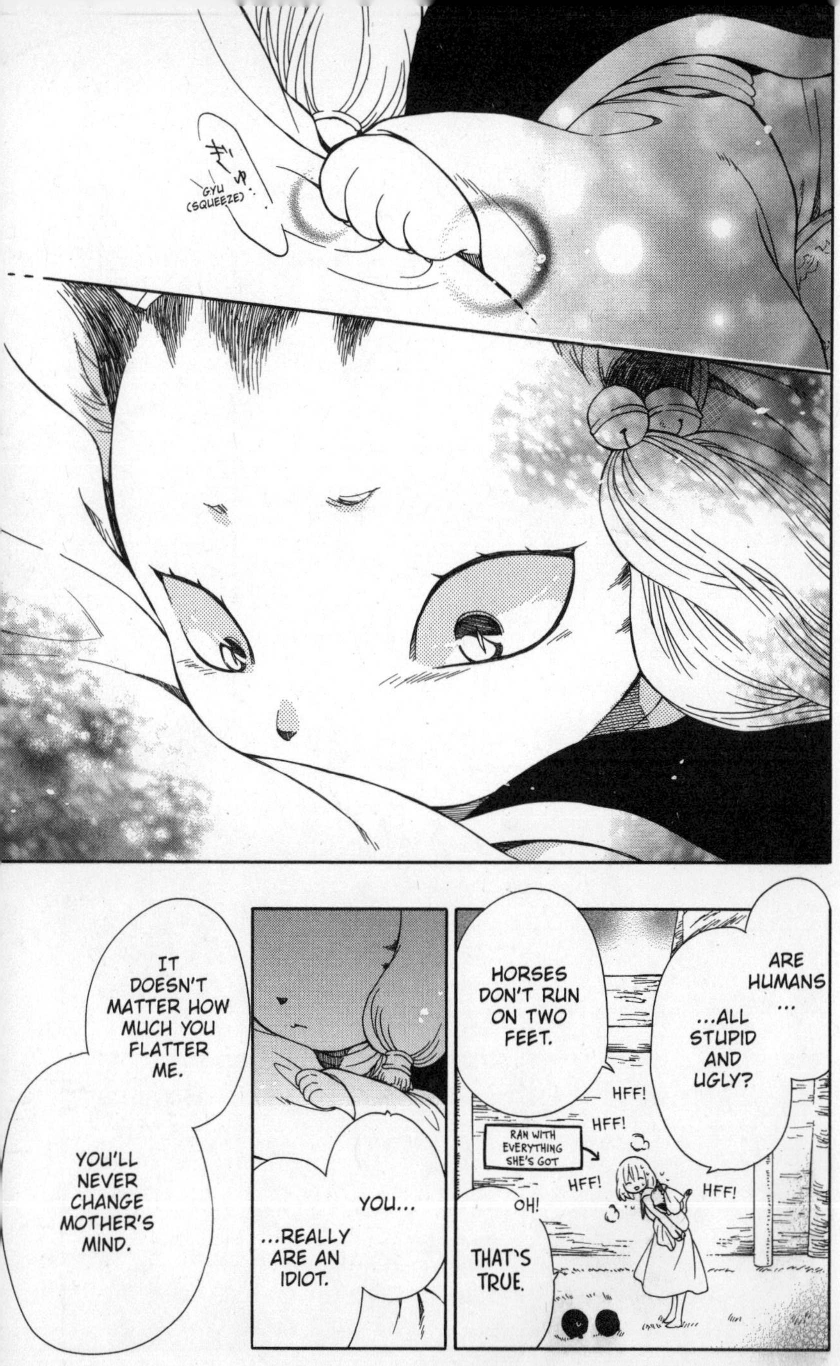
GYU (SQUEEZE)
ARE HUMANS...
...ALL STUPID AND UGLY?
HORSES DON'T RUN ON TWO FEET.
HFF!
HFF!
HFF!
HFF!
RAN WITH EVERYTHING SHE'S GOT
OH!
THAT'S TRUE.
YOU...
...REALLY ARE AN IDIOT.
IT DOESN'T MATTER HOW MUCH YOU FLATTER ME.
YOU'LL NEVER CHANGE MOTHER'S MIND.

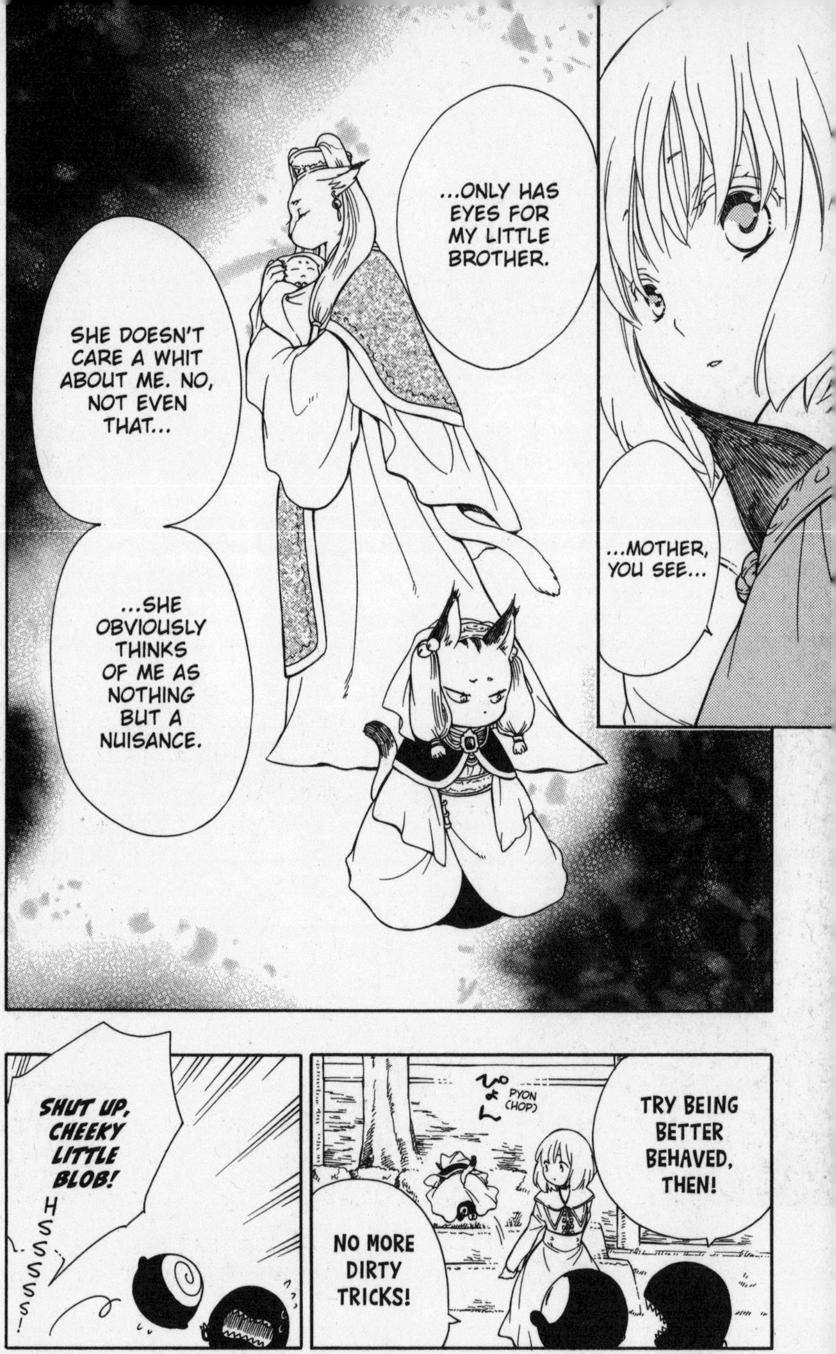
...MOTHER, YOU SEE...
...ONLY HAS EYES FOR MY LITTLE BROTHER.
SHE DOESN'T CARE A WHIT ABOUT ME. NO, NOT EVEN THAT...
...SHE OBVIOUSLY THINKS OF ME AS NOTHING BUT A NUISANCE.
TRY BEING BETTER BEHAVED, THEN!
ぴょん
PYON (HOP)
NO MORE DIRTY TRICKS!
SHUT UP, CHEEKY LITTLE BLOB!
HSSSSSS!

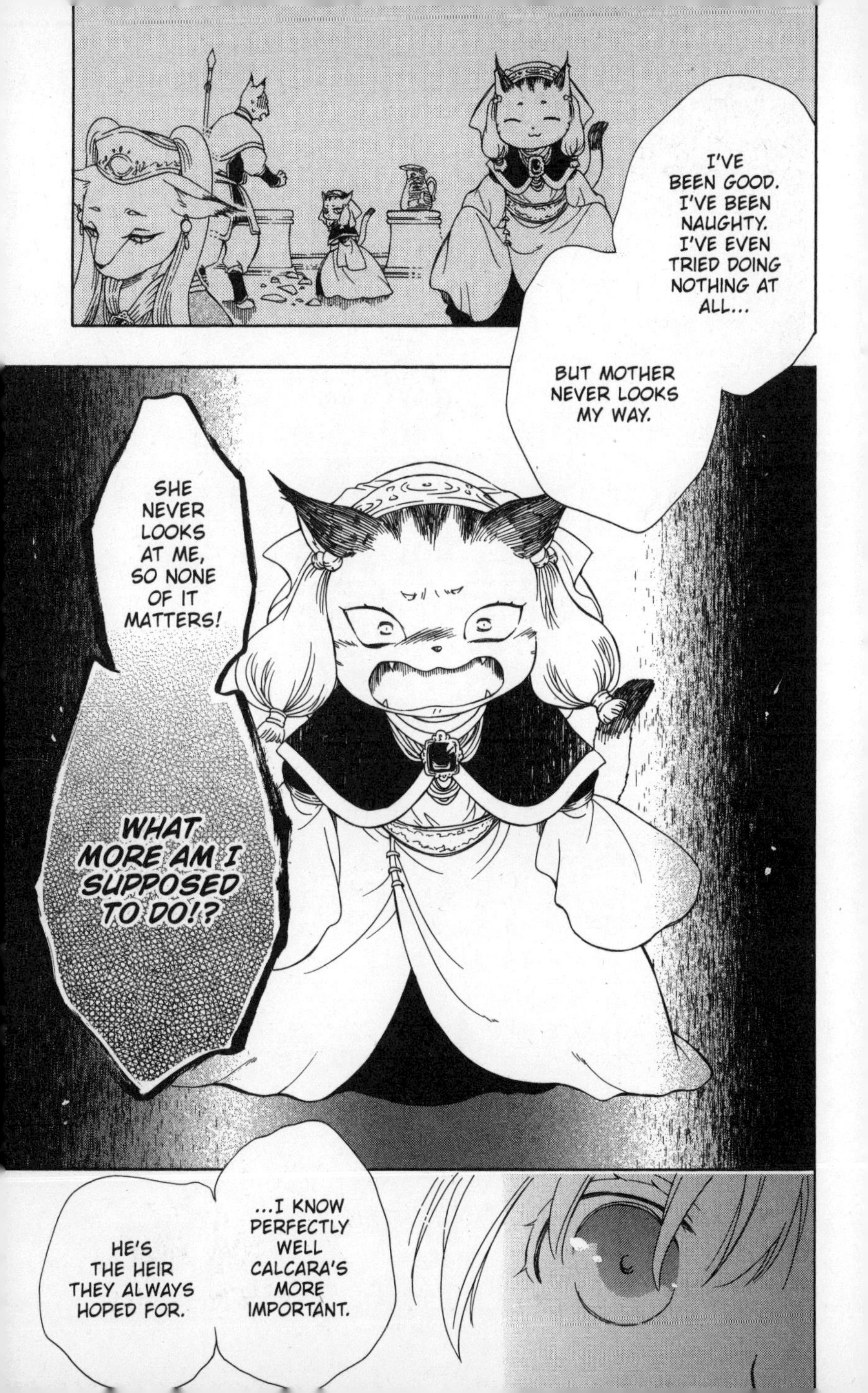
I'VE BEEN GOOD. I'VE BEEN NAUGHTY. I'VE EVEN TRIED DOING NOTHING AT ALL...
BUT MOTHER NEVER LOOKS MY WAY.
SHE NEVER LOOKS AT ME, SO NONE OF IT MATTERS!
WHAT MORE AM I SUPPOSED TO DO!?
...I KNOW PERFECTLY WELL CALCARA'S MORE IMPORTANT.
HE'S THE HEIR THEY ALWAYS HOPED FOR.

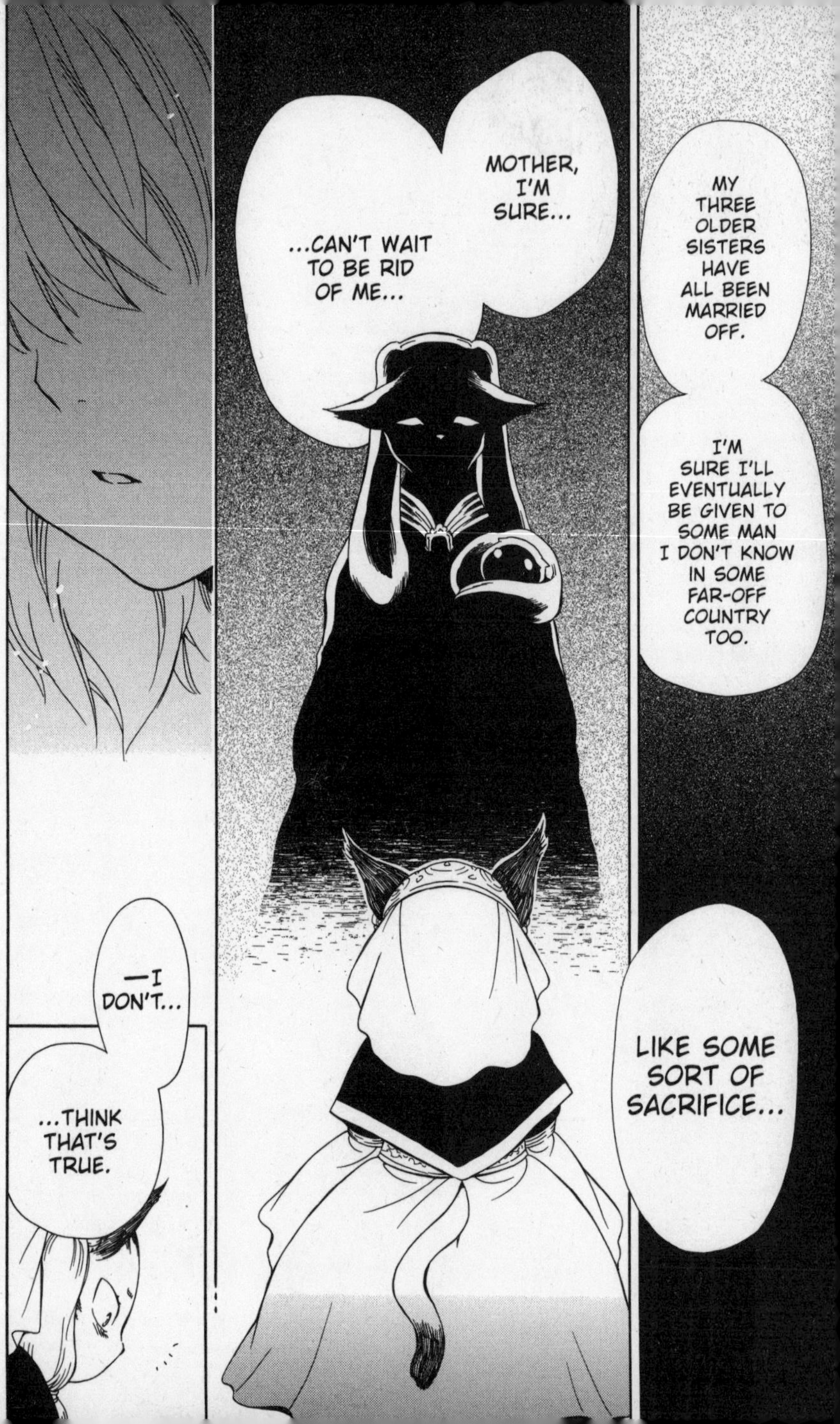
MY THREE OLDER SISTERS HAVE ALL BEEN MARRIED OFF.
I'M SURE I'LL EVENTUALLY BE GIVEN TO SOME MAN I DON'T KNOW IN SOME FAR-OFF COUNTRY TOO.
LIKE SOME SORT OF SACRIFICE...
MOTHER, I'M SURE...
...CAN'T WAIT TO BE RID OF ME...
—I DON'T...
...THINK THAT'S TRUE.

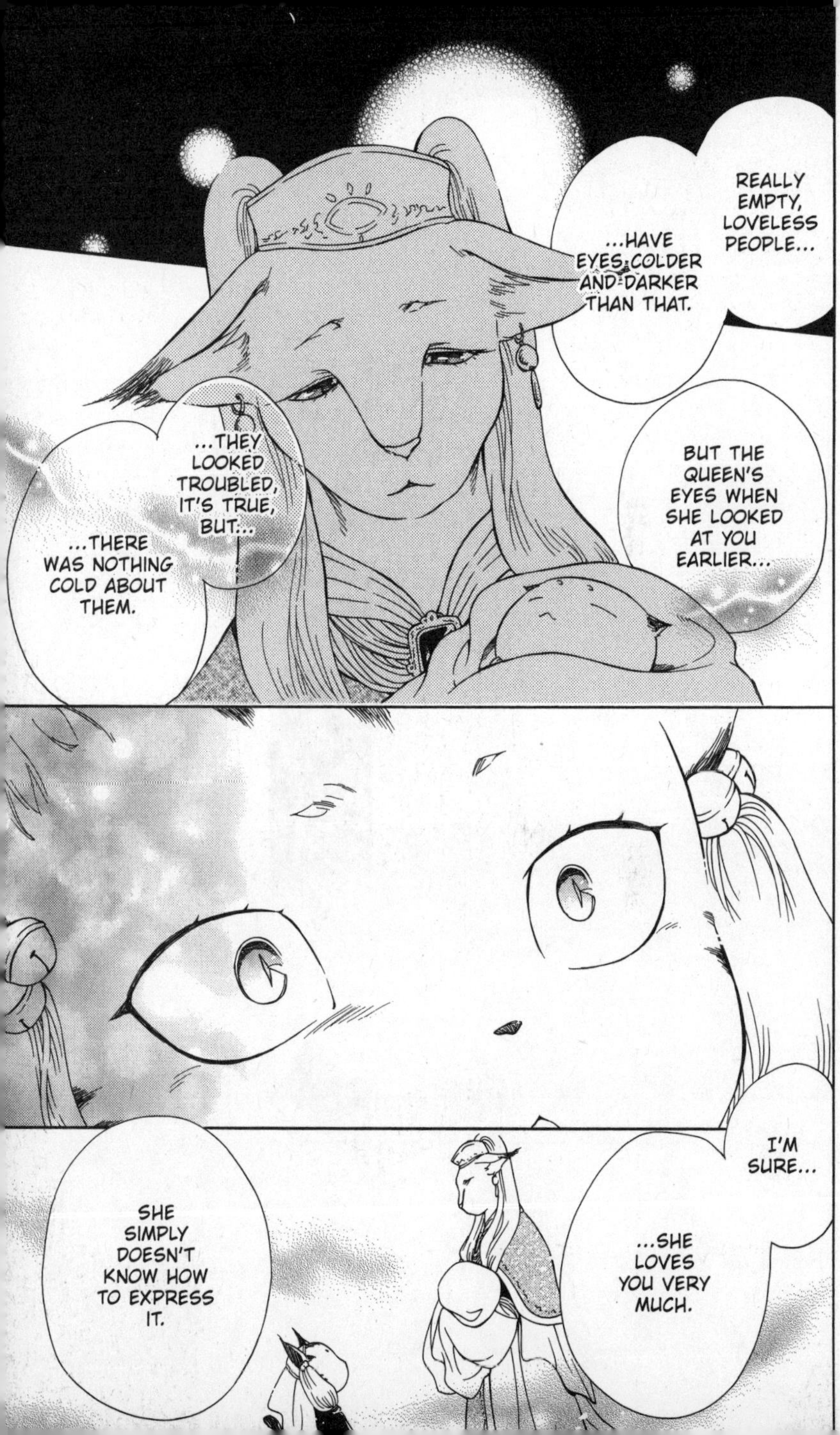
REALLY EMPTY, LOVELESS PEOPLE...
...HAVE EYES COLDER AND DARKER THAN THAT.
BUT THE QUEEN'S EYES WHEN SHE LOOKED AT YOU EARLIER...
...THEY LOOKED TROUBLED, IT'S TRUE, BUT...
...THERE WAS NOTHING COLD ABOUT THEM.
I'M SURE...
...SHE LOVES YOU VERY MUCH.
SHE SIMPLY DOESN'T KNOW HOW TO EXPRESS IT.

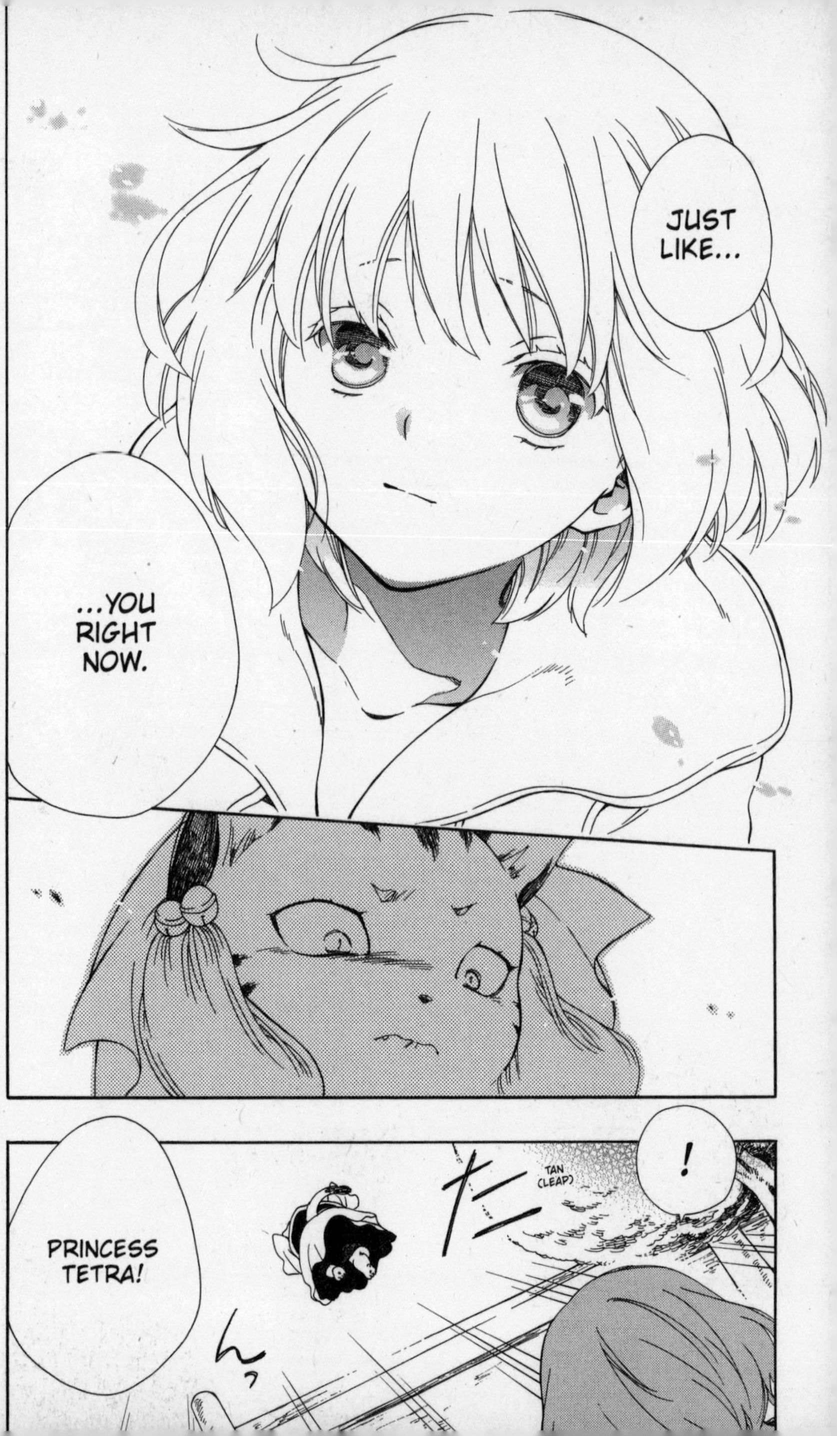
JUST LIKE...
...YOU RIGHT NOW.
!
TAN (LEAP)
PRINCESS TETRA!

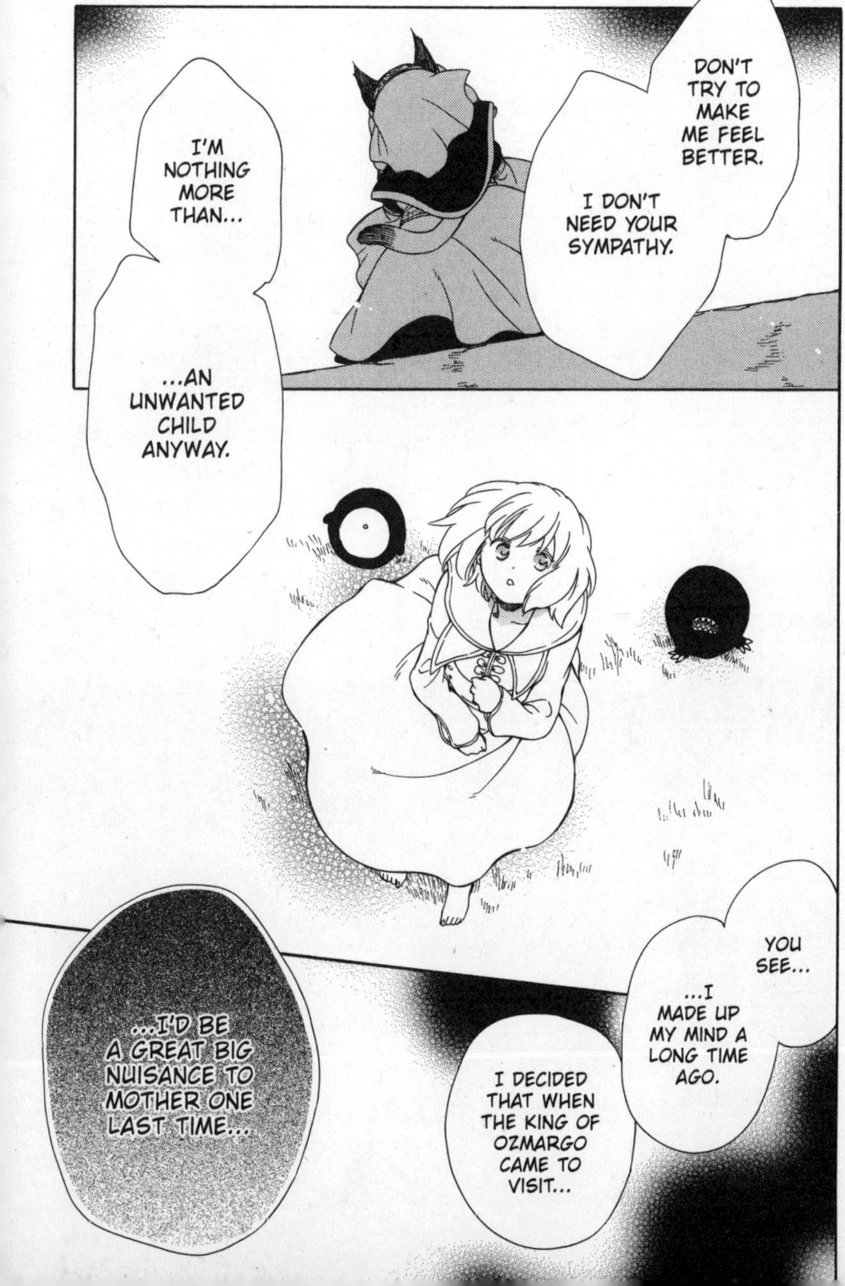
DON'T TRY TO MAKE ME FEEL BETTER.
I DON'T NEED YOUR SYMPATHY.
I'M NOTHING MORE THAN...
...AN UNWANTED CHILD ANYWAY.
YOU SEE...
...I MADE UP MY MIND A LONG TIME AGO.
I DECIDED THAT WHEN THE KING OF OZMARGO CAME TO VISIT...
...I'D BE A GREAT BIG NUISANCE TO MOTHER ONE LAST TIME...

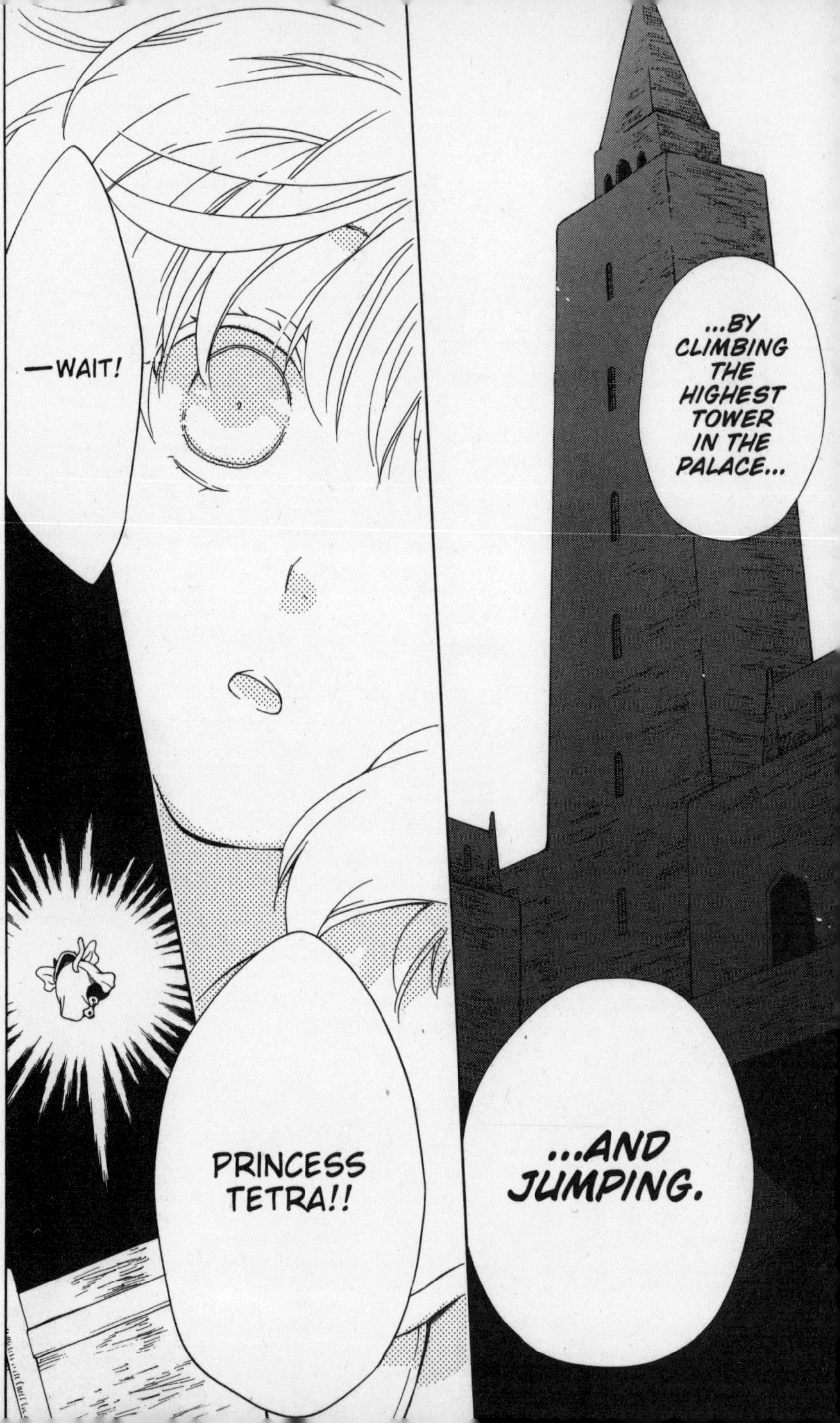
...BY CLIMBING THE HIGHEST TOWER IN THE PALACE...
...AND JUMPING.
—WAIT!
PRINCESS TETRA!!

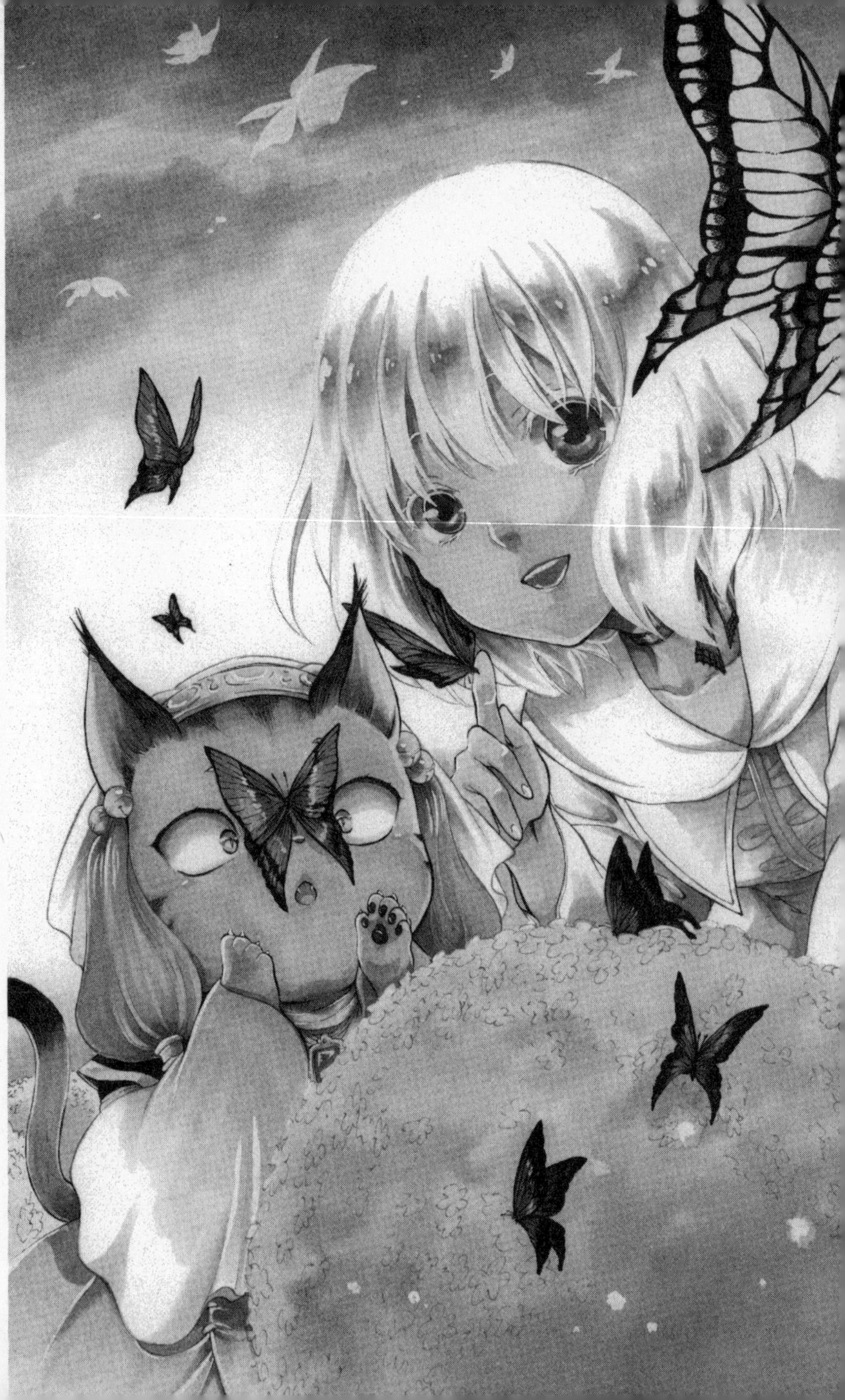

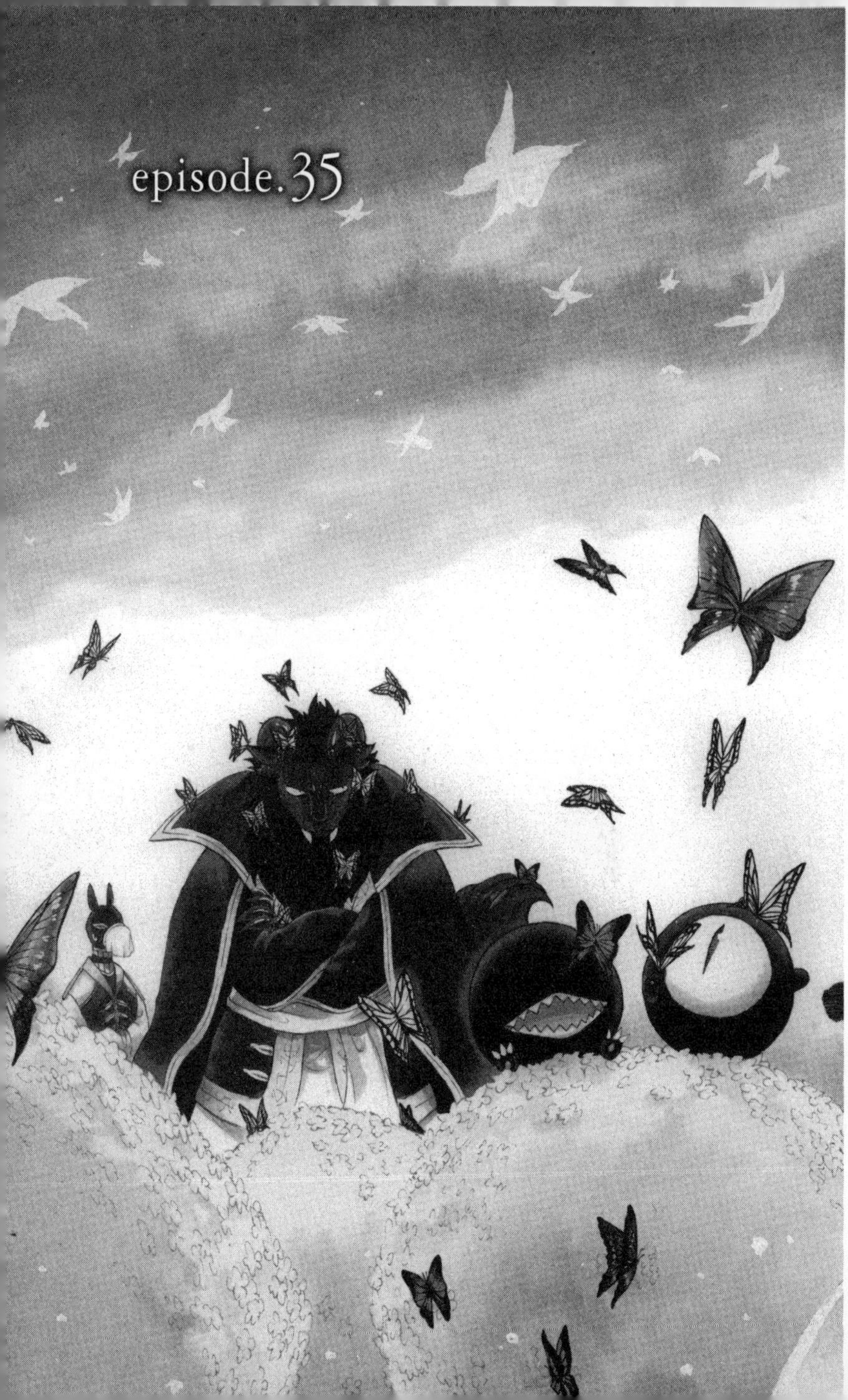
episode.35

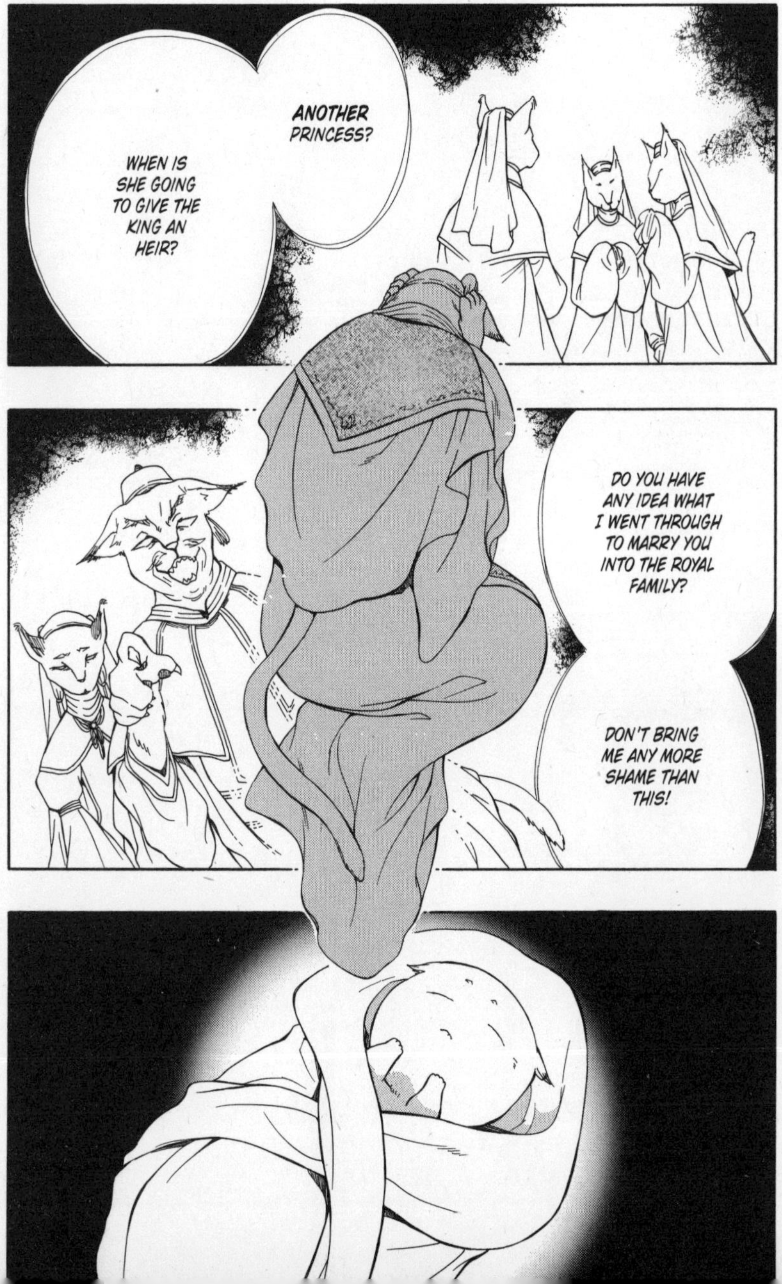
ANOTHER PRINCESS?
WHEN IS SHE GOING TO GIVE THE KING AN HEIR?
DO YOU HAVE ANY IDEA WHAT I WENT THROUGH TO MARRY YOU INTO THE ROYAL FAMILY?
DON'T BRING ME ANY MORE SHAME THAN THIS!

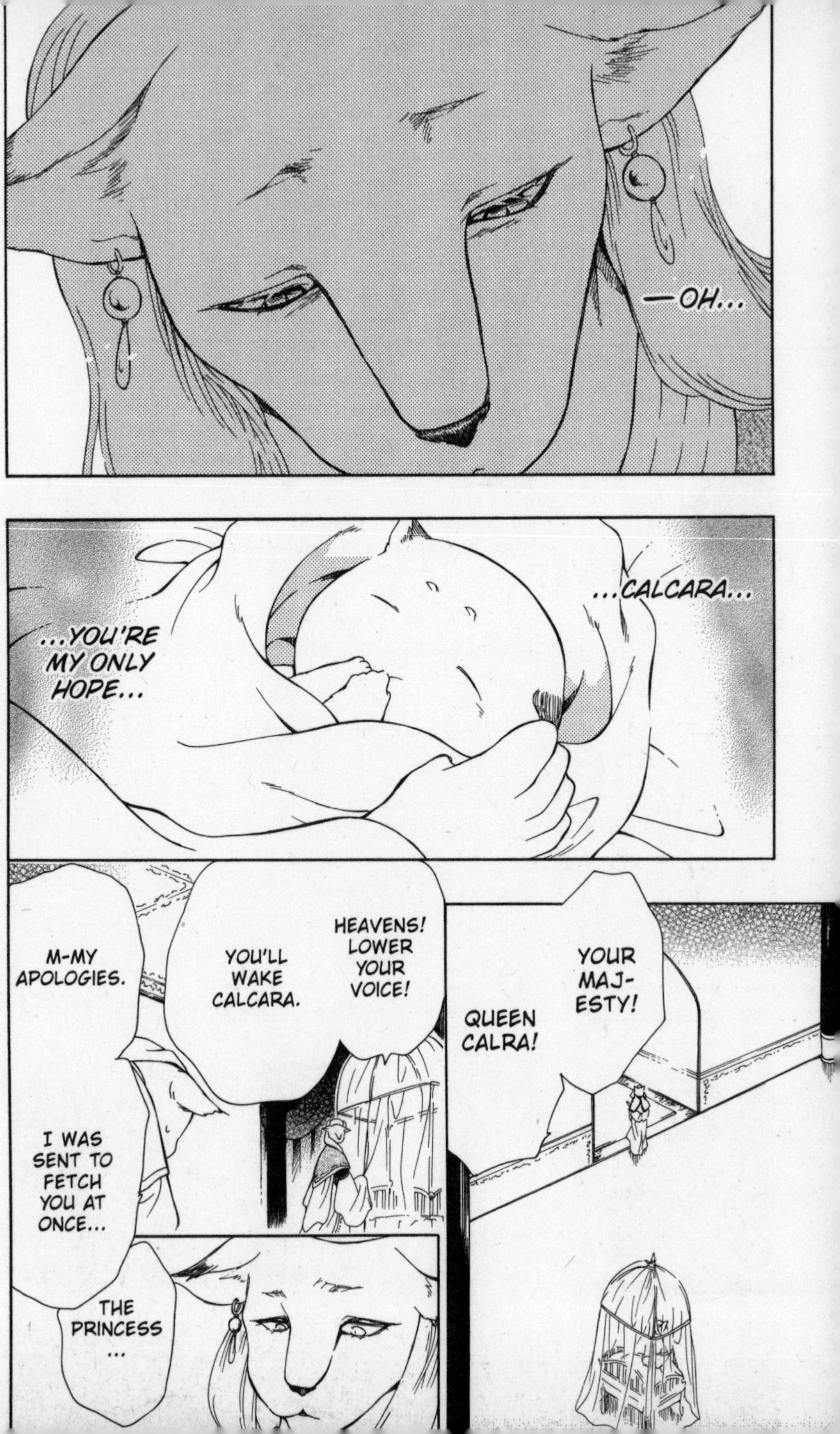
—OH...
...CALCARA...
...YOU'RE MY ONLY HOPE...
YOUR MAJ-ESTY!
QUEEN CALRA!
HEAVENS! LOWER YOUR VOICE!
YOU'LL WAKE CALCARA.
M-MY APOLOGIES.
I WAS SENT TO FETCH YOU AT ONCE...
THE PRINCESS ...

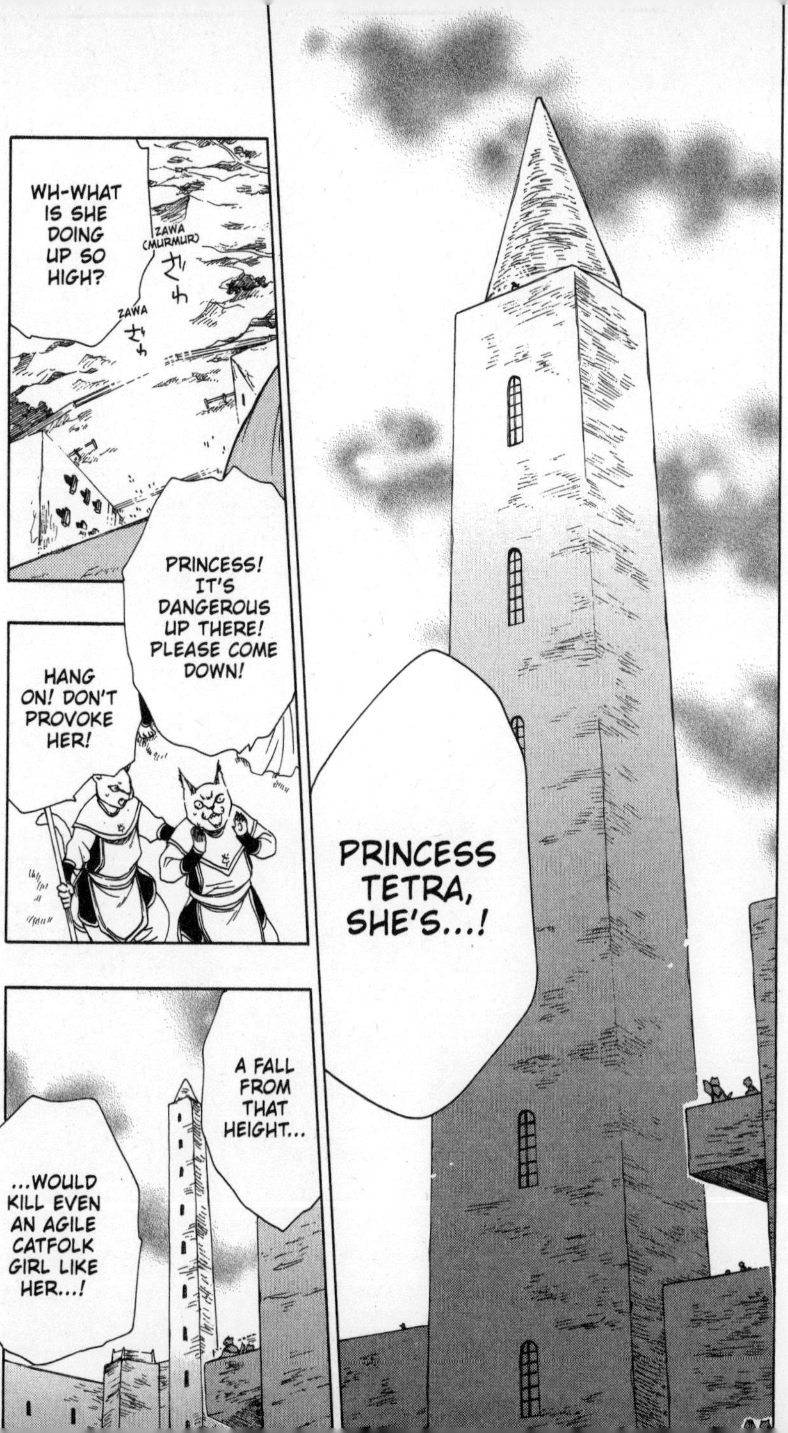
PRINCESS TETRA, SHE'S...!
WH-WHAT IS SHE DOING UP SO HIGH?
ZAWA (MURMUR)
ざわ
ZAWA
ざわ
PRINCESS! IT'S DANGEROUS UP THERE! PLEASE COME DOWN!
HANG ON! DON'T PROVOKE HER!
A FALL FROM THAT HEIGHT...
...WOULD KILL EVEN AN AGILE CATFOLK GIRL LIKE HER...!

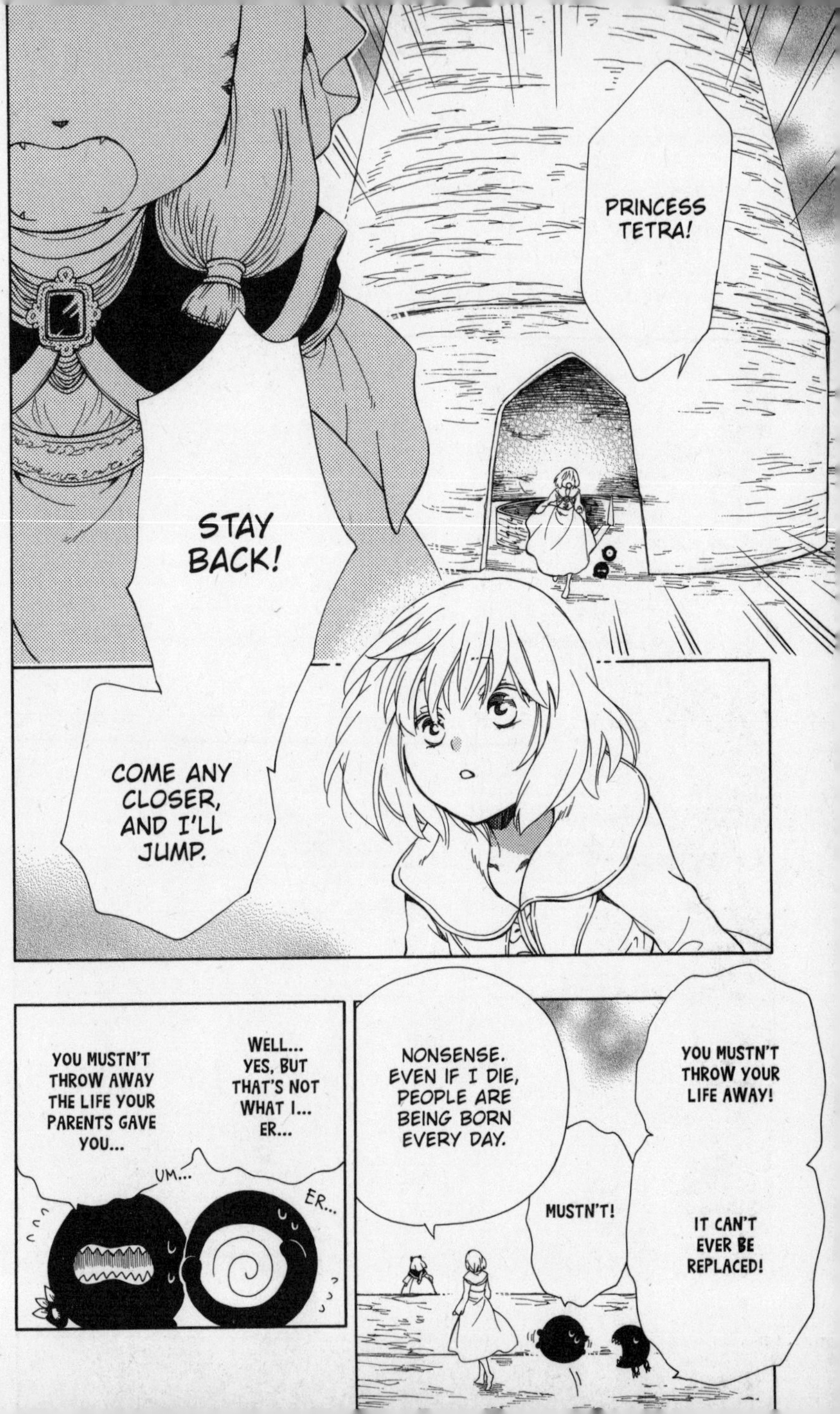
PRINCESS TETRA!
STAY BACK!
COME ANY CLOSER, AND I'LL JUMP.
YOU MUSTN'T THROW YOUR LIFE AWAY!
IT CAN'T EVER BE REPLACED!
MUSTN'T!
NONSENSE. EVEN IF I DIE, PEOPLE ARE BEING BORN EVERY DAY.
WELL... YES, BUT THAT'S NOT WHAT I... ER...
YOU MUSTN'T THROW AWAY THE LIFE YOUR PARENTS GAVE YOU...
ER...
UM...

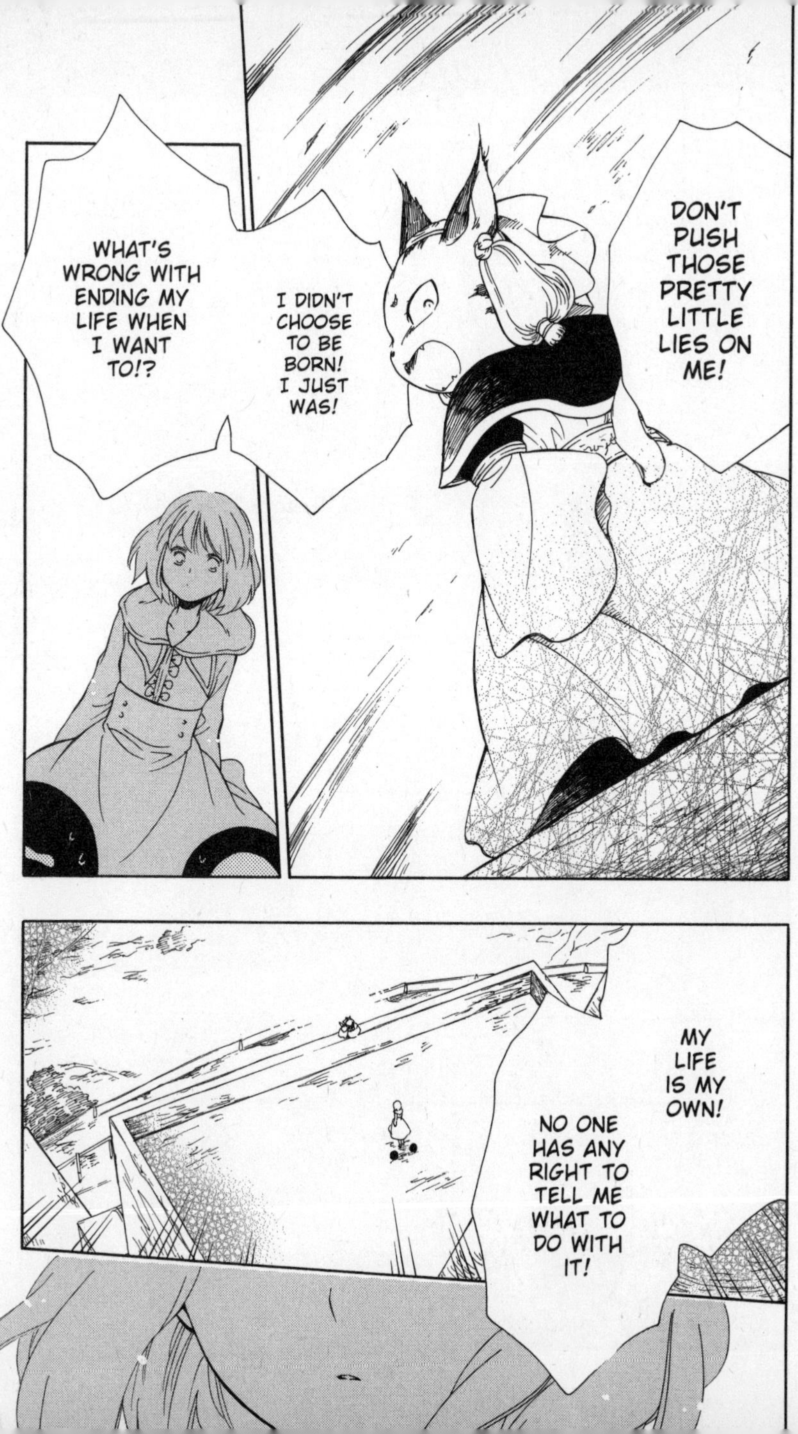
DON'T PUSH THOSE PRETTY LITTLE LIES ON ME!
I DIDN'T CHOOSE TO BE BORN! I JUST WAS!
WHAT'S WRONG WITH ENDING MY LIFE WHEN I WANT TO!?
MY LIFE IS MY OWN!
NO ONE HAS ANY RIGHT TO TELL ME WHAT TO DO WITH IT!

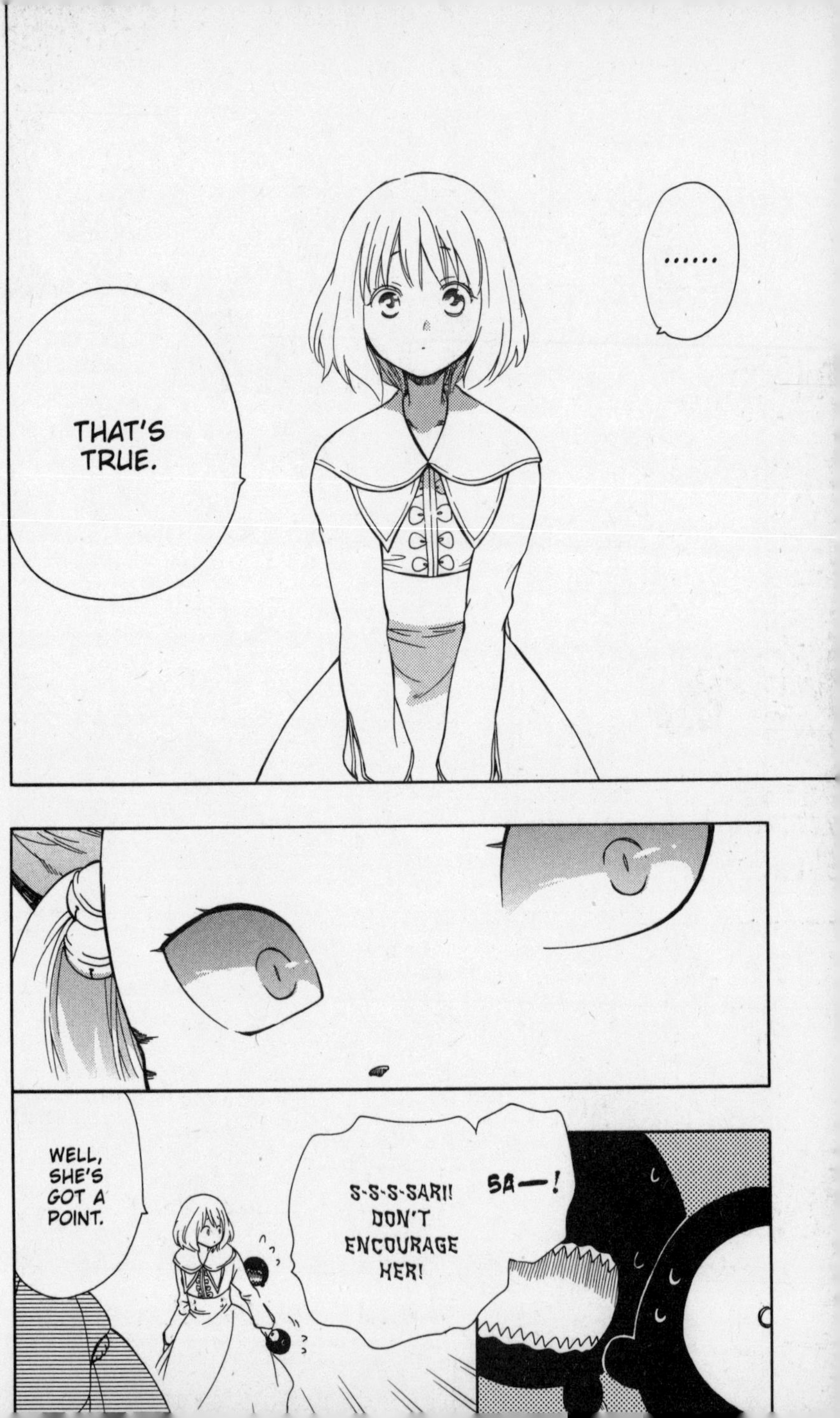
......
THAT'S TRUE.
SA—!
S-S-S-SARI! DON'T ENCOURAGE HER!
WELL, SHE'S GOT A POINT.

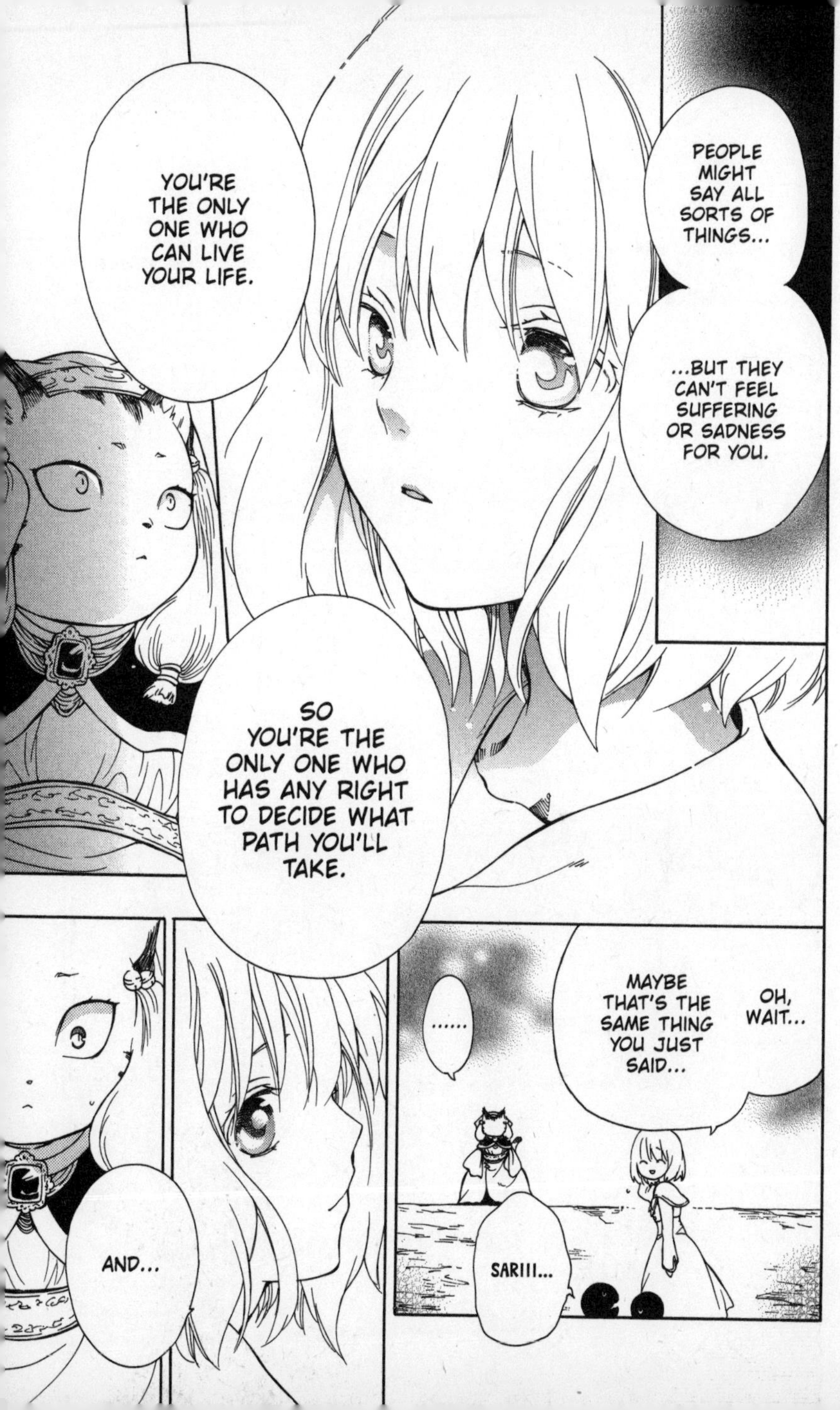
PEOPLE MIGHT SAY ALL SORTS OF THINGS...
...BUT THEY CAN'T FEEL SUFFERING OR SADNESS FOR YOU.
YOU'RE THE ONLY ONE WHO CAN LIVE YOUR LIFE.
SO YOU'RE THE ONLY ONE WHO HAS ANY RIGHT TO DECIDE WHAT PATH YOU'LL TAKE.
OH, WAIT...
MAYBE THAT'S THE SAME THING YOU JUST SAID...
......
SARIII...
AND...

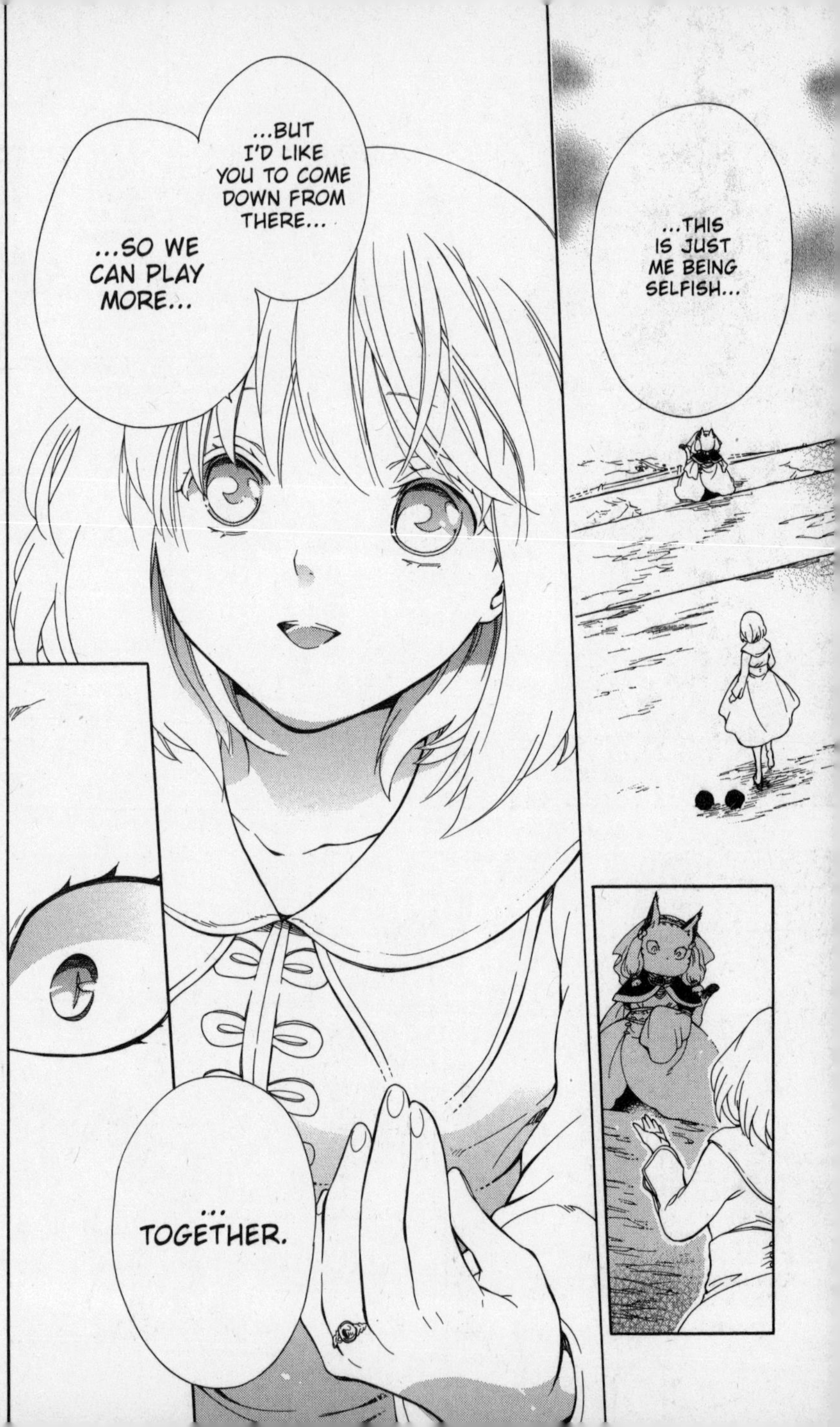
...THIS IS JUST ME BEING SELFISH...
...BUT I'D LIKE YOU TO COME DOWN FROM THERE...
...SO WE CAN PLAY MORE...
... TOGETHER.

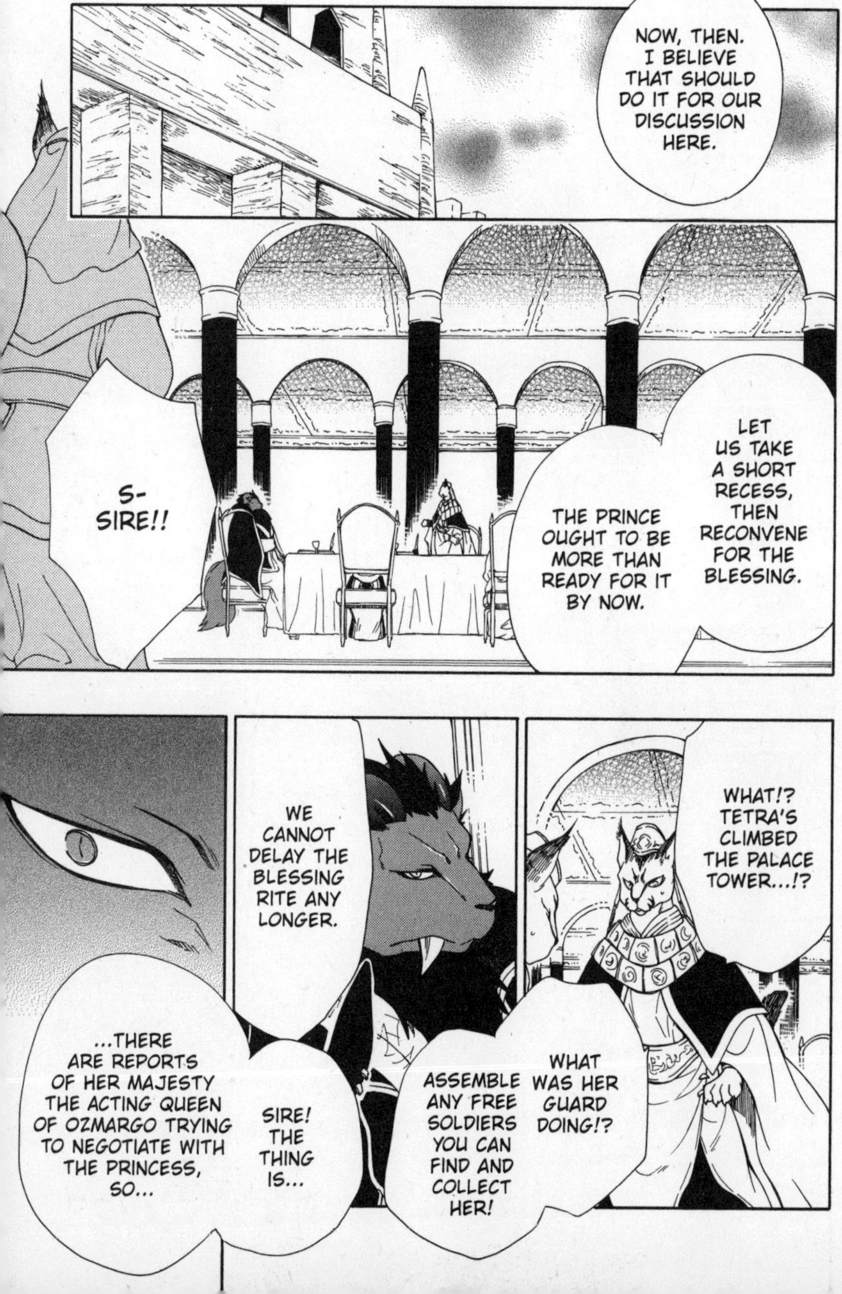
NOW, THEN. I BELIEVE THAT SHOULD DO IT FOR OUR DISCUSSION HERE.
LET US TAKE A SHORT RECESS, THEN RECONVENE FOR THE BLESSING.
THE PRINCE OUGHT TO BE MORE THAN READY FOR IT BY NOW.
S-SIRE!!
WHAT!? TETRA'S CLIMBED THE PALACE TOWER...!?
WHAT WAS HER GUARD DOING!?
ASSEMBLE ANY FREE SOLDIERS YOU CAN FIND AND COLLECT HER!
WE CANNOT DELAY THE BLESSING RITE ANY LONGER.
SIRE! THE THING IS...
...THERE ARE REPORTS OF HER MAJESTY THE ACTING QUEEN OF OZMARGO TRYING TO NEGOTIATE WITH THE PRINCESS, SO...

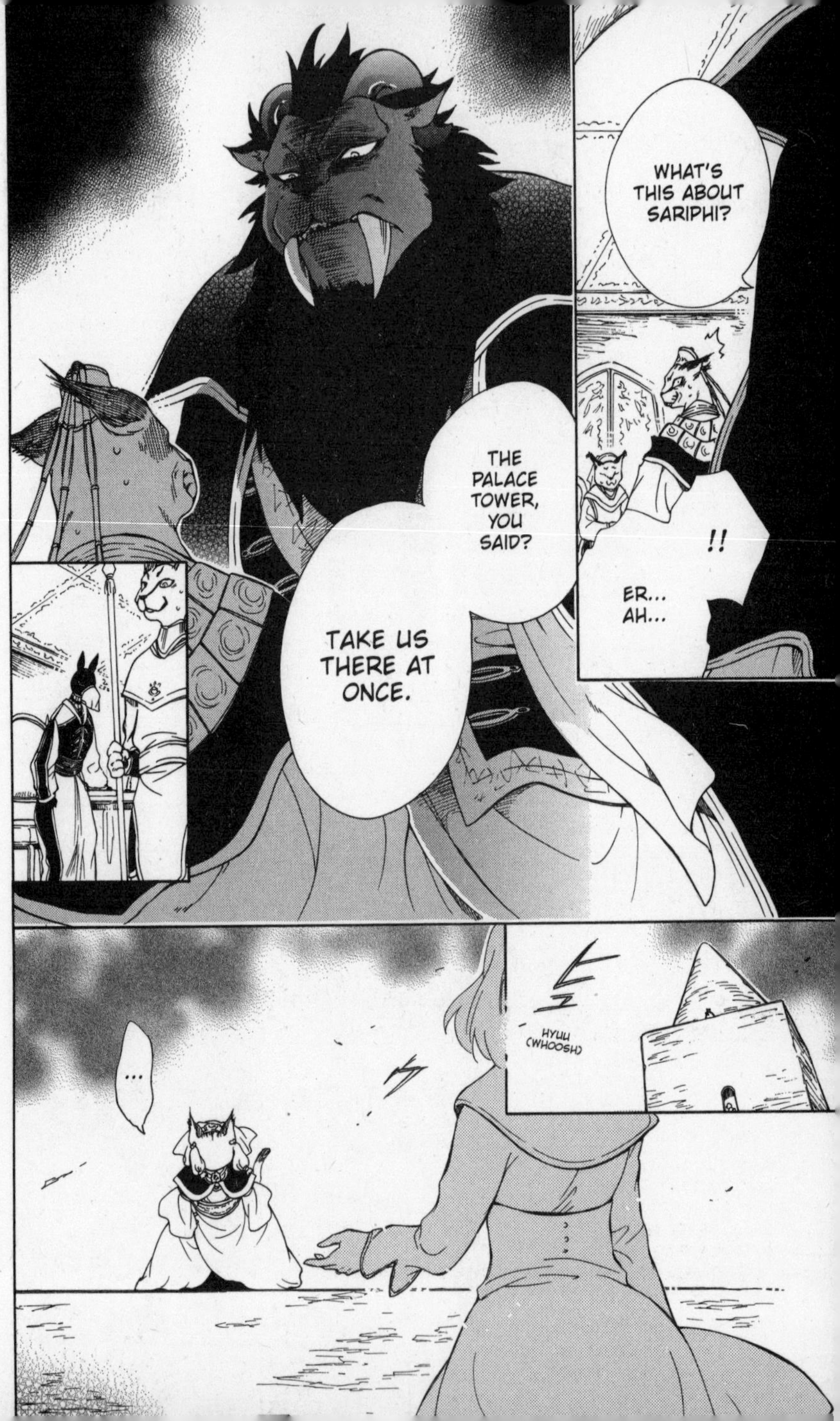
WHAT'S THIS ABOUT SARIPHI?
!!
ER... AH...
THE PALACE TOWER, YOU SAID?
TAKE US THERE AT ONCE.
HYUU (WHOOSH)
...

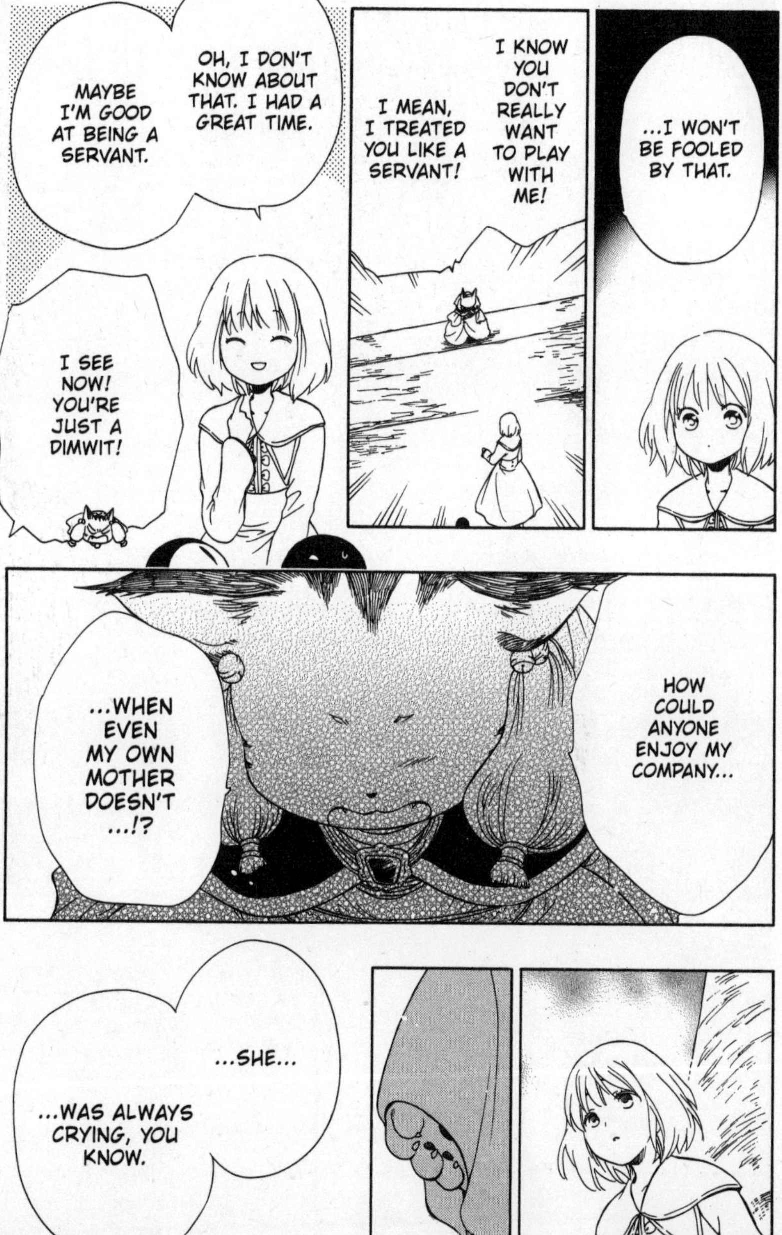
...I WON'T BE FOOLED BY THAT.
I KNOW YOU DON'T REALLY WANT TO PLAY WITH ME!
I MEAN, I TREATED YOU LIKE A SERVANT!
OH, I DON'T KNOW ABOUT THAT. I HAD A GREAT TIME.
MAYBE I'M GOOD AT BEING A SERVANT.
I SEE NOW! YOU'RE JUST A DIMWIT!
HOW COULD ANYONE ENJOY MY COMPANY...
...WHEN EVEN MY OWN MOTHER DOESN'T ...!?
...SHE...
...WAS ALWAYS CRYING, YOU KNOW.

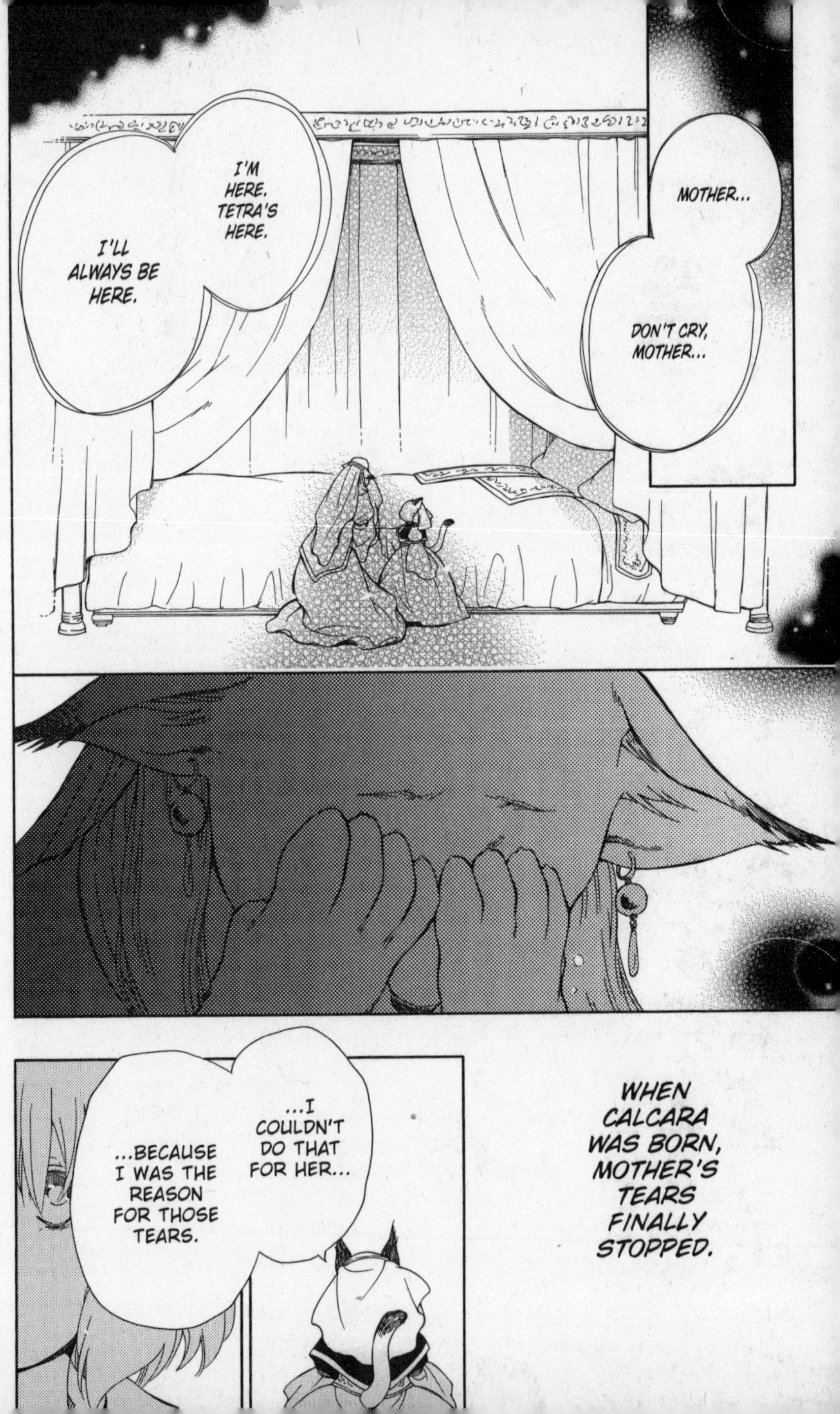
MOTHER...
DON'T CRY, MOTHER...
I'M HERE. TETRA'S HERE.
I'LL ALWAYS BE HERE.
WHEN CALCARA WAS BORN, MOTHER'S TEARS FINALLY STOPPED.
...I COULDN'T DO THAT FOR HER...
...BECAUSE I WAS THE REASON FOR THOSE TEARS.

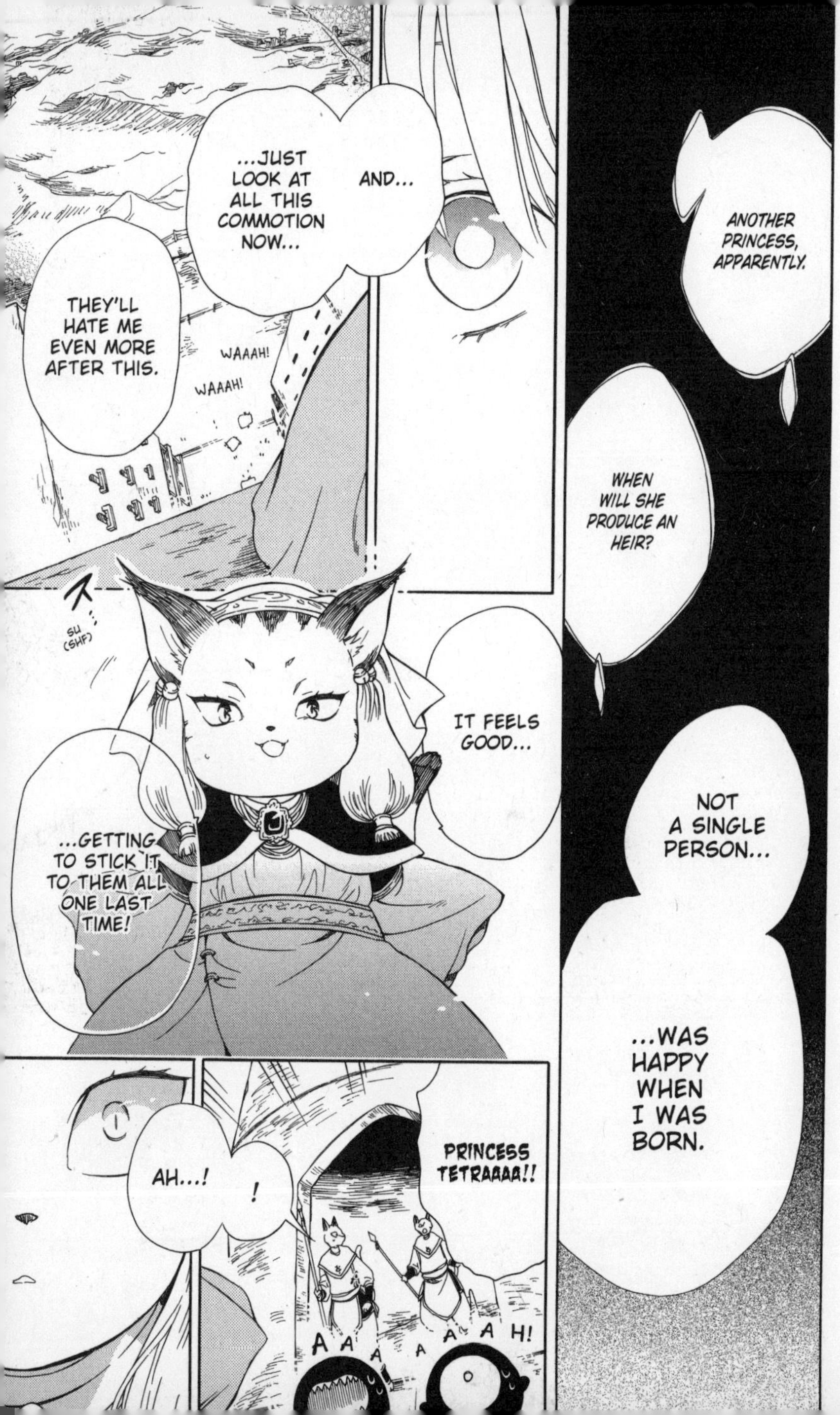

ANOTHER PRINCESS, APPARENTLY.
WHEN WILL SHE PRODUCE AN HEIR?
NOT A SINGLE PERSON...
...WAS HAPPY WHEN I WAS BORN.
AND...
...JUST LOOK AT ALL THIS COMMOTION NOW...
THEY'LL HATE ME EVEN MORE AFTER THIS.
WAAAH!
WAAAH!
SU (SHF)
IT FEELS GOOD...
...GETTING TO STICK IT TO THEM ALL ONE LAST TIME!
PRINCESS TETRAAAA!!
AAAAAAH!
!
AH...!

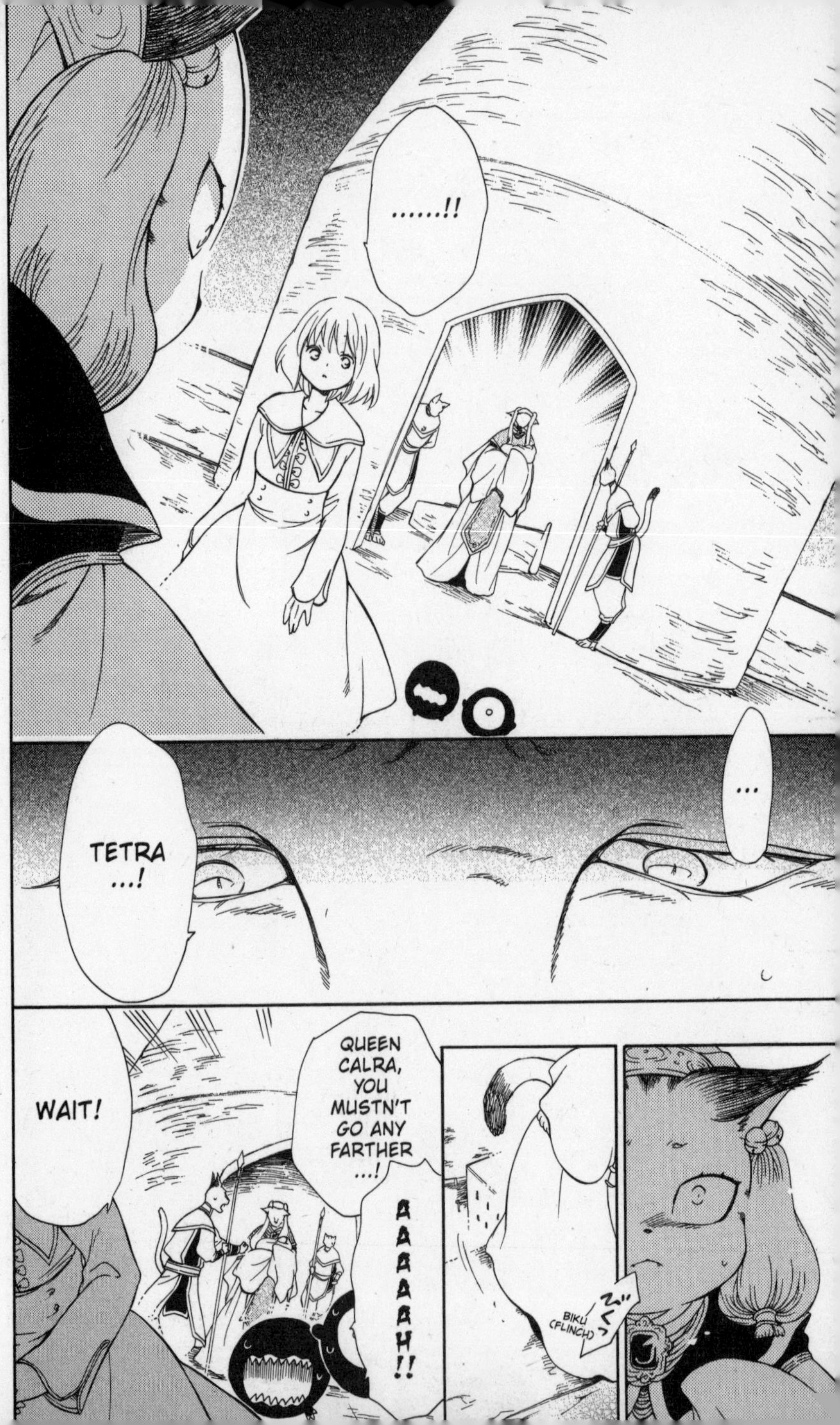
......!!
...
TETRA ...!
BIKU (FLINCH)
QUEEN CALRA, YOU MUSTN'T GO ANY FARTHER ...!
AAAAAAH!!
WAIT!

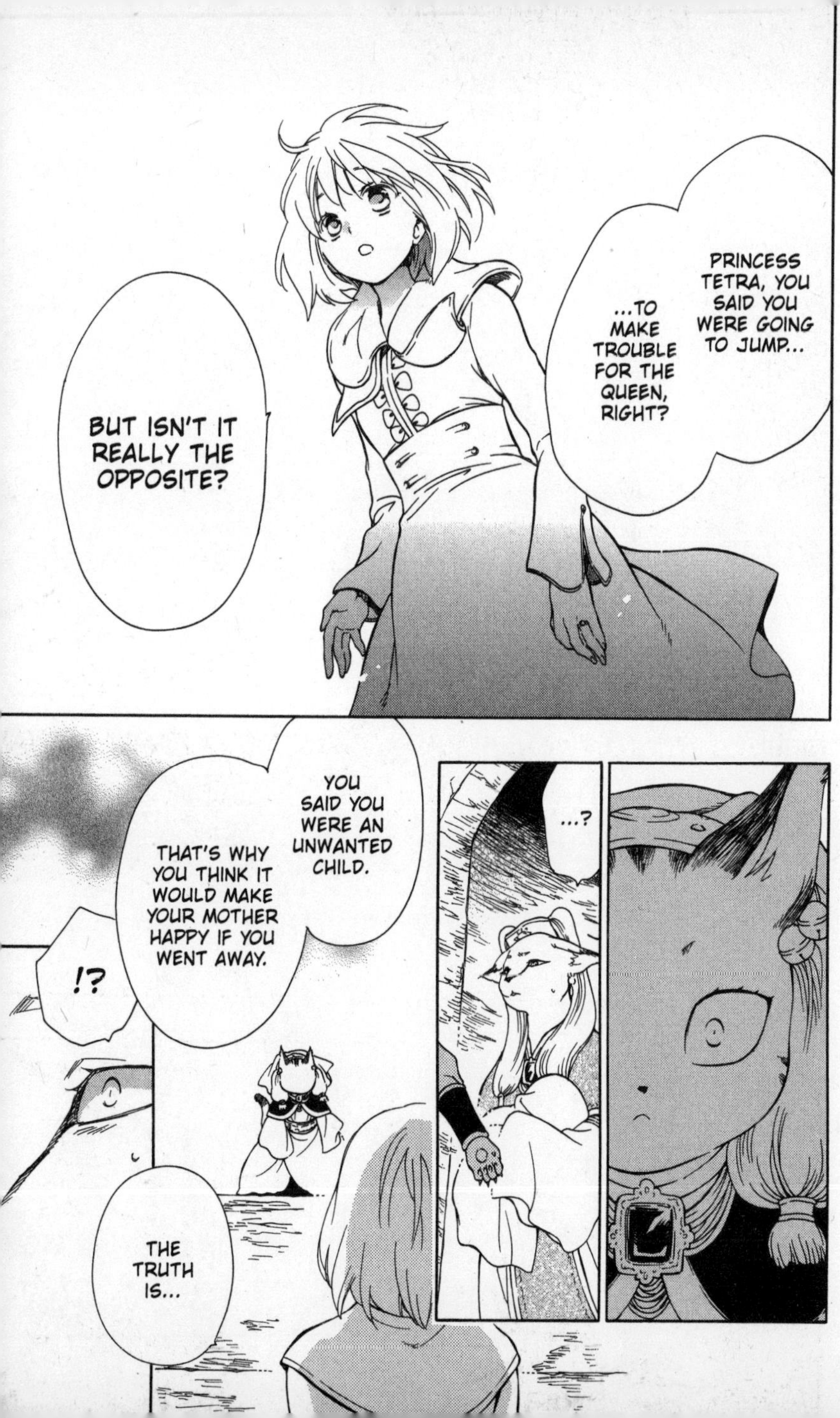
PRINCESS TETRA, YOU SAID YOU WERE GOING TO JUMP...
...TO MAKE TROUBLE FOR THE QUEEN, RIGHT?
BUT ISN'T IT REALLY THE OPPOSITE?
...?
YOU SAID YOU WERE AN UNWANTED CHILD.
THAT'S WHY YOU THINK IT WOULD MAKE YOUR MOTHER HAPPY IF YOU WENT AWAY.
!?
THE TRUTH IS...

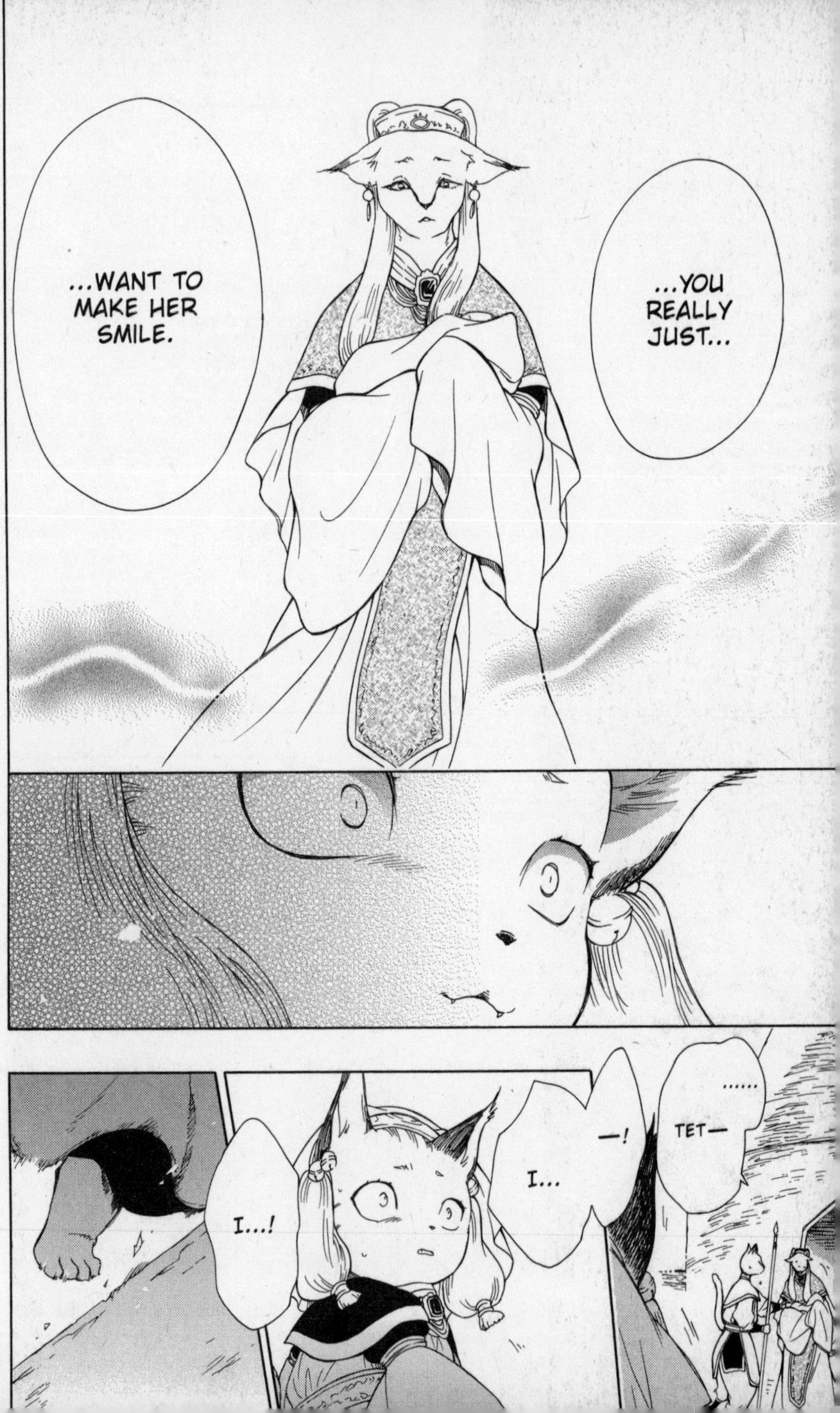
...YOU REALLY JUST...
...WANT TO MAKE HER SMILE.
......
TET—
—!
I...
I...!

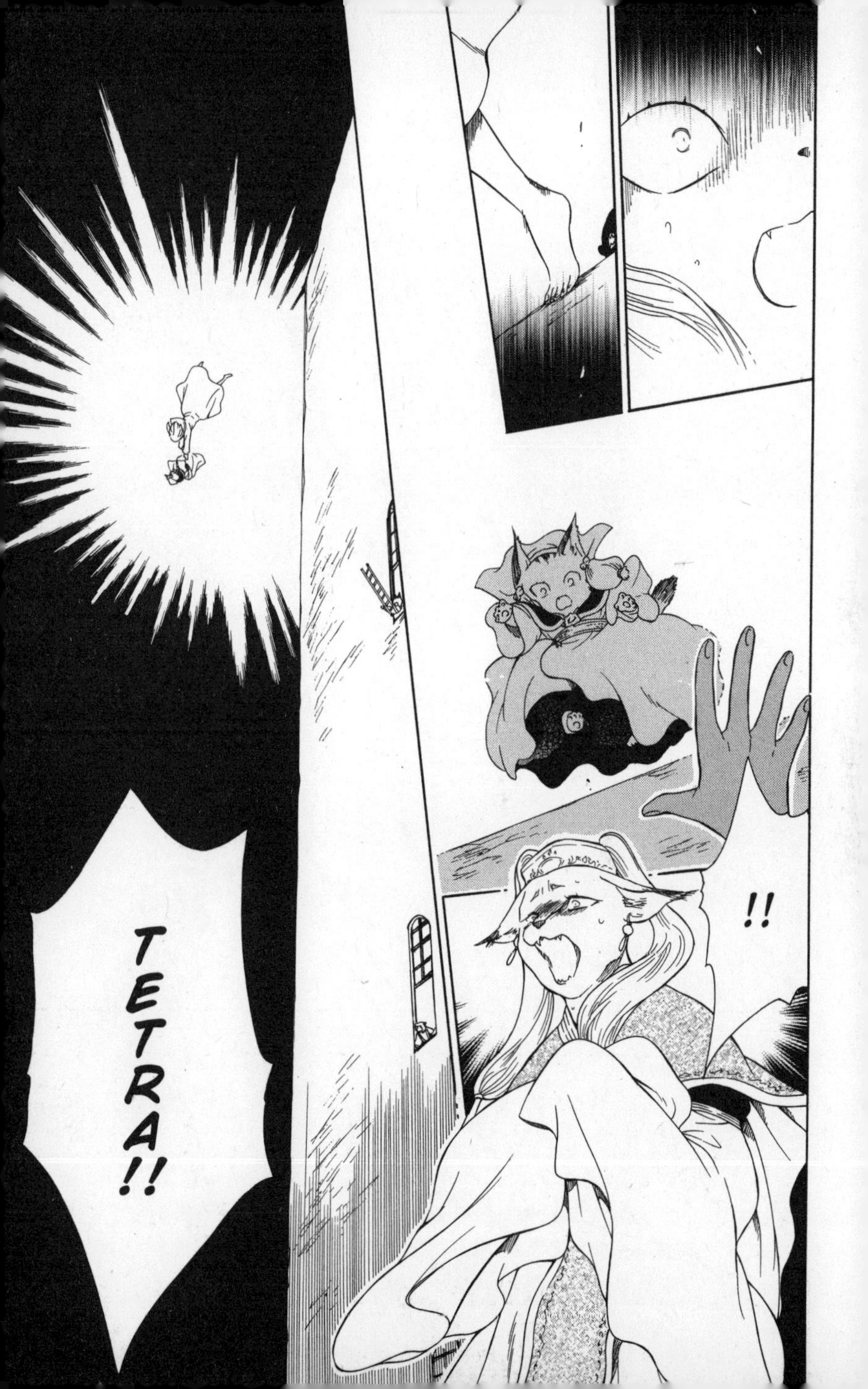
!
!!
TETRA!!

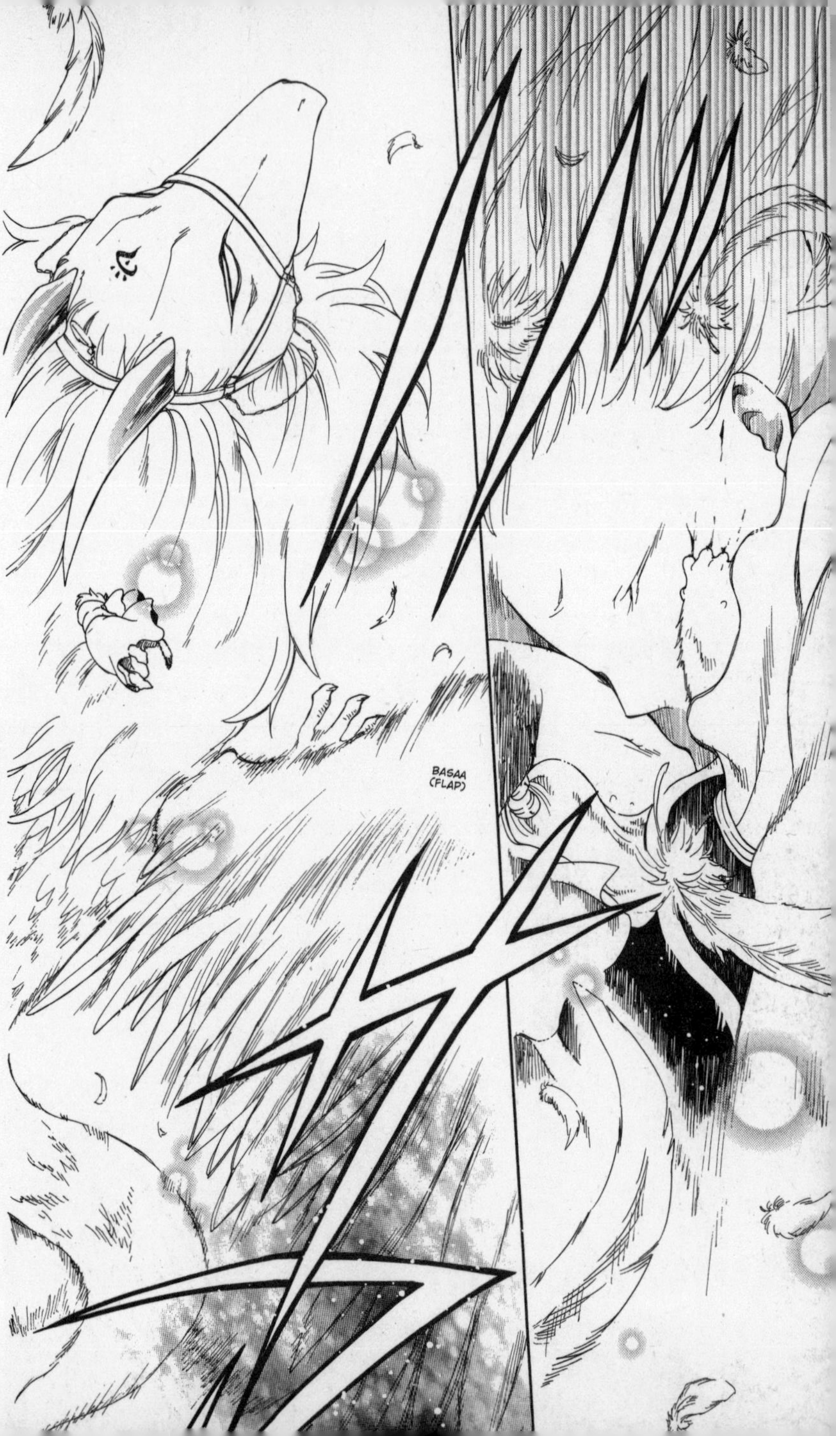
BASAA
(FLAP)

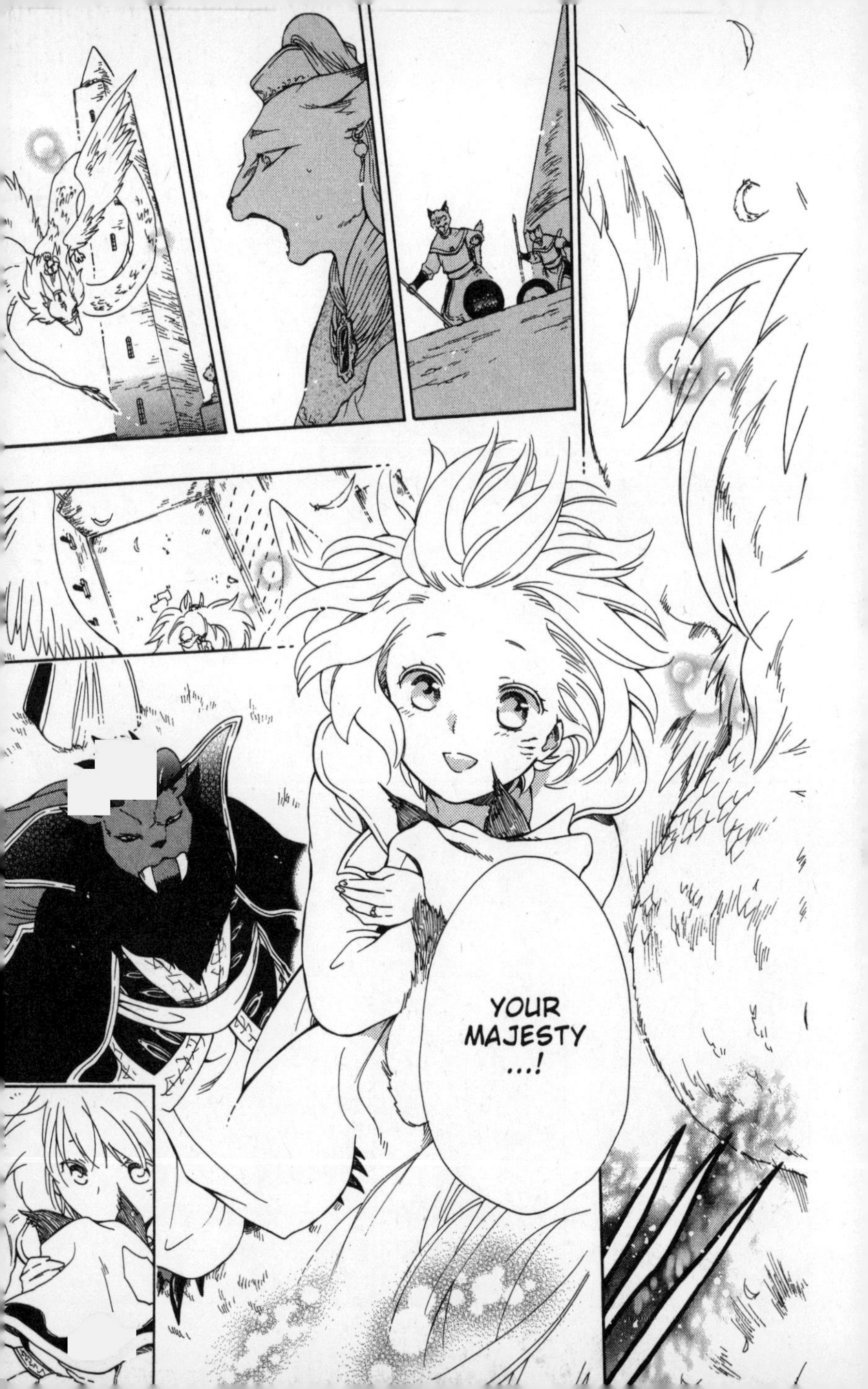
YOUR MAJESTY ...!

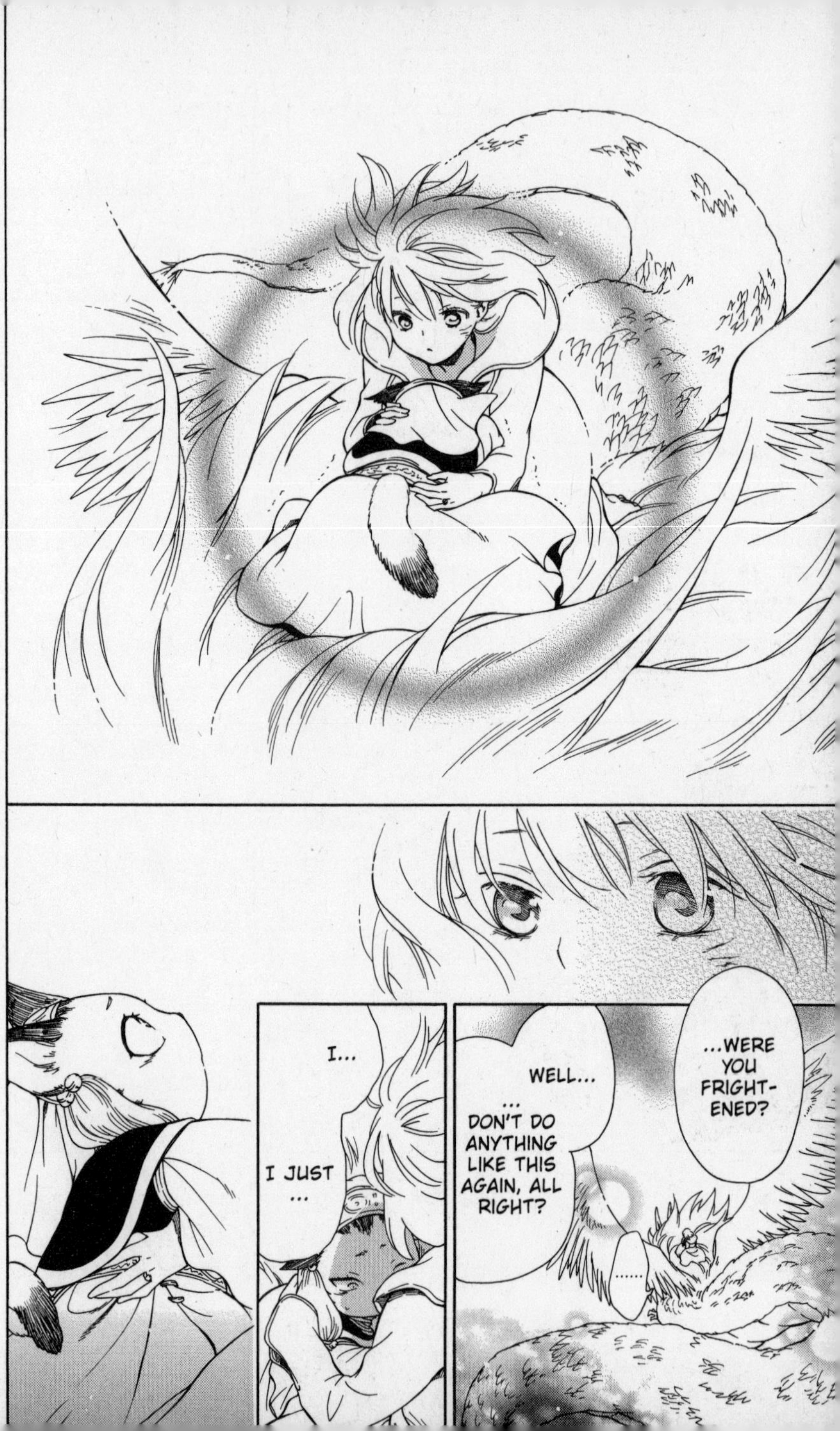
...WERE YOU FRIGHTENED?
......
WELL... ... DON'T DO ANYTHING LIKE THIS AGAIN, ALL RIGHT?
I...
I JUST ...

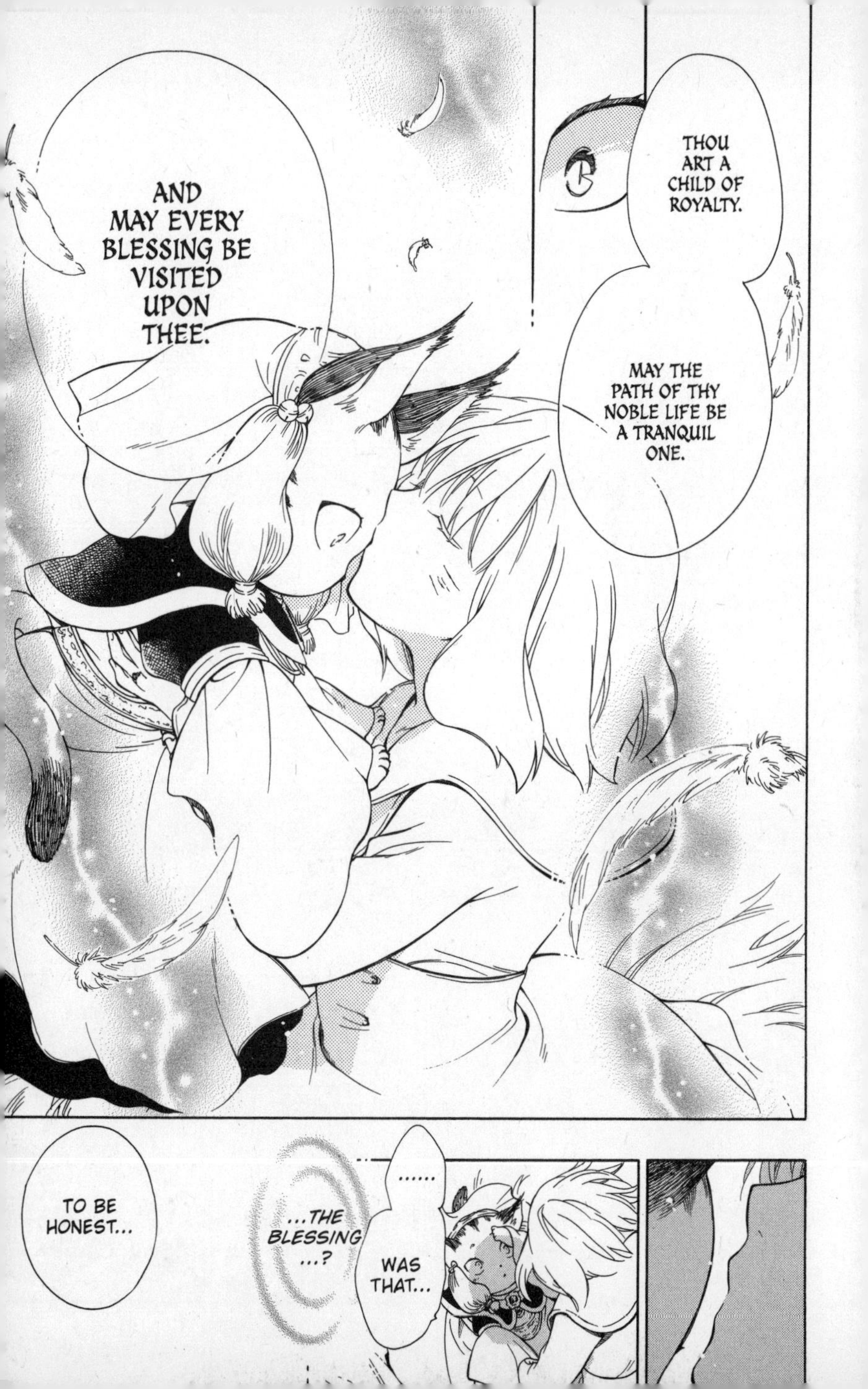
THOU ART A CHILD OF ROYALTY.
MAY THE PATH OF THY NOBLE LIFE BE A TRANQUIL ONE.
AND MAY EVERY BLESSING BE VISITED UPON THEE.
......
WAS THAT...
...THE BLESSING ...?
TO BE HONEST...

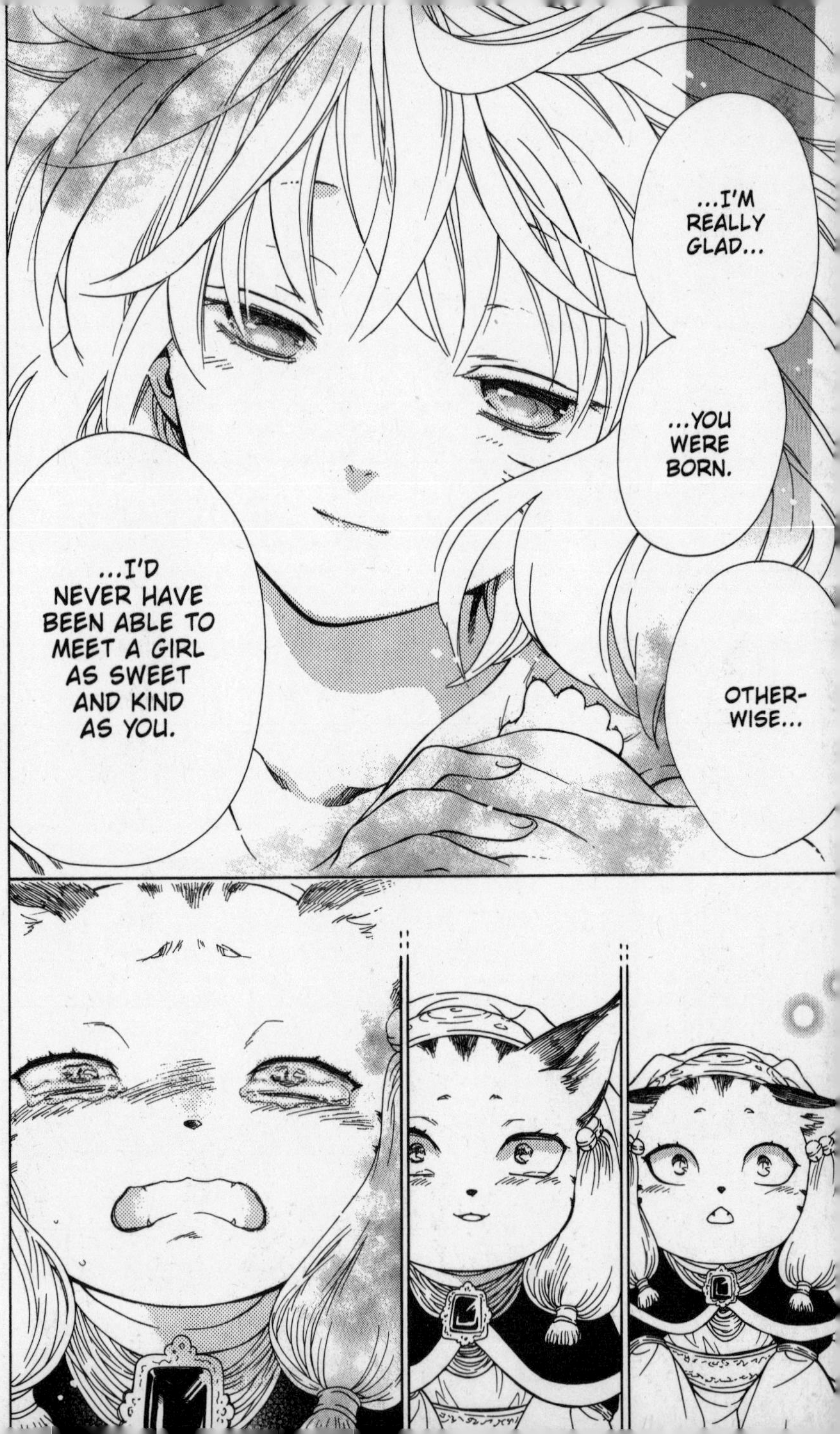
...I'M REALLY GLAD...
...YOU WERE BORN.
OTHER-WISE...
...I'D NEVER HAVE BEEN ABLE TO MEET A GIRL AS SWEET AND KIND AS YOU.
!!
!!

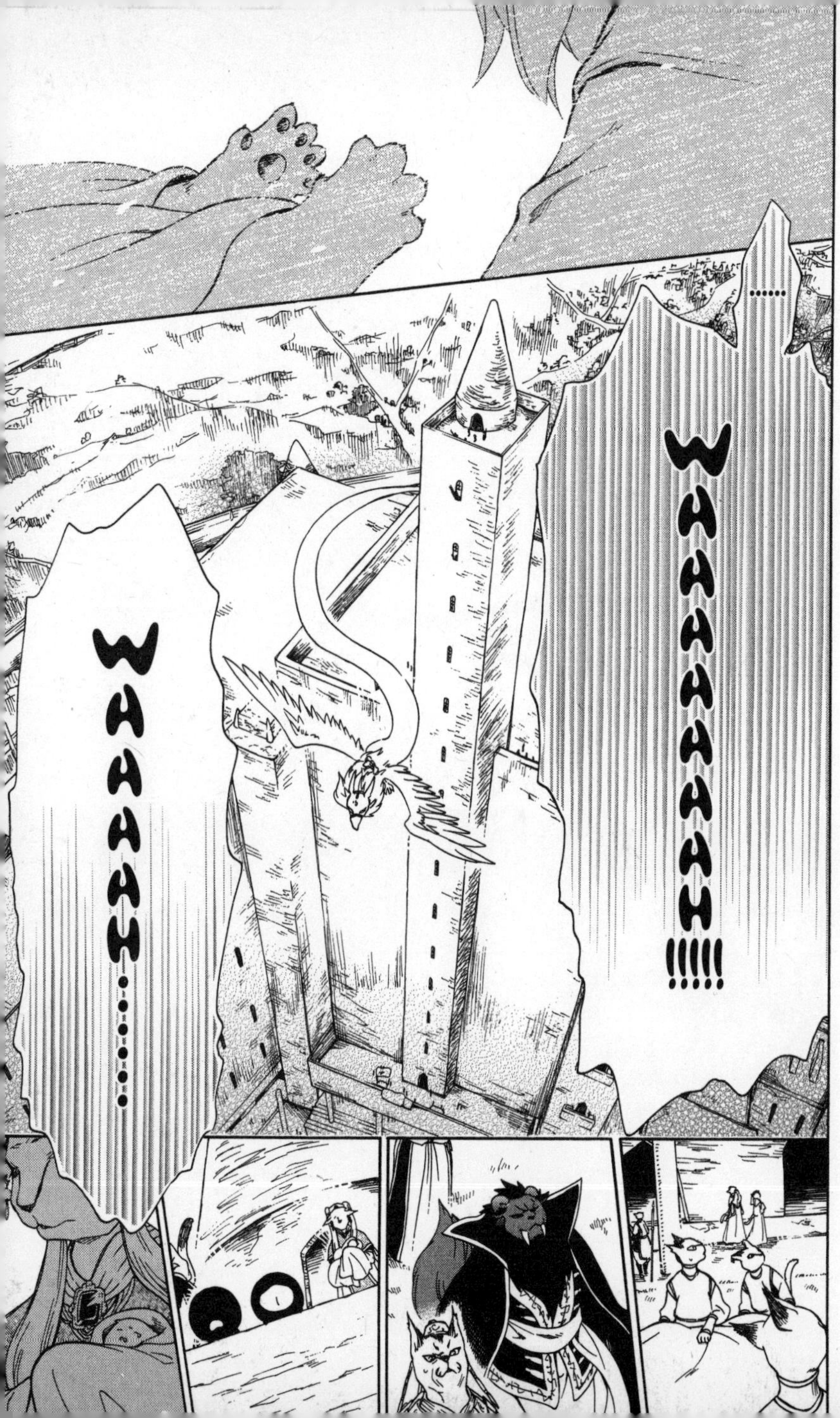
......
WAAAAAAAAH!!!!!
WAAAAH......

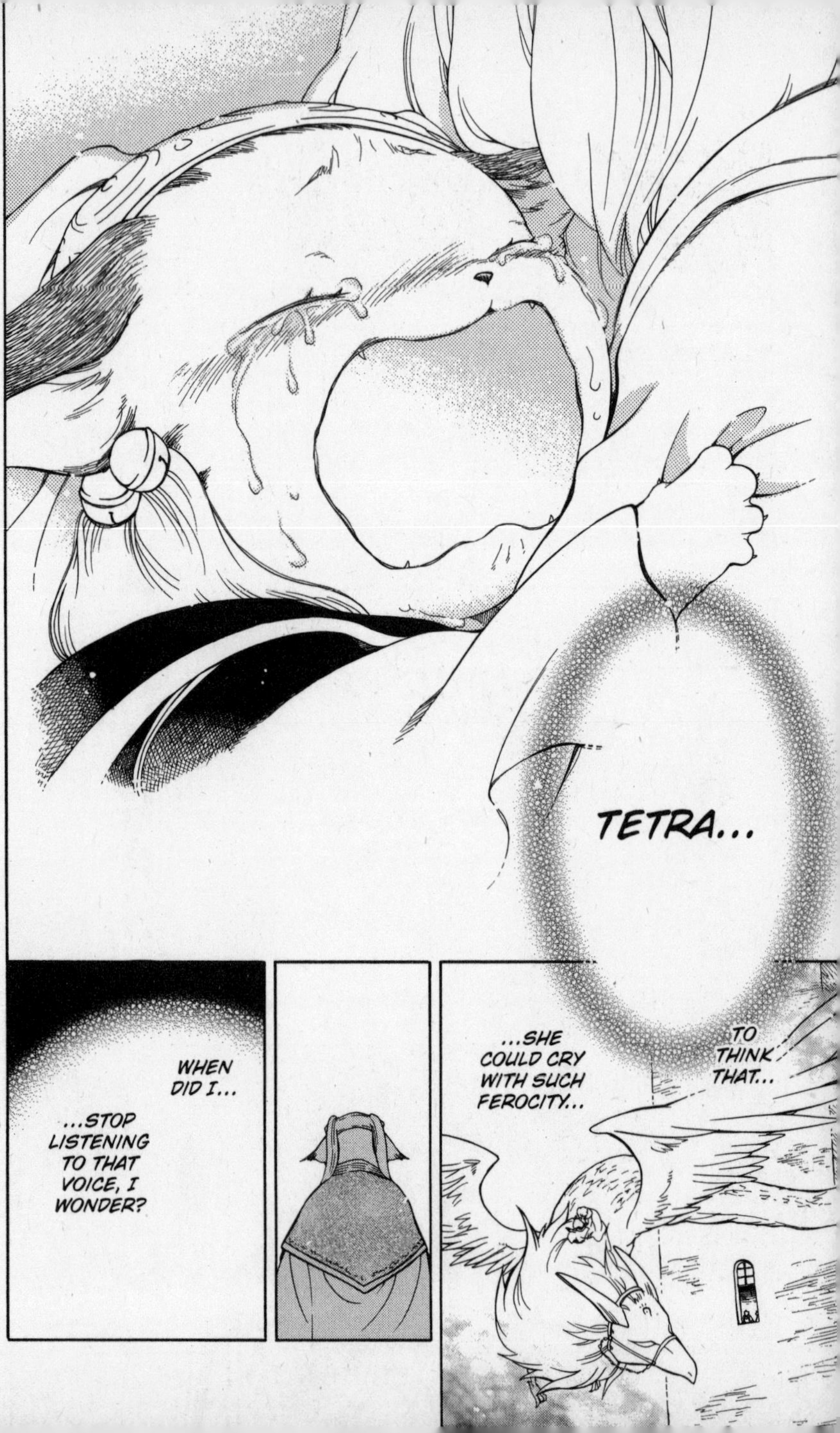
TETRA...
TO THINK THAT...
...SHE COULD CRY WITH SUCH FEROCITY...
WHEN DID I...
...STOP LISTENING TO THAT VOICE, I WONDER?

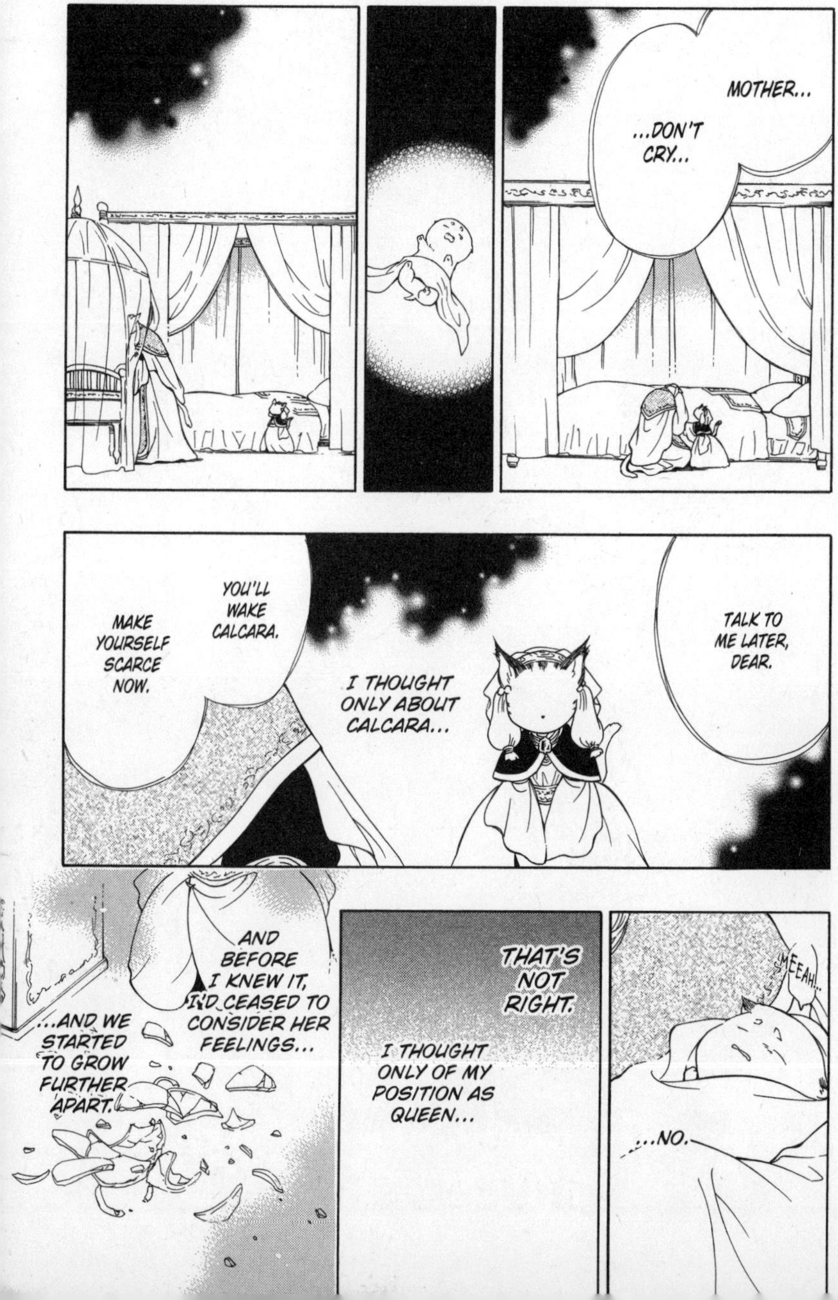
MOTHER...
...DON'T CRY...
TALK TO ME LATER, DEAR.
I THOUGHT ONLY ABOUT CALCARA...
YOU'LL WAKE CALCARA.
MAKE YOURSELF SCARCE NOW.
MEEAH!...
...NO.
THAT'S NOT RIGHT.
I THOUGHT ONLY OF MY POSITION AS QUEEN...
AND BEFORE I KNEW IT, I'D CEASED TO CONSIDER HER FEELINGS...
...AND WE STARTED TO GROW FURTHER APART.

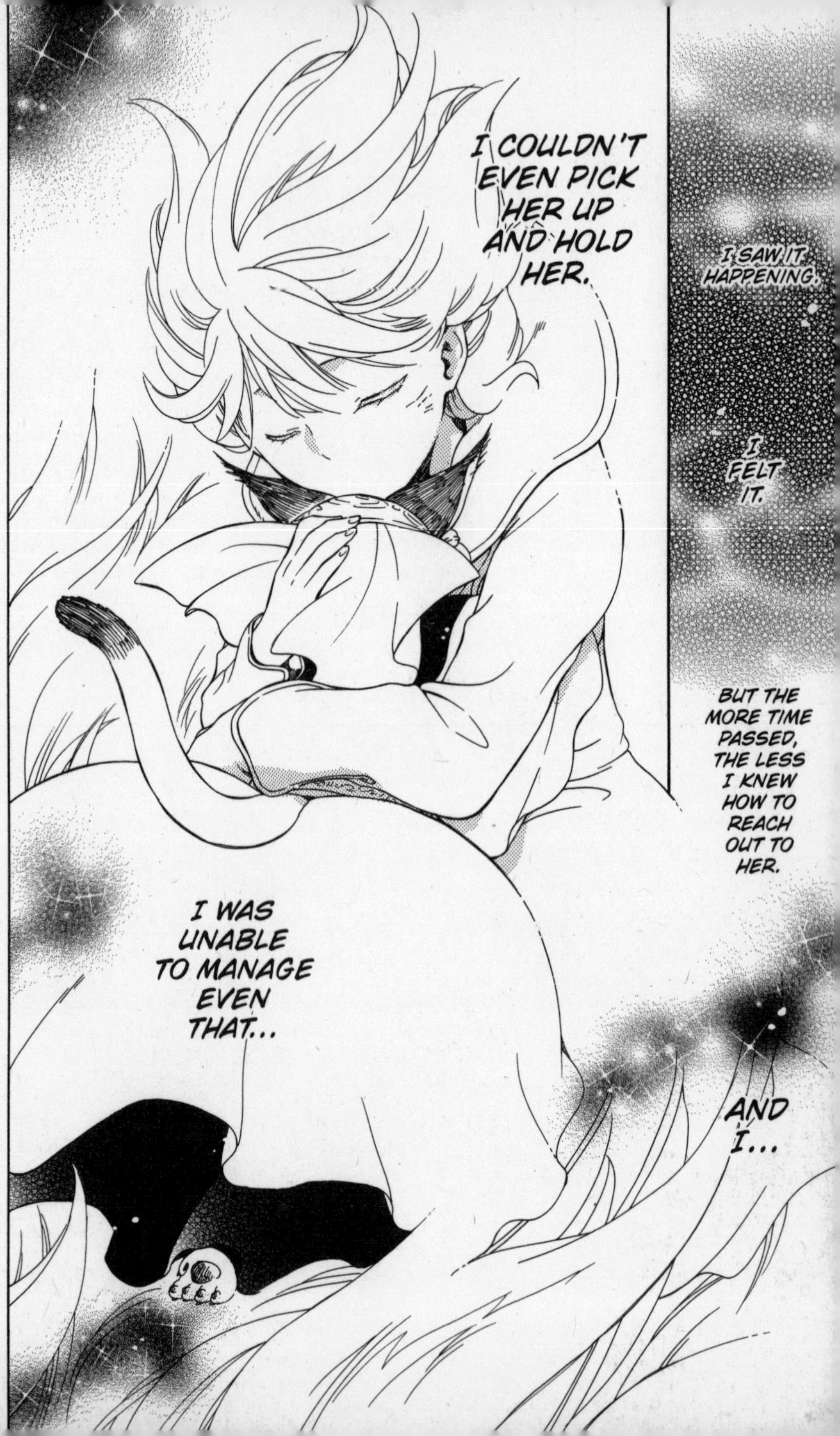
I SAW IT HAPPENING.
I FELT IT.
BUT THE MORE TIME PASSED, THE LESS I KNEW HOW TO REACH OUT TO HER.
AND I...
I COULDN'T EVEN PICK HER UP AND HOLD HER.
I WAS UNABLE TO MANAGE EVEN THAT...

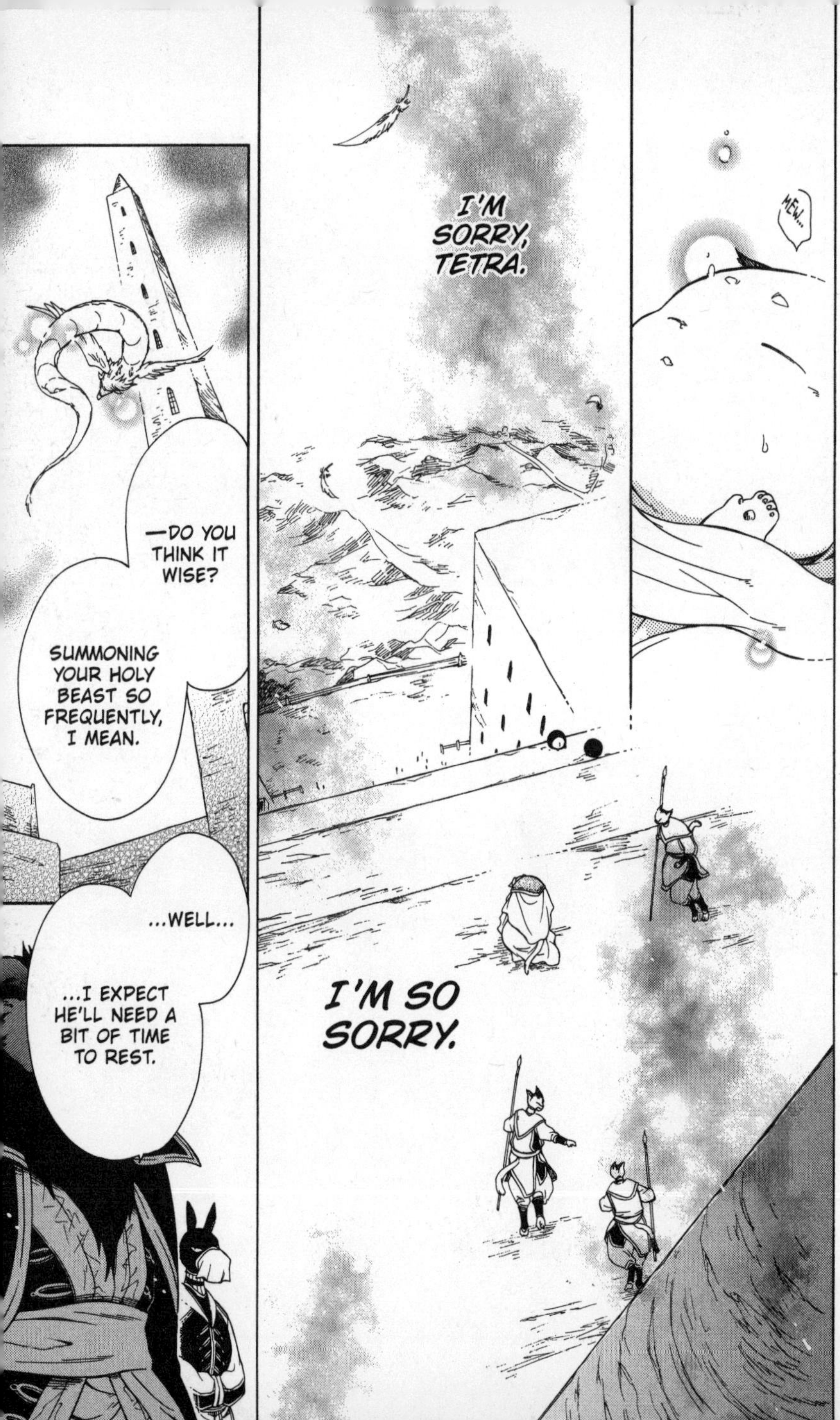
MEW...
I'M SORRY, TETRA.
I'M SO SORRY.
—DO YOU THINK IT WISE?
SUMMONING YOUR HOLY BEAST SO FREQUENTLY, I MEAN.
...WELL...
...I EXPECT HE'LL NEED A BIT OF TIME TO REST.

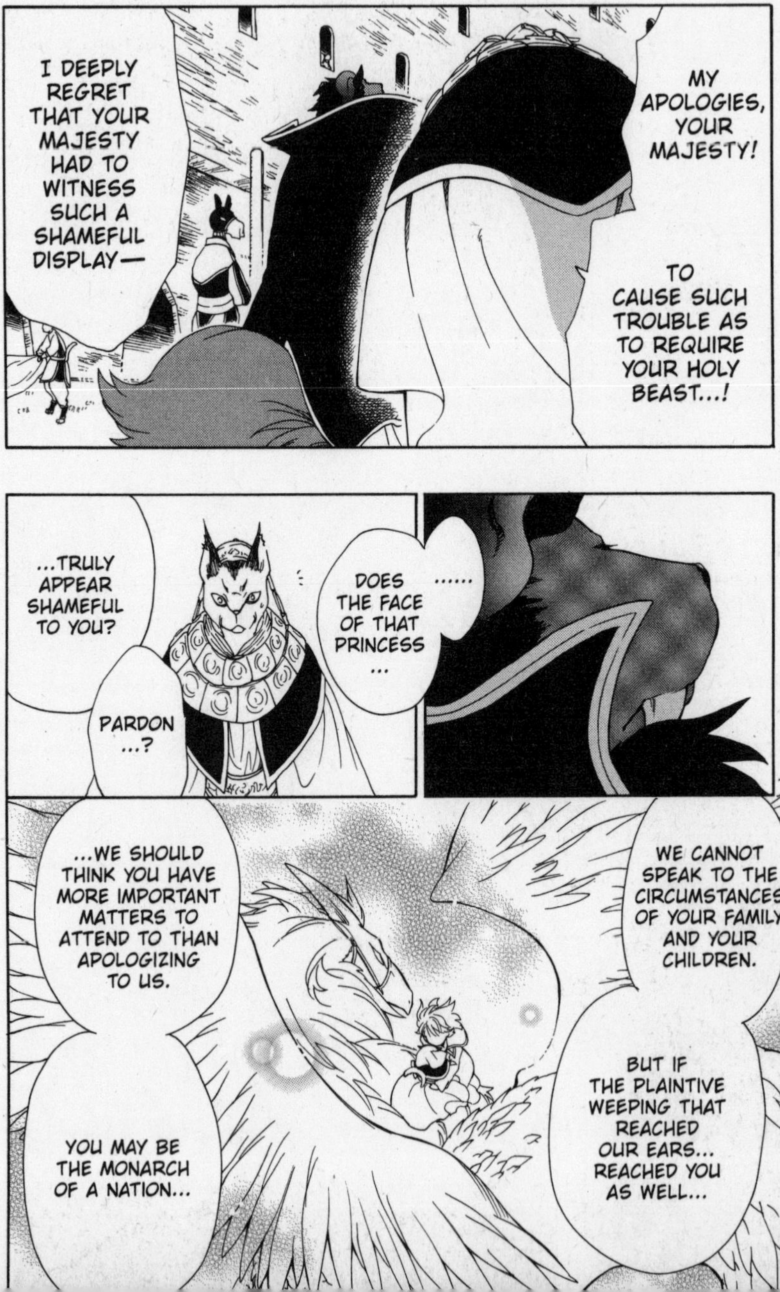
MY APOLOGIES, YOUR MAJESTY!
TO CAUSE SUCH TROUBLE AS TO REQUIRE YOUR HOLY BEAST...!
I DEEPLY REGRET THAT YOUR MAJESTY HAD TO WITNESS SUCH A SHAMEFUL DISPLAY—
......
DOES THE FACE OF THAT PRINCESS ...
...TRULY APPEAR SHAMEFUL TO YOU?
PARDON ...?
WE CANNOT SPEAK TO THE CIRCUMSTANCES OF YOUR FAMILY AND YOUR CHILDREN.
BUT IF THE PLAINTIVE WEEPING THAT REACHED OUR EARS... REACHED YOU AS WELL...
...WE SHOULD THINK YOU HAVE MORE IMPORTANT MATTERS TO ATTEND TO THAN APOLOGIZING TO US.
YOU MAY BE THE MONARCH OF A NATION...

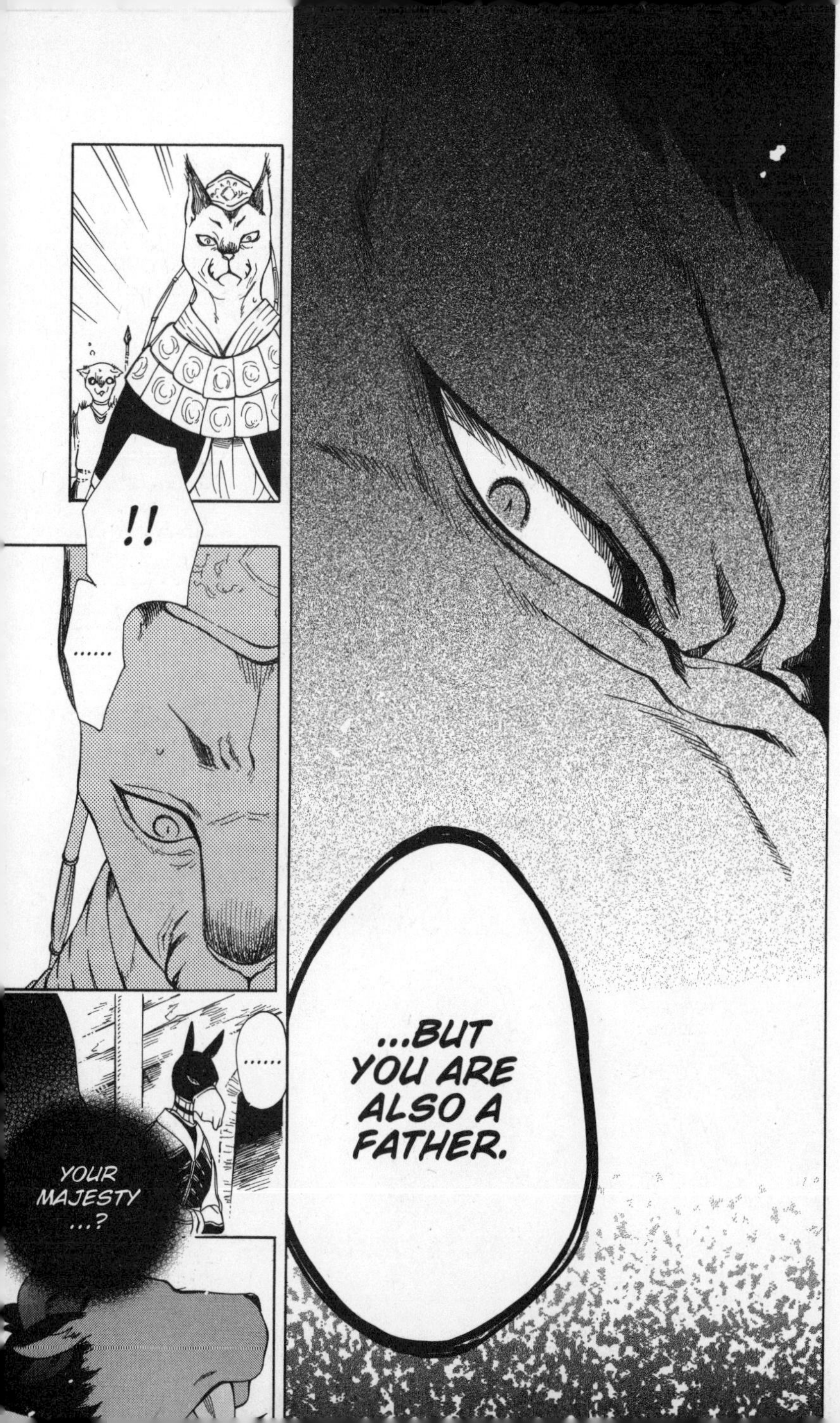
...BUT YOU ARE ALSO A FATHER.
!!
......
......
YOUR MAJESTY ...?

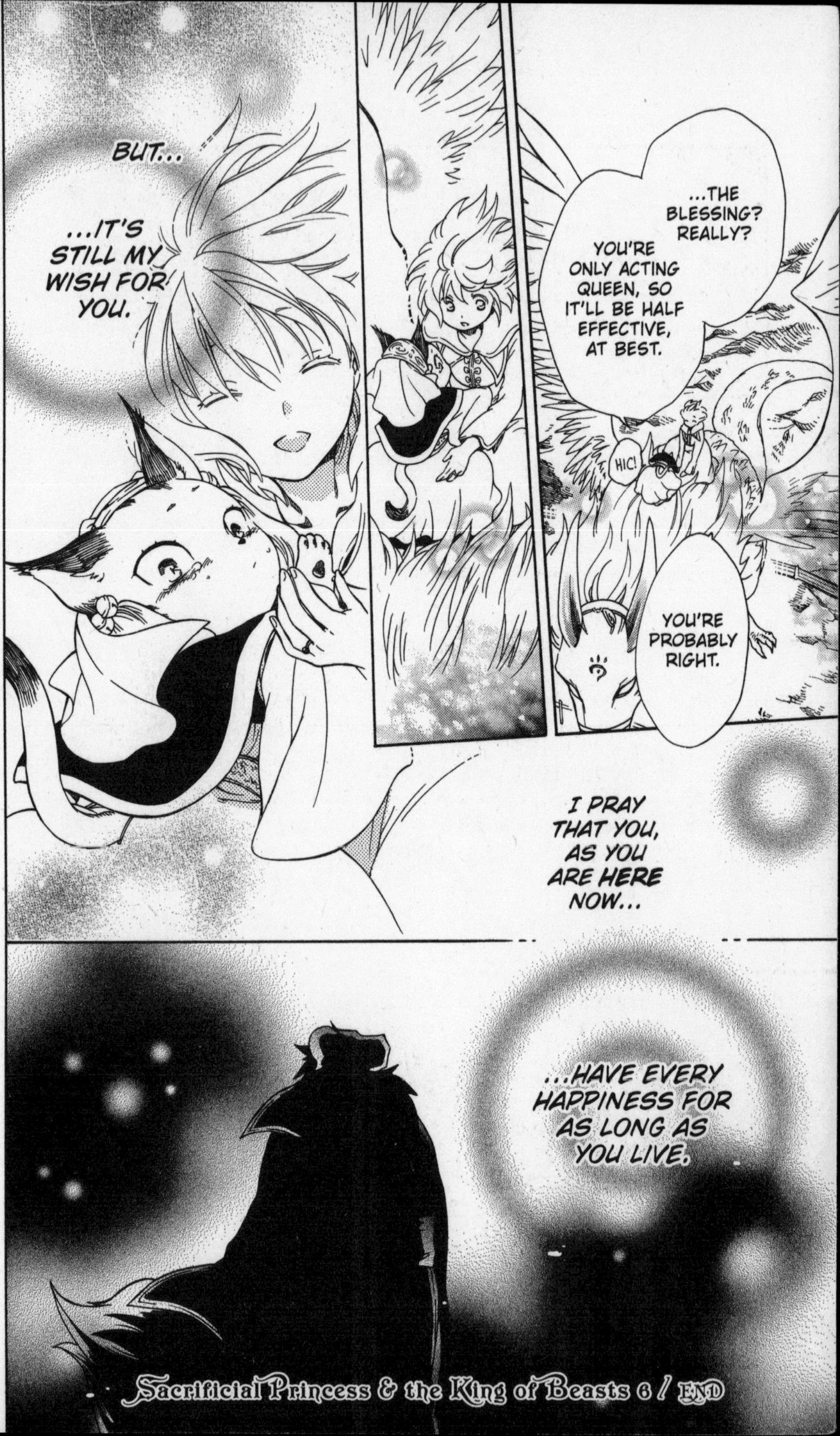
...THE BLESSING? REALLY?
YOU'RE ONLY ACTING QUEEN, SO IT'LL BE HALF EFFECTIVE, AT BEST.
HIC!
YOU'RE PROBABLY RIGHT.
BUT...
...IT'S STILL MY WISH FOR YOU.
I PRAY THAT YOU, AS YOU ARE HERE NOW...
...HAVE EVERY HAPPINESS FOR AS LONG AS YOU LIVE.
Sacrificial Princess & the King of Beasts 6 / END

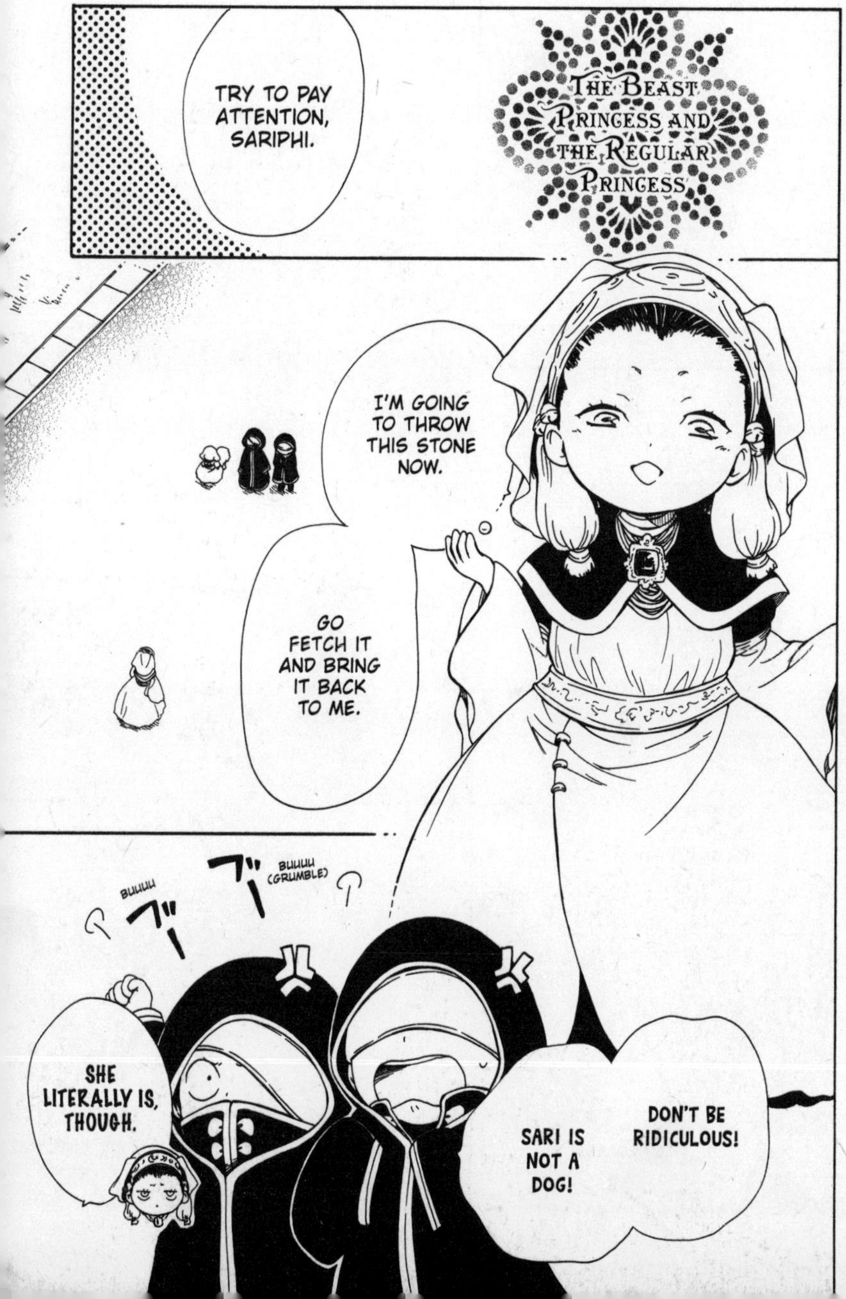
THE BEAST PRINCESS AND THE REGULAR PRINCESS
TRY TO PAY ATTENTION, SARIPHI.
I'M GOING TO THROW THIS STONE NOW.
GO FETCH IT AND BRING IT BACK TO ME.
BUUUU (GRUMBLE)
BUUUU
DON'T BE RIDICULOUS!
SARI IS NOT A DOG!
SHE LITERALLY IS, THOUGH.

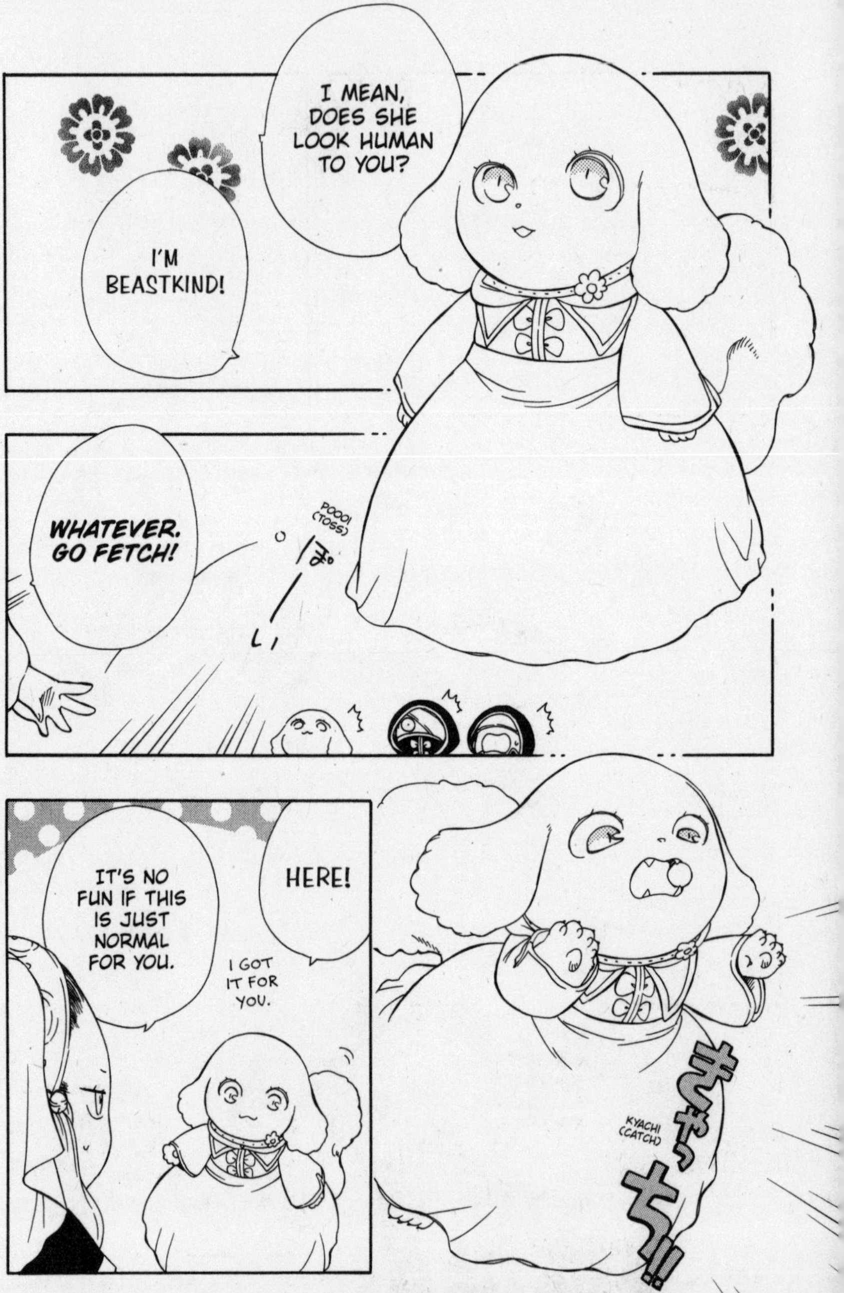
I MEAN, DOES SHE LOOK HUMAN TO YOU?
I'M BEASTKIND!
POOO! (TOSS)
WHATEVER. GO FETCH!
KYACHI (CATCH)
HERE!
I GOT IT FOR YOU.
IT'S NO FUN IF THIS IS JUST NORMAL FOR YOU.

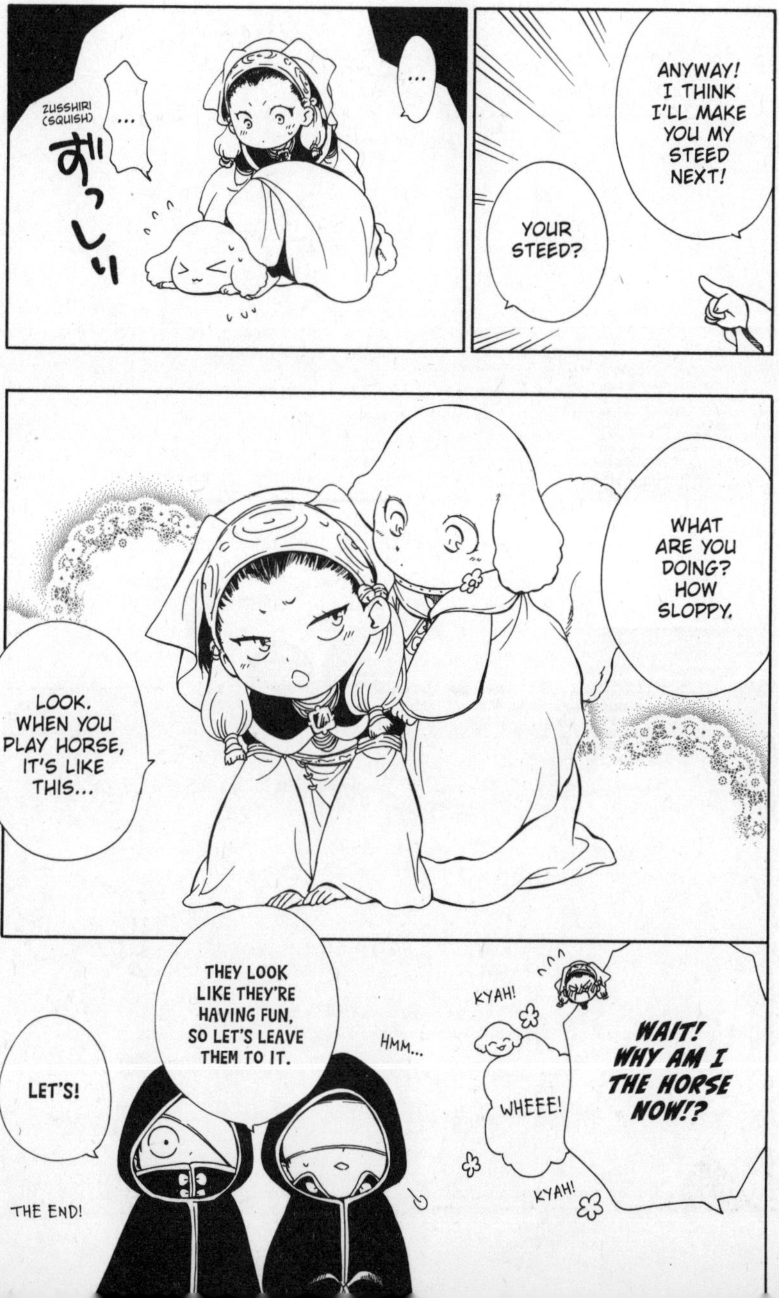
ANYWAY! I THINK I'LL MAKE YOU MY STEED NEXT!
YOUR STEED?
...
...
ZUSSHIRI (SQUISH)
ずっしり
WHAT ARE YOU DOING? HOW SLOPPY.
LOOK. WHEN YOU PLAY HORSE, IT'S LIKE THIS...
WAIT! WHY AM I THE HORSE NOW!?
KYAH!
WHEEE!
KYAH!
HMM...
THEY LOOK LIKE THEY'RE HAVING FUN, SO LET'S LEAVE THEM TO IT.
LET'S!
THE END!

SACRIFICIAL PRINCESS AND THE King of Beasts

6

Yu Tomofuji

TRANSLATION: Paul Starr
LETTERING: Lys Blakeslee

This book is a work of fiction. Names, characters, places, and incidents are the product of the author's imagination or are used fictitiously. Any resemblance to actual events, locales, or persons, living or dead, is coincidental.

NIEHIME TO KEMONO NO OH by Yu Tomofuji
© Yu Tomofuji 2018
All rights reserved.
First published in Japan in 2018 by HAKUSENSHA, Inc., Tokyo.
English language translation rights in U.S.A., Canada and U.K. arranged with
HAKUSENSHA, Inc., Tokyo through Tuttle-Mori Agency, Inc., Tokyo.

English translation © 2019 by Yen Press, LLC

Yen Press
150 West 30th Street, 19th Floor
New York, NY 10001

Visit us at yenpress.com ❦ facebook.com/yenpress ❦ twitter.com/yenpress
yenpress.tumblr.com ❦ instagram.com/yenpress

First Yen Press Edition: July 2019

Yen Press is an imprint of Yen Press, LLC.
The Yen Press name and logo are trademarks of Yen Press, LLC.

The publisher is not responsible for websites (or their content) that are not owned by the publisher.

Library of Congress Control Number: 2018930817

ISBNs: 978-1-9753-0437-9 (paperback)
978-1-9753-0438-6 (ebook)

10 9 8 7 6 5 4 3 2 1

WOR

Printed in the United States of America

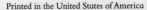